When the Willows Weep

Susan Agatha Davis

ERCILDOUNE PUBLISHING
Newport, Vermont 05855

WHEN ROSES WEEP
Copyright © 2013 by Susan Agatha Davis All Rights Reserved.
No part of this book may be reproduced or transmitted in any form or by any means, electronic, mechanical or by any other means, without written permission of the publisher or author, except where permitted by law.
Cover Art by Joseph Fletcher
Cover Design by Karen Karlovich
Editing by Tracie Ashman
Published by: Ercildoune Publishing, 25 Northern Ave., Newport, VT 05855
ISBN-13: 978-1491238509
ISBN-10: 149123850X
Published in the United States by Ercildoune Publishing.

ERCILDOUNE PUBLISHING
Newport, Vermont 05855

CHAPTER 1
FRIDAY

Francesca Simone never thought of herself as a murderer. She was a smart, reasonably attractive, successful Las Vegas criminal attorney with a spunky 12-year-old daughter and all the perks that came with her job. She only thought of murder when Max called. Lately, Max had been calling a lot.

Fran grit her teeth as she read the latest text message, turned off the ring on her cell phone and felt her gut tighten into a painful knot. She had changed her phone number a half-dozen times, which made it difficult for clients to reach her. Max, her estranged father and the mayor of Las Vegas, wasn't easily deterred. He knew every backdoor into her life, even in her nightmares.

Fran perched on the hard metal stool in the wing of the busy television studio. Her legs were crossed at her runner's thighs and the high heel on her lower foot was crooked into the stretchers of the stool. Her soft blue eyes squinted into the stage lights. The air around her was hot and dry. She was keenly aware of every sound, from the plop of change and drizzle of coffee into a paper cup from a vending machine to the soft twitter of the audience as the stage lights were flicked on. Her shrink told it was called hypervigilance. She balanced her coffee mug on one knee, took a slow, deep breath and inhaled the smells of waxed floors, steel cables, and stale donuts.

At the sound of a man's footsteps, Fran tensed, only to receive a strange look from a technician walking by. *He's not here, she reminded herself. He's not here. Calm down.* Her racing heartbeat pounded in her ears. It was too early in the morning to be this awake. *He's not here.*

The last thing she needed right now was another message from Max. There was nothing she could do about him except maybe, just maybe, dethrone him politically. At least, that was her working plan. Without his talons sunk into the heart of the city, without his claws wrapped tightly around the throat of the police force, then, maybe then, she could get some peace. If not, she might have to kill him. For barely a second, she relaxed and smiled.

The phone rang again, or more accurately, it vibrated in her pocket. She closed her eyes, took a deep breath, offered up a silent prayer and pulled it out. In a brief second, all the tension was gone. A wide smile spread over her face as she got up from the stool and crossed the large, warehouse-structured room to a quiet corner, the coffee cup still gripped in one hand, the phone pushed to her ear with the other.

"Hi," she said, just above a whisper as her eyes landed on a tiny spider crawling up the wall. She cradled the phone against her shoulder and flicked the creature to the floor with her fingernails. "Why are you calling me? You're supposed to be in class." The words may have been critical, but the tone was gentle.

"Hi, Mom," came a girl's voice. "I forgot to say happy birthday."

Fran could hear someone else on the phone – an adult in the background – urging the girl to be quick.

"Love you, Mom," the child added. "Gotta go. Bye."

"I love you, too," Fran returned, but the hang-up came so fast she wasn't sure her daughter had heard it. Instead, a woman's critical voice jolted her back to her surroundings.

"You *so* need to upgrade your makeup. I can help with that, you know."

Fran, startled, jumped slightly, spun around and nearly spilled her coffee. Her eyes scanned the room instinctively before focusing on the speaker. *He's not here.* She let herself breathe and turned off the phone.

A young woman dressed in vintage clothes and dangling earrings had emerged quietly from the darkness. She wore an eyebrow pencil stuck into the knot of her raven hair and a mauve smock that hung loosely over her hipless frame. A clipboard covered her chest and a collection of assorted

2

chains and beads dangled from her neck.

Fran thought of Mardi Gras, of Girls Gone Wild, of one-night stands on a starlit beach, of being that young again.

"Oh?" Fran asked through tight lips. She slipped the phone back into her pocket, steadied her coffee mug with both hands and glared at the girl. Yes, girl, Fran realized. Barely twenty-two. Maybe. Or was that merely a side effect of working in the television business? Fran self-consciously tucked a strand of her unruly long red hair behind one ear.

"You're running a political campaign. You think people won't notice how you look on his arm?" The woman delved into the deep pockets of her smock, felt around and finally shoved a business card into Fran's hand. "Call me."

Fran's neck burned red at the remarks; her infamous temper spat to flame. "It's retro," she snapped. She narrowed her eyes.

The woman put a hand sympathetically on Fran's arm, then withdrew it just as quickly when Fran pulled back. "It's not retro, sister. It's Donna Reed." She then turned and trotted off with an all-knowing look on her pert young face.

"Biatch," Fran mumbled under her breath as she jammed the card into the hip pocket of her skirt nonetheless. "Donna Reed, my ass. She has no idea who Donna Reed is. Was." Scowling at the retreating makeup artist, Fran wondered if she'd been talking to a woman at all. She instantly chided herself for being petty. The woman was right, of course. It was a political campaign. People would notice, but it wasn't as if she was his wife. It really wasn't, at least not yet.

Fran returned to the stool, a mix of emotions bubbling inside of her: Her love for her daughter, her fear of her father, her anxiety over her future, and him.

She closed her eyes a second and thought of Alex – Alessandro de la Rosa

– her candidate, her boss, her friend, her fantasy, and the man she had nursed, prodded, groomed, and dragged into running against Max Simone for mayor of Las Vegas. Now, she would be on his arm when the bombs fell and victory was declared. The smile returned.

My secret weapon, she called him.

Fran squeezed her coffee mug and slowly lifted it to her lips. Hot, black and bitter, the coffee burned through her pearl pink lip gloss. She sipped tentatively and quickly pulled her tongue back in retreat before being scalded. Lowering the mug and forcing her hands to remain steady, she could hear her heartbeat pounding rapidly in her ears.

It was only a television interview, she repeated in her head. It was only the mayor's race. If they didn't win, they didn't win. If HE didn't win, she reminded herself. He. Her eyes bypassed the television monitor with its slightly delayed airing of the live show and focused instead on the man onstage.

Across the worn, wooden stage floor, Alex leaned back in his eggplant leather chair and gave Fran a discreet wink. She immediately warmed but the tension remained. He was five years her junior, but the age difference had stopped registering the day he took her aside and slowly, passionately kissed her. He had been responding to a dare on her part. She had harbored an obvious crush on him ever since, but he had successfully eluded her. That wink was like tantalizing bait, teasing and, she knew, promising nothing. She winked back.

To Fran, Alex was the perfect image of the successful Vegas politician with his chiseled jaw and his thick, wavy, black hair that curled down slightly over his ears. Stage lights highlighted a few gray strands at his temples. He looked seasoned, matured, but not old. His dark brown eyes were calm and steady. She reminded herself that appearances can be deceiving.

Fran watched as Alex tilted his head slightly and turned his attention back

4

to the alluring host of the early morning talk show. He stretched his legs out territorially, his black loafer-clad feet nearly touching the woman's silver sandals. She didn't withdraw. Alex's gaze lowered to where the blonde's silky hair caressed her throat.

A sudden flash of heat rushed through Fran. She blamed it on the coffee. She blamed her trembling hands on the coffee, as well, forcefully shoving Max's image into a tightly locked closet in the back of her mind. Too much caffeine, she thought, and too little scotch. Lowering her eyes to the mug, she took another sip and grimaced at the bitter, burned taste, but at least it wasn't so hot, now. She looked up at Alex and forced a confident smile.

My secret weapon.

***

Onstage, under the hot, flooding spotlights and surrounded by the TV crew and an attentive live audience, Holly Butterfield leaned seductively back in her upholstered chair, flipped her blonde hair over one shoulder and angled her body to flaunt the perfect calves that prefaced silver sandals. Her backless dress dazzled under the lights against her evenly-tanned skin. Holly had been a Paris Hilton wannabe before Paris Hilton was. She had the air of a woman who had been used once too often but managed to hide it well. Now, as host of LV:AM, she seemed to hold Alex in her grasp.

Seemed to, Fran reminded herself.

Alex breathed slowly. He knitted his fingers together as his eyes lowered from Holly's throat to her shapely legs without lowering his head. He smiled when she tensed. He knew the effect he had on women, and even though it still surprised him to see the charisma at work, he enjoyed it.

He wondered what Holly's real name was, how old she was and how many men she'd used – or used up – on her way up the local ladder. He wondered what plans the socialite was plotting for him. Would she make him a local celebrity? Or expose his darkest secret and destroy his life? Would she do it from her green room or from his bedroom? Alex took a long, deep breath.

Holly's caressing voice, pitched for the audience, broke through his thoughts. "It must be difficult handling such famous cases: Max Simone, Autumn Bartlett and now Ivan Callas. How do you work off all that stress?" Her eyes were on Alex.

"I lead a simple life," Alex responded, his own eyes smiling. His voice had a deep, haunting timbre and the hint of an Italian accent. "Outside of work, I'm a very boring person."

Holly smirked. "No wine, women and song?"

"Holly, you know better. I couldn't change my socks in this town without you knowing about it." A smile played on his lips.

Her eyebrows arched upward. "You're not accusing me of stalking you, are you, Alex?"

She was teasing, and he rolled with it. "I'd be flattered if you were." Alex leaned back. "The truth is, outside of work, I'm just your average single guy." He glanced quickly at Fran and back again.

"Oh, I doubt that," Holly retorted. She frowned slightly and focused on his eyes. "Callas is accused of raping and murdering a 12-year-old girl. I'm sure people have asked you this before, but how do you sleep at night? Knowing you might get him off?"

How do you? Fran wondered. How do we?

The audience hushed.

For the first time, Alex's face became somber. His dark eyes hardened and darted apologetically to Fran before focusing on Holly. He leaned forward, his elbows on his legs, his hands clasped together almost in prayer. "It's easy. The man is innocent," he said with granite certainty.

"But the evidence...."

"Is far from complete."

6

"So, you'll be attacking the forensics? That has been your pattern on past cases."

Alex darted a look at Fran and caught her startled expression. He stiffened momentarily. The question was meant to illicit Alex's open and very public hostility towards a certain member of the city crime lab. They hadn't planned for that question. They hadn't expected Holly Butterfield to be that astute, but in hindsight, they should have.

"If you want to talk legal strategy, Holly, you'll have to quit your day job and come work for me," Alex said with a practiced warning smile while sidestepping the bait.

Holly took the hint and backed off. "I'm so sorry," she cooed. "I just find the whole thing very interesting."

Holly dipped into her interview bag for another tactic. "Rumor has it you're entering the race for mayor against one of your former clients. Care to make an official announcement on this program?"

Alex kept his cool. "When I'm ready to announce, you'll be the first to know."

Holly jumped at the innuendo. "So, you ARE going to announce, just not here and now?" She leaned forward with an excited blush on her cheek.

Are you picking out drapes for the mayor's mansion? Fran thought.

"We're certainly overdue for some fresh leadership," Alex said. "At the very least, the residents of Las Vegas deserve a mayor who actually spends time in this town."

Holly nodded. "It's true that Simone seems to have earned his reputation as the absentee mayor, but you must admit, since the city workers started renegotiating their contract, he's been front and center, working hard to keep costs down and services affordable while avoiding a strike."

"True, Holly, but Simone was elected to serve four years, not four months."

7

"Which brings us back to...." She urged him to keep talking.

"It's an open game." Alex's voice was soothing and knowledgeable. "Anybody can run. Who knows what the future will bring? Maybe someday you'll be mayor of Las Vegas."

"And the fact that your law partner is his daughter?" Holly ignored the remark.

Alex glanced at Fran and nodded. "She's her own woman. Always has been. She can think for herself."

The audience liked the answer and responded with a ripple of applause.

He watched as Fran unclench her hands from the coffee mug one at a time, shaking them out. He could read her body, her tension, even her thoughts. He looked back at Holly.

Holly, meeting a solid wall, changed course. She never once looked in Fran's direction. "Tell us, Alex, how does a successful and handsome widower like you manage to stay single in a town with so many wedding chapels?" A flirty smile played on her lips.

The audience giggled on cue.

Alex leaned towards her and flashed his famous and slightly skewed smile. If the reference to his late wife affected him, he didn't show it. Under the hot stage lights, he looked calm and cool as the proverbial cucumber to everyone but Fran.

Cucumbers sweat more, Fran mused.

"It's very difficult, Holly, especially with so many beautiful girls like you to tempt me," Alex said as his eyes grazed the host's lips.

Holly's eyelashes fluttered. She leaned back a little as if suddenly hit by a warm but powerful ocean breeze and she unconsciously held her breath.

Damn you, thought Fran. After five long years, she still melted at the sound of his well-rehearsed voice. He was one of those rare men who could call a woman "girl" and turn it into a compliment. She sipped again on the coffee and found it had cooled enough to be undrinkable.

Holly suddenly grinned foolishly and made an exaggerated fanning motion with her hand. "Oh! You are so hot!" Her cheeks were slightly flushed. The audience hooted and cheered.

When everyone finally calmed down, Holly asked the question that had sold local newspapers for a month earlier that summer. "Please, Alex, I know I shouldn't ask, but everyone here is just dying to know."

I just bet they are. Fran suddenly felt a twinge of nausea in her gut. She scrutinized Alex's face for any hint of discomfort but didn't see it.

He smiled calmly but, this time, didn't look at Fran.

"Is it true that when you represented the sultry soap star Autumn Bartlett..." The host glanced at her audience as if confiding a great secret, "during her scandalous divorce trial..." Alex leaned closer to her. "...the two of you were caught, red-handed so to speak, doing the nasty in the courthouse elevator?"

Holly's hand slipped forward, and she brushed his arm with her long fingers as if eliciting a confidence from a dear friend. A photo of the actress with her jade green eyes and long auburn hair appeared in the lower right corner of the television monitor. Fran pretended not to see it.

A slight gasp surfed across the room, followed by silence.

What if he simply says 'yes?' Fran suddenly panicked. She shifted again, chafing at the memory of those rumors. She didn't know the answer. She didn't want to know. She never wanted to know. The knot in her gut tightened.

Alex continued to smile. He reached out and rested his hand gently on Holly's, the touch sending an obvious shiver up her back.

"Holly, Holly, that's not fair," Alex crooned without skipping a beat. "Attorney-client privilege, you know." He winked.

They loved it. They loved him. She loved him. The nausea left Fran as fast

9

as it had come.

Holly blushed deeply under Alex's steady gaze. The red heat rose up her neck and under the streaming hair, barely visible to anyone.

He saw it and his smile deepened.

Holly quickly pulled back her hand as if touching the business end of a curling iron. In the heartbeat of confusion, she was forced to glance at her cue cards and resort to the carefully crafted lines.

"Well." She cleared her throat to get past the weakness in her voice before trying again. Some of the audience members laughed. "Well, with so many cartoon... excuse me, I mean so many courtroom wins, so many celebrity clients and such handsome..." She looked up a moment and then glanced away again. "Um... It's... It's no wonder you've been named...." She stopped to take a deep breath, fanned herself again and grinned like a school girl. "Oh, my. You do have a way about you." The audience laughed. Holly started again. "It's no wonder you have been named Las Vegas Man of the Year. Congratulations, Alex."

Relaxing a bit, Holly returned her eyes to him and leaned forward just enough to give him a gratuitous peek at her lace bra and pink cleavage as she extended a handshake. "And good luck in your campaign to be the next mayor of the City of Las Vegas." She quietly waited for his reaction with the air of a teenage girl expecting her first kiss.

"Thank you." He gently took her hand, lifted it slowly to his lips, smiled and kissed her fingers. His eyes met hers straight on, and he avoided the obvious bait. "Now, if someone could just point me to the elevator...." Alex teased, still holding Holly's hand. For the briefest of moments, his eyes flitted down and back up.

Holly choked, the audience broke into laughter and Fran looked up to heaven with a short prayer.

Alex slowly stood up and pulled Holly to her feet before he allowed her hand to slip out of his grasp. His athletic six-foot frame towered over the petite woman when he bent and kissed her cheek. Then he gave the audience a quick nod and a casual wave before he was escorted offstage.

Bastard, Fran thought. You little bastard.

The hot lights followed Alex as he strode across the wasteland between the stage's warm glow and the wing's shadows. Fran stood up and set the coffee mug on the stool. Alex tilted his good ear to her. His fingers glided softly around her neck as he brushed her hair back with a familiar intimacy.

"Some skinny jerk told me my makeup was shitty," Fran complained, pressing her shaky hand to his chest and looking up at him with eyes begging for reassurance.

A stagehand slipped quietly up to them and quickly removed Alex's mic, then just as quickly disappeared. Fran wondered if 'the jerk' had heard the remark.

"She must have been very pretty to make you that mad." He kissed her on the forehead. "You look beautiful, Bella. You always do."

"But she said I looked like Donna Reed!" Fran was not easily placated. She rested her head against his strong chest a moment and drew her strength from him.

Alex rubbed the back of her neck with his thumb and frowned. "Who's Donna Reed?" he asked.

Fran groaned and glanced back to the stage where Holly had taken a sip from her signature mug before regaining her composure and continuing with her show. "Isn't he just a dream?" Holly glanced briefly in the direction of Alex's exit and momentarily locked eyes with Fran. "And now, for my next guest...."

A burly man Fran vaguely recognized as a local casino owner was hustled past her and Alex and into the spotlight. He passed between the two women and broke their stares.

Fran plucked Alex's silken handkerchief from his breast pocket to dab at the spot of sweat over his lips. He reached up and steadied her hand as she did so. Grinning, she pulled her hand easily out of his warm grasp and gave him a little wink. "Time to schmooze," Fran told him.

Alex groaned and leaned forward to whisper in her ear. "I've done enough schmoozing for one day, Bella. Time to go home."

By 'home,' Fran knew he meant the office. There was no home for them. She sighed as she thought of how he'd kept the famous Holly Butterfield off balance when he had abandoned their carefully plotted script.

"They're too busy to talk anyway. Just shake a few hands and smile," Fran instructed. She pulled out her phone, glanced at it, turned it back on and erased the last three messages without comment.

"Is he bothering you, again?" Alex asked, frowning.

"I'll live."

Alex pulled out his own phone and scowled. He had silenced the ringtone. Fran knew the look.

"Toni?" she asked, referring to Alex's older sister.

Alex nodded. "Only four calls this morning. She must be getting lazy." He chuckled a bit and pocketed the phone.

"She needs some help, Alex. Counseling, therapy, meds. Something." He ignored her.

Slipping her arm through Alex's, Fran steered him around the room and gave him time to briefly meet each of the television crew. He then pressed his hand to the small of her back and steered her out to the sun-drenched parking lot and her convertible, silver Mercedes with its warm leather seats. They didn't speak about the interview until they were on the road and cruising the Vegas strip, Guitarra del Sur on the radio and only the hot wind listening.

"Well?" Alex asked. He studied himself in the visor mirror and wiped the last residue of makeup from his face with tissue paper and a dab of Fran's

12

cold cream, brought just for these occasions. He screwed up his nose as he cleaned his hands with a moistened paper towel, put the supplies back into Fran's tidy pink cosmetics case and set it in the backseat, on top of a stack of newspapers.

"Do you remember when you showed up at the nurses' association lunch still wearing lipstick?" Fran unsuccessfully brushed her windswept bangs from her eyes. He had done a live news interview regarding the Autumn Bartlett case and the makeup crew had gone a little overboard.

Alex snapped the mirror shut and tilted the visor back into place. "Don't remind me." He slipped on his sunglasses. "It took me two days to get that color off."

"Just be glad it wasn't fingernail polish." A broad smile lit up Fran's features as she thought about the show, the campaign, the adventure they were on. It seemed the gods were smiling on them with the same radiance as the Vegas sun. She forced the televised image of Autumn Bartlett out of her mind. Her eyes sparkled beneath her sunglasses. "Not too shabby." Fran tried to sound clinical. Her fingers lightly strummed the steering wheel to the music as buildings became a blur of sun-bleached colors and glinting windows. "Of course, you'll get better with practice."

Alex turned his head slightly and glared at her, wide eyes burning through his shades. "Bella, they loved me."

A soft laugh escaped Fran. She bit her lip to stifle it. "They sure did." Her fingers sped up as the tempo increased. "But all you did was flirt with the audience and with that little donnina. The real test will be the debates."

Alex frowned.

"Still, you did good," she reassured him.

The air had a thickness that foreshadowed rain despite the clear sky. Fran could taste it.

Alex leaned back in the bucket seat, stretched his legs a bit, closed his eyes, and relaxed. He let the wind brush his face as his long fingers matched hers and played on the window rim of the car door.

"We still need to make an official announcement." Fran's well-calculated statement interrupted his thoughts. Her eyes darted to him and back to the road. There was something about the quality of his stillness that disturbed her. She recognized the mood as easily as she recognized the heaviness in the air. She thought of his late wife.

Today was the five-year anniversary of her murder.

Alex glanced at Fran with a slightly worried look. His fingers stopped tapping. "Will you be there?"

It always surprised her when he showed these momentary flashes of insecurity. She frowned. "I got you this far and I intend to finish the job." She bit off the words.

Alex studied her tense body language a minute. "I don't want things to get worse between the two of you because of me."

"Worse?" Fran snapped the word like a whip. Her eyes darted back and forth between him and the road. Her lips tightened. "How can it get any worse?"

She knew Alex was talking about Max Simone, the invisible elephant in the backseat of her Mercedes. Well, perhaps not so invisible, she thought. She could still feel her father's hot breath on the back of her neck. She shuddered.

Fran's lips tightened into a straight line as she grabbed the stick and shifted. She hit the gas and passed three cars in one sweep as she tried to outrun her panic attack. Alex's eyebrows shot up and his fingers curled into the car's armrest, but he didn't say a word. She stabbed off the radio. For the next few minutes, they rode in tense silence.

"Do we really need to discuss this?" She looked straight ahead and clipped her words through clenched teeth. Thoughts of Max Simone and

14

what he had done to her and her mother had triggered an emotional spiral she couldn't control. She angrily brushed her bangs back yet again as if challenging the wind.

A mustard-yellow convertible Mustang loaded with college-age kids flew by, music blaring and a red UNLV Rebels sticker glued to the black bumper. One of the kids leaned over the back seat and threw Fran a sassy kiss. She softened slightly at an old memory. Her shoulders relaxed.

"Do you really believe I have what it takes to be mayor, Bella? Or are you just doing this to get back at him?" Alex's words cut through the wind and silence.

She bit her lip in thought. *He had to pick NOW to ask this question? Why now?* She thought he trusted his abilities as much as she did, but what if she was wrong? His question must be rhetorical, she surmised, meant to elicit any doubts she might have about the campaign.

"Having second thoughts?" she asked.

When he didn't answer, her grip tightened on the steering wheel. "Both." She shoved her sunglasses further up the bridge of her nose to conceal her angry eyes. Her heart seemed to constrict in her chest.

"Did you ever tell anyone else what he did to you?" he asked. He started to reach out to touch her but quickly pulled back.

"No!" she snapped back. "I couldn't…. No one would have…. I was only twelve." Fran took a deep breath." Yes! I told my ex and I told my mother. I told my mother and she tried to leave him and…." She choked. "She'd still be alive if…." Hot tears stung the back of Fran's narrowing blue eyes as the pain boiled out of her. "Shut up, Alex."

"That was an accident, Bella. She was drinking. She was driving too fast."

"Shut the hell up." There was no way she would let Alex pull the rug out from under her now.

The road and buildings transformed into a sun-streaked, watery carnival ride. Fran quickly glanced about when she heard a child screaming and sobbing in fear. Fran expected to see the girl fallen on the sidewalk somewhere, but there was no girl. No one responded to the crying, no one stopped, no one looked.

She sped by people at a dizzying speed. A loud banging noise exploded in Fran's head when some teenagers set off firecrackers on the sidewalk. She hated fireworks. She hated the sound they made, like gunfire. She hated loud noises. Her fists tightened on the steering wheel.

Fighting her panic, Fran glanced quickly over her right shoulder to check traffic, then shifted down, crossed two lanes and pulled off into the parking lot of an aging convenience store. The car narrowly missed the gas pumps. The tires left long black skid marks on the broken pavement of the lot as she braked. She was out of the car in seconds.

Alex, stunned, had sunk his fingernails into the armrest and now eyed her warily.

"Enough is enough!" she screamed at him as tears spilled over her cheeks. She stopped briefly to kick the front tire before marching off.

"Get back here, girl!" he yelled at her. He immediately regretted his tone. "Bella! I only meant...."

"I don't give a fuck what you meant!" she screamed at him. The sick feeling she'd had earlier suddenly erupted from her gut to her throat and drove her forward. In the reflection of the door window, she could see Alex lean forward on the hot leather seat and slam both fists down hard on the dashboard.

The young clerk behind the counter secreted her half-smoked joint and looked up at Fran as she entered the store. A spike of hot pink hair capped pierced eyebrows, a nose ring, and Goth makeup. She reeked of pot, garlic, and incense. A thick trail of smoke escaped the clerk's lips. She batted it away with her hand. "Can I help you?" she asked as she cautiously eyed the

16

crying woman from head to toe.

"Ladies' room."

The girl pointed to a swinging gray door in the back of the store. As Fran disappeared, the girl finished the joint and brushed some fallen ashes from the shelf to the stained linoleum floor.

Fran found a gray, concrete, cold-storage area filled with cardboard boxes and crates of groceries and cases of beer and wine. The room smelled of soap, stale potato chips, and pot. The floor was pitted. The lighting was weak. Small windows were covered with a streaked, uneven splash of dark gray paint. Winding around the stacks and wooden pallets, she stepped gingerly over a dirty, string mop and came on a battered wooden door with a scrawled, handmade, cardboard sign that read "Employees Only." She banged on it loudly to make sure the room was empty before she yanked the door open.

Inside, a weak fluorescent light, attached to the dirty tiled ceiling with what looked like duct tape, barely lit the cramped bathroom. Fran squeezed behind the sink, slammed and locked the door, and gripped the edges of the worn counter. She glanced up at her reflection in the smudged mirror and shivered.

The light was ghastly on her pale complexion and swollen eyes but her waterproof makeup had survived the unexpected flood of tears. She wet her bangs a bit and brushed them back the way her mother used to do. That motion triggered the grief that poured through her like a bottle of straight scotch and reached into every vein, every muscle, and every cell. Her face twisted with pain as an agonized cry escaped her lips. She grabbed handfuls of toilet paper and pressed them to her face to catch the tears.

"No, no, no!" she yelled at herself. "No!" Her fingers slipped into the thickness of her red hair and grasped it as she shook. "No, no, no!" She surrendered to fresh sobs as she collapsed against the wall behind her. Her

17

hands fell to her side. The room seemed to spin in her head. As calmness returned, she bent over the sink, turned on the faucet and splashed the tears from her face.

"Bella, stop it," Alex ordered from the other side of the door. "Get out of there. We need to talk about this."

Fran turned off the water with a squeak of the faucet, but she didn't respond. She knew he was standing right there, a few inches away. She wanted to teach him a lesson about messing with her mind. She cursed herself for not grabbing her purse and she wished she had a mint to wipe out the acid burning in her mouth.

"Bella! I don't want to fight."

"When will you learn to shut up?" she screamed at him. She bent her head to the sink, scooped up some more water in the palm of her hand and gargled with it before she yanked a paper towel from its metal container and wiped her face and hands.

"Bella!" He sounded frantic. "Should the next mayor of Las Vegas have to beg his best friend to come out of the bathroom?"

Fran heard an unfamiliar crack in his stern voice. He was worried. She began to relent.

"I won't bring it up again, girl. Do you hear me? Just get that cute ass out here! Whatever you do is fine by me." He was silent a moment. "Bella? Honey?"

Fran grunted, swung the door open and nearly knocked him over. She eyed him critically from head to toe like a cook inspects a cockroach on her clean kitchen counter. "Don't ever call me honey," she snapped, eyes flashing, as she yanked the handkerchief from his jacket pocket and blew her nose hard into it. She slapped it back into his hand. "You know how much I hate that!"

He glanced at the thing and quickly threw it into a trashcan. "It got you

18

out of the bathroom, didn't it?" He tilted his head and looked relieved.

"I mean it!" For a second they stared at each other; then Fran gave him a weak smile, a consolation prize for his obvious concern.

"Damn, girl, that was worse than the interview!"

Exhausted, Fran grabbed the lapel of his jacket for support. She pressed her forehead into his strong chest and inhaled his scent. When she could breathe again, she looked up and found herself close enough to his lips to feel his warm breath on her tear-dried cheeks. She considered kissing him but the residual taste in her mouth voted against the impulse. His large warm hands grasped her arms and steadied her. He bent his head to her, his lips soft on her temple. Startled, she stepped back. "Don't ever do that to me again!" she ordered with half-feigned rage.

"Do what? Kiss you or nag you?" He threw his hands up in mock wounded defeat and smiled. "Whatever you say, Bella. Whatever I did, I promise, I will never do it again."

"Ooo!" For a moment, she hung on that smile, then she straightened her suit and gave him her best maternal glare. "That's better." She pretended to brush a bit of lint from his jacket. "I really love that new cologne of yours," she noted.

He swallowed another laugh. With his arm over her shoulder and hers around his waist, they made their way through the store under the curious gaze of the clerk. They stopped briefly to buy a pack of peppermint gum before heading to the waiting car.

"This time, I'm driving." Alex pulled the keys out of his pocket and dangled them in her face. "I want to get home in one piece today."

She pouted but didn't argue as she slipped into the passenger seat, returned her sunglasses to her nose and settled down.

Alex got behind the wheel, reached over and buckled her seatbelt. He started the car and gave her a sideways glance. "Now behave, Bella," he ordered. The engine roared and the coupe squealed out into mid-morning Las Vegas traffic.

CHAPTER 2

All Detective Tom Sadler wanted was a quiet lunch. He was used to not getting what he wanted.

His partner, Toni de la Rosa, her dark eyes flashing mischievously under her curly, boyish haircut, angrily shoved her cell phone to the middle of the table and kicked him in the shin for the third time since sitting down at the crowded Vegas diner. Fortunately for him, she was wearing high-top Converse sneakers below her skinny black jeans.

"Ow!" Tom winced, nearly spilling his juice. Even though he should have seen the kick coming, he didn't manage to pull his leg out of the way fast enough. "It's not my fault he doesn't return your calls."

He plucked a radish from his salad and propelled it at her nose with a flick of his fingers. It hit its intended target once and bounced before disappearing under the table.

"Ow!' She mimicked his distress as she rubbed her nose.

"Serves you right." He softened the comment with a shy grin that made him look much younger than his age. "You're lucky I didn't shoot you for assaulting a cop."

Toni's eyes dropped involuntarily to the Glock Tom wore over his snug-fitting, blue polo shirt.

They faced each other at high noon across the retro-styled table flanked by glossy, red vinyl benches. An amber, translucent plastic shade separated them from the sun's sparkling glare as it skipped across the hoods of the cars in the parking lot and landed on the glass sugar container on their table. The air was thick with the smell of fried potatoes, onions, and burgers, carried on the chilly draft of a humming air conditioner. The lunch crowd – a mix of business types, blue collar workers, and tourists – streamed in and out through the art deco glass doors. Elvis crooned quietly over the din of conversation.

"The show was over hours ago. He should have called by now," Toni muttered.

"Maybe he had to work. Maybe he's busy. Maybe his battery died from taking all your calls. Maybe he found some pretty young thing to have sex with. Maybe, just maybe, you are NOT the center of his universe," Tom suggested with a prickly grin.

"Fuck you," she said, just barely quiet enough to not be heard across the aisle.

Tom's eyes drifted and his face softened. He flashed a beguiling smile at a young waitress with deep brown hair and eyes as she sashayed past in a pink dress and red, heart-shaped apron. She held a pot of steaming coffee in each hand, black lid for regular, orange for decaf. She winked. He cranked his head around, his hazel eyes following the shape of her hips as she turned a corner. She didn't look back. He unconsciously let out a small sigh.

Toni reached across the table and pinched his arm. "If you're doing that for my benefit, forget it. She's way too young for you," she chided.

Tom looked amused. "She is not too young," he said. "Definitely NOT too young." He turned his attention back to Toni and rubbed his arm. "Besides, why do you care? The only man you ever think about is Alex."

Toni wore jeans and a black "wife-beater" shirt that showed off the rose tattoo on her muscular upper arm. She was without nail polish or makeup, although her skin hardly needed any. She had a few strands of gray hair around her temples and small lines around her eyes and lips that belied her age. She looked, on the one hand, slightly weathered, and on the other, like she could nail anybody's ass to the floor in two seconds. She had none of the style, charisma or sophistication of her younger brother, Alex, but she had a presence – unmistakable, powerful, daunting.

Threatening, Tom thought, as he studied the emotions that seemed to cascade from her eyes whenever they talked about Alex.

22

The lanky brunette offered up a tight-lipped smirk, grasped her thick hamburger with two hands and plunged her teeth into it. The ketchup and meat juice dribble onto her plate of soggy chips. She barely stopped to dab a bit of food from the large silver cross nestled in her small breasts before she took another bite. He wondered if the cross was there to ward off vampires. She was the kind of person who would know vampires, he thought, or perhaps demons.

"Hey, we're friends, remember?" Tom hesitated as memories of the last few weeks with her ran through his mind. "Well, we were once. Before you got bitchy on me." He took a stab at his salad.

"I'm not…."

He didn't let her finish. "I know. It's that time of the year. But I worry about you." He gestured towards the hamburger with his fork. "You eat wrong, you drive too fast, you drink too much, you don't sleep, you work crazy hours and you don't have a social life, despite those tight jeans." His eyes crinkled up in a smile. "It's no wonder you're so damn cranky all the time." The curly-haired former jock spoke with a slight Georgia twang.

"What do you mean, that time of the month?" She snapped.

"Year. That time of the year." He sighed in frustration.

She kept her head down and continued eating.

He envied her ability to eat what she wanted and stay broom-handle thin, but he wouldn't tell her that. He could almost wrap his hands around her tiny waist. He distracted himself by spearing a large tomato wedge and shoving the whole thing into his mouth.

"You called me fat," she argued, her mouth full and her deep eyes blazing. "And I'm NOT cranky!" She glanced up momentarily at an elderly couple inching their way up the aisle, the woman's frail hand clinging to her partner's reassuring arm. They wore matching golfing outfits in lime green, even though their pale skins and bent posture indicated a serious lack of sun.

Toni turned her eyes quickly back to her plate and continued eating.

"I said you had a nice round ass," Tom countered in a low voice as he chewed. He had followed her look but said nothing about it. "If you didn't want me to notice, you should have worn something else."

"It wasn't for your benefit," Toni told him.

"Then whose was it for? Alex's?" Tom cringed when he heard the words come out of his mouth.

"Nobody's!" Her face flared red in rage. Her eyes went to the phone and quickly back to Tom.

He shook his head, plucked a paper napkin from its metal box and reached across the table to wipe some of the grease from her chin. "It was supposed to be a compliment – the ass thing," he explained.

"I got it." Toni snatched the napkin from his fingers and roughly wiped her face. "Stop babying me."

"I thought that's what you wanted, to be babied. That's why you got the hots for every old goat in the department except me." His voice had gone from teasing to accusatory. "Or maybe I'm just not old enough for you." The words came out of thin air. He didn't mean them. Well, maybe he did, but he never intended to say them. He kept asking himself, why was she being such a bitch? Why was she pushing all his buttons these days?

Toni leaned forward menacingly and lowered her voice. "It was one date with one idiot and I wasn't IN the department yet."

Tom matched her position and tone. "It was one date with the sheriff and it got you the job, didn't it?" Tom didn't know why he felt the need to attack her, but the words were out before he could blink.

Toni stared at him, her mouth full of hamburger and rage.

He quickly pulled away, regret in his. He took a drink and licked his dry lips. "I'm sorry." He rubbed his suddenly hot neck. "I've been under a lot of stress, what with the Callas case and the mayor's office breathing down our

24

necks and all the publicity. I shouldn't have said that." He didn't mention her recent attitude change.

Toni slowly lowered her hamburger. "Just don't you ever bring that up again." She took another swipe at her chin with the napkin.

"I said I was sorry," he countered without looking at her. He swallowed more water to get rid of the fuzziness in his mouth.

"Not good enough."

He nodded. "You're right. I was way out of line. I was just being...."

"Jealous," she finished.

His eyes rose to meet hers again. "No. Envious."

"Get over it."

"You're right. You're always right." He looked for a way to break the tension. "I should know better." He closed his eyes a moment, leaned back and smiled as the waitress passed by again. "Damn, she smells good."

"It's the coffee." Toni scowled at the waitress

Tom opened his eyes and shook his head. "Lighten up."

"You're a goddamn ass, Tom."

"And you're a...." This time, discretion got the better of him.

"How long have you known me?" she parried.

"Since Sarah was murdered," he said quietly. "Five years to the day."

Her eyelids flickered for a moment in reaction to the name of Alex's dead wife. It was that time of the year and they both knew it. Tom's comment had hit the mark, but she didn't bite. "You give me that shit again, and I'll nail your ass to the wall, again." A slip of a smile escaped her pert lips. Her teeth sank back into the burger without further comment.

"You caught me on a bad day." He recalled a certain grudge match on the gym floor. He knew she was convinced he had let her win. He would neither confirm nor deny.

"Have a lot of those, do you?"

Tom's phone beeped, and Toni glanced at hers. He unclipped the phone from his belt and frowned at the caller ID. Putting the phone to his ear and raising a finger to Toni to keep her quiet, he said, "Hi, Mom."

Toni stifled a laugh.

"Yes. Sunday. I'll be there." Tom tried to sound casual. He turned his head towards the window to keep the conversation private. "Charlie wants to know if we'll have Thanksgiving at his place or at yours this year. What do you want to do?"

Toni reached up and grabbed his floating finger, forced his arm back to the table and held it there. He darted a look at her, seized her fingers and hung onto them tightly as she tried to pull away. He smiled.

"I know it's three weeks away, but...."

Toni yanked harder.

"Right. Sunday. We'll talk about it then. Want me to bring something?" He was silent a moment as he listened to the voice on the phone. "Besides her." Tom sounded annoyed.

There was a brief silence as he glanced back up at Toni. "No, Ma. I told you, we're not dating." He squeezed his partner's finger again. "Please let it go." He sighed heavily and noted how Toni's deep brown eyes widened as he spoke. He shrugged. "Okay, see you then. I have to go. Work." He quickly flipped the phone closed and released her hand.

"It's not about you," he said curtly as if reading her mind.

"Like hell it isn't."

"It isn't."

"Not the thing to tell a woman you're on a date with," she retorted. She withdrew her hand, picked up her phone and checked for messages. She hit a button and listened while the familiar dial went through. It rang – and rang – and rang until she got a voice message that said the mailbox was full. She put the phone back down with a sigh.

26

"It's not a…. Never mind." Tom shook his head and picked up his glass of lemon water. "So, truce?"

She shrugged and kept eating. Her eyes were vacant as she stared at the uncooperative phone.

Tom picked at his salad before venturing into another line of conversation. "So, Alex wants to be mayor, huh?" From Sarah to Alex. Tom wondered just how predictable that was.

Toni scowled and exchanged the hamburger for her milkshake. She took a long sip through the peppermint striped straw and then glanced around the diner to see if anyone was listening to them. Then she leaned towards him, elbows on the table, voice low, dark eyes narrowed behind thin bangs. "He's nuts. Totally and completely nuts. I don't care how many goddamn TV talk shows he does, he's got no damn business running for mayor. He's setting himself up for a fall."

She set the drink down, nervously picked up the phone and punched in Alex's number one more time. She got another "mailbox is full" response, shut off the phone and stuffed it into the pocket of the leather jacket next to her.

"He wants revenge," Tom noted. He stabbed another tomato slice and munched on it thoughtfully before continuing. "He still blames Simone for the botched investigation of his wife's murder, the leaks to the press, everyone saying he killed her. Bad way to do business, prosecution by press."

"Bad way to get revenge, using politics – using Fran."

Tom shrugged. "Maybe she's using him."

Toni appeared to consider the possibility. "It's been five years," she said. Her hands trembled slightly as she took another long sip.

"People don't forget something that gruesome, especially since the killer was never caught." Tom felt a knot form in his gut and wondered if another fight was brewing. He considered retreating from the topic when Toni completed his thought.

"You're right, Tom. People don't forget when someone is accused of murdering his wife," she answered with disquieting numbness.

"Accused but not charged," Tom reminded her as he looked up into her intense eyes. "The media made the accusation, not the police. Alex was cleared. More than cleared. The press crucified him and then made a martyr out of him: Poor widower dragged through the mud by misguided cops. Something like that."

"Vindicated." Her voice sounded hollow as if she was unconvinced.

"That, too." Tom watched emotion return to her face. "The sheriff still thinks Alex is guilty," he added. "He can't seem to scratch deep enough to reach that itch."

"Those bastards are idiots. They should have known better. They should never have even considered him a suspect," Toni added.

Unlike her famous brother, Toni had managed to squeeze most of the accent out of her voice by disguising it behind a quasi-southern drawl, something she had learned from Tom. The accent only escaped when she was angry. At this moment, Tom heard it loud and clear.

"He's too temperamental for that job. He flies off the handle at the drop of a hat. He's just like his father," she said.

Tom looked confused. "Randall?" He referred to the sheriff.

Toni matched the look. "Randall's not his father."

"No, no. I mean Randall is too...."

Toni understood. "No, Alex. Alex is too temperamental."

"Your father, you mean, then," Tom interjected. You, he thought.

Toni flashed a nasty look. "For the record, we do not share the same father."

Tom looked surprised but when Toni returned to her hamburger he merely made a mental note of the fact and didn't pursue it. "Then there's Max

28

Simone. Young girl murdered. Alex still a newcomer. A first case no one will forget." Tom glanced back at the parking lot and shook his head.

"It was only a prelim. The charges were dropped before they walked into the courtroom. Max walked."

"You think he did it?" Tom asked.

"You have any doubt?" she countered.

"Rank has its privileges," Tom said. "It didn't look quite like that from the public's point of view. It looked like Alex got him off."

"Are you pumping me for information?" she asked.

"No, no. I just...."

"Well, Max is still in office, isn't he? The publicity didn't seem to harm him any." She finished her milkshake with a loud slurp.

"You can bet the press will bring it up, though, once Alex announces. They'd have to." Tom impaled a second radish and scowled at it with disdain. "You know how the press is. It sinks its teeth into a bone and won't let go until the thing is sucked clean. The rest of the world could explode around them, but they have to stick to that bone. Lazy bastards. This election will make one long, tough news blitz."

She handed him the salt. "You're beginning to sound like Alex with his conspiracy theories," she noted, somewhat approvingly.

"Are we talking Simone or Callas?" He referred to the child murder case Alex was handling.

"Alex says he's innocent." Her words flashed in the air like the swooshing tail of a wild salmon.

"I don't believe in conspiracies," Tom countered as he quickly cut the line. "I believe in evidence." He held the salt shaker in one hand and the pierced radish in the other and he gestured with both.

"The evidence is circumstantial at best."

"We're still talking about Callas, right?" he asked.

She nodded.

Tom thought quietly a moment. "Still, do you know anyone besides Alex who is ballsy enough to run against Simone?" He leaned back a bit, popped the radish into his mouth and waited for an answer as she finished another bite of her burger.

"He's NOT…." She snapped at Tom with her mouth full. "He's just… just…." She glowered at him. "He's just Alex, and don't look at me that way." She kicked him again and nearly caused him to choke.

"I said stop that!" Tom snapped at her around a mouthful of radish. He glanced nervously about to make sure they weren't being watched and shrunk back from the glare of a few sets of annoyed eyes. Irritated, he finished the radish, frowned slightly, leaned towards her and lowered his voice. "Forget about Alex. Let's get to what's really bothering you," he snapped. "When were you going to tell me?"

Toni's expression turned hard as she swallowed. She unsuccessfully put on her most innocent look. "Tell you what?"

"That you're quitting the force." He had identified the source of his anger. "That you're leaving me."

"I'm not quitting, exactly. I'm just transferring. Phoenix, I think." Her eyes widened. "Have you been reading my e-mails again? I swear, Tom, if…."

"Oh, no you don't. You're not going to weasel out of this one. I don't have to read your emails or anything else for that matter." He dropped his gaze and looked very uncomfortable. "I know when a partner is bailing on me. It's happened enough times. I can smell it in the wind." His voice was tinged with resentment; his mind wandered down some invisible path in his head.

She hesitated a second and then lowered her voice to a deep, soothing timbre. "It's not about you, Tom."

He looked skeptical.

30

"It's not your fault. You've just had a run of bad luck with partners, that's all."

"Our business runs on luck." Tom took a deep breath. "I thought it would be different with you." His eyes glanced momentarily at the large red clock over the restaurant's front door. They would have to get back to work soon. "You've done this to me three year's running. The anniversary comes up and you talk about splitting. I'm tired of it, Toni."

Toni shoved her lunch plate away angrily, wiped her fingers with the napkin and glared at him.

"It's not about you." Her shoulders slumped, surrendering to the weight of his obvious disappointment. Her voice could barely be heard over the muffle of conversations and the clatter of dishes.

He met her eyes. "I know that."

Toni leaned forward to concentrate on Tom. Her hand rested on his arm. He covered it with his own hand, his thumb sliding back and forth over her fingers.

"I've been cleaning up Alex's messes my whole life. It's like I can't breathe without him being there. Like we're connected at the hip. This election thing is making it worse." She stopped a few seconds to catch her breath. "I need a fresh start. I need to go someplace where I can have a life - a REAL life - my own life. Where I don't have to apologize for him, or fix things for him, or chase ghosts for him, or deal with his ex-lovers or late wife or whoever he's screwing these days. Where I won't.... You know. Someplace where no one knows me, where no one knows him."

"It's not your job to do any of those things, Toni. You were just a baby when your parents died. Seven? Eight? And Alex was what?" He did the math in his head with no success. "He's a grown man. You don't need to take care of him anymore. You're the one who makes a big show out of this; no one else does. You need to let it go. Let him go. Let the whole damn business

31

with Sarah's murder go."

"He was six, I was ten, and..." She began to tremble.

"I know."

"He... I...." Toni swallowed back the sudden rush of hot tears.

He didn't remember ever seeing her this upset before. "I know. I read your file, remember?" Tom hung onto her hand reassuringly and watched the ghosts flicker in her eyes. "You have to move on, hon. You have to let it all go."

"I can't. Not unless I can get away from him." She shook her head sadly. "What else can I say, Tom? What do you want me to say?"

Tom shook his head and then a grin crept into the edges of his mouth as he arched an eyebrow. "A kiss before you go?" he asked.

Toni went to kick him again but this time he managed to move his legs out of her way and she slammed her foot into the metal post of the bench instead.

"Ouch! Damn you! You're incorrigible." She yanked her hand back and threw down the napkin like some medieval gauntlet. "Just for that, you get the check." She stood up. "Coming?" she asked, slipping on her jacket and checking the gun holstered on her hip.

He was dizzy from the speed of her mood changes. "Unfortunately, no." Tom responded to the pun under his breath. He looked up and saw her puzzled expression. "Yes, I'm coming. Just remember, partner, no one runs away from their problems – not me, not Alex, not even you. The road isn't that long."

"If I really wanted to run away, trust me, no one would be able to find me." She glowered at him, turned and walked away.

"Hey," he called after her, "don't forget we're on call tonight."

"Not me," she shot back as she spun on her heel and walked backward for a bit while speaking. "Chuck is covering." She turned around and kept going.

32

He sighed and watched her hips sway down the narrow aisle to the front door as he admired her snug black jeans one more time. She really did have a nice ass, he mused. She turned her head to look at him, slipped on her sunglasses and gave him a brazen smirk as if she could read his mind. Tom groaned, picked up the check, grabbed his jacket and followed her.

CHAPTER 3

Fran's ex-husband, tall and blonde with a banker's suit and a tennis player's tan, stepped out of the driver's side of his Audi, squinted in the bright sunlight and smiled broadly across the hood of the car to his 12-year-old daughter as she ran out of the school building, her long, red hair flowing behind her. He glanced at the jostling kids in their uniforms, the strewn backpacks along the sidewalk, the yellow buses, and the sun-soaked cars. He froze, the smile gone. His eyes narrowed at the sudden bounce of sunlight off a white stretch limo's tinted windows. It stood away from the main drive, slightly down the street. Paul couldn't be sure who was in the vehicle, but he had an idea. His stomach twisted sickeningly.

"Daddy! Daddy!" Lauren distracted him as she dropped her bookbag at his feet and threw herself into his arms. She was one of those fair-haired, freckle-faced kids you see on television commercials for soup or cereal. She had her father's cool gray eyes and her mother's fiery hair and matching temperament. "I knew you'd come! Are we going to your house? Did Nilly make homemade ice cream?" The girl stared up adoringly at her father and squeezed him as tightly as she could.

"Just for a little bit, Lauren." He absentmindedly ruffled her hair. "Mom had to work late, and no ice cream until after supper!"

Lauren scowled and stomped her foot.

"Don't give me that look," Paul Burns scolded as he bent over slightly and shook a finger at his daughter. "Now, get in the car or I'll take you straight to your mom's condo and leave you there with that tobacco-spitting doorman!"

Lauren shrieked in mock distress and climbed into the car. Paul looked up the street and noted that the limo was gone. He could have been wrong, he told himself. He hadn't seen the plate number. There were lots of limos in Las Vegas: white, black and other assorted colors. But all the reasoning in the world didn't quell the fear in his gut. He turned and got into his car. Lauren already had the radio cranked up and a local broadcaster was talking about the upcoming mayor's race.

"I want music," she demanded. She wrinkled up her nose at the radio and tried to turn the knob.

"Not yet." Paul pushed her hand away and turned up the volume. He frowned as he heard excerpts from that morning's talk show and the political commentary that followed.

"Is he going to be mayor?" Lauren asked. She didn't have to say who.

"We'll see." Paul shook his head as he turned down the radio and put the car in gear.

"Well, I won't vote for him!" Lauren scowled and crossed her arms over her chest.

"Oh? Why not?" Paul was suddenly curious. He glanced over his shoulder to check traffic before he pulled out.

She sat back in her seat and stared out of the window as the school disappeared from her sight. With that stubborn look on her face, she reminded him of Fran.

"You know." Lauren looked uncomfortable. She kicked her bare legs against the seat.

Paul slowed down for a stop sign, studied her a moment and wondered how much she knew about the divorce allegations. "What do I know?" he asked.

"He's so, so – ewwww!" Lauren had the look of a girl who had explained the functioning of the universe in exact detail. She screwed up her pert little nose and squished her eyes closed.

"Ewwww?" he asked in amusement.

"Yes, EWWWW! With that 'hi-there-little-girl' stuff and that fancy cologne mom is always raving about." She brought her voice up a few pitches in a sarcastic imitation of Alex. "Come here, girl. Have a seat, girl.

Don't you look pretty, today, girl? YUCK. He calls EVERYONE girl! Even mom! It's disgusting. And he's always working out as if it will ever do him any good!"

"You saw him working out?" Paul tried not to sound surprised.

"Yeah. Once. Mom took me to his place to get some stuff. He's got this machine, you know, and he was all sweaty." She glared at the radio. "Please, can I change it? Please, please, please?"

Paul smiled in relief. "You're right. He is ewwww." He wasn't going to get more out of her. He would have to wait her out.

"And in other news," the announcer continued, "police say they have more than enough evidence to convict school janitor Ivan Callas...."

Paul changed the station.

The long drive was peaceful except for Lauren singing to the radio in her untrained voice. Paul kept his eyes on the rearview mirror; he didn't see the limo again. When they got to the sprawling ranch house with its sand and rock garden yard and seasoned cacti, he checked the street again before he hurriedly escorted his daughter out of the car and through the front door. A plump woman in her mid-sixties met them inside. He turned and locked the door without comment.

"Oh, my, you look like a hungry child," Nilly teased as she wiped her already clean hands on the apron she wore over her baggy jeans. Her curly, silver hair floated like a cloud over her ruddy face and she smelled faintly of hairspray. A starched butcher's apron, its bib folded down, was cinched around her waist.

"Ice cream! Ice cream!" Lauren yelled. She dropped her backpack in the middle of the tidy hallway floor and dashed for the kitchen.

"Did Matthew make it to scouts on time?" Paul interrogated Nilly.

"Yes, sir. In full uniform."

"Good."

"And your wife is still at the hairdresser's," she announced. "They were running late. She should be home soon."

"Sure, she is." He sounded unconvinced. "I need to call my ex." Paul nodded nervously in Lauren's direction. "Keep her busy, will you? And don't let her outside."

Nilly nodded in understanding as she slid the child's bag out of the way of foot traffic and went to find her.

Paul stepped into his orderly den and locked the door. Surrounded by the comfort of his books, blueprints, and paperwork from his engineering job, he moved to the back of his desk and stood there a moment, a lone figure framed in an oversized print of Da Vinci's Vitruvian Man. He wondered if he was doing the right thing. After tapping his cell phone thoughtfully a few times, he decided on a plan of action and dialed the number from memory.

"Law office," came the clipped voice of Margo Katzenberg, the firm's office manager.

"Put her on," Paul ordered without identifying himself.

A brief silence followed. "I'm sorry, Mr. Burns, she's not available now. She..."

"Is with a client? Has an appointment? Accidentally locked herself in the broom closet? I know. I've heard it all before. Now cut the crap and put her on."

Before the receiver could switch to a soft Latin tempo, Paul heard the woman mutter, "Asshole." A few seconds later, Fran was on the line.

"What now, Paul?" Fran's voice was groggy.

He wanted to ask how much scotch she'd had for lunch, but he resisted the temptation. "I've got Lauren." He hesitated a moment at the sound of her voice. "Is everything okay?"

"You were supposed to get her. Why the call?" she asked.

Paul's focus was outside, through the curtains and blinds, to the street beyond. He thought a white car had flashed in his peripheral vision but now it was gone. "You don't need a lame excuse for me to get her, you know. She's my daughter, too. Just ask me."

"It wasn't a lame excuse. I had to be in court this afternoon. I told you that." Fran slammed a file down on her desk and rubbed her blue eyes.

"You sound like you've been sleeping." Or drinking, Paul thought.

"I dozed off a second," she said. "What's it to you? I've had a rough day. It happens."

"Yes, I heard. Maybe you'd stay awake more if you left the scotch at home."

"That's why you called? To chew me out?" The tension in her voice crackled over the phone.

A headache was building behind Paul's eyes. "No."

"Spill," she ordered.

"Do you want me to drop her off or are you coming to get her?" He didn't know why he was avoiding the obvious, other than he really didn't want to get into a discussion with her about her father. The topic made him sick. When he found out what Max Simone had done to Fran, he flew into a rage. The marriage was never the same after that.

Fran took a deep breath. "You know damn well I'm coming for her. So, what's the real reason you called?"

"I just thought, given how 'tired' you are that maybe I should drop her off," he suggested.

"Paul!"

He hesitated a second. "Are you having problems with Max again?" His voice was tense. He planted one hand in his pants pocket and breathed slowly. His disdain for his ex-wife's father was evident in the way he clipped the name off his tongue.

"No. No more than usual. Just the mayor's race. Why?" She picked up a

39

pen and began to play with it.

"I heard about de la Rosa on the radio, running against him. I thought...."

"You knew about that." Fran's voice changed. She sounded worried. "What happened?"

"I thought I saw his car at Lauren's school." A soft streak of light appeared in the far distant horizon beyond Paul's window. It caught his attention. The weather was changing. He drew closer to the window and looked at the ominous sky. "Is it supposed to rain?" he asked.

"Whose car?" For an irrational moment, she hoped he'd say it was Alex's.

"Max's."

"Thought?" she asked cautiously.

"I saw a car like his. I'm not sure." Paul leaned against the window and watched the clouds.

"What do you mean, like his?" Fran asked.

Paul sighed. "A big, white, stretch limo with tinted glass and Nevada plates."

"If Max was after Lauren, you can bet he wouldn't show up in his signature car," she stated. "It probably wasn't him."

"Or it was him and he was just trying to send you a message," Paul offered.

She didn't argue with him. "Is she okay? You didn't scare her, did you?"

"No, I didn't scare her," he snapped, his attention now back on the phone call. He turned away from the window and went to the back of the desk, pulled out his large leather chair and plopped down. "I don't want any more trouble from him." Picking up a pencil, he tapped its eraser nervously on a pile of papers.

"No trouble. You worry too much." Fran nervously clicked the end of her pen with her thumb.

"Someone has to," Paul argued.

40

"Bullshit."

"Watch your language, Fran."

A second of silence was followed by the distant rumble of thunder. The wind picked up.

"By the way," he added, just for the dig, "Lauren thinks your boyfriend is *ewwww*. That's her word." He smiled, leaned back in his chair, checked his watch and wondered why it was taking his wife so long to get home.

"He's not my boyfriend. He never was," Fran yelled at him.

"Sure." He clearly didn't believe her.

"Damn it, Paul. Drop it already, will you? That's why we broke up. You shut me off, you turned me away, you practically drove me into the arms of another man and then you claimed jealousy!"

"Practically, huh? Looked like more than practically from my point of view."

"I never...." She objected.

He cut her off. "You never with me, either."

"Lauren is living proof that's not true," Fran snapped.

"Oh, right. I forgot. There was THAT time." He looked up at the sound of a car pulling into the driveway. Pushing the curtain to the side, he saw his wife climb out of her Jeep, her newly-coiffed hair blown wildly by the wind, a bag of some kind tucked under her arm, and her purse shoved tight against her breasts. Her loose pant legs fluttered as she strolled to the house. He dropped the curtain when the hall door opened and then shut with a loud bang.

"You were jealous then and you're jealous now. And there's no reason...." Fran was yelling.

Paul had almost forgotten she was on the phone.

"Jealous?" His voice came up in timbre. He tossed the pencil aside and covered his eyes as he spoke. "This is not jealousy you're hearing, Fran. This

41

is worry. De la Rosa is dangerous. It's beyond me why you don't see it. Even Lauren senses it."

Fran leaned forward and nearly spit into the phone. "The only thing Lauren senses is your dislike of Alex. GET OVER IT!" She slammed the phone down.

Outside, lightning streaked across a gray sky and thunder followed as the storm front moved in. Paul Burns threw his phone across the room and watched it slide harmlessly across a small leather sofa. He closed his eyes and listened to the pelting rain. "Happy birthday, Fran," he muttered.

*****

Las Vegas Sheriff George Randall tilted his massive six-foot-six body back in his chair in the precinct break room and propped himself up against the wall. He planted his size 14 cowboy boots onto a second chair, narrowed his eyes at the muted television set in the corner and growled between bites of a salami sandwich. At nearly 50, he looked like a darker version of Dodge City's Matt Dillon: tall, broad-shouldered, and somewhat weathered. His hair looked like steel wool. He had managed to squeeze himself into an obviously uncomfortable navy suit. He took a long slow drink of cold coffee, scowled one last time at the television set and stood up.

A young detective, still in civvies, poked his head in and nodded at the sheriff. "Milo asked me to give him a hand at the Leary crime scene, so I'm head out," he stated.

"Wait," Randall ordered. He tossed the last of his late lunch into the trash, picked up his Stetson hat and fingered the brim in thought. "Scrap that. Milo can use someone else." Randall glanced at the television and then back at the detective. "I need you to do some discreet surveillance work for me. And I mean discreet. Got it?"

"Sure, boss." The younger man stepped fully into the room and closed the door behind him. "Who we looking at?"

42

"You still got that old pickup truck of yours?" Randall asked.

"Yeah. I had an offer but...."

"Use it," Randall ordered.

"Something wrong, boss?" the detective asked.

Randall nodded his head quietly a few times as he chewed, then he stopped and looked up at the man. "There's blood on the wind," he said.

"Boss?" The detective looked confused.

"It's from a book I read once." Randall stretched. "There was blood on the wind and the sand tasted like ashes." He shrugged. "I have a hunch. Go with it."

CHAPTER 4

"Working late again?" Fran leaned against the shiny wooden door frame of Alex's office, her leather briefcase slung from a strap on her shoulder and her peach-colored suit jacket draped over her arm. Her small feet were tucked into crew socks and sneakers. A pair of expensive, spiked heel shoes dangled from her fingertips. Her reading glasses, tucked into the V-neck of her silk blouse, drew Alex's eyes lower than he knew they should go. For a moment, he ogled her over the top of his glasses and wondered how low those freckles went and if she did that thing with her glasses on purpose.

"You changed clothes," he commented, tilting his head slightly to hear her better.

She caught his look and scolded him with a shake of her head.

The law firm was located on the second floor of a reddish, adobe-styled structure that was built, as so many were, to look older than it was. The walls were sheathed in imported light oak, the floors flaunted flagstone tile and the shelves of books and arched windows gave the place the feel of a library. The walls reeked of old cigars and fresh coffee. A photo of Alex's late wife and an incongruous figurine of a black cat with oversized eyes, a gift from his sister, were the only intimate touches in the room. Alex had turned the cat to face the wall.

Alex pulled his eyes out of Fran's cleavage. What was that old nursery rhyme? When she was good she was very good, but when she was bad.... He followed the curve of her tight jaw, the angle of her throat, the pout on those lips he had once kissed. Only once, he reminded himself, but once had been enough to give him fair warning not to do that again. He turned his chair part way around and peered out the window.

The sky had darkened, and a hard rain fell on the city. Streetlights blinked on. Cars, their tires splattering in puddles, slunk down the narrow side street

45

below his window as they escaped into the wider avenue with its bright lights and pedestrians rushing to get out of the rain.

"We really needed the rain," she said.

"I'm reviewing my notes for the Callas deposition." His voice was apologetic and heavy with fatigue as he turned to face her. He rubbed his eyes and the bridge of his nose and pushed the glasses up slightly with his fingertips. "Rick is serving the subpoena. I have it set up for two weeks from tomorrow."

"On a Saturday?" she asked.

"It was the only time we could all meet." He closed the file.

"You're deposing Elliott?" She referred to the city's forensic investigator, the name Holly Butterfield had failed to dredge from Alex's lips during that morning's television interview, Roger Elliott, Alex's nemesis.

"Of course. Who else?" he asked.

Fran frowned in irritation. "I wish you hadn't taken that case. It's open and shut. Why bother? It could hurt you politically if it goes south."

"Some things are more important than politics." He saw her scowl. "I'm convinced he's innocent."

She was quiet a moment. "This won't fix anything," she finally said.

He looked at her with the pained eyes of a man who had heard this argument one too many times. "I'm not trying to fix anything, Bella – past, present or future," he snapped. "I'm just trying to get some justice for the poor guy, that's all."

"You can't save everyone who comes through that door." She matched his volume and pointed vaguely in the direction of the lobby with a nod of her head.

Alex leaned back and pursed his lips together, tapped his pen in the palm of his hand and studied her in a minute of aching silence before continuing the argument. "Don't do this, Bella. Don't presume he's guilty. You know

46

better. This is a law office – MY law office, and this is what we do. This isn't about Sarah, or Max, or you. You can deal with it or you can leave."

Fran shuddered, leaned back against the door jam and sighed. He had threatened to fire her at least a dozen times in the last two months. That part didn't mean anything. It was just him venting. As for the rest of his comment…. "You're right. Maybe he is innocent. Maybe." She shut her eyes a second and tried to keep her emotions contained. "Such a waste," she murmured.

He'd seen her like this before. He didn't like where it could take her. He knew the effort it took Fran to believe that a man, any man, could be falsely accused of child abuse.

"I filed a motion to suppress and a motion for sanctions," he said with a frown. "Elliott is building his whole case on a few drops of blood."

"Our client's blood," Fran reminded him.

Alex nodded gruffly. "If Callas is telling the truth, and if he cut his hand on a box cutter earlier, then found her sweater at the school and tossed it into the lost and found box, that would explain the blood. It would also explain why there was no trace of her on him."

"But there were small traces of him on her. Besides, it's a lot of ifs." She shook her head. "Well, at least he's not working at a school anymore."

Alex tossed down his pen. "Trace evidence is just that, trace. Without more, it's not worth the paper it's written on. We don't know that he's guilty. No one knows. The guy is clean – no record, no reports, no substantiations, nothing. Or haven't you been listening?"

"You never know who the bad guys are until you catch them the first time." Fran stared at him to make her point.

He didn't answer.

Fran glanced at the floor and shifted her weight. "So, you think Elliott is lying about the DNA?"

"Lying? Why would he lie? No, I don't think so, at least not this time. Incompetent and lazy? Yes. There's got to be more evidence, he's just not looking for it." He opened another file and groaned.

"You've been saying that for the last three years, ever since he got to Vegas," Fran countered. "I'll admit I don't like the guy, but this is a damn tight case. Callas is – was – the school janitor. He knew the child. He had access, and the girl's body was found about a block from his apartment."

"All circumstantial." Alex shook his head as his frown deepened. Lightning flashed behind him, followed by the low roll of thunder.

"The sun coming up in the morning is circumstantial," she countered.

He studied the pain in her eyes. "This isn't about you, Bella," he reminded her again.

"Like you said, this isn't about Sarah, either."

Perhaps it was the rain. It had been raining the night Alex's wife had been murdered. Their eyes locked and they both remembered. Her ploy to yank Alex off the topic of her father had worked for the moment, but only a moment. His ploy to drag her into the here and now was failing miserably.

Alex stiffened. "He just assumed I did it. He never even tried to find her killer. He let politics get in the way of his job." It was a bitter argument sharpened on the whetstone of time.

"By politics, you mean Max," said Fran. In her world, all roads led to Max Simone.

"I mean Sheriff Randall," Alex clarified.

She shifted her weight slightly. Her back ached from standing so long. Her eyes moved from the storm to him and out again. "I should get on the road. Lauren will be waiting. Paul will be pissed."

"I never said that – I never said Max had anything to do with it." Alex gestured as if dismissing the idea, but he dropped his eyes, avoiding hers.

"But?" She waited.

"Go! Get out of here! It's your birthday. Don't you have something birthdayish to do?" Alex stretched his own tired back. His thoughts drifted momentarily to a little Thai massage place he knew about on Fremont Street with red lacquer walls, loose silk robes, soft music and sensual company. But Fremont Street only reminded him of the body of the girl found in the dumpster, clothed in her school uniform, her delicate little fist clutched around a small painted rock. That brought him full-circle back to Ivan Callas, the janitor accused of her rape and murder. "Why the rock?" he mumbled to himself.

"What?" Fran was roused back to the present.

"She went to your daughter's school." He brought his voice back to normal and looked up over his glasses. "That's what really worries you, that this could have happened to Lauren."

Fran scrambled to put the pieces together. "Amelda Pena?" she asked. "Yes. She went to Lauren's school. They were in the same class. I'm just relieved they caught the guy."

"Maybe," Alex reminded her.

Fran's hand tightened around her briefcase and she dug her fingernails into the soft leather. "He's not the only pedophile in this city," Fran murmured, her thoughts skipping from one train of thought to another. "And it didn't happen at the school. It probably wouldn't have happened at all if she hadn't...." Fran went quiet. The girl had gone with friends. She hadn't waited for her ride. She hadn't gone home. Now, she'd never go home.

"Callas?" Alex asked.

"Callas what?" Fran looked dazed.

"He's not the only pedophile in the city." He reminded her of the dropped thought.

"Oh." Fran scowled. "Max."

This time, Alex let it go. "What time is it?"

"Almost 6:30." Fran glanced at her watch. "I've got to get home. The sitter called and reminded me he has a date." They exchanged humorous looks. Both knew she was poking fun at her ex. Her eyes went from Alex back to the rain.

"A date? What's that, Bella?" He flashed a teasing smile.

Fran made a clucking sound as she turned to leave. "Like I would know!" She hesitated a second before she glanced over her shoulder and continued. "For someone with the reputation of an Italian playboy, you don't get out much."

He answered with a smile and a Bogey drawl. "I owe my reputation to you, sweetheart." The elephant in the room had been abandoned, again.

She stuck her tongue out at him. "You got that right. If you need me, just whistle."

He grinned at the old movie line but decided not to finish the thought.

Fran gave him another of her luscious winks before she sprinted down the hall.

"Happy Birthday, Bella!" he yelled after her.

She didn't turn around.

Alex immediately felt the room grow damp and chilly. He looked over his work and wondered if it was worth staying an extra hour or two and decided against it. He could work just as easily at home. Callas wasn't going anywhere, at least not tonight.

Pushing himself out of his chair, Alex yawned and headed for the front office while rolling his sleeves down, tugging them into place and buttoning the cuffs. Except for him, the office was now eerily deserted. From the desk, he called Margo to give her detailed instructions for Monday. He got her answering machine. She probably was on a date, he thought with a grimace, as he glanced at a photo of her with her latest girlfriend.

He wandered back to his office and collected his suit jacket from the sofa, slipped it on and rummaged in the pockets for his keys. Lightning lit up the arched windows, followed immediately by a roaring clap of thunder as the rain turned into a torrent and the power flickered and went out. The computers issued a brief and uncomfortable clicking sound and the office, now cast in shadows, hissed into silence.

Swearing, Alex stood still in the dark a few minutes and listened to the pellets of rain that slammed into his rattling window pane. He could see lights on in other office windows across the alley. The streetlights still glowed on the wet pavement. It must be us, he thought. A fuse maybe. Something.

When the power didn't come back on, he used his cigarette lighter to rummage around his desk for some files and to slide them neatly into a briefcase. He then grabbed his overcoat from the closet and headed out the door and into the gray evening.

Alex blinked the rain out of his eyes as he scanned the large, nearly empty parking lot. His sports car was the only one near the front, but a few cars and an old pickup truck were parked near the side entrance. Through a rain-sheathed back window of the truck, Alex could barely make out the back of a man who appeared to be talking on a cell phone. Checking his pocket, Alex was relieved to find he had his phone on him.

It doesn't rain much in Vegas, but when it does the ground seems to repel the water like an alien substance. It pooled along the sidewalk and parking lot and created obstacles between the building and the car. Alex, his coat wrapped tightly around him and his briefcase balanced on his head in lieu of an umbrella, stepped quickly and carefully around the deepest puddles as he tried to protect his shoes. When he finally slipped into the seat of his BMW Boxster, he was damp and chilled. His breath fogged up the window as he started the engine. A minute later, the beams of his headlights splashing on

51

the wet asphalt, the car slid down the highway towards his condo in Turnberry Place as he hummed to Luther Vandross.

Alex tried to ignore the images of his wife's dead body, now blurred with that of the victim in the Callas case. They were one and the same to him: an innocent victim, a false accusation, a crooked investigator. He wondered why the press hadn't latched on to that story now that he was campaigning for the mayor's job. He imagined the headlines: Murder Suspect Turns Politician: A Killer Race. Alex groaned.

The darkened sky transformed the city into a gray, unfocused photograph of its usual self; the glitter and glitz were drowned in a semi-transparent haze. The rain grew heavier. Wind gusts cuffed the car with airborne sheets of water.

Alex turned the corner onto Paradise Road and suddenly slammed on the brakes. "What the hell!" he yelled to no one. His tires slid on the slick pavement as the car came dangerously close to rear-ending a diesel tanker that was stopped for a traffic jam in front of him. The slapping windshield wipers matched the loud thumbing of Alex's heart as he spun around to watch an ambulance race by, its lights flashing and siren wailing. His hands trembled.

Trying to calm his rattled nerves, Alex took a long, slow breath, then opened his glove compartment, pulled out a Cohiba, and gave himself a three-second argument about why he should not smoke cigars in his car. Nevertheless, he clipped the end, flipped open the cigarette lighter with shaking hands and lit up. The fragrant smoke merged with the car's distinctly leather smell. Now, if only it was legal to drink scotch behind the wheel, he thought, his life would be almost perfect. He cracked the window to allow the smoke to escape and resisted the urge to pull out his wallet and fondle the worn photo of Sarah, taken in front of the school where she had taught.

******

"Stand still and smile," he told Sarah as he leaned a bit to focus the 35 mm Nikon on her smiling face. A soft wind stirred up some dirt from the sidewalk. The bangs of her short dark hair dangled in her eyes and she brushed them back.

"Alex, hurry, please. I'm on the clock," she argued, posing flirtatiously for him.

"Just a minute more, honey. Almost done."

A click and a whirr finished the session. He stood straight and grinned. "Dinner. Seven. Then we'll talk."

She frowned slightly. "No talking, Alex. We've talked for three years. I want babies. Cute little bouncing boys and girls that look like you and are smart like me." She smirked. "At least five of them, but you have to stay home long enough to produce them!" Despite her evident frustration, she chuckled.

"We'll talk," he reiterated.

She glared at him.

The sun melted into rain and the old ache settled deep in his heart.

*****

Alex wiped the blurriness from his eyes.

A policewoman in an orange nylon poncho jogged towards Alex in the steady rain, a flashlight bouncing in her hand, her face hidden by the waterlogged hood. She stopped at his car and tapped lightly on the window with the edge of the flashlight.

Groaning, Alex lowered the window some more and put on his best politician's face. "Can I help you, officer?" he asked. He squinted against the rain as he looked up at a pair of beguiling eyes, a sassy mouth and long blond hair wound into a damp braid that hung over one shoulder.

"I don't know. Can you?" she asked with a lopsided smirk.

Alex broke into a broad smile and turned to face her more, to take advantage of his good ear. "What the hell are you doing out there?" he asked

Carol McEnroe. "Don't you know enough to get out of the rain, girl?" He had to raise his voice over the sound of windshield wipers, sirens, and honking horns. He had an instant hormonal reaction to her presence. In short, she turned him on.

"I knew that had to be you. Who else would ruin a perfectly good car with a cigar?" Her voice had a sexy tease to it as she leaned on his car door, her face barely inches from his.

"I thought you were in L.A." It was more a question than a statement. He watched the droplets of water wind down her rosy cheeks. He saw the way she licked them up with her tongue.

A slight blush crawled up Carol's neck. She shrugged and glanced in front and behind his car, her eye on traffic. "Didn't like it. No one to play with." She grinned.

"That's highly unlikely!" He motioned to the traffic ahead with his cigar-holding hand. "What happened?" He took a slow drag and exhaled the smoke that swirled around his head.

"Hit and run." Her eyes narrowed. "Pretty serious. Three dead."

Alex heard her words but was more focused on her full mouth. He could have sworn her lower lip quivered a bit. "When did you get back, girl?" he asked, emphasis on the word 'girl' as a warm feeling built up in his gut.

She stared into his penetrating dark eyes. "So many questions. So little time." Her voice was low and sultry, and she trembled a little from the dampness. "Why don't you take me to dinner tonight and I'll tell you all about it."

Alex felt his muscles tighten with anticipation at the suggestion. So many memories. "When do you get off?" He took another long, slow draw on his cigar and enjoyed the feeling of power over her.

Her blush deepened. She glanced at her watch. "About an hour. Where should I meet you?" Their conversation was interrupted by a roar of thunder.

54

He thought a minute. "I will be generous tonight. Your choice."

She rolled her eyes. "How about the Viaggio?"

"In Henderson?" he whined.

"Well, you said it was my choice. Besides, I live near there."

"I thought it closed," Alex said.

"New management. Again." She shrugged.

Alex stared as Carol reached into his car, plucked the cigar from his fingertips, put it to her lips and took a drag. Her cologne drifted in the air around him. Her eyes closed as the smoke wound its way through her lungs. Slowly licking her lips, she grinned and gently exhaled the smoke back into his face. She then ran her tongue seductively over the length of the cigar before handing it back to him with a sigh, the tip now encircled with lipstick. He took the cigar, reached out and drew a finger delicately over her chin.

"Okay, the Viaggio. but you had better make it worth my time, girl. Be there at nine." He found it hard to pull his eyes away from her lips. "Be on time. Wear red."

"Yes, sir." Carol winked and disappeared back into the rain.

Alex, the cigar secured in his grasp, hummed through smirking lips as he pulled into the parking garage of his condo building. He peeled his raincoat off in the elevator and shook it out. Droplets of water splattered on the steel walls. He felt particularly pleased with himself. Date? Hell. Who needs a date when you got Carol? He grinned broadly as he stepped into the dimly lit hallway leading to his condo. Callas was temporarily forgotten.

Alex heard the music halfway down the hall: Led Zepplin's "Stairway to Heaven." He frowned and slipped the key in the lock. He was in no mood for company right now, especially *hers*. He had to get ready for his date. The lock turned, and he strode into the contemporary room with its streamline furniture and gray walls. The place was anally immaculate. Cringing at the volume, he quickly crossed the room, hit the power button and plunged the space into a relieving silence broken only by the latching door and pounding rain.

A pair of wet, Converse, high-top sneakers dried in a shoe box next to his door. A black Glock rested in its holster on the kitchen counter. Black Velvet, his Burmese Cat, was licking the gun grip.

Alex dropped everything except the cigar, now tightly clenched between his teeth, and stepped quickly around the counter. He gently lifted the cat up and lowered her to the floor. "Bad kitty. Daddy is going have to give you a spanking." He opened a fresh can of tuna-flavored cat food, scooped some into a porcelain bowl and slid it to her on the floor. As she ate, he gently rubbed her nose with his fingertip.

"Hey! What happened to the music?" Toni stepped out of the bathroom still wet from her shower. She wore one of Alex's velour robes and her long hair dripped down her shoulders as she toweled it. "Why didn't you return my calls?" she asked on seeing him.

He hadn't seen her approach and was startled when she suddenly appeared. He tilted his head and eyed his sister critically.

"That's funny, I distinctly remember you having your own place," Alex growled as he stood up. Like Toni, his accent grew sharper with his irritation. He traded the cigar for a light beer from the fridge, taking a moment to pour some in a glass for himself and some in a bowl for the cat. Then he rinsed out the bottle and slipped it into the recycle bin.

"You didn't return my calls!" It was an accusation.

"I was busy," he snapped. "Make sure you clean up after yourself."

"You're such a neat freak," Toni observed.

"Do I tell you how to keep your apartment?" he asked as he turned towards her.

"You've never been to my apartment," she shot back.

"Well, if you ever cleaned it, I just might show up."

"You've got Italian marble and a Jacuzzi tub in your bathroom. Why would I shower at home?" Toni glanced at Black Velvet. "I already fed him."

Alex drank deeply of the beer as he stared at the water running down Toni's strong legs and soaking into the carpet. "Sometimes I think you gave me that cat just to make sure I'd come home every night and feed her," he growled.

"Him," Toni corrected, ignoring her brother's angry glare.

"Wishful thinking." Alex shrugged and took another swig before continuing. "All cats are girls; all dogs are boys. Or didn't they teach you that in cop school?"

"If all dogs are boys, why are so many bitches?" Toni countered with a grin.

"You still haven't told me why you're here," he said.

"You still haven't told me why you didn't return my calls."

He shrugged and took a drink of the beer. "I'm not on your leash anymore, sis. Get over it. Your turn."

She scowled at him. "It's an hour ride home and an hour ride back," she began, crossing her arms defensively in front of her. "If I'm going to keep an eye on Elliott tonight, I have to be at the lab when he gets out of work." She glanced at the clock and swore softly under her breath. "And I need to borrow your camera; mine needs a new battery. Besides, like I said, you have a nicer bathroom." She thought a second. "Although, what's with all the candles?"

"They smell good." Alex rolled his eyes in a manner reminiscent of his sister. "You'd better get going. I'm not paying you to shower."

"You're not paying me at all," she reminded him. "And I don't even want to hear the word 'girl' cross your lips."

Alex acknowledged her with a brisk nod as Toni turned on her heel and headed back to the bathroom, her bare feet leaving damp footprints behind. "You can brief me in the morning," he shouted after her.

Toni caught the undertone, stopped and turned to face him from the bathroom doorway. "Oh? Got a hot date?"

"None of your business." He settled into his sofa, pulled off his shoes and planted his heels on a gray leather ottoman. He opened the briefcase on his lap and started pulling out files.

Toni's eyes widened a bit. "A clean house? Candles in the shower? You do have a new girlfriend, don't you, little brother?" she grinned.

"I always keep my house clean and Bella gave me the candles. She gives me candles every year at this time, for Sarah." He paused a few seconds. "As for a date, I told you, it's none of your goddamn business."

"Oh my god! Who is she?" Toni bounced back into the living room.

"Go away!" Alex grabbed a small pillow and threw it at her.

"I'm only looking out for you, bro," Toni insisted.

"No." He sat up and leaned forward, planted his beer on the table and glared up at her. "I don't want you looking out for me. You've got to stop digging into my life. You've got to stop following me around. You've got to stop investigating my girlfriends. You've got to leave me the hell alone. Got it?"

Her eyebrows went up. "I distinctly recall you making a highly scandalous comment on a certain morning news program today."

"Your point?" he asked.

"It's her, isn't it? That actress. You're seeing her again." Toni stood in front of him with her arms crossed.

"It was not scandalous and, no, I do not have a date with her tonight." Alex dropped the briefcase on the floor, stood up and paced the room. "Stop

58

it, Antonia. Stop it, now! Get the hell out of my personal life. I am warning you for the last time."

Toni hugged the robe to her damp skin. Her eyes glazed over with tears. "Then just tell me who it is!"

He stopped pacing and eyed her for a second. "Okay, if you must know, it's Carol."

Toni looked confused. "Carol? Carol who?"

"The policewoman. She moved to L.A. Remember?" He could see her mind working.

"Her? You're seeing HER? Damn, Alex, are you nuts? After all the hell...."

"Shut the hell up!" he yelled. "NOW you know why I don't tell you these things!" He stomped off to his bedroom and slammed the door behind him.

Toni's lips clamped shut in anger as her eyes watched him disappear from her sight.

CHAPTER 5

De la Rosa's one and only investigator, Rick Brandt, pushed his way through the heavy metal and glass door and marched into the airy main lobby of the newly remodeled Las Vegas Metropolitan Police Department, the steel heels of his black boots clicking on the neatly tiled floor. People automatically moved aside to let him through, glancing at him quickly and then away as if afraid to be caught staring. Brandt's tanned and tattooed muscles, combined with his black clothes, slick alligator boots, military crew cut, hard features and arrogant attitude, cut a swath through the small group in front of him like Moses splitting the Red Sea. All he lacked was the staff and the beard. A semi-reformed gambler and former bounty hunter from Philadelphia, Brandt handled his job with fierce loyalty and deadly seriousness mapped across his craggy face.

He approached the desk, his jaw clamped around an unlit cigarette. His piercing, steel gray eyes made the clerk tense. "Elliott," he barked.

"He's tied up, Mr. Brandt." The young woman shuffled some papers and looked about for someone to rescue her. Her eyes caught those of a security guard who sat up in his chair and carefully watched the interchange. She struggled to avoid looking at the scar that ran from the top corner of Brandt's forehead into his graying, dirty blonde hair. "Would you care to wait?"

Brandt fingered the folded paper he had in his hand as he eyed her. "No. I got a subpoena."

"I'll see if I can page him for you." She reached for the phone.

Brandt didn't wait for her. Turning, he headed towards the labs and strolled through the metal detector without slowing down. The alarm went off. Rick was stopped by a door: steel, locked, impenetrable by even his defiant will. He looked back at the woman and growled as he waited for her to buzz him through. The security guard jumped to his feet and approached, hand on his holstered weapon and one eye on the receptionist as she put down the phone.

Brandt, his hands at his sides like some mythical gunslinger from the Old West, faced the guard.

"It's okay," the clerk called out across the room. "The director cleared him. Make sure he's not carrying a weapon. Then he can go in." Relieved, she settled the phone back into its cradle.

The guard nodded as his face hardened. "Hands up," he ordered.

Brandt obliged with a murderous look. "Fuckin' night shift. Can't even think for themselves." He knew better than to carry a weapon into the place, even with a license.

The guard ignored the comment with a practiced look of indifference. A pat down and hand scan later, the guard tapped a code into a security panel and the door clicked open.

As if by scent, Brandt tracked Elliott through the halls and into one of the labs. The clerk ran after him with a visitor's badge in her hand. "Wait! You need this!" she yelled.

Deputy Director Roger Elliott, still looking fresh from court in his navy suit, starched white shirt, and burgundy bow tie, pulled himself away from a microscope, rose to his full five-foot six-inch height in elevated shoes, and brushed back the edge of his handlebar mustache. "Brandt! You're not supposed to be back here!" he snarled in a surprisingly low voice.

"He was cleared," the clerk tried to explain. "The director said...."

"It's been six months, Elliott, and you still reek from that cheap cologne." Brandt talked around the unlit cigarette clenched in his teeth and took an exaggerated sniff. "If that IS cologne. Smells more like you've been sleeping in the morgue. What's the matter? Your old lady throw you out again?"

Elliott turned red. "I can still smell white trash when it's standing in front of me. What do you want?" His eyes were level with the barbed wire tattoo that encircled Brandt's neck.

Brandt took the folded paper and stuffed it in Elliott's jacket pocket. "Consider yourself served." He turned and marched out the door, brushed past the stunned clerk and left Elliott swearing behind him.

"Where the hell's security!" Elliott screamed. "I want a guard here! Now!" His neck and face glowed redder with his rising blood pressure.

"But the director said...."

"Neophyte," Elliott waved his hands in the air and shouted as he backed the terrified woman out the door.

"But she SAID...."

"HER, not you, woman! Hell, both of you! Goddamn females!"

The clerk went from fear to rage. She spun on her heel and escaped back to her desk.

Brandt smacked his lips around the cigarette and smiled as he walked away. The argument faded behind him. "Neophyte," he muttered to himself. "Good word. Gotta remember that one."

When Brandt reached the parking lot, the rain plastered his black shirt to his muscles like an oil slick. Climbing into his rusted white Jeep, he noticed a familiar sedan with its lights off at the far side of the lot. A slender figure ducked behind the steering wheel. Smiling, Brandt drove out of the lot and down the road.

***

Toni Rose was exhausted. She scrunched down in the shadows of her car, her black denim jacket collar turned up against the damp air. She peered through the rain-sheathed windshield and across the glistening parking lot. From time to time, her eyes went to the neon green readout of the dashboard

63

clock. Then she looked up again, waiting and watching, her fingers playing with the silver cross strung on its chain around her neck.

She was too fixated on the lit entryway of the building to notice the Jeep pull up behind her. When Rick Brandt wrapped his knuckles on the passenger side window, Toni jumped. She hit the unlock button and let him in.

"What are you doing here? I thought you were headed back to the office." Her attention immediately returned to the doorway of the crime lab.

Brandt plopped his damp body into the seat next to her and handed her a Philadelphia Eagles travel mug. "Just thought I'd get ya some fresh coffee." He chewed on the dead cigarette and eyed her suspiciously. "What's your excuse?"

"That thing stinks! Get rid of it!" Toni ordered, indicating the cigarette.

Looking disgusted, Brandt rolled down the window and tossed the offending butt into the rain.

Toni huddled down further, wrapped her pale hands around the warm mug, took a sip of the brew and screwed up her nose. "There's nothing in it."

"Tom said you're watching your carbs." Rick closed his eyes and rested his head against the seat back.

"Asshole." She pointed to the glove compartment. "Fetch," she ordered.

"Huh?" he opened his eyes.

"Fetch!"

Brandt smirked, flicked open the compartment and took out a small metal flask with something illegible engraved on the side. He unscrewed the top. "Hold her steady," he ordered Toni, who had removed the cap from her coffee mug. Brandt poured in a jigger of bourbon, took a swig himself, screwed the top back on the flask and returned it.

"I take it you served him." She took a drink of coffee and made a satisfied sigh. The liquid cleansed her as it burned down her throat.

64

"A yup." Brandt's gaze went from the building back to the girl as he studied her.

"Keep your mind on business," she said without looking at him. Toni was staring straight ahead as she handed the mug back to Brandt.

Roger Elliott, wearing a tan trench coat and carrying a large black umbrella and his briefcase, paused briefly in the doorway of the building. His eyes scanned the parking lot quickly before he spotted Brandt's Jeep. Recognizing it, he fumbled the keys and dropped them in a puddle. Elliott bent over, fished the keys out of the dirty water, shook them out and made a run for his red Mustang.

"He looks kinda rattled. How'd he take it?" Toni asked. She started the engine but kept the headlights off until Elliott's car was ready to enter traffic.

Brandt just shrugged.

"That's what I love most about you, Rick." Toni flashed him a warm smile. "You're such a stimulating conversationalist."

"Oh? You love me?" he bantered back. "I wondered when you'd finally smarten up and do that."

"Pfft."

He smiled. "Well, at least I know when to keep my mouth shut." He could almost hear her hiss.

"You are so full of shit." Toni pulled forward and merged into traffic a couple of car lengths behind Elliott.

Brandt chuckled. "I'm not the one who talked myself into a suspension."

"That was a goddamn year ago!"

"Still…." He enjoyed tormenting her.

"I take it back. You do talk too much. Now shut up and let me work." Her windshield wipers emphasized her words.

Brandt drank some of Toni's coffee and squirreled up his face. "Burned," he growled as he rolled down the window and tossed the drink into the street.

"Hey! That's good bourbon!" Toni yelled.

"I've had better." He threw the plastic mug over his shoulder to the floor of the backseat. "You ruined it with the coffee."

She growled. "I did NOT talk myself into a suspension. I tried to talk myself out of it. I can't help it the department is run by mindless twits."

Brandt shrugged off the remark. "You piss off the sheriff again and you'll be walking the Mexican border looking for illegals."

Toni knew that could never happen, of course, but she got the point. "And here I thought you didn't love me."

"Somebody's gotta watch your sexy ass," Rick told her.

Toni groaned. "You and Tom. Always watching my ass. Men!"

With familiar ease, Brandt slid a hand up her thigh. She felt it quiver under his touch.

"It's only 'cause we care, darlin'," he muttered.

She slapped his hand away. "Where the hell is he going?" Toni asked as Elliott's car bypassed the usual spots and headed southwest.

"Henderson?" Brandt suggested.

Toni groaned. "It's going to be a long night."

Toni drove a few cars back from Elliott. She kept in different lanes when possible, occasionally slowing down as if trying to read passing house numbers in the dim light of streetlamps. If Elliott noticed her, he didn't show it. He drove deliberately, slightly over the limit when he could, his eyes straight ahead. As they reached the suburbs with neat rows of copycat adobe houses, the traffic thinned out.

"Pull back," Rick instructed.

"I know what I'm doing." The rain stopped, and Toni rolled down her window. The night air was cool on her red cheeks.

Rick didn't respond. He watched as Elliott turned left at a corner and down a narrow street lined with sparse palm trees and rock garden front yards.

Toni drove straight through the same intersection and pulled into a parking area adjacent to the neighborhood tennis courts. The green surface of the court was nearly black in the night except where the streetlamps bathed the edges. She slowly turned the car around.

"Whatcha gonna do?" Rick asked.

She headed back down the street and turned right, following Elliott's path, while reaching into the backseat and picking up a map. "Here, unfold this all the way and read it and try to look lost."

"I am lost." Rick hadn't been paying attention to the streets as they were following Elliott. He slipped another unlit cigarette into his mouth before he pressed his face deep into the map to hide himself and Toni.

A few minutes later, they saw Elliott's car parked in the driveway of one of the homes. The lab director stepped out into the night, glanced at the passing vehicle with little interest and headed towards the house. The street was eerily silent.

"Distracted. Got something else on his mind," Rick noted.

"Or someone," Toni added.

At that moment, a beautiful blond woman walked out of the house and onto the front stoop. Her hair was swept up in a ponytail and her trim body was barely covered in retro capris pants and a tube top. Toni watched them through her rearview mirror as she turned the car down another side street to put the couple behind her. Elliott and the woman embraced with a long, deep kiss. Toni groaned.

"Watch it!" Rick yelled.

Toni hit the brake and slid two feet past a stop sign on the oily pavement. Fortunately, no vehicles were coming. She gripped the steering wheel tightly with both hands as her heart pounded in her ears. "Don't DO that!" she yelled.

"Next time, I drive." Brandt loosened his grip on the dashboard. He slapped the map out of his face and screwed his body around to look out the back window.

Elliott and the blond were framed in the light of the doorway; they were just turning to enter the house, Elliott's arm wrapped intimately around the woman's hips.

"Funny, he doesn't look worried about being served," Brandt muttered.

"I need a drink." Toni drove across the intersection and executed a three-point turn, shut off the car's headlights and parked with the house in her front window. She pointed to the glove compartment with a silent order to fetch while she kept her eyes on Elliott. From somewhere nearby, a dog barked.

"Don't think booze'll help," Brandt reluctantly offered, refusing to get out the flask.

"Just pass me the damn thing," Toni insisted. "Christ, I'm not even tipsy yet."

"Hey, baby, you know I like you. Hell, I'll sit down and put away a fifth with ya but, right now, you're drinking, driving, carrying a gun and pissed. I think more booze is a bad idea."

"You don't get to think, period." She was instantly sorry for yelling at him. "I didn't mean that. I'm just…."

"Yeah. I know. It's that time of the year." Brandt ignored her anger. He glanced in the direction of the barking dog and frowned.

The memory of Sarah's tortured body was in and out of Toni's mind faster than a bolt of lightning. "We're not talking about that, remember?" Her cell phone went off and she jumped. "Damn!" She glanced at the caller ID and saw Tom Sadler's name. "Now what?" She put the phone to her ear.

"Where the hell have you been?" Tom yelled before she could say a word. "I've been trying to reach you for hours!"

"I'm off duty." Toni skipped her end of the hello part as well. She ran her fingers through her damp hair.

"We're on call," Tom reminded her. He stood in a hospital corridor, his jacket soaked from rain, the phone pressed to his ear. He needed sleep, a lot of sleep.

"Tonight? No way! Chuck said he'd cover for me. I told you at lunch. I had to have tonight off." Toni reached into the backseat, grabbed Alex's camera and handed it to Rick as she pointed to the house.

The second before the front door closed, Rick focused and took his shot.

"That was then. This is now," Tom argued.

Rick balanced the camera on the dashboard to keep it steady for the slow exposure and clicked a few more photos for good measure

Tom grew increasingly irritated with Toni. "Chuck's out of commission and I need you at Desert Palm Hospital immediately."

"Why there? Of all the hospitals…. What do you mean, out of commission?"

"Home with the flu," Tom explained.

"The blue flu, I bet." Toni snickered.

"No, the one that's going around. So, shut up and get your ass here now!"

"My fucking ass! Why is everybody after my fucking ass?" She heard someone yell "Move" in the vicinity of Tom's phone. "What have you got?" Toni groaned inwardly. She stared at the house as if committing every aspect of its mundane architecture to memory.

"Hit and run on Paradise. We got three dead, a fourth critical, and three we can interview if you hurry," Tom said.

"Paradise?" Her heart skipped as she clenched the phone. "Alex…."

Rick looked back at her.

69

"No! He wasn't there! This is work. Get over here."

Toni closed her eyes a moment and breathed a long sigh of relief. "How many vehicles?" She glanced at Rick and shook her head as if telling him everything was all right. He nodded and returned his attention to the house.

"Two. The dead were pedestrians," Tom explained.

Toni swore. "Alright. I'll be right there."

"Hurry!" Tom yelled.

Rick took another photo.

"I said I'll be right there! Keep your goddamn pants on!" She shut off the phone and turned to Brandt. "Gotta go."

"Yup. Got that." He nodded.

"Work. 401A. Fatality. Tom calls and I go running." She dropped the phone in her jacket pocket. "I need to change that."

"You on swing?" Rick asked.

"Backup."

"Tom's a lucky bastard." Brandt grinned. He examined the camera. "If you want, I'll come back out and keep an eye on things."

"Don't bother. By the time you get back, he'll be long gone," Toni said.

Brandt reached into the depths of his jacket pocket, pulled out several mints and handed them to her. She took them without comment.

As Toni prepared to pull back into the street, Elliott walked out of the house and back to his car, his arm around the blond. He opened the passenger side door and helped her in before he got in the driver's seat.

"That was fast." Toni reached for the camera, but Rick held onto it.

"Who is she?" Brandt asked with a tone of appreciation. He focused the zoom lens and clicked off a round of shots as the shapely body disappeared into the car.

"Not sure, but she looks familiar." Toni couldn't put a name to the face. "Well, if he's spending the night with that, it won't do us any good to watch him anyway."

Rick aimed and took more shots of the couple as the car backed out of the driveway and turned to leave. "Got 'em."

Toni drove back into Vegas, left Brandt at the crime lab to get his Jeep, and headed for the hospital. When she arrived, she found Tom angrily pacing the hall floor, a lone figure in a black LVPD windbreaker in a sea of white and pastel hospital uniforms.

"Where have you been?" he asked the second he saw her.

"In Henderson, working a case." She sucked on the mints.

"You smell like a bar," he noted.

"I was off duty, remember?" She crossed her arms defensively.

"Off duty? On a case? Which is it? What case?" Tom's eyebrows shot up. "You mean one of Alex's cases? When are you going to get it into your thick skull, DETECTIVE, that you work for the City of Las Vegas, not your brother?"

Several of the hospital staff turned and hushed him at the same time.

Toni propped her fists on her hips and glowered at him. "For your information, bozo, I was working the Callas case."

"Not drunk, you weren't. Besides, that already went to the D.A. We're done with it," Tom argued with a lower voice. He rubbed his tired eyes as a headache loomed.

"Alex said...."

"That's my point, Toni. We..." he waved a finger back and forth between them, "...the Las Vegas Police Department, arrested the killer, charged him and built our case against him. It's our job to get him convicted, not get him off. Got that?" He stepped into her space and tried not to yell. "You don't

71

work for Alex! You work for the city! How many times do I have to remind you of that?"

"But...."

"Don't make me repeat myself, detective." Toni stiffened with rage.

"You should listen to your partner." Sheriff George Randall's deep voice punctured the argument. His large frame was stuffed into a rain-soaked business suit and he looked irate. He jerked a handkerchief from his pocket and sneezed.

No one knew how long the sheriff had been standing there or how much he'd heard. Randall handed the officers the preliminary reports on the accident.

"This is what we got so far," he told them as he wiped his nose. "Finish the interviews and then report back to the office – and no detours." The last remark was made for Toni's benefit. Randall started to walk away when his phone rang. He stopped to answer the call, his back to them.

"One of these days you're going to get us both fired," Tom whispered.

Randall sneezed. "You tell that woman to be in my office in ten minutes," he yelled into the phone. He wiped his runny nose again. "And the next time that little vulture shows up, you call ME! Got that?" He clicked off the phone and hurried out the door.

Toni, red with embarrassment, groaned and glanced down at the accident report drafted by one Patrolman Carol McEnroe. Suddenly she put a face to a name and knew who the woman was at the house in Henderson. Toni wondered how McEnroe had managed to seduce Alex, report the accident and make it home in such a short time. "That little slut," Toni hissed.

Tom looked at her, bewildered. "Something you care to share?" he asked.

Toni ignored him and marched towards the nurses' station.

CHAPTER 6

The rain was beginning to let up as Fran drove into the barren lot of the half-vacated shopping center and easily found a parking spot in front of the obscure little bar. She turned off the slapping windshield wipers and studied the place a moment. She hadn't been there for a while. The windows were tinted too dark to see inside. A few beer signs flashed in neon.

She pulled her scarf tight around her head, held her jacket closed with one fist as the other gripped her purse, and made a dash to the large, heavy front door. It gave way with a serious pull. Fran stepped inside, removed the scarf from her head and shook it out. Raindrops splattered on the tiled floor of the tiny foyer. Her eyes adjusted to the dim light.

To her right was a row of small booths; the dark vinyl seats could have been black, or navy, or even eggplant, it was hard to tell. The walls were darkly painted in something bordering on burgundy. To her left, the bar ran the length of the room, flanked by salvaged stools that didn't match but somehow looked as if they belonged together. The only other customers were a man and woman in business attire seated opposite each other in a booth who tried to look casual.

Fran strolled to the farthest end of the bar, slid onto a stool, and smiled apologetically at the young man behind the counter.

"Scotch, neat?" he asked.

"Add some ice for flavor," she joked. She crossed her legs, propped her elbows on the bar, and rested her chin in her hands. "How's it going, sugar?" she asked.

It was one of those relationships where they knew each other only in context. She would never recognize him in a grocery store or at a party. She didn't know his name and he didn't remember hers. It didn't matter. At some level, they were old friends.

"Oh, same old thing." He poured her drink and placed a napkin on the bar before setting it down. "I haven't seen you in a while. What brings you out, tonight?"

The couple got up to leave and placed the tab and cash on the bar. The bartender nodded politely as he collected the money. Fran waited until he was done with the cash register before speaking up again.

"It's my birthday." The words hung in the air.

He looked up and grinned. "Well, happy birthday, honey."

She smiled back.

"I take it this is your party." It was more a statement than a question.

Fran looked down at her drink and swirled the ice around with her fingertip. "I'm not much into parties anymore, not since I turned 29." She laughed softly at the old joke.

The bartender leaned on the counter and studied her a minute. "I don't believe that," he teased. "You can't be a day over 24."

Fran shook her head. "Damn, you're good. No wonder I keep coming here." She glanced at the glass. "I'm going to pick up my daughter from my ex, rent a movie, maybe order Chinese tonight. I have a taste for crab rangoons – lots of them."

"Didn't you used to jog?" he asked.

"Still do. Every morning. How else do you think I can drink and keep this girlish figure?" Fran grinned over the top of her glass. The room seemed to darken a bit. She could feel the stress of the day begin to lift and fatigue start to settle in. "So, what's new with you?"

He shrugged and leaned back against the bar. "Not much. I've been following this Callas case. Pretty interesting. You think he's guilty?"

The question caught her off guard. She thought for a few minutes before answering. "I don't know. Maybe."

"You know he's gay, don't you?" the bartender asked.

Fran set her glass down. "Where did you hear that?" she asked. Callas had never mentioned anything to her or Alex. Well, at least not to her. Besides, Callas was married with kids.

"Scuttlebutt." The bartender shrugged his shoulders. "I hear a lot of things in here." He avoided her eyes a moment as he spoke.

Fran frowned. "Why is it that when a man is gay they assume he molests kids. It's ridiculous."

"I was thinking just the opposite," the bartender responded. "Why would anyone believe that a gay man would molest a little girl?"

Fran studied the bartender for a moment and, for the first time in the five years she'd been coming here, realized that he, too, was gay.

"Good question," she murmured.

That question was still in Fran's head when she parked her Mercedes in her ex-husband's driveway and glanced in the rearview mirror to touch up her lipstick with the tip of her little finger.

Why would a gay man molest a little girl? Indeed, why would he? More to the point, why didn't Callas tell them he was gay? Maybe it was just scuttlebutt and there was no truth in it. Damn. Damn. Damn. Why did these things always have to get so complicated?

Fran popped a Listerine strip and a chocolate covered cherry into her mouth. For a fleeting second, she concentrated on the sugar melting on her tongue. Taking a deep breath, she stepped out of the idling Mercedes, hurried up the walkway and reached the door just as Paul opened it.

"Where have you been? Do you know how late it is? If you wanted me to give her supper, you should have said so." Paul's stern voice rattled through his house as Fran pushed past him and let the door slam behind her. A cold chill ran up her back and goosebumps formed on her arms – because of the dampness or because of him, she wasn't sure.

He stood over a foot taller than her and he brushed his blonde hair back as if disciplining it. He was still in his white shirt and tie and smelled like money.

For a moment, she remembered why she had fallen in love with him.

She tugged at her rumpled jacket as she attempted to gloss over a sudden attack of insecurity with feigned bravado. "Lauren? You ready to go?" Fran called out, ignoring his tirade. She ignored the squeaky-clean slate floor and polished furniture. She glanced quickly in the hall mirror to assess her appearance, then took a second to wipe a bit of chocolate from the corner of her mouth with her finger. "For god's sake, Paul. It's only seven."

"Seven forty-five and you still didn't tell me where you've been," he said.

"I don't need to tell you where I've been. I'm not married to you anymore." Fran took a deep breath.

"I need to know, Fran." His voice went from irritated to worried. "Anything could have happened to you."

They both knew what he meant by "anything."

"I told you, you worry too much." She turned to face him. "Where's my daughter?"

"Lauren is OUR daughter, and she worries, too. She needs consistency in her life. If you say you're going to be here by seven, be here by seven. It's that simple."

"Lauren is used to me being late," Fran argued, feeling a bit guilty.

"That doesn't make it right. Just call and tell us where you are."

"It's none of your business." Fran didn't look at him. It would have been easier just to tell him, she knew, but she was beyond the point of giving him anything easily.

"Coming, mom!" the girl yelled from the kitchen.

"Were you giving her Nilly's ice cream again? You know that'll spoil her supper," Fran chided. "Must be the sexy little wife isn't home yet. I wonder where she's hiding."

"As a matter of fact, she is," he countered.

Fran started towards the kitchen, but Paul stepped around her and blocked her path. Fran crossed her arms and glared at him.

"I want custody, Fran," he announced, invading her space. "I mean it this time. You've got that bastard father after you, again. I'm sure of it. Your schedule is erratic. You work ridiculously long hours. You drink too much. You sleep around. You consort with known felons. You...."

Nilly peeked around the kitchen door but kept silent, her small eyes nearly lost in her plump face.

"Sleep around? Consort with known felons? What are you talking about?" Fran would have laughed if she wasn't so angry. Her neck flushed a deep red. She planted her fists on her hips. "You are one hypocritical bastard! I never slept around! And as far as those felons? It's my job, Paul! It's what keeps food on the table. It's what keeps Lauren in private school. It's what pays the bills! Not like you and your corporate gang of thieves! Unless you have another idea how to...."

"You got a nice big settlement check. You don't need to work for that creep." Paul's jaw tightened as he spoke with chilling authority. She thought he would crack his teeth.

Fran attempted to stammer out a response as Lauren ran out of the kitchen, her eyes blazing. "Stop it!" she yelled, stomping her feet and swinging at the air. "Both of you! I hate you! I hate you both! I hate you!" She ran out the front door and slammed it behind her hard enough to make the windows rattle.

"Now see what you've done!" they both yelled at once, eyes dueling.

Fran, embarrassed and angry, grabbed her daughter's backpack from the floor, turned, marched out and added her own slamming door to the mix. She stomped down the sidewalk, threw the bag into the backseat of her car and climbed in behind the wheel. The car was cool inside from idling with the air conditioner on. Taking a deep breath, Fran closed her eyes a second to compose herself. She slipped on her sunglasses, checked her lipstick again and put the car in gear as Lauren seethed beside her.

As her tires peeled out and she headed down the street, Paul screamed after her from his front stoop, "And you drive too damn fast!"

Fran might not have heard him, but she knew what he was saying. She quickly slowed the car, lowered the air conditioning and tried to calm down.

"I'm sorry, Lauren," she told her daughter without looking at the child. "I'm really, really sorry."

Lauren sulked next to her mom, her bottom lip jutting out in a pout, her arms crossed angrily. She kicked the bottom of her seat and didn't speak again for the entire 45-minute trip home.

When they arrived at the building, Lauren darted ahead. Fran – loaded down with office work, her briefcase, a jacket and Lauren's book bag – struggled into and out of the elevator and down the hall with her keys in her teeth. Dumping everything on the floor in front of her door, she fiddled with the lock while Lauren stood frozen and continued to glare into space.

Exasperated, Fran turned on her. "That's enough, young lady! Go to your room now and don't come out until you're ready to apologize to me!"

The door swung open and Lauren ran sobbing into her bedroom.

Fran gathered up her things and half-dragged, half-kicked them into the condo. She peeled off her suit jacket and flung her shoes angrily across the room, just missing a lamp. She poured herself a large glass of scotch and collapsed into her favorite, overstuffed chair. Her eyes drooped from fatigue and her hands shook from the adrenalin rush of her argument with Paul. She was barely settled when the door buzzer went off. Cursing, she slammed the liquor glass down on the end table, kicked the ottoman away and got up to answer the door. She was greeted by a large crystal vase of white lilies and a nervous, tobacco-chewing doorman whose timid eyes hid behind the arrangement.

Fran's first instinct was to find a gun and shoot the doorman and then shoot her father. Instead, she seized the flowers, vase and all, lugged them across the hall and sent them crashing down the garbage chute. The stunned doorman hurried out of sight. When Fran returned to the apartment, she spotted the flashing red light on her answering machine. She stabbed at the message button.

"How long are you going to keep this up?" Max's deep, rolling voice asked. "I just wanted to wish you a happy birthday. I love you, pumpkin."

Fran shuddered. She forwarded to the next message.

"You can't be serious about helping that boyfriend of yours beat me out of my job! He's dangerous, Frannie. I know what I'm talking about. Call me." As the message ended, the phone rang.

She answered it with a shriek. "Get the fuck outta my life!"

"You're my daughter…." Simone began.

"Don't you DARE go there!"

"I'm only thinking about Lauren," he argued.

"Bullshit! Like you only thought about me when I was her age?" Fran gripped the edge of the table, her head spinning, her stomach sick. She had trouble breathing.

"All I ever did was love you," he said. "I still love you. I want the two of you to be happy. I don't know why you don't understand that."

"Love? You call that love?" Fran inhaled deeply as she fought for control. "Don't call here again. Don't come here again. Don't go near my daughter and don't send any more of your damn flowers!"

"I just want to make sure she's safe," Max shot back. "I can do that. I can protect her."

"From what?" Fran asked.

"From ending up dead like those other girls," he said.

Fran closed her eyes; her heart squeezed tight with fear. The pictures from the Callas case flashed through her mind again: the dead child, the dumpster, the small painted rock. "Lauren is my concern." She quietly forced the words out. "The only person I'm afraid might hurt her is you. Got that?" She slammed down the phone.

"Grandpa's really pissed at you." Lauren poked her head out of her bedroom. The child had dried her eyes and had slipped into some jeans and a sweatshirt. She licked a gooey glob of peanut butter off a large spoon.

"Lauren Burns, don't use that language in this house! And how many times have I told you not to eat in your bedroom?" Fran instantly regretted her tone of voice. Her anger was with her ex-husband and her father, not Lauren. "I'm sorry," she said for what seemed like the twentieth time that day. She rubbed the nape of her neck to ease the tension.

"You're always sorry." Lauren wasn't so easily appeased. "Why don't you just talk to him?" She looked sour and took another lick.

Fran studied her daughter a moment. She noted the tilt of the chin and the defiant attitude. Fran saw much of herself in her daughter, and maybe a bit of Max, too, which scared her. "How about a movie?" she asked, avoiding the question.

"What have you got?" Lauren finally trusted her mother's mood enough to inch out of the safety of her room.

Fran went over to her desk, opened her briefcase, pulled out a collection of DVDs and flipped through them. "I've got *Babe*, *Babar the Movie*, *Balto* and *Beauty and the B*east."

Lauren grimaced. "What did you do, hit all the B's in the store? Must have been in a hurry."

Fran smiled guiltily. "I was. So, which shall it 'B'?" She turned around and leaned against the desk, her lips turned up into a weak, exhausted smile.

Lauren sighed at her mother's silliness. "Well, I'm really too OLD for this, but we can watch *Balto*, if I get ice cream, too."

Fran didn't bother to argue. She glanced up at the five unlit tea candles on the bookcase, quietly crossed the room and lit each one. "For you, Sarah," she prayed softly to herself.

"Those are pretty," Lauren noted.

"Yes, honey. Very pretty."

"Happy birthday, Mom."

"How about Chinese for supper?" Fran asked without looking at Lauren. The candlelight flickered in Fran's blue eyes.

***

Randall leaned back in his squeaky, rolling, vinyl chair and stewed. He glanced repeatedly at the clock on the wall and imagined how many times his wife would yell at him for being so late. He cringed at the thought. He turned his legs to the side and stretched them out. His scuffed black loafers stared up at him. The government-issued desk was too cramped for him. The chair was uncomfortable, too. He wondered how many men his age had asses that small. He crossed his hands in his lap as he twirled his thumbs over each other. He needed to be calm. His phone blinked. He checked the clock again.

"She's here," a woman's voice said over the speaker.

Randall stabbed the button. "Send her in." He didn't bother to turn around.

The room filled with a vanilla scent as Dr. Candace Knight entered. She had an exotic and yet undefinable look. Her bobbed dark hair brushed her shoulders and her brown eyes were tucked behind rimless glasses. She wore her standard lab coat and carried a file of notes in her hand. She'd been in that same office a half-dozen times before, but her eyes still wandered over the paraphernalia he had managed to collect in his fifteen years as sheriff.

"Sit down, Candy," Randall ordered. He hurriedly grabbed some toilet paper from a roll in his desk drawer and sneezed into it. His chair squeaked under him.

"If this is about Brandt...." she began, still standing. She gathered her file to her chest like a shield.

"Sit down." Randall's voice was stern as he looked up at her and blew his nose.

She sat. The arms of the narrow, uncomfortable chair pinched her thighs.

"You let that son of a bitch into my lab." His voice was level and cold. He wiped his nose and swore.

"He was here to serve a subpoena," she began defensively. "He didn't have a weapon. We all know him. The security guard...."

"You let that son of a bitch into my lab. No one else did it. You did it," Randall reiterated, cutting her off. He sneezed again and slammed his fist on the table. His chair squeaked. "I don't care what kind of security he goes through; he doesn't get into the lab. Got that?"

Dr. Knight jumped a bit at Randall's tone. "He just wanted to...." she began, again.

"What in hell possessed you to do that?" Randall asked as calmly as he could muster. He turned the bulk of his body towards her and leaned forward on his desk, his legs still shoved out of the way, his face flushed. "He didn't have to go in there. Elliott could have come out. The receptionist could have accepted service for him. Hell, I could have accepted service for him. I don't understand why you did that." He sneezed again. "What kind of cologne are you wearing, anyway?" he suddenly asked.

"It's not...."

"Never mind. Damn stuff is making my cold worse." He rubbed his nose and tossed the tissue into the wastebasket.

"I was told that we were to cooperate in these matters," she said. "That we're a public agency and...."

"Who told you that?" Randall asked.

Dr. Knight burned red. "I asked," she stated. "I did as I was instructed."

"By whom?" He leaned closer, his jaw clenched. His chair squeaked. He swore.

"By the director. The former director, that is, when I was working for him. He said...."

"Son of a bitch!" Randall's voice lowered to the level of near silence. He slammed his fist on his desk in a flash of anger before regaining his composure. "Didn't it ever occur to you that there's a reason he's a FORMER director?"

"Do you ever let someone finish a sentence?" she shot back.

"Not when they're spewing bullshit." He grabbed more tissue and sneezed.

Dr. Knight sat with her mouth half-open; she was searching for words. She closed her mouth and shook her head.

Randall leaned back and eyed her. He liked the woman. She was bright, attractive, sexy and honest – maybe too honest. She was also impulsive, argumentative and politically insensitive. "Pick up your things. I want you cleared out in thirty minutes." He held his eyes steady, challenging her to object. "Will you go nicely, or do you need an escort?"

She stared at him. "You're firing me? Over this?"

"See, I knew you weren't stupid." Randall leaned back and plopped his hands back on his belly, his deed done.

"I didn't do anything wrong!"

"You opened the door to the enemy. Brandt works for De la Rosa. You know that, and you know what De la Rosa is: a wife beater and a murderer with connections to the Italian mob."

"There's no evidence of any of that," Knight argued. "He's just a smart lawyer doing his job and that's it. As for his wife...."

"You weren't there when she died. I was." Randall snorted. "I saw what he did to her. I saw the look in that dead woman's eyes. One of these days I'm going to get that perverted, murdering bastard. I stake my career on it."

Knight stood up. "One of these days? I'll tell you what's going to happen one of these days, George." She leaned towards him, her white knuckles pressed into the gray paint desk. "One of these days you're going to find out who the good guys are around here and who you can really trust." She turned to leave. "You'll hear from my lawyers. And fix that damn chair!"

Randall nodded and pursed his lips. "I've been in this game a long time, Candy. You won't win this round."

She walked stiffly out of the office.

Randall exhaled slowly and checked his pulse. He picked up the phone and dialed Elliott's number. "Get in here, Roger. I got a new job for you." He sneezed all over the receiver.

"But — but — I'm in bed!" Elliott squeaked on the other end of the line.

"Do I sound like I care? Send the slut home and get here now!"

***

"We got a serial," the young patrolman said. He glanced nervously at the battered dumpster.

The alley reeked of beer, urine, and cigarettes. Small puddles of dirty rainwater still collected in cracks in the pavement. A rat darted in front of him and disappeared into a drain.

Tom wanted to tell the patrolman that he, Tom Sadler, was the detective, and that he would make that call, but he couldn't. He stood on a shaky crate in the dead cold night and stared into the dumpster. He held a tissue over his nose to lessen the stench. His flashlight illuminated the very white body of a very small girl, still wearing her school uniform skirt, coated in rainwater and filth. Tom, groaning, flicked off the light and stepped down.

"You don't look so good," the patrolman noted.

"My 'on call' just turned into a double shift. Seal off the area and call the lab boys. I need to call the sheriff."

"Done and done. He's on his way." The patrolman had also called for backup and a second car arrived in time to both draw the curious and shoo them away.

"You taking lead?" the patrolman asked.

Tom's head churned with memories of the last victim – the fragile body, the grieving parents, the waste of an innocent life. It played like some bad, late-night rerun. "We got an ID?" He knew the answer but asked anyway.

"Nope. Not yet," said the patrolman.

Tom glanced at the cruiser's flashing lights and pulled his windbreaker tighter against an unexpected shiver. What irked Tom the most was that it was the same part of town, the same alleyway, the same goddamn dumpster. Shreds of the original crime scene tape still clung to the plastered walls. He muttered under his breath.

"Well?" the patrolman asked again, interrupting Tom's thoughts. "You lead or what?"

"That's Randall's call." Tom had put in a long day already, plus overtime, plus missing supper and now this. The body looked fresh and Ivan Callas had been in prison awaiting trial for the last three months. Tom checked his watch, grateful the rain had stopped.

Elliott and Randall arrived together; neither one of them looked happy. Both looked sleepy and crumpled. Tom stepped back to give them access to the crime scene.

"We got another one," the patrolman repeated.

"Impossible," Randall shot back. "We got the guy." He glanced at Tom. His eyes narrowed in concern even as he voiced skepticism.

Elliott snatched Tom's flashlight, stood on the same crate and peered over the edge as far as he could. "Could be a copycat," he noted.

Tom felt his stomach tighten. "You haven't even seen her yet. How can you tell?" He tried to keep his voice calm and curious, but a bit of sarcasm managed to escape.

Elliott shined the flashlight in Tom's eyes. The glare made the detective blink and turn away. "Because it's my job," Elliot countered.

"Any chance you're wrong about Callas?" Randall asked Elliott.

Elliott stiffened and stepped down from the crate. "I know what I'm doing, George." He forced his voice into strained deference.

Randall nodded, not convinced. "You damn well better, Roger, or you're going to find yourself following Candy out the door. I will not let you or anyone else embarrass me on this one."

"Candace is gone?" Tom stared at Randall in surprise. "What happened?"

Randall's look was enough to convince Tom not to pursue the matter any further.

"I want the lead on this," Tom told the sheriff. "No one knows the Callas case better than I do. If it's a copycat, I can prove it. If not, well, I can prove that, too."

Randall nodded, yanked a tissue out of his pocket and sneezed into it. "Damn!" He wiped his now red nose. "Okay, but I don't want your partner on it, got it? She's already up to her neck in conflicts of interest and she's got plenty to handle with the car crash."

"Conflicts on the Callas case, you mean." Tom glanced at Elliott.

Elliott glowered back.

"Yeah. Whatever." Randall blew his nose hard enough to make the patrolman cringe. "I'm going home. Drink hot tea. Crawl into bed. You guys will have to sort this out without me."

"Sure thing, George." Elliott nodded. "I'll call you when we get something."

"No, you'll call me sometime after twelve noon tomorrow, got that? I don't want to hear from either of you unless it's a goddamn emergency."

"I'll give you a hand," Tom told Elliott, less concerned with assisting than with making sure the evidence wasn't compromised. He grabbed the flashlight back. The more Tom thought about the little girl in the dumpster and Toni's ranting, the more he wondered about the Callas case. He didn't realize he was staring at Elliott.

"What are you looking at?" Elliott snapped as he pulled on his latex gloves.

Tom narrowed his eyes. "Let's get to work."

He walked the lab crew through every inch of the alley, inside and outside the dumpster. He checked for any video surveillance at neighboring shops. There were none. He checked for tire treads. Nothing stood out. It wasn't until they pulled the girl out of the dumpster and laid her on a plastic body bag on the ground that he noticed her hand, bruised and curled into a tight fist.

Elliott knelt at her side. His body shadowed hers and blocked Tom's view. Elliott pried open the girl's soiled, bruised hand. From the small fingers that once held pencils and crayons and dolls, Elliott extracted a small, painted blue rock and held it up for Tom to see.

Tom looked at Elliott. "We didn't release the info on the rock. Still think it's a copycat?"

Elliott ignored him and bagged the evidence.

"I want copies of everything," Tom told the crime lab guys. "Whether you think it matters or not. The whole shebang. Got it?"

They nodded silently around him.

Elliott bristled. "I'll have you know I'm the director of the crime lab, now." He pulled his small frame up as tall as he could. "I'll decide what you get and what you don't."

Tom approached Elliott slowly. With the streetlamps behind Tom, the bulk of his body formed a menacing shadow that fell across Elliott's angry face. "I want everything," Tom said quietly and slowly, his lips drawn back tightly. "I know this scene. I know what we did. If you hold back on me, I'll know it and you'll have a lot more to worry about than some over-zealous defense attorney. Got it?"

Tom turned slowly on his heels and confronted the piercing gray eyes of Rick Brandt.

CHAPTER 7

Alex inhaled the aroma emanating from the elegant Italian restaurant. It took him back to his childhood in the Tuscan town of Cecina on the Ligurian Sea. He and Antonia would run home from school along the narrow walkways to escape the bullies who taunted the slender, delicate Alex, while Antonia reached down and hurled rocks at them. The Cecina air was rich with the smell of marinara, onions, garlic, and ripe cheeses. Their small fourth-floor apartment overlooked the beach. The house was surrounded by hand-painted, terracotta pots of weeping roses, the family's signature flower, their soft yellow tips transformed like a sunrise to a pale pink center.

Alex's mother – a slender woman with strong arms, a quick tongue and a prematurely gray hair that forever dangled over her nose – spent hours trying to sweep the fine, wind-blown sand from her balcony. She leaned from time to time on the broom handle as her mind drifted out to sea. She had been a poet, Alex and Toni learned a few years later when they uncovered her secret trove of writings in their grandfather's attic just after his death. Shortly after that, the children were shipped to America to live with relatives; they never saw the trunk or her poems again.

From the moment the children stepped out of the hot sun and into the shade of the winding wooden staircase, they knew what every family was having for dinner. They would race each other up the creaking stairs and Antonia always won. After a full meal and sweet wine, they would lie down on mats near the balcony doorway with Antonia holding her baby brother safely against her, her ears alert even in sleep for his father's footsteps. A soft breeze lulled them into a sonnellino as it filtered through the colorful, ribbon-like strips of cloth that hung in lieu of a screen door.

Perhaps it was the restaurant's warm atmosphere, or because he was already exhausted from a long day, or because Carol was an old flame, but Alex felt completely relaxed. He followed the hostess to the dark-paneled bar where he propped himself up on a stool, ordered scotch and waited for Carol to appear as he watched the reflected images caught in the mirrored wall. He lowered his eyes to his drink, swirled the golden contents around and coated the sides of his glass. Memories of Sarah invaded his thoughts. Closing his eyes, he chugged the last of the scotch and ordered another.

He smelled Carol before he saw her; the familiar scent of her coconut shampoo drifted over his shoulder. The fragrance brought with it a host of titillating memories. He glanced up to see her reflection in the mirror behind the bar. "You're late." He turned his head around and his eyes locked on hers.

She sparkled in the warm lights. Her body pressed against his back and her hands circled his chest. Her long, jewel-polished fingernails slipped between the buttons of his shirt. Startled by the sudden intimacy, he grabbed her wrists and roughly pushed her hands away.

"Ah, come on. It's not like we're strangers." She breathed in his ear.

His eyebrows went up as he turned to look at her. She wore a deep red dress with a plunging bodice top, a very short skirt, spiked heels and little silver earrings in the shape of handcuffs. The earrings caught his eye and he squinted in the dim light to focus on them, his finger involuntarily reaching out to caress her earlobe.

"Nice," he murmured.

"Like them? I wore them in memory of you." Her smile broadened. Her eyes were wide, searching, teasing and only a few inches from his.

He had trouble breathing. "It's been a long time, Carol." He kept his voice level and took her hands in his to keep her from becoming too playful.

"True, but I haven't changed," she told him.

He was sure she hadn't. "I have. I've regained my sanity," he said.

She laughed, slowly pulled one hand free and drew her thumb across his lips where he captured it for a moment in his mouth. "Prove it." She moved closer.

90

He suddenly seized the invading hand, lowered it and pinned it to his lap. "You always were a handful."

She leaned over to softly nibble on his neck. His eyes had nowhere to go but down into her shapely breasts. Despite himself, he let out a soft groan.

"Stop," he finally whispered. He pushed her roughly away and smirked. "Our table is waiting."

She pouted. "You've turned into a tease, Alex."

He let out a soft sigh and stood up, grabbed her arm and led her to the dining room where fine china twinkled in the candlelight on floor-length, ivory, damask tablecloths. They were barely seated when she slipped off a shoe and ran her toes up his leg beneath the table. A shiver streaked up his back.

"Stop that!" He whispered the command as he reached under the table to slap her foot away. He glanced around the room and noticed a few bemused looks, but most people were too involved in their own dramas to pay attention to his. He wondered how many of the customers had seen the morning's live broadcast of LV:AM.

"Hothead!" She was pouting again. Her soft, full lips tempted him. "I haven't seen you in over four years, Alex. Don't you want to play?"

Alex wasn't relaxed anymore. "I'm running for mayor. I can't be seen playing footsy in a public restaurant," he argued halfheartedly. He denied the part of him that warmed to the thought.

Her eyes narrowed, and she leaned towards him. "What's the matter? I'm not good enough for you anymore?" Her tone was critical.

Alex put down his menu and leaned towards her. His eyes locked with hers. "It's not about that and you know it. You are good enough. You're more than good enough. You are...." He hesitated a second as he searched for an excuse that would cool them both down. "I already have a reputation...."

"So, I've heard." Carol's fingertips reached out to stroke his tie. Her smile reappeared. "I'm no Autumn Bartlett, but I could help it along."

She was trouble. She had never listened to him. She had come to him at the lowest point in his life, shortly after the death of his wife. She had appealed to his baser needs. When he couldn't control her outbursts of jealousy, she suddenly abandoned him to his grief. The sliver of bitterness raised by that memory was just enough to distract him from her mouth.

"If you can't behave yourself, we'll have to leave," he warned her.

"Promise?" Her tongue slowly licked her parted lips. "I brought the handcuffs. You know the ones, with the yellow fuzzies on them? They're right here in my purse."

She picked up her bag from her lap and started to open it, but Alex quickly seized her hand to stop her. His eyes darted about the room as his thumb pressed deep into her skin. Who saw? Who heard? Who knew?

"May I take your order?" a waiter asked. He glared reprovingly at them.

"Yes." Alex held her hand. The back of his neck burned.

"No." Carol snapped her purse closed.

The mind games began.

Dinner was excruciatingly painful for Alex. From the minute Carol pressed her body into his back until the last cup of coffee, he fought his arousal. She wasn't subtle. Everything she said and every move she made was geared to one result, and she was succeeding. When the bill was finally paid, and they stepped out into the warm city night with its flashing neon lights gleaming off passing cars, he breathed a sigh of relief. At the very least, he no longer had to worry about an audience.

"Take me home?" Carol pleaded. She pulled him to her and smeared his white dress shirt with red lipstick as her hand ran seductively down his thigh.

He wanted to grab her ass and take her right there. Instead, his arm tight around her waist, he glanced up and down the sidewalk. "Behave, you little sl... wench." Alex's gruff voice was loud enough to penetrate her apparently alcohol-induced haze. "You've had too much to drink. It is time to get you home." It never occurred to him to ask how she'd gotten there.

He propped her up with one arm while the valet retrieved his car. Settling Carol into the passenger's seat, Alex reached over to hook her seat-belt. Carol tilted her head back. Her hair fell to her cleavage and she blew softly in his ear. His skin tingled. Alex quickly retreated from the car and bumped his head slightly on the door frame in the process. He shut the door, climbed in the driver's side and rubbed his head.

"You're too self-conscious," she told him.

"Where to?" He checked the mirrors for oncoming traffic.

"My place?" Her fingers reached for his thigh and found a soft spot. She dug in.

He slapped her hand away. "Where's your place?"

He watched, impatient and somewhat perplexed, as she opened his glove compartment with an uncanny familiarity and pulled out two of his cigars. She clipped the ends, lit them, blew a soft wisp of smoke into his face and handed one to him. Her lips seductively played with the tip of her cigar as she reached into her purse and pulled out a car rental slip with the directions written in pencil on the back.

"You don't know where you live?" he asked in surprise. His teeth clenched the cigar as he glanced at the paper.

"I just moved back this week. Sometimes I get confused. You can find it, right?" Her free hand returned to his thigh.

He grabbed it and roughly placed it back in her lap. "Not while I am driving. I might hit something." He took a minute to plug the address into his GPS unit and set the unit on the dashboard. A soft and sultry British female voice instructed him, "Turn right."

Carol smiled. She tried playing with him a few more times until he threatened to pull over and make her walk home alone with her hands cuffed

93

behind her back. The rest of the trip, she puffed on her cigar and sulked. When they pulled up to her small ranch house, the GPS unit announced, "You have arrived at your destination." Carol waited for him to open the door and extend his hand. She took it as she feigned intoxication and leaned against the car. Alex grabbed her and held her. Her lips closed hungrily in on his. Her fingers knit into his wavy black hair; her knee bent and pressed tightly into his groin.

Next door, a dog barked, protecting its fenced-in territory.

"Let's get you inside." Alex's voice was husky as he came up for air. The cigars fell to the sidewalk and were crushed underfoot.

They stumbled to the front stoop, his arm wrapped tightly around her waist. Her tongue ran over his lips. She handed him the key. He opened the door and reached for the light. Carol placed a hand on his arm and stopped him.

"Leave it." She looked up into his eyes. Her features were barely illuminated by a streetlight.

Alex, his heart pounding loudly, took a deep breath, tuned out every alarm in his head, steered her into the sparsely furnished living room, and kicked the door closed behind them. He shoved her up against the hallway wall and pinned her with his body. His breath was hot on her cheeks and his eyes burned into hers. The light of the streetlamp illuminated the room enough for him to see it was almost empty. The only other light was a small lamp over the kitchen stove in the next room.

"Where's your stuff?" He glanced quickly around before being drawn back to her.

"Movers come Monday." She shifted her body slightly to rub against him while her fingers played with the buttons on his shirt. "I have some guys from work coming to help me unpack." She paused a second and gazed at his lips. "Unless you'd like the job."

He shook his head. "Sorry, beautiful. I don't work for you, remember?" He slipped one hand around her neck as his thumb played with the handcuff earring. Memories tantalized him.

She snuggled closer. Her hand slipped down to his belt buckle. Her fingers found their way beneath his waistband and touched skin. He shuddered.

"I need to get you to bed." His body tensed under her touch as his need silently screamed in his head.

"Yes, you do." She nipped at his chin. She managed to squirm her way around in his arms until her back was to him. "Zipper?"

His fingers numb from anticipation, he fumbled in the dark as he looked for it. "You don't have one," he concluded. He leaned in tight against her as his hands firmly gripped her arms and his lips found the nape of her neck. She tasted sweet. Her scent was subtle. He wanted to lick her from the toes up.

"Oh." She giggled softly and leaned back into him. Her buttocks nestled into his hips.

Alex closed his eyes as his hands slipped the spaghetti straps off her shoulders, followed them down her arms and peeled the dress away from her cool, smooth skin. He let the dress fall to her tender ankles until she was left in only a thong. When his teeth found her shoulders, she squealed. His hands slipped around her waist and up, cupped her bare breasts and found her nipples already hard. She gasped and arched her back. Her hands reached behind her and slid down his muscular thighs. Without another word, he spun her around and lifted her up in his arms, her legs straddled around his waist.

"Damn, girl. Do you realize what you do to me? I think we both need a cold shower," he said as he carried her into the bathroom.

She was a roller coaster ride moving way too fast for him. The smell of her desire was intoxicating. He had to seize control.

"No! No!" she squealed, throwing her head back and laughing. Ignoring her protests, Alex kicked off his shoes, dropped his wallet on the floor and, fully clothed, carried her into the shower stall.

As the water flowed down and plastered his clothes to his skin, he lowered her to her feet. Carol slipped off her thong and began undressing him: first undoing his belt, then his pants, and then unbuttoning his shirt, nibbling on his nipples as she did so. He stood still and let her fingers and lips do all the work until his own clothes were shed in a puddle on the shower floor. With one hand on her shoulder and the other on the top of her head, he shoved her down to her knees where she slowly and expertly worked him into blissful agony. He gasped, his head tipped back, and his eyes shut tight as he steadied himself. Despite the cold shower, he had to press his hands against the wall to hold himself up.

As he swelled to near climax, she suddenly stopped and stood up, backed out of the shower and motioned with a curled finger and a mischievous grin for him to follow her.

"Come here, bitch," he ordered playfully. "Finish what you started!"

She ignored him.

He left the water running and followed her round ass and trail of wet footprints to the bedroom. Carol stretched on top of the still-made bed. She sank into the soft green comforter catlike and purred for him to come to her, her body bathed in the sliver of streetlights that filtered through half-closed blinds. Her wet hair was plastered against the pillows like an image of Venus rising. "Turn on the light," she whispered.

"You're giving me orders, now?" Alex asked.

"Please?" she begged sweetly. "I want to see you. All of you. Every goddamn inch of you. Don't you want to see me?"

He flipped the wall switch as his eyes hungrily took in her glowing skin. She was trouble. The mantra ran in the back of his head and he ignored it. He

96

couldn't peel his eyes away. Like someone walking in a dream, he followed where she led as he tried to swallow the lump in his throat.

"Like old times," she whispered, her hands reaching up to the headboard behind her.

Throbbing with his need, he settled between her legs and his eyes followed her arms. He reached up, pinned them in place and reveled in the hint of fear that danced in her eyes. Her breath quickened.

"You know what to do. You know what I like." She shifted slightly beneath him. Skin rubbed on skin. Her eyelids flickered half-shut and she moaned softly.

"I don't have the handcuffs," he smirked. She'd left her purse in the other room.

Carol bit her lip in thought. She glanced at the lamp.

Reading her thoughts, he reached over, grabbed the cord and unplugged it. Jerking on the extension until it fell out of the socket, he reeled it onto the bed and eyed it with narrow concentration as he laid the cord between her teeth and ran it slowly across her mouth. "This will do," he stated. His hot lips found hers and he kissed her hard with the cord between them.

She smiled as her tongue wrapped around it.

"Are you sure you want to do this?" Old memories banged warnings on the locked door of his conscience. He was in genuine pain and wanted only to thrust himself into her and relieve his own tension, but she was right, he did know what she liked.

"Please." Her eyes widened to appeal to him.

He loved it when she begged.

Propping himself up on his elbows, Alex took the cord and studiously wrapped it around her throat. He drew it just tight enough to make her groan with pleasure. Next, he took the ends and wrapped them around her wrists until they were secured to the headboard. Her eyes were closed. She began to writhe beneath him with pent-up sexual energy. He tightened the cord. She groaned again and arched her back. Driven by her lust, his eyes flickered closed and his mouth, nibbling and biting, found her breasts until she begged him to take her.

"I need you! Damn it, Alex! Now! Fuck me, now!"

The taste and sound and smell of his late wife unexpectedly flooded his mind. "Shut up," he hissed repeatedly as he slammed into Carol.

All he could think about was the pain that had built up inside of him since Sarah's death. He wanted release. He begged for it, cried for it, screamed for it until he reached orgasm and exploded. Exhausted, he collapsed on her and feigned a coughing fit to disguise an escaped sob.

"Hey, it's okay. You're okay. I know it's been rough on you. The memories. Everything." Carol tugged on the cord that secured her hands over her head to see if she could break free. Her arm muscles twitched slightly, and she was covered in sweat. Her calm and soothing voice washed over him. "It's okay. Everything's okay, now."

Alex pulled himself up on his elbows and stared down at her with glassy eyes as he blinked away the tears that had erupted. "I was too rough."

"It's not your fault, you know." Carol tugged again and felt the cord give a little.

Alex was dizzy as he shoved himself to his knees by her side. An angry heat welled out of him. "Wasn't my fault? What are you talking about?" He ached from the unaccustomed exertion. He rubbed his closed eyes with the palms of his hands and willed away a growing headache.

Carol tried the bonds again. She was getting nervous. "We can't help what we are. You and me. Things happen, and it changes us, you know. I'm sure you didn't mean... "

Alex stood up, even more perplexed. "To do what? You begged me. You said...."

"No. I didn't mean... I wasn't talking about THAT."

"Sarah?" He flinched at the sound of her name.

"No. Alex, I'm sorry, I shouldn't have brought it up. I just wanted you to know that I understood. It isn't your fault. Your mom…. You were just a kid," she continued. "She was easy, that's all. She wanted a good time. It had nothing to do with...." She didn't get to finish.

"What the hell are you talking about?" Alex demanded to know. He glared at her with a stabbing black look that made her cringe.

Carol struggled harder against the cord. "I know about your mom, about the abuse, about how she died. I know what happened. Those things leave their mark on a person. You needed to get it out. You needed to vent. I understand."

"My mother was not a whore!" he screamed.

"I didn't say she was!"

The room was suddenly as cold as a walk-in cooler. For a few seconds, Alex couldn't breathe. When he did, he spat the words out between clenched teeth. "How did you know about that? How? Tell me! Now!" His open hand came down hard on her cheek and left a red mark. Every muscle tightened to a sharp edge. His teeth ground against each other in his tight jaw.

"Ow!!!" Carol, trapped between his rage and her bondage, choked a bit as she fought the cord. "I don't remember! You must have told me!" she blurted out. She looked up at him with pleading eyes. "Don't just stand there, Alex. Help me! I can't get loose!"

"Never! I never told anyone!" He was oblivious to her situation. He hit her again.

She screamed. "Then Toni...." She tugged more but only managed to tighten the knot. She kicked and twisted in panic. "Stop it! You're hurting me!" She was sobbing.

"Toni hates you. She would never tell you anything like that. Never!" He

99

shook his head. "You bitch! You slut! Who put you up to this? Who?" A third time his hand came down hard on her face.

He stood up and fear fell on him like a collapsing building. His knees weakened. He leaned on the headboard and steadied himself a moment as he glanced about the room.

"Alex! It's not like that! I swear!" Carol shouted. "Get me out! Please! Help me!"

He turned back to her and licked his dry lips. "Get yourself out!" He marched out of the room to the bathroom, fell to his knees and vomited in the toilet. He heard her screaming in the next room.

"Get in here now, you son of a bitch!" she yelled. "I need help! Untie me!"

Using the sink, Alex pulled himself to his feet, rinsed out his mouth, and continued to ignore her. He wrung them out his clothes as best he could, accidentally dumping the contents of his pants pockets on the floor. Growling obscenities under his breath, he scooped up the handful of items, stuffed them back into the pocket and wrestled to put on the pants. The wet material clung like two-sided tape to his legs.

"Alex!" she screamed again.

"Tell me!" he yelled back from the bathroom. "Who put you up to this?" She screeched in rage.

A few minutes later, Alex picked up his shoes and jacket and walked out the door.

SATURDAY (Just after midnight)

Trembling in his wet clothes, Alex unlocked the door to his condo and entered his retreat, dark and cool, meticulous and clean. Contemporary. Sterile, except for the nearly dead weeping rose bush near the window and the cat dish on the kitchen floor. For a moment, he just leaned his back against the door as if he was bracing it against some evil power. He was exhausted. He was angry. He was drunk, more so than he should have been for what he had imbibed.

Alex stripped down to his boxers and left his clothes in a laundry basket in the middle of the kitchen floor. He swallowed some sleeping pills with a scotch chaser as he struggled to bring his heartbeat back to normal. Something nuzzled at his ankle and he jumped; then he relaxed and glanced down at Black Velvet.

"Come here, girl." Alex picked up the cat with trembling hands. "You must be hungry."

He set the cat on the kitchen counter while he rationed out the rest of the cat food. The animal's soft purring soothed Alex's nerves. After giving the cat one last stroke, Alex picked up the drink and the pills and dragged himself to his bedroom. It occurred to him that one dose might not be enough. He set the glass and pills on his nightstand and gazed at the photo of him and his late wife. The scene was a beach in Hawaii. The photo had been taken a few days into their honeymoon. He picked it up and his heavy eyes glistened with grief-laden tears. With his last ounce of energy, he put some soft music on the radio, turned on a small fan for white noise and collapsed on top the covers, the photo gripped in his hand. After two more pills and the last of the scotch, he sank into oblivion.

***

Tom tossed his keys on the small kitchen table as he entered his darkened apartment and tripped over a pair of boots he'd left by the door. He needed a wife, he thought, or a maid. He decided a maid would be cheaper. He flipped on the kitchen light that bathed the place in a sleepy glow. He was trying to decide if he should eat something or just crawl into bed.

Tom set his Glock down on the counter and peeled off his coat. He had barely opened the refrigerator door when his cell phone rang.

"Damn!" he yelled, knowing no one would hear. "Enough is enough

101

already!" He snatched the phone and was prepared to make some belligerent remark when he noticed the number. He frowned. Tom sagged against the counter in fatigue with his eyes closed. He had expected it to be his mother. He had expected Toni. He had expected more information on the recent child killing. He hadn't expected this call.

"Sadler. You know what time it is?" he asked.

"They got a homicide in Henderson." Candy Knight's voice was soft and matter of fact.

"I thought you were fired." Tom instantly regretted his bluntness.

"I am. That's why I called you," she told him.

"Then how do you…?" he started to ask.

"Don't ask," she said.

"Look, I put in my tour of duty tonight – twice. Why are you calling me?" Tom reopened the fridge and peered in. He decided food should come before bed.

"Alex de la Rosa is being arrested for murder."

Tom froze. His throat tightened. "You're bullshitting me." He instinctively knew that she wasn't.

"Better get going if you want in," Candy told him.

"Who the hell did he kill? Elliott?" He couldn't help but allow a little wishful thinking to creep into the situation.

Candy sighed in understanding. "Some woman cop."

Tom was stunned. His first thought was Toni, but that didn't make sense. Candy would have said if Alex had killed his sister. "Of all the people you could have called, why me?" He was suddenly suspicious.

There was a minute of silence before she answered. "You know why. Besides, someone in that department has to do their damn job."

"You heard about the other dead girl, then, huh?" He could almost see her nodding on the other end. "Elliott is calling it a copycat."

102

"I'd explain different but right now you have other problems," said Candy.

Tom hung up the phone and wondered if Randall was out of bed already. "Sounds like an emergency to me," he muttered as he grabbed his coat.

.

CHAPTER 8

VERY EARLY SATURDAY

Tom rubbed his tired eyes as he drove his unmarked car slowly through the high, gated entrance to Turnberry Place. He leaned forward into his window and glanced up at the magnificent white towers that plunged into the night sky, their bases firmly planted in greenery, their porticos framed with palm trees. *So, this is how the very rich live,* he thought as he bore left around the clubhouse. He had always wondered where Alex got his money, even while Tom ignored the innuendos tossed about by Sheriff Randall. Alex's law practice seemed solid enough. Tom glanced again at the towers. Maybe not this solid.

A security officer checked Tom's credentials before directing him to park by Tower 2. Tom wedged his vehicle between a patrol car and a news crew van along the circular drive that served the tower. He stepped out of his car, stretched his tired back and took a minute to look over the scene. The signal lamps of several cruisers, flashing like strobe lights at one of the area's many nightclubs, lit up the building and bounced off the glass and trim. Several police officers stood guard behind them. One nodded at Tom in recognition. Tom saw Randall and a few heavily-armed men poised at the entry. Yawning, he felt like he was slogging through mud as he jogged to catch up with them.

Randall, looking much older and even more tired than he had a few hours earlier, glanced at his watch and then at Tom. He was obviously pissed. He wore a frayed sweater, sagging blue jeans and wet sneakers that squished when he walked. He ran his hand through his curly, gray hair and his bloodshot, dark gray eyes were nearly black as he stared at Tom. He was still groggy from cold medicine and he smelled like Vicks.

"What the hell you doing here?" Randall asked.

Tom stopped a few feet away and silently asked himself that same question. "You want me to leave?" He wasn't sure if he wanted to hear yes or no.

Randall grunted. "Well, you're here."

If Randall hadn't been so tired, he would have put up more of an argument, Tom realized as the team entered the building. Behind them, a young reporter and an older cameraman jumped out of a KVBC television van. The reporter quickly straightened his tie and took his spot before the camera's beam of light. Tom, propping open the front door for Randall, paused a second to listen.

"We are reporting live from the exclusive Turnberry Place, home of the once famous and now possibly infamous Las Vegas attorney Alessandro de la Rosa. Our sources tell us that De la Rosa is wanted suspect for the brutal rape and murder of 29-year-old ex-stripper turned police officer Carol McEnroe at her Henderson home earlier tonight. Unconfirmed rumors say the attorney and the beautiful female cop had been carrying on a steamy and rocky affair for a number of years since the untimely and unsolved, brutal murder of De la Rosa's wife."

What the hell have I gotten into? Tom thought.

"You coming?" Randall barked the question.

Tom spun on his heel, left the chaos behind and followed the sheriff and a couple of men into the elevator. Others took the stairs. A few minutes later, the half-dozen police officers, in vests and helmets and with guns drawn, huddled in the soft gray carpeted hall on the fourth floor of Turnberry Place, their boots leaving clots of mud behind them. Randall towered over them. He handed Tom a slip of paper with the apartment door's security code on it, gripped his gun snugly and banged on the door.

"Open up! This is the police! Open the door now!"

The dark hall closed in around Tom Sadler and choked the air out of him. He ran a finger under the collar of his shirt to loosen it as he watched the officers shuffle about half-stooped.

"The guy doesn't even own a gun," Tom remarked, gripping his own. They ignored him.

Tom shook his head and fingered the paper. He hadn't told the sheriff he had the code memorized – a symbol of trust from Toni to be used in case of emergencies. His jaw locked as he felt the betrayal in his bones. His eyes darted from Randall to the door and back again.

"Well, you were stupid enough to show up for this," Randall muttered. "Now open it." Tom reluctantly did so.

Inside the otherwise quiet townhouse, Black Velvet, curled up on the back of the sofa, turned his head to look at the strangers. His eyes reflected the glare of flashlights in the darkness. He hissed, jumped down and bolted under a chair. A trail of water led to the wet clothes in the basket next to an empty cat dish. A ring of keys, a silver and turquoise cigarette lighter and a damp wallet were abandoned on the counter. A long-dead cigar was crushed in an ashtray. Randall picked up the cigar with a pair of tweezers and sniffed at it. He put it back. "Elliott will want to see this," he mumbled.

Behind Randall, a snapshot of Alex, Fran, Toni and Tom at a local bar, neatly framed, sat on the kitchen counter. Tom grimaced. Randall pretended not to notice. With silent gestures, the sheriff directed the police to enter the bedroom. Guns drawn, they quietly pushed through the door and circled the suspect.

They found Alex fast asleep and snoring softly. He was face down on his bed and still clutched the photo of Sarah. He wore a pair of dark socks, blue striped boxer shorts, and a sleeveless undershirt. The fan hummed created a cooling breeze and a soft noise. A half-bottle of sleeping pills, the lid tossed to the side, sat next to an empty glass and Alex's reading glasses. The only light was the flickering of candles on the bureau. The soft strains of Diana Krall streamed from an Amazon Echo player on the nightstand.

All or nothing at all; half a love never appealed to me....

Alex never heard the police bang on the door. He never heard it open. He never heard anyone enter his home until he was dragged from his warm bed and slammed to the hard floor. Shocked into consciousness and blinded by bright flashlights, he lashed out, only to be beaten about the head and neck with batons. He screamed in rage.

All or nothing at all; if it's love, there is no in between....

Cringing, Alex curled into a fetal position on the floor and covered his head with his hands as the toe of a boot slammed into his ribs. He gasped in pain. Obscenities flooded the room. As he tried to turn away, another boot got him in the small of his back and he cried out. A baton smacked his jaw.

Please don't put your lips so close to my cheek....

"Stop it!" Tom yelled. He grabbed several officers and shoved them back. "What the hell are you doing?" He quickly holstered his own gun.

The kiss in your eyes, the touch of your hand makes me weak....

"Enough! Damn it!" Tom yelled again. "Cuff him and put him in the car, and I don't want to see another mark on him! Got that?"

The officer looked from Tom to Randall for confirmation. Randall, looking sullen, nodded.

"Get up," an officer ordered Alex.

Alex forced himself to his knees, clutched Tom's coat, and looked up. "What the hell happened?" he asked as he struggled to breathe. "What's going on? Tom? What...?"

"On your feet, Alex." Tom's hazel eyes were steady. He didn't try to help Alex up. He knew how it would look to the others; he knew they were watching. He should have gone to bed. He should have stayed a million miles away from here.

Alex stared back and nearly lost his balance.

I would be caught in the undertow....

Two officers grabbed the attorney by the arms and steadied him, then they yanked his arms behind his back to cuff his wrists. Alex doubled over with a yell. Tom reached out and grabbed Alex by the shoulders to keep his friend from falling face forward.

"Shit, that hurts! My ribs! They're broken! Tom! What the hell?" Alex cried.

Tom shook his head sadly. "Sorry about this, Alex. Just doing my job."

"Your job? This is your job? What the fuck is going on?"

So, you see, I've got to say no, no. All or nothing at all....

Alex was dragged into the hall, down the elevator and out of the building – barefoot, battered, still in his underwear and swearing loudly the whole way – into the view of police, onlookers and the KVBC Channel 3 news. That's when he shut up.

In the large living room, Tom drew back the window curtain.

An enthusiastic reporter pushed through the police line and stuck his microphone in Alex's face. Alex tried to duck the camera's glaring spotlight and hide his face while the reporter pelted him with questions. Tom couldn't hear them. He was too far away, and the windows were soundproofed. He stood in the thick silence and watched.

Stumbling, Alex didn't speak. An officer pushed Alex's head down and his body was shoved into the sticky, hot, vinyl backseat of the squad car. The officer joined him, and the car peeled off into the night.

Tom let the curtain fall back into place.

So, you see, I've got to say no, no. All or nothing at all....

Roger Elliott walked into the room and gave Tom a cold stare. "Don't even think of interfering. I don't want you on the scene at all. You'll compromise the investigation."

"And you won't?" Tom turned away from the window and faced Elliott.

Elliott ignored the remark, ordered his crew into the bedroom to process for evidence, and followed close behind. A few seconds later, the music stopped.

Outside, the reporter wrapped up his story. The squad cars pulled out of the driveway, one at a time. The parking lot was soon empty and quiet as the crowd dispersed. Tom stood in the window of Alex's home and stared at the cat.

***

Sgt. Pedro Martinez, a soft-bellied, round-faced, family man with silver-tinged hair, had better things to do in the middle of the night, but it was one of those nights. He snapped his nicotine gum with his teeth and leaned against the entrance to the garage of the Clark County Detention Center as a squad skirted a gathering of newspaper reporters and slipped into the garage. The doors shut with a clang.

Martinez could have stayed in bed. He could have been cuddling his wife, eating onion rings and watching an old movie, but when the news bulletin flashed across his TV screen, he was dressed and out the door in seconds. He watched his men carefully as they led the stumbling and disoriented attorney into the cool blue halls of the building. The sergeant's brow twisted in thought; his lips pressed together. They knew he was watching them. They kept their heads down and their minds on the business at hand.

The police bypassed the booking room with its airport-styled rows of black seats and crowds of drunks, prostitutes, wife beaters, and assorted detainees. They dragged Alex directly to a small room and shoved him in. Tripping and with his hands still cuffed behind him and no way to break his fall, Alex slammed head first into the hard wall before he landed on his knees on the concrete floor. He gasped in pain. A bump swelled on his head.

"That's enough," Martinez barked as he shoved his burly weight into the gathering guards. "You're outta here. I don't want any of you within a hundred feet of him, you hear me?"

One guard started to say something and thought better of it.

"Hey, who's in charge? You want a paycheck at the end of the week? Get out!" Martinez ordered as he physically pushed them into the brightly lit corridor and slammed the door behind them with a heavy clang. The guards huddled outside the security window like a clique of gossiping schoolgirls peering into a fishbowl.

Alex turned to look up at the sergeant as the pain in his chest worsened.

Martinez reached down, unlocked one of the handcuffs with a sharp click, carefully pulled Alex up and helped him to a gray, utilitarian chair bolted to the floor. There, Martinez cuffed Alex to the chair's steel arm. "You hurt, Alex?" Martinez asked as he leaned against the table and crossed his arms over his bulging gut.

"My ribs. I think they're broken," Alex whispered. "Who's dead, Pete?"

"The sheriff will be here shortly. I'm sure he'll fill you in. In the meantime, you have to be processed." Martinez looked apologetic as he gestured to the window behind them to remind Alex that they were both being watched by more than a handful of curious people. "The next few hours are going to be the worst. You'll be searched, fingerprinted, stripped and then a guard will do a cavity search. I'll find you something to wear and see if there's a medic to check you out. With a little luck, you could spend the weekend in the infirmary."

Alex nodded silently.

"We've known each other a long time, Alex, and I shouldn't have to ask this." Martinez leaned over until he was inches from Alex's ear. He voice was soft enough not to be heard over the room's hidden surveillance equipment. "Tell me. Did you do it? Did you really kill her?" Old suspicions about Sarah's death surfaced in Martinez's mind.

"Who, damn it?"

Martinez sighed and glanced down at the floor a second. He felt like a man sitting on a train loaded with dynamite and knowing the bridge was out

111

ahead. "Carol McEnroe."

Alex nearly tore himself out of his chair and his eyes widened with shock. "Carol? Carol is dead? That's impossible! I just...." He froze.

"Just answer the question, Alex. For me. Just between us."

"No! Never! Of course not! That's crazy! You know me better than that!" Alex yelled.

Martinez looked confused, skeptical and slightly relieved all in one glance. "Whatever you do, don't fight these guys. They want nothing more than to use you for soccer practice, you hear me?"

Alex nodded but his eyes raged.

Someone knocked at the door and a guard entered with Randall and Elliott. The guard took his position at the door; one hand rested menacingly on the stick secured to his belt.

Alex's whole body went taut when he saw Elliott, who had a camera in one pudgy hand and a forensic kit in the other. The man's bow tie was missing but he still wore his usual starched shirt and sickly stiff persona, and, to Rick Brandt's credit, Elliott really did smell like a morgue. The dark circles under his eyes told of hours without sleep.

"We're ready." Randall pulled out a chair and settled his portly frame into it. Elliot sat next to him, playing Jeff to Randall's Mutt, and taking his cues from the sheriff.

Martinez pulled a small tape recorder from his pocket, turned it on and set it down in front of Alex. He tapped it a few times and played the sound back to make sure it was working right. "You have the right to remain silent," Martinez said clearly and slowly. He crossed his arms as he continued to lean against the table. "Anything you say can and will be used against you in a court of law. You have the right to an attorney. If you cannot afford an attorney, one will be provided to you at no cost. Do you understand these rights as I have read them to you?"

112

Alex closed his eyes, tipped his head back and moaned.

"You need to speak loud enough for the tape recorder to hear you," Martinez directed, watching Alex carefully.

"I understand." Alex opened his eyes and glared menacingly across the table at Elliott. "I know my rights. I have nothing to say."

Martinez clicked off the recorder, pocketed it and solemnly left the room. He stationed himself at the window outside the door and watched, aware of the war between Alex and Elliott. As the questioning continued, the loitering guards wandered away.

Inside, Randall instructed the guard to remove Alex's handcuffs. "Stand up and take off your clothes," he told Alex. He slapped a search warrant down on the table as Elliot checked his camera.

Under the watchful eyes of Randall and the guard, Elliott photographed every part of Alex's body, then took scrapings from under his fingernails, swabbed the blood from his forehead and lip, swiped saliva from his mouth and combed through his head and pubic hair. Elliott never spoke to Alex but, for a second, with the help of Elliott's platform shoes, they were nose-to-chin and their eyes locked.

Martinez could read the unspoken fury between them. Elliott's hands trembled slightly as he worked. When the investigator had finished and left Alex cold and naked in the air-conditioned room, the guard took finger and palm prints. Then he donned latex gloves and examined Alex's ears, nose and mouth. "Bend over," he said finally.

"I thought there was a rule against cavity searches on detainees," Alex noted.

"Sue me," Randall told him.

Martinez, his hand on the doorknob, considered intervening but decided to wait it out.

Alex wrapped his arm around his damaged ribs, grit his teeth against the

113

pain, hung onto the table and complied. He felt the warm red blush crawl up his spine and neck and expose his embarrassment. He said nothing. When the guard finished, Alex was given a navy jumpsuit with CCDC in white letters across the back and a pair of bright orange boxer shorts and slippers. He was instructed to dress. Grasping the jumpsuit for a moment of dignity, he spoke directly to Randall. "I need to see a doctor. My ribs are broken."

Randall ran his fingers through his gray hair but didn't answer.

"You'll see one soon enough," the guard responded.

Alex slipped the jumpsuit over his bruised and aching body before he was handcuffed back to the chair. He shuddered. Goosebumps crawled up his skin.

Elliott, the deposition subpoena that Brandt had served on him still sticking out of his jacket pocket, gave Alex one last smirk behind the handlebar mustache, gathered up his materials and left. Sheriff Randall remained, joined again by Martinez who knew better than to leave the two men alone in a room together.

"You know he is out to get me," Alex told Randall. Everyone knew he meant Elliott. "You know he tampers with evidence. You know he can't be trusted. I want him off this case. Now!"

"Where should we begin?" Randall ignored Alex's complaints. He turned on his tape recorder and laced his fingers together as he leaned across the table.

"I told you, I'm not saying a thing," Alex stated.

"Then I'll do the talking. You knew Carol McEnroe. That much we know. You two were lovers several years ago. We know you had dinner together tonight." He glanced at his watch. "Last night. We even have paparazzi photos of you at the restaurant. We know you took her to her place. The valet heard you talk about it. We know she was quite drunk. We know you showered there. Cleaning up after the crime, perhaps? Water was found on

114

her hallway floor. Her sheets were wet. Your car seat was wet. Your clothes were soaked. We know you left her apartment around midnight, about a half-hour before she was found – dead. We found your cigar…" He tossed an evidence bag with a crushed cigar onto the table. "…at the scene. She was tortured with a burning cigar."

Randall didn't miss the shocked look on Alex's face.

"I invoked my right to remain silent, remember?" Alex slammed his emotions into a dark box in his mind.

"You don't have to say a word. We have all the evidence we need to get the death penalty." Randall took a deep breath and reined in his own anger over Carol's brutal death. "A neighbor heard yelling and identified your car as the one pulling away in the middle of the night. We found Carol…." He fanned a large stack of photos of the dead woman in front of Alex, whose locked jaw defined a frozen face.

"I want a lawyer." Alex tried to focus on Randall, but his eyes were dragged back to the photos.

She was naked and dead and tied to her headboard, her eyes open and her mouth gagged with a washcloth. Small red blotches could be seen on her breasts and face and throat – the throat that was still securely wrapped in the extension cord.

Carol had been photographed from every angle in excruciating detail, but what struck them most was how much this looked like a previous crime scene. The years peeled back, and they saw another woman strangled, gagged, raped and dead – Sarah de la Rosa.

Martinez was a detective in the field, then. He was the first officer to arrive on the scene. He had found Alex curled in a ball and sobbing in Fran's arms. Now, as he faced Alex, Martinez's mouth went dry. What if Randall was right all along? Sure, Alex had coughed up an alibi then, but what if…?

"You want to talk about it?" Randall asked.

115

"I'm being framed." Alex's eyes burrowed into the door like bullets aimed at the back of Elliot's head. "That goddamn son of a bitch is setting me up."

"Who? Why?" Randall asked.

"Elliott! The fucking idiot. He was a fucking idiot when I met him, and he is still a fucking idiot." Alex acted like a man with little to lose. "I told you. He tampers with evidence. He did it to Callas and now he's doing it to me. I was onto him and he knew it. He's covering for somebody. You know it. You probably know who the hell it is, too."

"That's a pretty serious allegation, especially from someone accused of murder." Randall's eyes narrowed. "Can you prove any of it?"

Alex tightened his jaw.

Randall nodded. "Didn't think so." He leaned forward. "I know you raped and murdered Carol McEnroe the same way you raped and murdered Sarah. You got away with it once, de la Rosa. You won't get away with it twice."

Alex paled at the sound of his wife's name. "You fucking bastard! I never touched Sarah! I loved her! I loved her!" His voice cracked as tears welled up in his eyes.

Randall pursed his lips and studied the beaten man. "You loved her too much, you mean – too much to let anyone else have her." The metal legs of his chair scraped across the concrete floor as he shoved back, stood up and loomed over Alex.

"She didn't want anyone else!" Alex protested. "We were happy. We were going to have children."

"Sarah died at your hands." Randall planted his knuckles on the table. "She found someone else, you got pissed and you killed her. I couldn't prove it then, but I'll prove it now. You're going down for murder, Alex, and I'm going to see to it you finally get what you deserve."

Alex thought of Bella. "I want a lawyer," he said. "Now."

Randall knew better than to argue with him anymore. Turning off the tape recorder, he closed his folder and got up to leave. "He's all yours," Randall told Martinez at the doorway.

Martinez nodded but didn't speak until he was alone with Alex. "They're going to keep you in the infirmary for a night or two and you'd better pray to god you make bail on Monday because you won't find your cellmates as nice as I am."

"Thanks," Alex whispered, grateful for the unexpected kindness.

"I'm not doing this for you, Alex. I'm doing it for Toni. I owe her. Remember that." He turned his back on the prisoner and walked out the door.

CHAPTER 9

Fran woke with a throbbing headache and the tinny strains of the Beach Boys in her ears. Trying to lick the cotton balls out of her mouth, she untangled herself from her satin comforter, rolled over and tried to shut off the music before she realized the sound came from her cell phone. The clock glowed 2:47 a.m. Frowning, she sat up on bed, grabbed the phone and brushed her bangs out of her sleepy eyes. "What the hell?" she mumbled, hitting the talk button twice before getting it right.

"Hello?" Her voice sounded like a nasal, hoarse squawk and she had to clear her throat and try again. "Hello?" Shivering, she pulled the blanket over her bare arms. The calming blues of her bedroom were gray in the dark. She reached over and flicked on the bedside reading lamp. The dim light revealed a clutter of clothes, shoes, work papers and old magazines.

"Bella, it's me. I'm in trouble." Alex's voice was shaky, and his words were clipped.

"So, what's new?" Fran groaned with relief and glanced at the clock again. "Can't this wait 'til morning, Alex? I'm exhausted!"

"No, Bella. It can't wait." He hesitated a second. "I've been arrested. I'm in jail."

She snickered, drew her knees up to her chest and wondered what kind of prank he was pulling this time. "Sure, you are. What do you need? A ride home from somewhere? A place to crash? An escape route from one of your adoring fans? What kind of trouble did you get into?"

The phone was silent for a few long seconds.

"Alex?" she asked, her voice tight with unexpected worry. A deep cold reached down inside of her and grabbed her by the gut. She pulled the blanket tighter. "Alex, just what kind of trouble did you get into?"

"Murder." He whispered the word.

The word crashed into her like lightning. She couldn't have heard him

119

right. It was a dream. That was it. She was having a nightmare. She looked at the clock again: 2:49. She waited for the punch line. When it didn't come, she took a deep breath and closed her eyes as the room spun around in her head.

"Bella?" His voice broke through her fog. "You still there?"

"Fuck." She swore under her breath. "Where are you?" If this was his idea of a joke, it was a damn sick one. Her fingers trembled as she covered her lips and tried to stay calm.

"Clark County Detention. I'm being held without bail pending a preliminary hearing on Monday. I'm allowed one call. You're it." He waited.

Dazed, Fran shook her head.

"Did you hear me, Bella? I've been arrested for murder," Alex repeated.

"This isn't funny!" Fran snapped. Her heart twisted into a knot. Tears stung at the back of her eyes. "Don't do this to me! Tell me this is a joke! Tell me now or I swear…."

"I'm in jail for rape and murder. Would I make that up?" His voice was pleading, breathless and tinged with anger.

"Rape?" Her bedroom grew chilly as a winter morning. "What happened? What the hell did you do? No, don't tell me. Don't tell anyone. Have you given a statement?" As the reality of the situation slammed into her, her mind slipped into lawyer mode. She curled herself up tighter.

"Are you kidding?" His sarcastic tone helped calm her a bit.

She nodded, now fully awake. "I'm on my way." She tossed the blanket to the side and slipped her sock-clad feet to the floor, the phone still planted to her ear.

"No. It's too late for that, Bella. Besides, you need to get over your hangover first," he said.

"I don't have a hangover," she argued.

"It's Saturday morning. Of course, you do."

"But…." She clenched her teeth.

120

"In the morning, Bella. I'll see you in the morning. Thank you."

A click and humming sound told her he had hung up.

Fran lowered the phone to the bed and stared at it. Rage boiled out of her. "Damn you, Alex! You son of a bitch! Damn you!" She felt the fate of Max Simone slip out of her fingers. The vacuum was filled with terror.

***

Alex leaned back in the tan office and stared at the phone until Martinez put down the receiver and looked up.

"Time to go," the sergeant said. He took Alex by the arm and helped him out of the chair. Martinez steered Alex toward the open door, clicked off the office light, closed the door with a metal bang and locked it. Alex winced at the finality of the sound.

A short, muscular guard waited for them in the dimly lit corridor, one hand resting casually on his nightstick. He was grinding away on a piece of gum as if he was trying to disintegrate it.

Martinez gave the guard a sideways glance and directed Alex to walk ahead of them. The guard followed silently.

As Alex stumbled along, unable to focus on the details surrounding him. Another door clanged shut somewhere around a corner. A fluorescent light glowed overhead. A buzzer went off someplace else. The guard flicked the lights off one by one as they walked. Darkness took over the space behind them. The rest was the silence of pain locked behind unadorned walls.

Alex closed his eyes a second and fought back an unexpected onslaught of rage. He remembered Carol's laughing eyes when she had hugged him that evening, the coconut scent of her hair, the look on her face when she'd begged him for sex. He remembered the feel of her skin against his and the cord in his hands. His face twisted into pain.

All or nothing at all. Half a love never appealed to me...."

At the end of the corridor, they turned right and made their way down a set of polished stairs. The silence was broken only by the clanging of Alex's chains and the padding of his orange slippers on the concrete floor.

He tried to shake the song out of his head. He almost remembered something. What was it? How drunk was he? What was he forgetting? For some strange reason he couldn't quite name, he was angry at Carol for dying and putting him in this position. She had done this to him. She was trouble. Was. Had been. Wasn't anymore. He licked his lips and tasted dry blood. He wondered if it was hers or his. The memories were like frightening bits of an old horror movie.

"If it's love, there is no in between...."

Alex was escorted into the antiseptic smell of the infirmary. Even here, with most of the staff long gone to bed and a few patients fast asleep, everything was dark and quiet. Martinez instructed an on-duty orderly to tape up Alex's side. They helped him into a hospital bed and removed the rest of his bindings.

Martinez casually tossed a lightweight blanket over Alex and turned off the light. The room was dark except for the red and white exit sign over the door, the flickering of the television set in the orderly's station and the flooding guard tower light from outside that bathed the bottom half of Alex's legs.

"Get some sleep," Martinez ordered.

"I don't think that'll happen," Alex told him.

"It may be the only time you do." Martinez's voice was calm despite the warning.

"I could use some painkillers." Alex shifted slightly to relieve the pressure on his ribs.

"You have to wait for the doc. He'll be here by nine," Martinez said.

"Not even aspirin?" Alex asked.

"Rules are rules, even for you," Martinez walked out the door.

Alex stared up at the dark ceiling. The sensation of Carol's skin against his flashed through his mind. He felt her warm breath on his cheek. He tasted the brandy and tobacco on her lips. He felt the extension cord slide through his hand. Her body quivered below him. *"Please don't put your lips so close to my cheek...."* Bile churned its way up Alex's throat.

Elliott had set him up. Alex was sure of it, but he needed proof. If only he had proof, but proof was the ghost that ducked into the shadows each time he came around the corner. Proof was a whisper from an unknown source. Proof eluded him.

What if he was wrong? What if he'd killed Carol and just couldn't remember? What if Elliott was telling the truth?

Alex closed his eyes against the dark despair that engulfed him. Despite himself, Carol's body was foremost in his mind. Her lips reached for his, but he pushed her away. She begged him to release her. He didn't. She had always been trouble. What the hell was he thinking? He should have listened to his gut. He should have listened to Toni. Carol was so different from Sarah, and yet they merged in his mind as if one and the same.

The reality of Carol's death slammed into him. Finally, the song was gone.

***

Fran sat on her bed and shuddered. She clasped the phone with two hands and stared at the lighted numbers. She tried Toni's number first with no answer. Of course, she'd be asleep. She probably had her phone turned off if she didn't want to be bothered, Fran thought. Fran considered calling her ex-husband but realized in the same breath that the first words out of his mouth would be something in the line of "I told you so." At the back of her head was the nagging fear that Alex might be guilty. She couldn't shake the thought, no matter how hard she tried. It was illogical, she told herself. It wasn't like him. He wouldn't do this to her.

She called Rick Brandt and was surprised when he answered the phone.

123

"What are you doing up at this hour?" Fran asked as she tucked her legs under her.

"Answerin' the goddamn phone, boss lady. I got news for ya on the Callas case. I'll meet ya at the office in the mornin' and fill ya in. No rest for the wicked." Rick chuckled.

Fran took a deep breath. Good old Rick, always there, always on the job, always had her back. She leaned on him a lot. She was about to wipe the smile from his face.

When she didn't answer, he asked, "What's up?"

Fran struggled to hear him over the distinct sounds of a casino in the background. She was surprised at how alert he was. At any other time, she might have chided him for his sarcasm, but this was not the time. "We got a problem. Big problem. HUGE."

"Yeah. I know, but it should work in our favor, right?" he asked.

She shook her head in confusion. "In our favor? How? How did you find out so fast? Alex just barely called."

Rick continued talking as if he hadn't heard her interruption. "They dug that poor girl outta the trash and it looks like your man was right after all. Callas was set up. You know what this means. We got a helluva lot more work to do on this case. Elliott is yelling copycat and…." His voice suddenly stopped. "What the hell you doin' up at this hour anyway, boss?"

"What girl?" Nasty thoughts exploded like synchronized dynamite in her head.

"The schoolgirl." Rick lowered his voice a bit to avoid being overheard. "About the same age: twelve, I'd guess, from the looks of her. Course, I only got a quick look before the damn lab boys hauled her away. Sadler was there, by the way. That boy sure does get around."

Fran panicked, suddenly nauseous. Murder, Alex had said. Rape and murder. Whose murder? Damn! Why hadn't she asked? She shook her head and tried to breathe. "No. That's impossible. I know Alex. He'd never do something like that. Never." She had trusted Alex. He had been around her daughter.

"Alex? What the hell does Alex gotta do with this?" Rick asked.

"Another school girl? From Lauren's school?" Fran's mind jumped from one image to the next.

"Yeah, complete with plaid skirt and that damn rock in her hand. But you still didn't tell me...."

Fran wrapped an arm around her embroiled stomach. "Alex was arrested for rape and murder tonight."

Rick was quiet far too long. She imagined him flipping the coin he had planned to slip into a slot machine. He'd bet on it. Heads, it went in. Tails, he walked.

"Rick! You there?" Fran yelled frantically.

"Hold on, boss." Rick's calm voice held her back and she waited impatiently for what would come next. "This ain't right. Ain't right at all," he finally said. "Let me check on it. I'll get back to you." He hung up.

Unable to go back to sleep, Fran turned on her bedside lamp, pulled on her pink terry robe and tiptoed down the dimly-lit, carpeted hall to her daughter's room. Lauren was sound asleep, her arm curled around a white faux fur bunny nearly as big as she was. She looked so innocent, so untouched. Fran breathed easier. Alex didn't do it. He couldn't have. The proof was in Lauren, wasn't it? Fran glanced quickly at the nightlight that she, not Lauren, insisted on having.

Fran leaned against the doorway and watched the child breathe. She had a million questions on her mind and no answers. On impulse, she finally headed to the kitchen, flipped on the light over the stove and opened the fridge. A blast of cold air hit her cheeks and drove the last shreds of sleepiness away. Nothing in the fridge appealed to her. She shut the door and pressed her forehead against the cool stainless steel for a minute.

Still shaking, she went to the living room, turned on the desk lamp and picked up her flask. Her fingers gently stroked the engraved metal. "You're the best. Love, Alex." He had given it to her at the office. It was her birthday present, five years ago, the day his wife was murdered. Fran poured herself a cognac. She spilled some on the rich rosewood of her secretary and wiped it up with the sleeve of her robe before she brought the glass and the flask to her favorite armchair.

She snuggled into the chair with her feet on the ottoman. With the five candles flickering lazily in their jars on the bookcase, she drank her way through the flask until sunrise as she waited for the craziness of her world to crash around her. By morning, the candles were drowned in melted wax and Fran was in a restless sleep filled with screaming children and watery carnival rides and small painted rocks that rested in the palm of her hand.

***

Across town, in the chill of the air-conditioned infirmary, Alex gave up trying to sleep and surrendered to a night of tortured memories.

Five Years Earlier

"Are you coming out or do I have to come in there and get you?" Alex asked.

He was still in his suit from court and was leaning against the woven wire fence that separated the kindergarten's playground from the sidewalk and road. Sarah, wearing a floral summer dress and white sandals, her pixie-cut black hair tossed by the breeze, smiled back at him. Three kindergarteners were seizing her skirt, screaming for her attention and begging her not to leave. Other children were tearing around the yard under the watchful eyes of the staff.

"You're going to have to rescue me," she laughed, her green eyes twinkling in the afternoon sunlight.

"Okay, but you'd better warn those guys. I'm coming in and I won't take no for an answer." Alex dropped his briefcase, mussed his thick hair, arched his back and spread his fingers like bear claws as he stomped towards the gated entrance and growled through his foolish grin at the squealing children who tried to hide behind their teacher.

"Stop, Alex! Stop!" Sarah laughed. "You're scaring them!"

"Yeah! You're scaring us!" one little boy repeated, taking his stand in front of Sarah, his fists planted on his hips and his eyes staring defiantly upward.

"Oh, you want scared, do you? Well, I'll show you scared!" Alex reached out to tickle the boy in the ribs. The child screamed delightedly and ran away, his two friends on his heels.

"You are such a meanie." Sarah draped her smooth, cool arms around Alex's neck and kissing him gently on the lips. "I love you, you know." Her fingers worked their way up through his dark hair.

He lived for that touch. Had lived for it. His thoughts dragged him to a darker place.

Alex picked up his office phone and called home. He could hear the disappointment in her voice when she answered.

"Please don't tell me you're working late again. You promised. It's Fran's birthday for heaven's sake! I have dinner planned. You can't keep doing this to me. We need to talk about it."

"I'm sorry," Alex told her. "This case is huge. Elliot is up to no good. I know he's been tampering with the evidence, but I still have to prove it. I'll get there as soon as I can."

"This is our marriage, Alex. You know that. We made plans," Sarah argued.

"I know, and I love you. I really do, but I can't sit back and let this bastard...."

127

"That's not your job," she continued. "The police should investigate him, not you. You're obsessed."

Alex sighed and rubbed his tired eyes. "Just an hour. Maybe two. I'll make it up to you."

It's not about making it up to me. I can't keep doing this, Alex. I told you. I don't want to be alone anymore. Please come home."

She hung up on him, and he knew she was crying.

How many times had he beaten himself up over that decision? She wanted him. She needed him. It was the last thing she ever said to him. How could he have put her off? And for what? Five years later, he couldn't remember the name of the client.

"Yes, Bella! I need those papers at my house tonight!" Alex pulled into his driveway with his cell phone attached to his ear. He turned off the windshield wipers. The rain had let up a bit. "You heard me. Tonight. I still have to review the last three statements and organize the exhibits." He smiled as he thought of the lie he was using to lure her to his house for her birthday dinner.

Alex clicked the phone closed without saying goodbye and grabbed his briefcase and jacket. The front door swung open without resistance. He made a note to remind Sarah to lock it behind her.

The house smelled of marinara sauce and the table was set for three. A chocolate birthday cake was decorated with a plastic redheaded doll in a cheerleader outfit. Alex smiled. Sarah had placed a small bud vase next to the cake with clippings from his weeping roses. He bent over to take a whiff and glanced around. Everything was immaculate as usual. He expected nothing less from her. The only clutter was the small stack of books and papers on the desk in the corner where Sarah scratched out her to-do lists. He checked the oven; dinner was still warm. He looked at the clock: a few minutes past eight.

Tiptoeing down the hall to surprise her, Alex approached the bedroom. A soft glow seeped through the opening in the door. Light spilled onto the hallway rug. He pushed gently on the door and looked in, his body framed by darkness as he stared at the bed where she was stretched out.

Not again, Alex thought, staring at the ceiling as the gray of early dawn seeped into the infirmary. I can't go through this again. I can't, Sarah. I'm so sorry.

***

At half past five, as the sun poked through the curtains of Fran's apartment, she awoke to a migraine, a stiff back and a sharp fear in her gut. The night's events plowed mercilessly into her consciousness. Panicked, she sat up in the chair, picked up the phone and called Rick.

His tired answer was simple: "I talked to Tom. Not the same case. We need to meet. When can you get there?"

"Oh my god, oh my god," she said, her voice cracked as she sank into the chair and the worst of her fears drained out of her.

"Boss? You okay?" Rick sounded confused. He would never have considered Alex as a child killer, Fran realized.

It was her ghost and her nightmare that tainted everything.

"I need to go to the prison first." Fran was breathing a little easier. "How about one? You're at the office?"

"Will be. See you there, boss. Don't worry, boss. We'll fix this," Rick assured her.

Fran nodded, hung up and called Margo. The woman growled, still half-asleep.

"We have an emergency." Fran leaned back in her chair and closed her eyes, the phone at her ear. Her hands were steady now. She felt guilty at being so relieved, but that didn't matter. "I need everyone at the office by one. And get a hold of Alex's sister, will you? She's not picking up. Go to her apartment if you have to. She has to be there."

"Do you know what time it is? It's Saturday! Can't it wait?" Margo whined. "I planned to...."

"Tom Sadler, too, if he can make it. He can fill us in," Fran interrupted.

"It's Saturday!" Margo reiterated.

"I told you. It's an emergency. Make the calls. Be there," Fran barked.

Margo was silent a second. "Who died?"

Funny, thought Fran, that was the one thing she should have asked Rick and didn't. "Alex was arrested for murder."

A moment of shocked silence filled her ear. "You're kidding!"

"No. I'm not," said Fran.

"But who...?" Margo started to ask.

"I don't know!" Fran yelled. She was on the edge of hysteria. She took a deep breath. "I don't know," she repeated calmly.

More silence. "This has got to be a joke. Somebody set him up. He wouldn't kill anybody. He...."

"Margo, I need you calm and I need you to call everyone. Can you handle it?" Fran asked.

"At one?"

"Yes, at one." Fran hung up and went back to her drink.

It would be another three hours before the jail would let her see Alex. She had time for breakfast: scrambled eggs and more scotch. She wondered if her ex-husband would notice she was drunk when she dropped Lauren off at his house. She had to drop Lauren off, even if it went completely against her own self-interest. The girl couldn't be in the middle of this. Fran wondered if Max already knew. She turned on the morning news.

"We are reporting live from Turnberry Place, home of Las Vegas attorney Alessandro de la Rosa who, over the last ten years, has represented some of Las Vegas's most famous and infamous defendants, from movie stars, to

130

politicians, to alleged mob bosses. Shortly after midnight, de la Rosa..." A
tape of Alex being arrested flashed across the screen. "...who was expected to
announce his bid for mayor of Las Vegas, was arrested for the brutal rape and
murder of 29-year-old police officer Carol McEnroe that occurred in her
home Friday night." The camera focused on a photo of the woman when she
was a young cadet at the police academy. She smiled from under the cap of
her uniform. The cameraman panned a shot of the condos before closing in
on the sheriff.

"This is a tragedy, a real tragedy," Randall was saying. "We will get to
the bottom of this as soon as possible. I have no other comment to make at
this time. Thank you."

Tom, looking worried, stood behind him.

Fran switched the channel to Saturday morning cartoons. The noise
roused Lauren. Sleepy-eyed, she dragged her blanket into the living room
and curled up on the sofa, her head resting on Fran's lap.

"How are you doing?" Fran asked as she stroked her daughter's hair.

"You smell funny. What time is it?" Lauren yawned.

"Way too early for you to be up." Fran took a sip of her drink.

"Are we going shopping today?" Lauren pulled the blanket up to her chin
as she focused on the television set.

"Actually, something came up at work. How about spending the day with
your daddy, huh?" Fran knew she'd regret that decision.

Lauren nodded and soon drifted back to sleep.

Outside, the streetlights went out one by one as the sun rose higher in the
clear Vegas sky.

*****

Every morning, Mayor Max Simone had steak and eggs for breakfast:
eggs runny, steak rare, both buried under steak sauce. If he could have eaten
both raw, he would have, but his doctor frowned on the idea. Today, however,

the steak and eggs grew cold and untouched on his plate. Instead, he stretched his long, thin frame across the leather sofa in the corner of his office and feasted on the news broadcast. The television was suspended on the wall, just over a small bar. It was flanked on one side by a modest aquarium housing Siamese fighting fish, and on the other by a small mermaid fountain; both looked incongruous in that setting. The area itself was visually separated from the main office by a free-standing, woven, Japanese screen. It was his private space.

Max's eyes took on a deadly glare, his brow arched in suppressed rage and he muttered a few obscenities to himself. He reached for the cell phone on the nearby table, but it rang before he could pick it up.

"I got it," Elliott told him.

"She's dead!" Simone yelled into the phone. "What the hell happened?"

"Can we meet?" Elliott asked.

"When?" Max's eyes never left the television screen.

"I can be there in twenty minutes."

Max grunted. His jaw tightened. "Talked to Randall, yet?"

"You kidding?" Elliott responded. "I'm not that stupid!"

"I know just how stupid you are, Roger," Max snapped. "Carol is dead and the clock is ticking. Get your ass in here." He hung up and called Randall. "Brief me," he ordered when the clearly exhausted sheriff answered on his direct line.

"I sent an email." Randall rubbed his eyes and leaned back in his office chair. It squeaked.

"I hate computers," Max stated.

"Yeah, well, you never found one you could coerce, threaten, bribe or blackmail," the sheriff countered.

"I take it you're not running for re-election," said Simone.

"Didn't you hear? I want your job." Randall sighed. "Where do you want

132

me to start?"

"From the top."

CHAPTER 10

Every time the phone rang, Toni winced. She had refused to answer it ever since she got the call from Martinez at some ungodly hour of the morning. She sat cross-legged in the middle of her rumpled bed, positioned in the very center of her cluttered studio apartment. She wore cutoff jeans and a faded shirt and was cleaning her gun with trembling hands. The weapon, oil, rags, and tools were spread over a pile of old newspapers at her knees. The cinnamon odor of gun oil mixed with the smell of the stale beer she was having for breakfast.

Toni's television played silently on the kitchen counter. Its cord trailed behind the toaster oven, well-used blender and some dirty dishes. She had heard the story once and once was enough. She had turned off the sound, but her eyes found their way to the ribbon of words sliding across the bottom of the screen. She soaked them in and glanced only briefly at the cell phone when it rang. She waited for Alex's number but all she saw was Tom's and Fran's and Rick's and Margo's. She took another swig of warm beer and settled the bottle between her folded legs. She wondered if anyone was feeding Alex's cat. She read the lines on the TV screen again: Famous lawyer arrested for murder. Clip at one.... We go live to Turnberry Place.... Sheriff George Randall....

Toni took another swig.

***

Tom, in day-old rumpled clothes and an overnight beard, tossed his cell phone onto the passenger seat of his sedan as he turned the corner into Paul Burns' driveway. Toni was deliberately not answering, he thought. By now, she had to know. When he tried Fran's number, all he got was busy signals. It was going to be one of those mornings – days – weeks.

The sun bounced off the hood of his car and hit him square in the face. He squinted behind his sunglasses. He carefully executed his hand-over-hand with the precision of a high school driving instructor and wondered again if he was doing the right thing. Fran would kill him. She would beat him to a bloody pulp and leave him in the desert for the ants to chew up. He left the engine running as he stepped out of his car and eyed the house.

The driveway was newly resurfaced. The lawn was an even three inches high. A neatly trimmed hedge divided the property between the Burns' house and that of the neighbors. The siding had recently been replaced and even the mailbox on the porch glistened with a fresh coat of black paint. Looking through the upstairs window and past sheer white curtains, he saw Paul's wife, Cheryl, staring back. She wore a thick terry robe and wrapped both hands around a coffee mug as she held it to her lips. Her long, wet, red hair clung to her shoulders. For a moment, Tom thought he saw Fran, but he realized it was an illusion caused by the orange sunrise reflected on the window. He smiled and nodded politely.

She withdrew into the shadows of the house without responding.

Fran's ex-husband met Tom at the door. "We heard," Paul growled as he motioned the detective in and swung the front door closed. Perfect teeth showed when he spoke. His starched white collar rubbed against a clean-shaven neck. His charcoal gray slacks sported a straight, ironed crease. Even his fingernails were buffed. He returned to the mirror where he worked on his tie.

Tom wondered why the man was dressed in a suit on a Saturday morning.

Paul finished his tie with a look of irritation, glanced at his watch and half-turned towards the stairs. "Three point five minutes, Matthew!" he shouted. He snatched a set of keys from the rack and slipped them into his pocket.

"Coming, dad!" The boy's voice was muffled behind a door. A toilet flushed.

"And wash your hands!" Paul yelled.

The boy never argued. Tom heard the sound of running water.

"She didn't send you for bail money, did she?" Paul turned his attention back to Tom and lowered his voice, so his son wouldn't hear.

"We're in the middle of a media circus." Tom ignored the question.

Paul just nodded.

"It's no place for a child," Tom continued. He pictured Fran running a knife through his chest.

Cheryl descended the stairs with Paul's suit jacket thrown over one arm and the coffee mug in her hand. She smiled shyly at Tom but didn't speak. Tom smiled discreetly back.

Paul immediately snatched the jacket from her and angrily shook it out before slipping it on. "You're getting it all wrinkled," he barked. "I told you: keep it on the hanger until I need it." He glanced up the stairs. "And get my son down here, now."

"I'll get dressed and take him," she said softly.

"No, you will not take him. This is a family matter. You're both riding with me. Now get going or we'll be late." Paul looked in the mirror again to check his hair.

Cheryl set the mug on the hall table and obediently headed up the stairs. Paul frowned, picked up an advertising brochure and slid it underneath the mug to protect the furniture.

"Going somewhere?" Tom asked, his curiosity getting the best of him.

"We're taking my parents out for breakfast. Their anniversary." Paul sighed. "They've probably heard by now...." The thought trailed off. He glanced up the stairs again. "That boy will never amount to anything if he doesn't learn to be punctual."

"How old is he?" Tom asked.

"Seven."

Tom nodded.

137

"We were talking about my daughter," Paul reminded Tom.

"Yes, I – I just thought…." Tom started.

"Of course, she should come here," Paul said, finally happy with his appearance. He turned to Tom. "I never trusted that sleazy Italian bastard and now look what he's done! Rape. Murder. My god! What the hell was my wife thinking getting mixed up with him?"

"Ex-wife," Tom corrected.

A tense pause followed. Tom felt as if he'd stepped on the paw of a sleeping lion. He waited for the beast to bite.

"EX-WIFE," Paul said coolly. He drew his lips into a sneer. "I must have been out of my mind to marry her."

"A lot of that going around," Tom muttered. His fists tightened in his pockets as he managed a courteous smile. "I'm headed to Fran's place now. I'll talk to her about Lauren coming here."

"You didn't talk to her first?" Paul's eyes widened in surprise.

Tom looked guilty.

Paul nodded and frowned. "You could have just called," he said. He reached into his pocket and pulled out his wallet, extracted a business card, retrieved a pen from the table and wrote out a phone number. "When you have her, call me. I'll give you directions."

"To where?" Tom asked.

"The restaurant."

Tom was beginning to appreciate Fran's opinion of Paul Burns. "I'd better get over to Fran's." He was anxious to get out of that house.

Paul opened the door for Tom and stood on the threshold as Tom stepped into the hot sun, pulled off his jacket and tossed it carelessly into the backseat of his car. He glanced briefly back at the house and spotted Cheryl in the upstairs bedroom window. She had loosened the tie around her robe and stood there wearing a smile, her white lace bra, and matching panties. He nodded politely, lowered his eyes, and met Paul's steely glare.

***

"What the hell!" Fran tossed her hair back and glared at Tom.

He stood in the doorway of her apartment and flinched. He had just confessed to going to the Burns' house. He stepped back slightly as he smelled the alcohol on her breath and expected the worst.

"Mommy?" Lauren peeked out from under the peach quilt on the sofa. She had fallen asleep watching cartoons and now rubbed her eyes with the back of her hand.

"Sorry, honey. It's okay. It's just Tom. Go back to sleep." Fran hurried to her daughter, tucked the blankets in nice and tight and gave the girl a kiss on her forehead as Tom stepped into the apartment and softly closed the door.

Lauren curled beneath the blanket and closed her eyes.

Fran then grabbed Tom by the arm, dragged him into her bedroom and shut the door behind them.

Tom tugged his eyes away from the vision of soft round breasts tucked into a mint green camisole and half-hidden by a pink terry robe. He glanced around the bedroom. A pile of clothes covered an overstuffed chair, the shoes were kicked to the side, the bed left unmade, and stacks of paperwork and magazines littered the floor. Fran had chosen a soft blue for the walls and blue and white toile for the bedding. His eyes drifted back to the camisole just as Fran self-consciously pulled her robe tightly around her and cinched the belt.

"You had no business going over there," she hissed.

"It was on my way. I was just thinking of Lauren. With Alex in prison, the press moved from his place to yours. They're camped out in the parking lot now, just waiting for you to show your face. I thought...."

"Don't ever meddle in my personal life, again!" Fran angrily crossed her arms in front of her. "Do you have any idea what kind of leverage this will

139

give him against me? He's been trying to get custody since day one!"

"I THOUGHT I could get her out of here, take her to her dad's. The press wouldn't have to know. I just wanted to be sure...." Tom tried to explain.

"And you never thought to tell me? To call me? Anything?" she raged.

"I tried calling, Fran. I couldn't get through." He looked annoyed.

Fran looked sheepish for a whole fifteen seconds, almost. "The phone's been ringing off the hook. First the cops, then the press, then our friends." She bit her lip as the sadness swelled to the surface. "I didn't want it to wake Lauren." She managed to slide back to indignant. "You still should have talked to me first!"

"Don't tell me you didn't consider it," he argued. "I know you. She would have been your first concern."

Fran fumed. "Irrelevant."

"Don't go lawyer on me." Tom stood over her and crossed his arms in mock imitation. He smirked and tried a diversionary tactic. "You're cute when you're mad."

Fran snatched a red stiletto shoe from the floor and swung it at him, but he easily grasped her wrist, wrestled the shoe from her tight fist and tossed it aside.

"This isn't funny!" she snapped. She yanked her arm twice before he released her. She stomped over to the chair and plopped down on top of the clothes.

The grin slowly disappeared from Tom's face. He leaned forward and planted his hands on the arms of the chair on either side of her, his eyes inches from hers. "You're right, Fran. This isn't funny." He paused a second to study the worry and pain in her eyes. "Okay, I should have talked to you first. I wanted a chance to size up your ex, to see what he was like for myself. This seemed like a good opportunity."

Fran let out an exasperated sigh. "He's a control freak. I told you."

"You were right, as usual." Tom held up a hand to stop her from speaking. "You were right, and I was wrong, okay?" Sighing, he slowly knelt in front of her and clasped his hands together on her lap. "Please forgive me, oh great and beautiful one." He clamped his jaw tight to avoid laughing.

Exhausted, Fran closed her eyes and fought back fresh tears. "Okay," she finally sighed. "You're forgiven. This time."

Tom grinned. "Good. My knees hurt."

"I forgive you, BUT, there's still the question of Alex's arrest. Why the hell were you there?" Fran was back to lawyer mode.

Tom pushed himself to his feet and buried his hands in his pockets. "I wasn't supposed to be. I got wind of it and showed up without an invite. I was afraid...." He pressed his lips together and thought about what he was wanted to say next.

"Go on," Fran urged.

"I thought he might get hurt," Tom admitted.

Fran's eyes narrowed. "Did he get hurt?"

"Yeah."

Her shoulders sagged. "I've called a meeting for one at the office. Did Margo get in touch with you, yet? Can you make it?"

"I work for the enemy, remember?" he said.

She nodded. "Just be there."

He smiled. "Say please."

This time it was a slipper, and it didn't miss.

"Ow," he yelled, teasing her.

"Okay. You can take Lauren to Paul's, for now, but I need a favor in return," Fran told him.

"What?" Tom asked.

"A ride to the detention center."

"You have to stop having scotch for breakfast," he chided.

141

Rick slammed his gloved fist into the punching bag with full force. He had arrived at the gym at his usual seven a.m. with plans to work out, grab a hot shower and take a quick nap before meeting with Fran at the office. Instead, he found the television, screwed into brackets and hung close to the ceiling in a corner of the room, blaring the news of Alex's arrest.

"Over the last ten years," the news anchor said, "De la Rosa has built his law firm into one of the best known in the country, representing some of Sin City's most famous and infamous defendants - movie stars, politicians and alleged mob bosses, even our own colorful Mayor Max Simone. De la Rosa, 42, was expected to announce his bid for mayor in a race that would have pitted him against his former client."

Photographs of Alex and Simone appeared on the screen. The reporter continued.

"De la Rosa was once suspected of murdering his wife, but alibi witnesses placed him somewhere else at the time of her death. This new charge could resurrect that still unsolved case. Unconfirmed reports say last night's victim, Carol McEnroe, was strangled to death in much the same way as Sarah de la Rosa, five years ago to the day."

Only two other men were at the gym and neither seemed to notice or care about the news report.

Usually, an hour was enough for Rick to work off any pent-up tension, but not today. Today, every hit, every slam, every punch seemed to drive him further into a rage. He finally had to stop. He hugged the bag with both hands, pressed his sweaty forehead against it and tried to calm down. His powerful muscles ached from the force of his blows.

No one approached Rick during his workout. The Marine bulldog on his upper arm, the tattooed circle of thorns around his throat and the fierce look in his eyes kept people away. When he stepped back and wiped his face with

142

a towel, an older man approached, a fresh towel wrapped around his neck. The man's bald head was glistening with sweat and his muscles sported aged tattoos

"You all right, Ricky?" he asked.

Rick nodded. "Hard day at the office, sir," he snorted.

"Hell, you ain't even started yet."

Rick shook his head. "Oh, yes, I have." He trotted to the showers.

Somewhere on the highway between the gym and the law office, Rick remembered who Carol McEnroe was. "Goddamn fucking son of a bitch. Fuck! Fuck! Fuck!" He pounded the wheel with his fists. "You IDIOT, Alex. You goddamn IDIOT!"

The orange sunrise struck Rick in the face. He shielded his eyes and squinted at the glowing city before him. Rick's head buzzed with questions and somewhere, out there, were the answers. He just had to find them.

***

Fran popped another mint in her mouth and pushed the buzzer to the prison's front door, then waited until she heard the familiar click of the electronic lock. She stepped out of the hot sun and into the first foyer. Its tan, neutral walls closed in around her. The door slammed and locked before the second door clicked open. She entered the main corridor with its painted concrete floor and paunchy guards in their uniforms. The second door locked behind her. Once inside, she stood in front of the reception window while a prim woman in office attire looked at her quizzically.

"I'm Francesca Simone. I'm a lawyer. I'm here to see my client, Alessandro de la Rosa." Fran nervously brushed her hair back from her face.

"You related to the mayor?" the woman asked, raising an eyebrow.

"Not by choice."

The woman nodded. "Sign in please and show me your license card and identification." She spun a ledger around, slipped a pin into the fold and slid it towards Fran.

Fran dug the documents out of her purse, handed them over and signed the guest book. The woman gave Fran a name tag and a tiny key and indicated she should leave her things in a locker. When everything was secured, Fran went through the security portal, followed by a sweep with a metal detector by the guard. A second guard motioned her to follow him. Beyond that door was a steel-gated box just big enough for two people while, again, the door clicked into lock behind her.

A guard in a security kiosk hit a button and the gate slid open, metal screeching as it slid on metal, and allowed Fran access to the concrete walls of the main corridor. Fran waited. Four locked doors now stood between her and freedom and she had two more to go through before she was led to a small room with a metal table, two chairs and a safety glass window to allow the guards to see clearly inside. Fran slipped into one of the chairs, propped her elbows on the table and waited alone for nearly twenty minutes until someone was gracious enough to bring Alex to her.

She caught her breath and her eyes narrowed when she spotted him shuffling towards her in his navy jumpsuit and orange slippers. He was limping. His eyes were on the floor as he tried not to trip. His shoulders drooped. His thick, dark hair was unkempt, and he was badly in need of a shave. Fran quickly cupped her hand to her mouth, checked her breath and took another mint as she tried to minimize the odor of alcohol that clung to her.

Alex and the guard stopped just outside the door as the man in the kiosk pushed another button; another electrically controlled lock slid open and the door allowed access. The guard waited in the hall until the door locked behind Alex and he was alone with Fran. When she stood up, he raised his eyes to hers. A large lump had formed on his forehead. He had a black eye, a cut lip, and bruises everywhere.

144

"You look like shit," she said.

"You should see the other guy, Bella." The joke fell flat as he carefully lowered himself into the chair and let out a small hiss of pain.

"Alex? What happened? I mean, to you. What happened?" She sank into the chair opposite him.

"They think I killed a cop. What do you think happened?" He frowned and turned slightly to hear her better. The shift made him look conspiratorial. His dark eyes poured into her blue ones.

"They can't do this, Alex," Fran said.

He hushed her. "Hey, we're not children here, right? We know what they can and can't do. It's done. Period."

She leaned forward, her eyes level with his. "Tell me what happened."

"Which part? The part where I dated Carol? Or the part where I got beat up?" he asked.

"Either. Both. From the beginning."

He shook his head. "Not here. Not now."

She nodded in understanding, but she had to put her hands under the table, so he wouldn't see how badly they shook. "You look like shit," she said, again.

"And you smell like booze and eggs."

She smiled slightly. "I didn't know eggs had a smell."

He tried to grin, but his face hurt from the beating. "They don't. I just know what you like for breakfast."

She blushed slightly; the color accented her red hair. "What do you want me to do?" she asked.

The humor disappeared from his eyes. He stared at her a minute and looked defeated.

"You have to do the Callas depositions. You can bring the file and I'll brief you. I can't let him down and I can't help him like this. Ivan is in your hands now, Bella. You need to believe in him. You need to believe in his innocence. If you don't believe in him, the jury can smell it. They'll convict," he told her.

"I mean for you." Angry tears burned the back of her eyes. "What can I do for you?"

"There's nothing you can do, at least not until Monday. I need to get bail set. I need to raise some cash. I need Rick investigating this thing if he isn't already. Someone set me up good, Bella, and until I find out how, there is nothing I can do. These bastards are not on my side."

She knew who he meant by 'someone.' She nodded in agreement as her eyes dropped to her lap. "I've called a meeting at the office. I'll fill everyone in. I…"

"Tom was there," said Alex.

She looked up. "Yes. I know. He dropped me off. He's taking Lauren to Paul's and then he'll be back for me."

"Paul? I bet you loved that," he said.

She didn't answer.

"Bella?" His face seemed to pale even as he spoke. "One last favor."

"For the man who just destroyed my life?" She tried to keep the tone light, but she wanted to strangle him. "Go on."

"Take care of Toni, will you? She going to be scared to death and pissed as hell."

"She's tough," Fran said.

"Not tough enough. Not for this." He shook his head. "You don't know her."

Fran nodded. "Of course." It was a hollow promise. She didn't know anything she could do that would make a difference for Toni. The woman was like a hot poker – you had to know where to grab onto her, so you wouldn't get burned, and Fran didn't have a clue.

"Thanks. I know you can handle it. You're strong, Bella, a lot stronger than I am." They both stood up as the guard unlocked the door. "Maybe you're the one who should be running for mayor," Alex added. He was quiet a few seconds. "Remember Callas. Don't let him down. Don't let the devil win. This is too important. This is the case that will break Elliott."

Fran's temper flared, and she forced herself to speak quietly. "We could have broken Elliott, and Randall, and Max, all in one fell swoop, if you hadn't been so damned – so damned – SELFISH! This was my chance – our chance – and you ruined it, all over some tail. Damn it. Damn it to hell."

Alex looked stunned. He didn't speak but just stared at her a minute. Then he was gone. It wasn't until he was out of sight that Fran remembered the murder of the second child. He has enough to think about, she told herself. It can wait. When the door locked behind him, she leaned in the chair to wait until it was her turn to be released. She closed her eyes.

Five Years Earlier

Fran clutched the stack of files to her chest as she crawled out of her car, shoved the door closed with her hip and gripped her keys in her teeth. The rain had let up a bit, but only for a few seconds. Fran carefully wove in and out of the small puddles as she made her way up the front steps of the house. Bending over, she reached under the stack of files and pushed the doorbell. No one answered. Shifting the files, she tried again. Again, no one answered. Fran glanced sideways through the drawn curtains and saw the lights were on. She listened and heard the soft sound of music. She pushed the bell one more time.

She decided to check the door. Finding it open, she tiptoed into the front room and carefully lowered the stack of files onto the coffee table. Then she turned to head out the door. That was when she heard the sobbing. The sound sent a shiver up her back.

Fran, afraid of intruding, stepped cautiously towards the noise. From the living room, she could look down the hall and see Alex collapsed on the

147

carpet, his face buried in his arms, his body shaking with grief. She hurried towards him.

"Alex, what's the matter? Are you okay? What happened?" Her cool hand rested on the nape of his neck.

He didn't respond. He didn't look up.

Fran's glanced into the bedroom. What she saw made her jump up and run to the bathroom to throw up. Gripping the porcelain toilet, she quickly flushed, washed her face and rinsed out her mouth. Then she called the police.

Sheriff Randall and Detective Martinez were the first to arrive on the scene. They found Fran sitting on the floor with the distraught Alex. Randall scowled; his imposing figure loomed threateningly over them. He looked over the bedroom. His eyes glazed, and his hands balled into tight fists. He nearly choked on his words when he called the crime lab.

"Get your ass to De La Rosa's, now," he ordered. "Sarah de la Rosa is dead."

His face ashen and his eyes dark with fury, Randall slipped the phone into his pocket and turned on Alex,

Alex, for the first time, pushed himself into a sitting position. He was white and shaking. He couldn't look at his wife. He couldn't look at Fran. The world seemed to be spinning around him.

"What happened?" Randall demanded to know. His eyes narrowed as he studied the lawyer. He resisted the urge to kick the man on the floor.

"I came home. That's how I found...." Alex's voice trailed off as he choked up.

"Where the hell were you?"

"With me," Fran said sharply, realizing Alex was unaware of Randall's growing rage. "He was with me the whole time, all day."

"I didn't ask you," Randall snapped.

148

Alex nodded, his head buried in his hands. "We were in court, then at the office." His voice was hoarse.

"When was the last time you saw your wife?" Randall demanded to know.

"When I stopped by the school about three this afternoon," Alex told him.

Randall didn't bother with notes. His fingers played with the gun on his hip. "Was she leaving you?" Randall asked.

Alex's mind cleared, and his eyes flared. He started to get up, but Fran held him back. "How dare you!" Alex yelled. Fresh tears spilled down his face.

"I need a statement." Randall signaled a police officer who had just entered the building. "Seal the whole place off and have someone take this man to headquarters." Randall glanced dismissively at Fran. "The girlfriend, too," he ordered.

Fran flushed in anger. "I am NOT his girlfriend. I'm his law partner!"

"Then you're his accomplice."

CHAPTER 11

Toni could avoid answering the phone all she wanted. She couldn't avoid Rick Brandt yelling for her and banging on her apartment door. She had to answer it if only to stop him from pissing off the neighbors. She staggered glassy-eyed to the door and cracked it open but left the chain in place. She peered through the slit of space, squinted at the sunlight and asked, "What do you want?"

"Are you gonna let me in or should I just make your life a living hell?" Rick looked like he'd slept in his clothes, except the bags under his eyes said he hadn't slept at all. He wore stained black jeans and a Harley tee-shirt pulled tight over taut muscles. He smelled of cigarettes, beer, and sweat.

"Go to hell," Toni retorted. She wanted him to come in. She wanted someone to hold her, so she wouldn't break, but she couldn't admit it.

Rick stared her down. "I ain't going. I'll break down this door if I gotta, but I ain't going."

Toni sighed in resignation and slipped the lock out of its cradle.

The apartment reeked of beer and about a dozen empty bottles were in the sink. Dirty dishes littered the counter. A small rose bush in a terracotta planter was the only sign of life and, like Toni, it struggled to survive. The television was on mute.

Rick frowned. He walked to the counter and shut off the TV.

"What do you want, Rick?" Toni asked. She fell face down on the bed and covering her aching head with a pillow.

"I take it you know what's going on." That was obvious. He tripped over some discarded clothes and kicked them into a corner.

Toni groaned.

"We gotta meeting at the office in an hour. Get in the shower and put on some clean clothes. I'll wait," Rick said.

"You need a shower worse than I do," Toni told him.

He crossed his arms and stared at her.

Toni rolled over on the bed, her body stretched out and as vulnerable as her mind. "What meeting? What office?"

"The law firm." He turned his back to her and ambled up to the sink and started dropping the beer bottles into the garbage can.

"Hey! Those are recyclable," Toni stated. She rolled over and pulled the pillow over her head again.

Rick ignored her. He shoved the basket under the sink and approached her. He could smell the beer-soaked sheets. "Come on, baby." He yanked her pillow before she could resist.

She grabbed for the blanket, but he snatched that, too, uncovering her gun, some newspapers and her cleaning kit under it.

"No!" Toni yelled, curling up in a fetal position as new tears broke through her anger.

Rick smacked her ass. "Get up, now. You wanna see that brother of yours get screwed? Or you wanna get up and do something about it?"

"He's already screwed," she sobbed.

"You tellin' me he did it?" Rick sat down on the edge of the bed and gently rested his rough hand on her shoulder. His voice was gruff, in sharp contrast to his comforting touch.

"No, damn it!" Toni flipped onto her back and stared at him.

"Then get up."

She rubbed her eyes a few seconds to drive away a looming hangover. "Okay. Okay." Resigned, she grasped his arm, pulled herself into a seating position and planted her feet on the floor. When she tried to stand, she had to lean against him to steady herself. Rick stood up and guided her to the bathroom.

"This is as far as I go, baby," he said as he gave her a gentle push.

Toni shut the door behind her and peeled off her rank clothes. A minute later, she leaned against the shower wall and let the warm water cascade down her slim body and carry her tears down the drain. When she emerged, she wrapped a towel around herself, ran a brush through her thick hair, stared at herself in the mirror with disgust and walked back into the main room.

Rick had stripped the bed and had the linens piled up for the laundry along with her dirty clothes. The dishes had been washed, dried and put away.

"Damn, I should hire you as a housekeeper."

Rick gave her some painkillers and a bottle of water.

"What? No bloody Mary?" Toni collapsed into a metal kitchen chair and accepted them.

"Only if you wanna stay drunk. You're dehydrated from the booze. Drink up." Rick headed to the bathroom to find clean sheets.

"Still love me?" Toni called out after him. A knife of pain drove through her skull. She winced.

"Always, baby!"

* * *

"She wasn't supposed to get killed." Max's eyes narrowed; his voice was cold. He sat behind the desk on its raised platform and stared down at Elliott as the small man slipped a hand into his jacket pocket and silently pulled out a DVD. Max leaned forward, lured like a mouse to cheese. "You said she wouldn't get hurt. You told me she knew what she was doing. And now she's dead and I'm holding you responsible."

"Carol," Elliott held up the disc as he spoke, "came through for us." He stepped one foot onto the platform, reached up and slid the disc onto the mayor's desk. Then he stepped back and stood at attention like a soldier reporting back from the front.

If Carol's death affected Elliott, he didn't show it. His eyes had dark circles from fatigue and his narrow lips were drawn tight, but his face had the

153

same hard scorn he always wore. "You'll never have to worry about Alex de la Rosa again."

"The police?" Max asked, not touching it.

"Never saw it. Good thing I got there first, huh?" He forced a smile.

Max didn't like the man but every so often even eels have their purpose, he mused. "This shows Alex killing her?"

"Not exactly," Elliott admitted.

"Then it shows that he didn't kill her." Max looked slightly confused.

Elliott leaned forward. "It shows him in bed with her. It shows him tying her up, fucking her and slapping her around. It shows her screaming. It shows him walking out of the room."

"And then?" Max didn't like waiting.

"Then it shows who did kill her," Elliott concluded with a grin.

"Are you going to tell me who killed Carol?" Max asked.

"No. It's too good. You have to watch this," said Elliott. "You can't make this shit up."

Max picked up the disc and gently tapped the table with it. "What do you want?" he asked.

"To make you a happy man and get De la Rosa the hell out of my hair once and for all," Elliott said.

Max nodded. "Since when do you care if I'm happy?" The question was rhetorical, and Elliott didn't answer. "I take it you have a copy."

"I have the original," said Elliott. The smile was gone.

Max put the disc down and folded his hands. "You don't even care about the dead girl?"

"Carol?"

Max frowned. "The one in the alley."

Elliott looked uneasy. "I told you, it could be a copycat."

"It could be the real deal and you've got the wrong janitor," Max barked.

"I'm not wrong about this." Elliott stared at Max with disdain.

The mayor grunted and stared back.

"Okay," Elliott conceded after a tense silence. "Maybe I am wrong, but why would the perp dump the bodies in the exact same way and in the exact same location?"

"Maybe he's an idiot," Max answered. "Or maybe he wants to get caught. Or maybe he's had enough. Maybe these aren't his only victims. Maybe he's trying to send a message. Maybe he wants you to stop him."

"Maybe. Maybe. Maybe." Elliott scowled.

"I want to know what you get when you get it, on both cases," Max directed.

Elliott nodded. "Of course, you do."

As Elliott turned on his heel and left the room, Max's eyes drifted back to the DVD.

***

"You goddamn fucking son-of-a-bitch!" Toni, her dark hair flying, charged like a mad dog at Tom Sadler in the parking lot of Alex's law firm.

Tom had barely stepped out of his unmarked cruiser as Toni and Rick were entering the building. Hearing a car door slam, she turned, saw him and attacked.

"Stop it!" he yelled as he tr4ied to pin her to the side of his car without hurting her. "Toni! You don't understand! I can explain! Ouch!"

She grabbed for his hair, but it was too short to get a good hold. She kicked him in the groin and elbowed him in the chin. He dropped to the pavement, landed hard on his knees and fell on his back. His hazel eyes stared up at her in shock. She pounded him wildly in her rage as he covered his face. He did his best not to hit back and used his arms to block the blows.

"Toni!" Rick stepped into the fray and pulled the screaming woman off her partner before she could inflict more harm. His muscular arms held her

155

tightly from behind. "Toni. Stop it. Stop it, now," Rick ordered.

Toni continued to struggle as she yelled. "Let me go!" She kicked at Rick's legs, struck his arms and tried to grab the strands of his butch haircut. He never flinched.

Tom rubbed his sore chin and stood up.

Rick released Toni and shoved her towards the building's front door. "Go on!" he ordered. "You can't do any good here."

"That son-of-a...." She turned towards Tom again, but Rick stepped between them.

"I know!" Rick barked, grabbing her by the shoulders and planting his face in hers. "Get inside, now!" He shoved her back toward the door again.

She turned belligerently on one heel and stomped towards the building with Rick close behind and Tom behind Rick. The two men avoided eye contact. When they got to the fourth floor, they found Fran dressed in jeans and a tank top and seated on the conference room table. Her legs swung nervously; her red hair was pulled into a ponytail. She held a fresh cup of black coffee and smelled like scotch. Her eyes were on the small television on the bookshelf. The volume was muted.

Rick nodded to her. "How ya holding up?" he asked.

She looked up and shook her head. "Not well," she admitted.

Rick rested a reassuring hand on her shoulder. "Hang in there, boss. I'll fix this."

Margo, flushed from her morning run, paced about like a tiger to relieve tension. Her black hair, accented with a yellow and pink streak, and her long, jewel-studded fingernails matched her pink and black jogging outfit.

Rick poured two cups of black coffee, handed one to Toni and straddled a chair backward.

Tom stood in the doorway like a rabbit about to enter a bear den. His eyes scanned the people in the room before returning to Fran. She was tired. Her shoulders were slumped and there were dark circles under her eyes. Her hand shook as she held her drink. His first instinct was to go to her, but he held back.

"You want to go first?" Fran finally asked him as she picked up the remote and flicked off the TV. She wrapped both hands around her coffee cup and raised her eyes to meet Tom's.

He flinched at the pain on her face. "Look, I know you're all pissed at me," he began.

"Got that damn right!" Toni snapped. She sank into the sofa, arms crossed, legs propped up on the seat of a chair in front of her and her coffee cup gripped in a right fist. Her dark eyes pierced what little was left of Tom's calm.

He turned on her. "I had to be there. Jesus, Toni, somebody had to be there, or they would have killed him!"

Toni silently processed what he said.

"The department is out for blood on this one. When I got a tip about what was going down, I broke five laws getting there. Randall didn't want me at the scene. None of them did," Tom explained.

A moment of tense silence followed.

"What happened?" Fran finally asked.

Tom broke free of Toni's stare and turned to Fran, his voice quieter. "Alex was arrested for murdering a female police officer last night. He's being held without bail until Monday." He watched her face for a reaction.

"That part I already know. Who's heading up the case?" she asked.

"Elliott, of course. He's in charge of the lab now. Randall fired Dr. Knight." Tom saw the look of surprise on Fran's face.

"You got to be kidding!" Margo sputtered.

"He didn't do it." Toni shook her head and fought back angry tears. "No way in hell. You know it and I know it."

"So, let's get out there and prove it." Margo bounced up and down on her sneaker-clad feet.

"This is a law firm. You're not cops," Tom argued. "You have to let the police handle this."

"Like they handled Sarah's murder?" Fran asked, her voice icy. Her eyes locked on Tom's.

"Bullshit!" Toni interrupted. "We won't just sit here and let Elliott railroad Alex into jail!"

"I'm with her," Rick chimed in.

Tom forced himself to turn away from Fran and look at Toni.

"You know better, Toni. You're a cop, one of us, or have you forgotten that again?" Tom asked.

"Someone ought to give that bastard a free lobotomy," Toni growled.

Ignoring her comment, Tom turned back to Fran. "This is a high-profile case. The media are watching this thing like a hawk, and Alex has a lot of friends in and out of law enforcement."

Fran looked so damn weak, so shattered. The more Tom looked at her, the more he wanted to strangle Alex.

"And a lot of enemies," Rick said, draining the last of his coffee. "Man, who we kidding here? Randall's been gunning for Alex since Sarah's murder. Alex was stupid enough to think he could be mayor. Made him a fucking target. You think they're gonna to try to clear him?"

Fran sought solace in her coffee grounds. The leering eyes of Max Simone stared up at her. She blinked and set the coffee on the table.

"There's a lot we still don't know," Tom said. "It's not their job to clear him. It's their job, our job, to solve the case. Period." He always felt intimidated by Rick. Perhaps it was all the muscles or those damn tee-shirts, or his surly attitude or that Marine haircut. Or maybe it was just the deadly look in the man's eyes.

"You're on the case?" Fran asked Tom.

Tom shook his head. "No. I thought I told you. It's hands off for me."

"Maybe you did. I can't...." She stopped speaking.

Tom took a step closer to her.

"What did you find out?" Fran asked Rick. If she'd noticed Tom's move, she didn't acknowledge it.

"The call about the homicide came across my scanner just before midnight. I didn't know they were looking for Alex, so I didn't bother with it until you called." Rick eyed Fran cautiously. He was watching her in case she fell apart.

"Who was she? When and where did she die?" Fran's unnervingly calm voice cut through the tension.

Everyone's focus turned from Rick back to Tom.

"Carol McEnroe," Tom said. "She was found tied to the bed at her apartment with an extension cord wrapped around her throat. She was naked and gagged and appeared to have been struck in the face and strangled. Police found cigar burns on her breasts and...," He hesitated. "...other parts of her body."

Toni shuddered and looked away.

"How does any of this relate to Alex?" Fran asked, compartmentalizing the horrific images into neat boxes in her head to look at when she was alone.

Tom passed the question to Rick.

"They were an item a few years back," Rick told Fran. "He was wild back then. Remember? It was right after Sarah died. No one could talk to him. Anyway, they had one of them hot, short affairs. She was a pistol." He paused for a second, recalling one particular night on the town with the now-dead cop." She was kinky as hell, and she wanted more. Alex weren't ready for it; not then; anyhow. She pestered him for about three weeks and he seemed to be fallin' for it, softenin' to her. Then she split. No word. Just like that. Left him high and dry and worse off. He hurt pretty bad. That's when he met that woman from the crime lab."

"Candy?" Tom asked. "I mean, Dr. Knight?"

"Yeah. Anyway, last I heard, she was working L.A., until we saw her on Elliott's arm last night," Toni interjected.

"You saw her? Where?" Fran asked in surprise.

"I didn't hear about that." Tom looked at Rick, but a hint of accusation filtered in Toni's direction.

"We followed Elliott to a ranch house in Henderson. She answered the door. The two were carrying on like lovesick birds," Rick explained.

"She was at the scene of the accident near Alex's place, too," Toni added. "Damn bitch gets around. I warned him about her."

"Warned him? When?" Tom asked.

"Last night. He told me they had a date," Toni said.

It was Rick's turn to stare at Toni. "Why didn't you tell me that last night?"

"I didn't realize it was her," Toni argued defensively. "I didn't recognize her at first. I guess I should've had you follow them after all."

Tom shook his head and absorbed the new evidence. Watching Fran's reaction, he picked up where Rick left off. "She moved back to Vegas about a week ago and was recruited by the LVPD. Last night she was working the hit and run out by Alex's condo. According to what I found out, she spotted him and went to his car to talk. She was apparently happy to see him. Later that night, they showed up at the Viaggio together. A waiter said she was drunk and coming on strong. A valet overheard Alex say he was taking her home. Dispatch tried calling her around eleven-thirty. She was supposed to cover for someone that night. When they couldn't reach her, Elliott went to her home and found her."

"First witness, first suspect," Toni muttered.

"And her boyfriend," Rick added.

"As much as you hate the guy, he hasn't got the guts for murder," Tom said.

"Not even if he caught his squeeze in bed with Alex?" Rick asked. "That would set me off."

Tom frowned in thought. "He'd go after Alex, not her."

"You never know who the bad guys are until you catch them the first time," Fran muttered, recalling her past conversation with Alex.

"Now what?" Rick asked.

"Well, Randall won't let us touch it." Tom indicated himself and Toni with a nod. "Conflict of interest."

Margo let out a short, sarcastic laugh.

"But we can," Fran jumped in. "We're going to need help. Are you in?" Her eyes met Tom's.

He nodded. "I want to help you, Fran." The statement was as personal as he dared to get in this crowd. "Between what I saw last night and what you guys just told me, you bet."

"It was bad?" Toni asked nervously. Her eyes didn't meet his.

Tom thought a minute. "Yes, but I don't mean Alex. I mean the girl."

"Girl? Carol? She's no girl." Toni said.

"No, the dead child. There's another child murder," Tom corrected her.

"They found another one," Rick explained. He glanced at Fran a moment. "Another dead twelve-year-old. Same M.O. Same everything."

Toni sunk lower into her seat.

"If Callas is innocent, then..." Fran hesitated a second before she continued. "...maybe this isn't about Alex. Maybe it's not even about Max." Until that moment, she was the only one who had considered the possibility that Max Simone would be behind a frame up.

"Maybe it's about Callas." Tom followed her train of thought.

161

"Who would set up Alex to screw with the Callas case?" Margo asked. She'd been struggling to keep quiet.

Fran and Tom looked at each other and spoke at the same time. "The killer."

"No fucking way," Rick broke in. "That's way too complicated. Don't make sense at all. A child molester is a child molester. Period. He doesn't need any other motivation. It's not the way these guys operate."

"Well, there's only one way to find out," Fran told Rick.

"I have to be careful. I can get canned over this." Tom looked back at Toni. "We both can."

She scowled at him. She looked like she wanted him thinly sliced and served for lunch.

"Are you bringing in help?" Margo asked Fran.

"Yes." Fran turned to Rick without further clarification. "Go back out there. Find out who the witnesses are in the child's case. See what you can get. I want every inch of background on the little girl. Photos, family history, her school report card, if you can get it." She turned to Tom. "You and I will cover the McEnroe crime scene and Alex's apartment." To Margo, "Don't you have an old girlfriend at the crime lab? See what you can find out about Callas. What they've got."

"I'm on it," Margo said with an eager nod.

"And get me the phone number of Charles Warner Smith," Fran told her. "Alex's case needs more than a big gun. It needs a legal weapon of mass destruction."

"Anybody here?" came a man's voice from the outer office.

Margo ran to see who it was and returned with a long flower box. "Care to guess?" she asked Fran as she pulled away the delicate lavender ribbon.

"Damn him!" Fran opened the box, found the note and read it out loud: "My sympathies. Don't say I didn't warn you." She crumpled it in her hand.

"Max Simone," Rick muttered. "Shit, is he still after you? Doesn't that man know when to quit?"

"Shut up!" Fran snapped.

"Fran…." Rick's voice was a quiet warning.

She sighed. "I'm sorry. Yes, he's still bugging the shit out of me."

"Anything you want me to do about it?" Rick asked.

Fran shook her head. "Not now. Not yet."

"What do you want me to do with these?" Margo asked, holding the long-stemmed roses in her arms.

"Burn them and send the ashes to the mayor's office," Fran instructed.

"And this?" Margo pulled a disc out of the bottom of the box and waved it in the air.

Fran scowled. "Yes, that, too, whatever the hell that is."

As the group dispersed, Tom lingered. Fran pulled her legs up under her as she sat on the table. Her fingers curled under the edge of the tabletop. Her head dropped. Waves of red hair hid her eyes like a waterfall.

"You need some rest," he told her.

She looked up, startled to find anyone still there. "What I need are answers." Even as she spoke, her tough girl demeanor cracked.

He walked up to the table and stood a few inches from her, close enough to feel her breath on his arm, yet not so close that she would feel the need to back away. "Talk to me, Fran."

"About what?" she asked.

He took the question as a stalling tactic. "About what's going on in that head of yours. About how you're doing. About…."

She cut him off. "I'm fine. I'll be fine. I'm just tired. Stop coddling me."

He leaned back on his heels, his arms crossed in front of him, and studied her like he would a fresh crime scene. "Okay," he said finally. "I'm here to help, and I mean it."

One of the advantages of being a homicide detective, Tom explained to Fran later, was that he could find out at any given minute where any police officer was in the city. That meant he knew when no one would be watching Carol's home. Slipping under the police tape and using a lock pick, Tom and Fran slid quietly into the house. Without speaking, they closed and locked the door behind them and shut all the blinds and drapes against the daylight and prying eyes.

Fran's heart was beating wildly, and her palms were sweating. She already knew what awaited them in the bedroom, so she decided to try the less obvious approach first. She moved from the living room to the kitchen and then to the bath, while Tom took a few minutes to make sure they hadn't been followed. She was gleaning, looking for the little things the crime lab might have overlooked, but she had to admit they had done a thorough job.

"Anything?" Tom asked as he began his own search.

"Nothing in here. I wish I knew what the police already took out of here." Fran shook her head.

"I'm sure we'll find out sooner or later." Tom glanced at her. "We'd better hurry. I don't want to get caught."

Fran nodded and continued in the kitchen. Like the living room, it was immaculate except for a few unpacked boxes. No dishes in the sink. Not even a damp towel lying about. The garbage can was empty. The fridge contained a half-gallon of skim milk, a small container of strawberries, some brie, and a spray can of whipped cream.

"Mmm. Yummy." Fran licked her lips and made a face. "I wonder what this girl ate."

The cupboards were also bare, with only a few spices, a couple cans of soup and some peppermint candy.

"How long has she been in town?" Fran asked.

"About a week. Why?" Tom asked.

Fran opened another cupboard and found a single box of cereal. She then checked the stoneware canisters; they were empty and had the price tags on the bottom. "Either she didn't plan on staying or she didn't have time to shop."

Tom shrugged.

Fran moved to the bathroom. Again, the place was spotless. She wondered if Elliott's crew had gathered up all the dirty laundry and towels as they looked for evidence that Alex had been there. Fingerprint powder covered the sink, toilet, and shower. Fran spotted a set of dusted handprints on the tile wall, one hand on each side of the shower head.

"Tom, take a look at these." She called him into the bathroom.

He found Fran standing in the shower, her hands posed in the air a few inches from the prints on the tiled wall.

"What do you notice?" she asked.

"A beautiful woman in the shower?" he quipped as he leaned against the door frame. He grinned as his gaze fell on her slender figure.

Fran threw him an annoyed look. "Don't let Toni hear you talking that way. How tall was Carol McEnroe?"

"About five-four." His back stiffened and his eyes narrowed. "And we're only partners."

"Sure, right." Fran rolled her eyes. "Have you told her that?" She turned back to the shower. "If Carol had leaned against this wall, her prints would have been much lower." She adjusted her arms to demonstrate.

"That means those aren't her prints. As for Toni, that's what she told me, just before she put in for a transfer. Besides, right now she hates my guts." He thought a minute. "They could be Alex's prints. They could have showered together."

"A transfer? I didn't hear about that." Fran failed to hide her reaction to the rest of Tom's comment. If Alex had showered with Carol, he'd had sex with her; if he'd had sex with her, he probably killed her. A shiver ran up Fran's back as she thought of Max's warning.

"Hate is just another word for love," she sighed. Her thoughts drifted back to Toni and Tom.

Tom mumbled his disagreement. He watched her as she looked around the room again. Opening the cabinet over the sink, she found very few toiletries and no clutter. She pulled open a bathroom drawer and found only a hairdryer in it. Finished in the bathroom, she pushed him out of her way and stepped into the hall as she worked up the nerve to enter the bedroom where Carol McEnroe had been tortured and murdered. Tom came up behind her, his minty breath raising the hairs on the back of her neck, his hand reaching for her arm. She jumped when he touched her.

"Are you ready?" He eyed her with concern. She nodded, took a deep breath and opened the door.

Pinstripes of light filtered through the closed blinds in the contemporary styled room and draped over the exposed mattress. The bed had been stripped and the sheets were in evidence, she realized. She carefully went through each drawer and then the closet. She noted the scarcity of things.

"Only two pairs of panties?" Fran held a bit of black lace up to the light. "What kind of woman owns only two pairs of panties?"

"The kind who doesn't wear any." Tom smirked.

"Get real!" Fran snapped. She blushed slightly and kept looking.

"Hey, you're asking the wrong person. My ex-wife had so much underwear she had a whole bureau just to hold the stuff," he said.

"My point exactly." Fran stopped and turned to stare at him. "When did you get married?"

Tom looked trapped. His eyes went wide. "We're not going to talk about that," he said, resuming his search of the room.

166

"Does Toni know?" she asked.

"It was a long time ago and it didn't last long." He refused to look at her.

"That's not an answer."

"It's none of her business." Tom scowled as he continued the search.

"Tom!" Fran said.

"It's none of your business, either!" He turned his back to her and didn't say anything else.

Fran gave up trying to get a response out of him. She stood in the darkened room and imagined what Carol McEnroe was like. She could feel the dead woman's spirit. She smelled what Carol had smelled just before she died: cedar chips in the closet, coconut shampoo, and lavender candle wax. She saw what Carol had seen: a poorly painted ceiling, a thin layer of dust on the chandelier, an old mirror. She heard what Carol had heard: passing traffic, a ticking clock, a yapping dog. Fran approached the bed with caution. She carefully stretched out on the stiff, new mattress and slowly raised her hands above her head, her eyes closed. She shuddered. For a moment, the sun turned to water.

"Where did the extension cord come from?" she asked without moving.

Tom stood in the doorway, hands on his hips, and stared at Fran in the dim light. "I don't know. The lamp, maybe?"

Fran rolled over and pulled on the lamp cord. It was unplugged. The socket was on the other side of the bed. "A weapon of convenience," she concluded. She propped herself up on her elbows and caught Tom staring at her. "What?" she asked.

"You really want to know how she felt?" He tilted his head.

"That's the idea. Why?" She was uncomfortable under his stare.

"Let me show you something. Lay back down." He removed his jacket and climbed on the bed, his knees straddling her hips, his hands sliding up her arms and clamping down on her wrists. "Now, try to get away."

167

"What?" she asked.

"You heard me. Try to get away," he ordered.

Fran's fought back the instinctive fear and twisted her body to unbalance him. Tom lowered himself on top of her, slid his legs between hers and pinned her to the bed. His breath was warm on her face. She panicked.

"You're not trying very hard." His eyes narrowed as they traveled downward and rested on her breasts.

Fran struggled harder. "Let me go!" Tears burned her eyes. She thought of Max, the children, the rocks.

"No." His grip tightened.

She gasped for air. "Let me go, now!"

"Like hell." He leaned closer to her; his lips brushed her neck.

She could feel his sudden and unexpected arousal through her clothes. Fear turned to fury. "Thomas Adam Sadler! This isn't funny!"

He nodded, his voice a whisper in her ear. "It's not supposed to be." Then he slid off her, retrieved his coat and held it discreetly in front of him.

"You bastard! You enjoyed that, didn't you?" Fran yelled, jumping out of bed and straightening her clothes.

"Being on top of you? Sure. Scaring you? No." He took a deep breath. "When are you going to realize it wasn't your fault?" he asked. "You're a grown woman and you couldn't stop me. How the hell were you supposed to stop Max when you were just a kid?"

She was seething. "I hate you! Don't you ever do that to me again." She considered slapping him but stopped herself.

"Tell someone about it, Fran," Tom urged. "Go to the cops. Report him. Sue him. Something. Stop trying to turn every case into a case about Max." He retreated to the living room.

Fran trembled as she made one last inventory of the apartment. She had a lot of evidence that didn't make sense: not enough clothes, very little makeup. She went back to the bathroom and looked at the bottles and tubes again. Everything was new, from the toothpaste to the shampoo to the face powder. It was like Carol McEnroe hadn't owned a single thing before that week. Fran tried to calm down, but her fear kept bubbling up. She swallowed her rage. She battled back tears. For a moment she allowed herself a sob and then angrily pulled herself together. She still felt Tom on top of her.

"We need to know more about this woman." Fran angrily dumped the bathroom items into a small trash bag to take back to the office. "We need to know what happened in L.A."

"I know people. I'll make some calls." He hid in the living room and watched her.

He'd gone too far, she thought, and he knew it. Fran tried to regain her earlier composure. "You know people?"

He shrugged his shoulders. "Anything else?" he asked. His voice was tentative.

"Yes. We should go to Alex's place. If the cops were there, they had to have a reason," said Fran.

"Probably looking for DNA," Tom suggested.

"No. They got that when he was arrested. They were looking for something else, something specific." She thought a minute. "You don't have a copy of the search warrant for Alex's place, do you?"

"No, but I can get it," Tom told her.

"Because you know people." Her panic seeped away.

He smiled a little and pulled out his phone. After chatting with someone for a minute, he hung up. "You'll have it Monday morning."

"I guess you do know people." Despite the lightness in her voice, she still felt uneasy being around him. When he suggested they leave, she was quick to agree.

169

CHAPTER 12

SUNDAY

Rick rolled over in his sleep and pulled the blanket up to shield his eyes from the late morning sun. They'd slept in. The small apartment still smelled of pizza and beer from the night before. Rick grunted, slipped his arm around Toni's bare waist and pulled her to him, her back to his chest.

"You're hot," she mumbled sleepily, her eyes still closed.

"Yes, I know." He kissed her neck.

She groaned. "No, I mean you are HOT. You give off enough body heat to warm a house." She kicked off the blankets, exposing their naked bodies to the sun.

He pulled her closer. "Better now?" He smiled, cupped a breast in one hand and kneaded it.

"I'm tired and I got a headache," Toni complained.

Rick chuckled. "Okay. I get it." He let her go, sat up and rescued the blanket, then pulled it over his head as he lay back down with his back to her. A few minutes later, he felt her warm hand circling his chest. "I thought you had a headache," Rick said.

"I got over it." Her breath breezed across the back of his neck and gave him goosebumps. He turned over to face her. His hand cupped her soft cheek as he looked into her eyes. "We shoulda done this a lot sooner."

She nodded in agreement. Her eyes lowered to his lips.

"What's the matter? Am I too hot again?" Rick asked.

She smiled. "No. You're just right." She kissed him quickly on the lips.

The next hour was spent in easy, relaxed, Sunday-afternoon lovemaking. When Toni finally collapsed from exhaustion, Rick pulled her into his arms and held her. She was silent, but he could feel the soft trail of a tear weaving through the hairs on his chest. "Are you going to tell me, or do I have to guess?" he asked, mentally preparing himself for another flood of emotion

171

over Alex's situation.

Instead, Toni quietly looked up at him and brushed the stray tear away. "You know, Rick, you're the only man on earth I can be honest with."

"I'm flattered." He squeezed her hand.

"No, I mean it. The only one. Well, other than Alex, and I keep a lot of secrets from Alex," she admitted.

Rick nodded and wondered where this was going.

"I need to tell you something."

"About Alex?" he asked.

"Sorta. About me. About both of us," Toni said.

Rick listened intently, his head tilted slightly to the side, his hand gently rubbing her back. "Go on."

Toni took a deep breath. "I killed two people."

Rick stiffened involuntarily but didn't let go of her. "Okay. Tell me the rest of the story."

Toni pulled out of his arms, sat up in the bed, crossed her legs in front of her naked body with the blanket in her lap and spoke softly.

"My mother was pregnant when she married Alex's dad. She'd had a – romance – to put it nicely, with a boy in town. He ran out on her and she was left pregnant with me and, well, you know how things were in those days. Especially a good Catholic family in Italy. There would be talk, scandal, embarrassment. But my grandparents had other ideas. They knew a family, a young man looking for a wife. He had problems, he drank, but then, what can you expect for a ruined girl? So, they arranged a wedding – between my mother and Alex's father, Vincenzo. We called him Vince. Of course, he knew I wasn't his child, but he was too proud to tell anyone."

She angrily wiped the tears from her cheek and glared at the back of her hand. "Vince was violent, in and out of prison, always in trouble, a blight on the family, my grandmother would say. When he wasn't there, life was good."

172

She smiled. For a second, she seemed at peace. "When he was there...." Her eyes went to the bed where she picked at the blanket.

Rick took her hand in his. "Go on."

Toni cleared her throat. "When Vince was there, Alex and I lived in the closet. Literally, in the closet. Either he didn't want us around or mom would shove us in there when he was in a black mood. We had to stay very, very quiet or else." She shuddered at the memory and withdrew her hand.

Rick nodded.

"We could hear them." She looked up, meeting his calm eyes with her haunted ones. "What he would say, what he would do to her, how they would..." she choked on the words. "...you know." She shrugged as if, in the end, it didn't matter.

Rick picked up every nuance of body language and every hint in her voice. He read her with the same attention he gave a crime report.

"One day, we came back from school. I remember. We were running. Vince wasn't supposed to be there." Her eyes clouded. "I was ahead of Alex on the stairs and I could smell dinner cooking. Then I heard mom scream and the sound of a kettle hitting the floor. I stopped but Alex kept going. I tried to stop him. I grabbed his shirt, but he was moving so fast it slipped out of my fingers."

She wiped away more tears with the heel of her hand. "I tried to stop him. I really tried. Alex was a few steps ahead of me, just a few, but when he pushed the door open and I saw them – mom shoved up against the wall, her dress torn and covered with spilled tomato sauce, her bloody lip. She was so scared; and Vince, that bastard, that – that monster...." Toni grabbed a pillow and held it tight against her chest. "He had a small gun in his hand. I didn't see it at first, but Alex did. Alex yelled at him, started hitting him with his fists, crying, screaming."

Toni's eyes darted back and forth across the apartment. "Vince was drunk, and he swung at Alex and knocked him down, but the gun fell on the floor. Mom screamed again and tried to kick him – Alex's dad, I mean. He smacked her and yelled at her... such words." Toni covered her ears as the memory propelled its way through her mind. "He yelled at her, called her... you know what he called her." She took a deep breath. "I grabbed the gun. I held it with both hands, and I was shaking like I was riding an earthquake. I was so scared. I aimed. I closed my eyes, and then Alex ran towards me and slid on the spilled tomato sauce and knocked me down." Toni swore under her breath. "It was his fault! He slid right into me! He was so scared I was going to kill his father! He didn't know what to do. The gun went off, right next to his ear, and mom...." Toni gasped at the pain of the memory, "...made this weird, weird sound, like the engine of a car when it runs out of gas."

Toni sobbed. "I didn't mean to shoot her. I didn't. I was trying to save her."

Rick pulled her closer and held her. "It's over, Toni. It was over a long, long time ago." He kissed her forehead. "Tell me what happened next."

"I was on the floor with Alex on top of me and his dad staring at me. Vince was furious. He kicked Alex, and I raised the gun and shot again. This time, this time, I kept my eyes open." She used the corner of the blanket to wipe her nose. "I'll never forget the look on his face: shock, horror, disbelief, and then – relief."

"Go on."

"He fell down and blood was everywhere," Toni said. "Alex and I were so scared; we hid in the closet for hours until someone came. Our uncle packed us up and took us to our grandfather's, mom's father. When he died, the family shipped us to America to live with cousins."

"The police didn't question you?" Rick asked.

She shook her head. "No. They called it a murder-suicide. They didn't ask questions. They knew better. The family took care of everything. We are De la Rosa. We always take care of each other."

174

Rick soothed and cradled her until her sobs quieted.

***

A warm sun flooded through the spotless window and into the yellow and white garden that was Maryanne Sadler's immaculate kitchen. A smattering of dirty dishes rested uneasily in the sink. The food had been put away except for a fresh cherry pie displayed on the counter. The tile floor gleamed and the white table was topped with a pot of chrysanthemums. A delicate, daisy wallpaper surrounded white cabinets.

"You don't remember it, do you?" Maryanne placed a plate of warm pie topped with vanilla ice cream in front of her son.

Rested and clean shaven, Tom Sadler looked better than he had all week. He grasped his fork, dug in hungrily and ignored the question. He remembered. He didn't want to, but he did. He smiled and relaxed in the familiar kitchen.

Maryanne wiped the ice cream off her hands with a dish towel, grabbed her own plate of pie and sat down opposite him. Her auburn hair, carefully colored and permed, framed a soft round face. Laugh lines edged her sharp hazel eyes. She was, as usual, dressed casually in a cotton long-tailed shirt, jeans, and clean, white sneakers.

"You were seven; she was nine. You looked so cute in that top hat! I wanted to cry. I'm sure I still have the picture around here somewhere." She spoke with a Georgia accent.

"It was her idea. Completely hers! If you ever find that picture, burn it!" Tom grinned.

"But you made the most adorable groom!" Maryanne smiled at her son.

Tom swallowed an impatient sigh. "That was then, mom; this is now. I'm not that little boy anymore." He leaned back and wiped ice cream off his chin with a napkin. "Besides, she got married and settled down."

"It was a beautiful wedding. She had these pink gardenias." Maryanne's thoughts trailed off. "Too bad it didn't work out for her but, then again, I never really liked that man."

"Don't worry, mom." He leaned forward and gently squeezed her hand. "When the right one comes along, I'll know it. You'll see."

"Yes, well, you thought you'd found the 'right one' when you eloped with whats-her-name, that college girl, only three weeks after the wedding."

Tom glared at her. "You know damn well what her name is, and it wasn't three weeks. It was more like three months."

"That didn't work out either," she reminded him. "Watch your language."

"Sorry." He went back to eating. "I was young. What did I know?"

"You were on the rebound and now you have another chance." Her eyes focused on Tom.

He shook his head and kept eating. "I told you, she's taken. She's in love with someone else, now. The past is the past."

Maryanne leaned forward on her elbows. "Is he in love with her?"

Tom was spared answering the question when his phone rang. He checked the caller ID. "Sadler. What have you got?"

Brandt's clipped voice could be heard over the sound of heavy traffic. "Two things. I did some diggin' and, well, it ain't good."

"What isn't?"

"Another dead girl," said Brandt.

Tom sat up straight. "When? Where? Today?"

"Nope. Two years ago. Emily Walkins. Age 12. Same MO. Same damn garbage bin," Rick said.

Tom relaxed a little and leaned back in his chair. "That makes it official, then. We have a serial killer on our hands." He rubbed his forehead. "Why didn't anyone pick up on that? If there was a pattern...."

"Why should they when they got their killer?" asked Rick.

"...someone should have caught it." Tom nodded. "Okay. Keep me informed." He hung up and set the phone aside.

"Is that boy innocent?" Maryanne asked, her fork poised in the air during the entire conversation. "He looked innocent to me. Poor kid."

"You know I can't talk about it, mom," Tom told her.

She nodded. "Well then, where was I? Oh, yes. Is he in love with her?"

Tom took a few minutes to remember what she was talking about before answering. "The only person Alessandro de la Rosa loves is Alessandro de la Rosa. But she loves him. So, that's that. No more top hat stories." He finished the pie.

"What did you get her for her birthday?" she asked.

"Damn! I forgot." Tom shook his head. "With everything going on, I didn't even think about it."

"Language!" she reminded him.

The phone rang again.

"And the SECOND thing is...." Rick began.

"Oh. Sorry." Tom rubbed his eyes.

"The rock."

"Rock?" Tom asked.

"The rock in the girls' hands. Remember? At least two of them had one. Not sure about Walkins."

"You're going to tell me it's some kind of sandstone, and it's common and can be found anywhere," said Tom.

"Well, if you're going to be a smart ass," Rick countered.

Tom mentally backtracked. "I'm listening."

"Yes, it's sandstone, and yes, it's common and can be found anywhere. According to the lab report, it had some stuff on it – residue – like it came from a fish tank, and the paint is the stuff you buy at Home Depot or Lowes or somethin'. Waterproof. Just thought you should know."

Tom laughed. "Okay. I find a fish tank with painted rocks and I got my

177

man." He could visualize Brandt shrugging.

"Just thought you should know," Rick repeated.

"Thanks." Tom hung up, shut off the ringer and slipped the phone into his pocket.

Maryanne picked up the plates and brought them to the sink. "People can't read minds, you know," she said as she rinsed the dishes and slipped them into the dishwasher. "They can't make logical choices if they don't have all the facts."

"What facts? What are you talking about?" Tom's thoughts had moved on to the murders.

She turned to face him and smiled. "Tell Fran you love her. You're not seven, anymore. Time is passing. Tell her now, before it's too late."

"Mom, stop." His voice was gentle but firm.

Tom finished his pie and escaped into the mid-afternoon sun. He tried to drive images of Fran out of his mind. He had more important things to think about, much more important. He slipped on his sunglasses, grateful that the rain had stopped. Now, if only the murders would stop. He slipped the key into the lock of his car door and hesitated, his instincts telling him something was amiss. His eyes traveled across the street to a white pickup that pulled away from the curb and slowly drove off. It was nothing, he told himself. Just random coincidence. They were probably visiting the neighbors. He was growing paranoid. Realizing his heartbeat had quickened, he turned his phone back on and it rang.

"Yes?" Tom didn't check the ID. He expected it to be Rick and was pleasantly surprised to hear a woman's voice.

"I left a package at your house." Candy said.

"Where?"

"In the living room by the picture of your dad."

Tom felt numb. "How did you get into my house?" If she could, anybody could, he reasoned.

"Good set of lock picks. You should find everything you need. I trust you'll know what to do with it all. Oh, and I did NOT look in the top drawer of your right-hand nightstand." She hung up before he could say anything else.

CHAPTER 13

SUNDAY NIGHT

Fran and Tom found the door ajar to Alex's condo. Inside, music blared. Approaching cautiously, Tom took the lead and pulled his weapon. He slipped through the door, swept the room and startled Toni.

"Oh my god!" Toni yelled, jumping. "Don't do that!"

She stood in the kitchen, a can opener in one hand and a small can in the other. She was nearly invisible in black jeans and a black tank top. The Persian cat wound around her ankles.

"Sorry. What are you doing here?" Tom holstered his weapon and glanced nervously around the room.

Fran quickly turned off the music.

"Feeding Black Velvet. Someone has to feed him. I don't want him to starve to death before Alex gets home."

Toni's face twisted up in pain and her voice broke. She set the can on the counter, opened it, scooped some of the contents onto a saucer and served it to the cat, who ate eagerly.

"See, he's starving. Poor thing." Her trembling fingers found some comfort from stroking the cat's arched back.

"It's going to be okay," Fran said.

Fran reached out to give Toni a gentle hug, but Toni pulled away. Fran let go.

"He'll be home soon. I promise," said Fran.

Toni stiffened. Her dark eyes were bloodshot, swollen and haunted. She didn't look at Fran. Instead, she sought out Tom as he watched from across the room. "I can't handle this. I can't. It's driving me crazy," Toni admitted in a strangled voice.

"Come on." Tom extended a hand towards her. "Let me take you home."

"Why the hell should I go with you?" Toni's behavior suddenly flipped as she glared at him.

It took a few seconds for Tom to switch gears and respond to her. He kept his voice soothing and low. "I did the best I could. I'm sorry if it wasn't enough."

"Best you could? Really?" Her eyebrows rose with her voice as she gestured, the half-filled can still in her hand. "Why the hell didn't you call and warn him? Why didn't you tell them he was innocent? Why didn't you call me?"

"Toni, that's enough," Fran said calmly.

Toni ignored her.

"It wouldn't have done any good." Tom withdrew his hand.

"Letting him get arrested did some good? You know Alex. You know he couldn't have done this," Toni yelled.

Tom's eyes hardened as they drifted from Toni to Fran. "Any man can rape, and every man knows it," he said.

Fran nearly choked.

Toni stiffened and hurled the open can of cat food at him.

Tom ducked as the can hit the wall behind him; the contents splattered on the wall and rug.

"Take that back! Take that back!" Toni screamed, clenching her fists and stomping her feet hysterically. Tears poured down her reddened face.

"That's enough!" Fran yelled at Tom. She grabbed Toni by the shoulders. "You're not doing Alex any good this way. We're going to fix this thing. I promise. Now, stop it!"

Toni looked from Fran to Tom. She wanted to say more but the words wouldn't come out. Her shoulders slumped.

"Let me take you home," Tom coaxed Toni, reaching out to her again as he saw the resignation in her stance.

"Not until you take it back!" Toni argued one last time as she hung onto the crumbling foundation of her life.

Fran stepped back, giving Toni room to feel safe.

Tom sighed as if exhaling every ounce of fatigue in his body. He rubbed his tired eyes with the heels of both hands. "Okay, Toni. I take it back." He kept his eyes level with hers.

"You mean it?"

"I mean it. I'm just tired. Don't pay attention to anything I say. Now, let me take you home."

Toni eyed the outstretched hand a minute and tried to determine the level of his sincerity. She chose to believe him despite her misgivings. "Not without Black Velvet, just in case."

"Okay," Tom said.

Toni handed some cans of cat food to Tom, gathered up the cat and held it lovingly. "I'll need the litter box," she added as an afterthought.

"I'll be back for you," Tom told Fran.

Tom was careful to stay out of Toni's orbit as he trailed her out the door. He carried an armful of cat food cans and the igloo-styled litter box.

"Don't spill anything!" Fran called after them. She closed the door.

Fran didn't want the others to know she was hurting: the way she hurt when her father betrayed her in the worst possible way, the way she hurt the year her husband left her with nothing to hold onto at night but a cold pillow, the way she hurt the night Sarah was murdered. She felt a painful absence in her bones, a total aloneness that she hadn't felt in years. With the radio now silenced and Alex's things around her, she felt as if she was standing in a mausoleum late at night with no one to commune with but ghosts. She was reminded of Hamlet, wandering the turrets of his dead father's castle and looking for answers.

"Where are your ghosts?" Fran asked as she gazed around the room. "What will they tell me?" She spotted the splattered wall and sighed. Some things, she told herself, take priority.

After cleaning up the cat food, Fran set aside her uneasiness about invading Alex's privacy and began a thorough search of his apartment. She knew that anything incriminating would have already been seized by the police. She was looking for something that wasn't incriminating, something that would tell the world that Alex de la Rosa was a normal man with normal interests, not just someone who defended perverts, screwed starlets in elevators, engaged in bondage and lived with a dead rose bush and a cat. Fran searched for the normal, but she didn't expect to find it.

Alex's furniture was largely leather, heavy and manly. For art, he hung old movie posters of Marilyn Monroe on his wall. A treadmill and some weights showed obvious use in one corner of the room. His music tended towards classical, jazz, and hard rock. Stacks of *National Geographic, Psychology Today, Playboy,* and the *American Bar Association Journal* were piled on his coffee table, all well-read.

On dust-free shelves, Fran found copies of Public Enemies, by John Walsh; Criminal Justice in America, by George Cole; The Anatomy of a Motive, by John Douglas and Mark Olshaker; The Perfect Murder: A Study in Detection, by David Lehman; Studies in the Psychology of Sex, volumes 1 through 5; and a copy each of The Sexual Man and Unmasking Male Depression, both by Archibald Hart. They stood side by side with Marcel Proust, William Shakespeare, Bernard Shaw, and copies of two of Nancy Friday's books, Secret Garden and Forbidden Flowers. They all looked well read. Fran realized that the cops must not have understood the implication of the last two books.

"They probably think they're about gardening," she thought out loud, picking up Friday's books and setting them aside to take with her later. She wondered what or who had prompted him to buy them. She spotted his camera on a side table by the sofa and wondered why the police hadn't taken

184

that. She picked it up and set it with the books.

She explored his kitchen and found things she would never have found when Sarah was alive: a six-pack of beer, leftover pizza carefully tagged in a plastic container, a box of donuts and other assorted items that told her Alex hadn't been eating well. In his bathroom, she found all his personal items, neatly lined up on the shelves, from tallest to shortest, their labels facing forward. The counter was decorated with a row of vanilla candle jars. Fran shook her head at the incongruity in his life. On impulse, she lit the candles.

His bedroom, with its heavy black shades drawn against the brilliant sun, had been ransacked. Drawers hung open, clothes littered the floor as if tossed by a windstorm, sheets and blankets were torn off the bed, and the mattress was tipped on the floor. Everything in his closet was piled the middle of the room. There was nowhere to walk except over it all. Footprints and a pair of crushed reading glasses attested to the fact that the police had done just that. Fran made a note to bring him an extra pair.

The photo of Alex and Sarah was on the floor, the glass broken.

A hundred memories ripped into Fran's heart. Fighting back tears, she clutched her gut and sunk to her knees on the mountain of clothes. They had violated him, she thought. She covered her mouth with her hand, stifling her sobs. They had violated him just like before, just like when Sarah had died. It was payback for what they thought he'd done to Carol. They weren't looking for evidence. They were looking for revenge and they knew how to get it.

Fran clenched the photo in her hand and wept for the first time since she'd learned of Alex's arrest. Tom Sadler found her in that spot almost an hour later.

"Hey, you alright?" He bent down to check on her. His hands rested gently on her shoulders.

She pulled angrily away from him, nodded and quickly brushed the tears from her cheeks. "We need to clean up this mess. I don't want him to see it like this. He's been through enough." She cradled the picture in her arm.

Tom helped her to her feet and didn't bother to argue that Alex might not be coming back.

"How long are you going to let this continue?" he asked. He hoped she wouldn't see the hurt in his eyes.

"What?" she asked.

He shook his head, disappointed with her. "Look, I'm not a bad looking guy, and I don't have a problem getting dates, but I've hit on you at least, what? A hundred times? And you still blow me off. I'm not an idiot, Fran. I can see what's happening here." He paused. "You're sleeping with him."

Her head shot up and she glared at him. "No! In the first place…. Oh, hell, you wouldn't understand, anyway. I'm too old for this shit. I shouldn't have to explain, not to you and not to anyone. Besides, it's none of your damn business."

Tom backed up a step as if he'd been slapped. "Can't you see how he plays you, Fran? He's not in love with you. He just wants to have you there when he needs you, how he needs you, his own private cheering squad."

"We're friends!" she yelled.

Tom's voice unexpectedly turned bitter. "He doesn't love you, Fran, not like… not like we do. We're your friends. Me, Rick, Margo. We love you…"

She set the broken picture frame on the night table.

"Is that Alex's camera in the living room?" Tom asked, changing the topic.

Fran nodded. "I'm surprised the cops didn't take it."

"They didn't take it because it wasn't here," he told her. "I was here, remember? They looked for it."

Fran tugged at the mattress to drag it onto the bed. Tom gave her a hand.

"How did it get here, then?" she asked. "Where was it?"

"Toni must have had it. She took pictures of Elliott Friday night. She was

186

following him around," Tom reminded her.

Fran stopped, straightened up and stared at him. "Pictures of Elliott," she repeated. "Elliott and Carol McEnroe."

Tom smiled.

***

"Hey, man!" A twenty-something kid with a wife-beater shirt, sunken eyes, and scraggly hair yelled at the guard through the small screened window of the courthouse holding cell. "You put me in here with that cop-killing perv! I don't want to be with no perv, man! Creep me out!"

"Shut up, Miller," the guard ordered, tapping his baton on the metal door.

"If it makes you feel any better," Alex said calmly and with a completely deadpan face, "being in here with you creeps me out, too."

Alex, in his prison-issued jumpsuit, sat on one of the two metal chairs in the small cell. A large leather belt was cinched around his waist and, from the belt, a chain ran to his ankles that attached to shackles with just enough play to let him shuffle through a room. His hands were also cuffed and secured to his waist, the chain barely long enough to allow him to unzip his pants, should the need arise, but nothing more. He couldn't even scratch his nose, which he wanted to do very badly.

"It's always the little things," he muttered to no one.

Miller, in similar shackles and chains, looked at Alex, sized him up and kept his distance. "You're the man, right? I saw your mug on TV. Hey, what's your name?"

"De la Rosa." Alex closed his eyes and took a deep breath. He had trouble focusing without his glasses, and his head was splitting. Every breath he took brought pain to his cracked ribs.

"De la what? Sounds Italian like a mafia name. Is that a mafia name? You in the family?" the guy asked.

Alex opened his eyes, looked at Miller as if studying a strange new life

187

form, and said, "Shut up."

"You do what they said, man? You kill that woman cop while screwing her? With your bare hands? Burn her all over like that? Were you lookin' in her eyes, man? Did she scream?" Miller, babbling and staring with curiosity, took the chair opposite Alex and leaned forward.

Alex was worried about surviving on the inside, but fear could be a good deterrent if played carefully, he thought. "What do you think?" he asked.

The young man tensed and was silent a few seconds before speaking. "I think you're screwed, man." The humor was gone from his voice.

"Yes, well, I hear that's what started it all," Alex said.

The guard unlocked the door. His burly frame filled up the small window. "Miller, you're with me. De la Rosa, your lawyer is here."

"Fran?" Alex asked with a sudden rush of relief, but he didn't get an answer.

A few seconds later, Fran entered with Charles Warner Smith, a tall and strikingly handsome man and one of the best criminal defense attorneys in Nevada.

"You hired a top gun? Shit! I am screwed!" Alex exclaimed on seeing Smith. He sank further into the chair and didn't dare meet Fran's reproving eyes.

"Nice to see you again, too," said Smith. He pulled up a chair and sat in front of Alex.

"I had to," Fran said. She stood with her arms crossed in front of her, ready to argue with Alex. When he didn't respond, she gently rested a hand on his shoulder. Alex looked up into her pained blue eyes. She turned her attention to Smith. "Rick get my file to you?"

Smith nodded. "Good stuff." He continued, "I don't mean to break up this reunion, but I need to talk to my client before arraignment."

"What good stuff?" Alex asked.

188

"Sure. Don't mind me," said Fran.

"What good stuff?" he asked a little louder.

"Alone," Smith told Fran.

She frowned, gave Alex a quick kiss on the top of his head and slipped out the door. It slammed shut behind her.

"I'll probably have to sell the farm to pay you, or at least my car." Alex's dark eyes focused on Smith.

"I know." Smith didn't seem to care. "I always liked your car. I'll take that as a retainer and consider the rest an act of loyalty to an old friend." He was referring to Fran. "But if I'm going to do this, I'm going to need some things from you."

"What?" Alex asked.

"The truth to begin with. The complete and unvarnished truth," Smith said. "There's nothing more damning to a defense attorney's case than to be taken by surprise during a trial. I need to know everything you know. You can't hold back any secrets from me. In this relationship, I'm the one in charge. You can tell me what you think, you can give me information, you can tell me to go to hell, but I call the shots. In that courtroom, I'm the expert."

"I slept with her. I didn't kill her. Is that good enough for you?" Alex snapped.

"It's a place to start. Anything else?"

Alex glanced nervously at the door.

"Alex?"

"I tied her up," Alex admitted. His eyes dropped to the floor and his shoulders sagged. "I didn't gag her. I swear I didn't. And I didn't burn her either. It was just sex."

Warner frowned as his mind kicked around all the angles. "And then what?"

189

"Then I went home," Alex said.

"She was fine when you left?" Smith asked.

"She was alive when I left."

Smith chewed over Alex's words. "Alive but not fine."

Alex looked up. "It got rough. She liked it that way. Then she got mad at me. I was pissed. We argued. I left her there, but I didn't kill her."

Warner nodded. "Rough sex? You call that a defense? Anything else you want to share right now?"

"Can you spell bail?" Alex asked sarcastically, closing his eyes again.

"You know better." Smith was critical.

"How's that?"

"That attitude. Make no mistake, this case will be tried in the press, and the press will fry you for comments like that," Smith snapped.

Alex didn't respond.

"What did you tell your law partner about the case?" asked Smith.

"She knows I was there. That's all," Alex said.

"That's too much. What will you tell anyone else?"

Alex, irritated, sat up in the chair. "I'm not an idiot," he said.

"Your employees? Your mother? Your girlfriend? What will you tell them?" Smith pressed.

"I – didn't – kill – anyone." Alex's neck turned red. The headache pounded.

"Wrong! The answer is NOTHING. You will tell them nothing because, no matter what you say, it will be turned around and used against you. Got that?"

Alex needed to confide in somebody, and he knew exactly who that somebody was. "Who can I talk to?" he asked.

"Me, or a wife. You got a wife?" asked Smith.

It wasn't the answer Alex wanted. "No. I got a cat."

190

"Then me and the cat."

"What about bail?" Alex asked again.

"The D.A. is going to ask that you be held without bail, and I'm going to object like hell. You are going to stand there and look upset. And I mean UPSET! I don't want any of that sarcasm leaking out to the press. I don't want anyone saying you're too unemotional. You're the victim here. Start acting like it."

"Funny. I've had Kafka on my mind lately." Alex smirked.

"Has anyone ever seen you cry over a dead man?" Smith stood up and picked up his briefcase.

"Yes," Alex said slowly, suddenly subdued. "My wife. I cried over my wife."

Smith responded with silence.

"They're ready for you," the guard said as he unlocked the door.

"Any last requests?" Smith asked Alex.

"Can you scratch my nose?"

Alex and Smith, escorted by two guards, entered the courtroom from a side door. The room was packed with reporters, off-duty police officers, and the curious. Alex remembered the last time he'd been the show. He wondered what Holly Butterfield was saying about him now.

Alex spotted Tom first, who looked straight ahead with a face like ice. Brandt, expressionless, curled an arm protectively around Toni. She tried to look tough, but her eyes were bloodshot from hours of crying.

One look at her face and Alex didn't have to pretend to be upset.

Fran stood next to Toni, her pain hidden behind a calm facade. Her eyes locked with Alex's and everything became slow motion until he was forced to turn around.

"All rise," the bailiff ordered.

The judge settled behind the bench. The bailiff motioned for everyone to be seated.

"Mr. De la Rosa, Mr. Smith, what's your pleasure?" the judge asked, slipping on his glasses, opening the file and scanning it as if he hadn't read it all the way through at least twice beforehand.

"We received the information and affidavit and enter pleas of not guilty on all counts," Smith said.

"All counts?" Alex mouthed, glancing up at his lawyer. He wondered how many there were.

"On the issue of bail?" the judge asked.

The prosecution opened.

"Your honor, the defendant is charged with a particularly gruesome crime involving the rape and murder of a policewoman. The evidence as presented in the supporting affidavits clearly shows that he was at her apartment, that they were intimate and that he was the last person to see her alive. Also, the victim was tortured with a cigar and one was found at the scene, identical to the kind the defendant keeps in his vehicle. DNA is still pending. The only prints found in the apartment were his..." He glanced at Alex. "...and hers. No others were found except her landlord's."

"This is a heinous crime carrying a life sentence. Mr. De la Rosa poses a high risk to the community and a high risk of flight. He has few ties to the community. He has no wife or children. He is not involved in any civic organizations, and a search of his apartment turned up a number of materials relating to sexually aberrant behavior, materials which we believe to be highly relevant to this case. Therefore, we are asking that the defendant be held without bail."

Fran felt lightheaded and she grabbed Tom's arm for support. His hand covered hers reassuringly.

"Mr. Smith?" The judge asked as he addressed defense counsel.

"Your honor, the state's case is purely circumstantial. They have no

192

evidence whatsoever that Mr. De la Rosa committed this horrendous crime. His presence in the apartment, if true, only proves he knew the victim, had been to her apartment and may have had an intimate relationship with her. That's all. My client has resided in Las Vegas for the last ten years and is one of the city's most renowned individuals. Any material found in his apartment is subject to interpretation, especially given his line of work. He has no criminal past except for a few speeding tickets, and he poses no risk of flight. We ask that cash bail be set in a reasonable amount to ensure appearance."

"Very well," said the judge, looking at the prosecutor. "While I agree that this is a horrendous crime and that sufficient evidence has been filed to support a finding of probable cause, the state's case is circumstantial. I won't hold it against Mr. De la Rosa that he's lucky enough to still be single. As for anything sexually aberrant, this is Vegas. Define aberrant. However," the judge directed his next remarks to Smith, "people are convicted every day on circumstantial evidence and the evidence is compelling. Therefore, I am setting bail at $500,000. Should your client manage to make bail, he is ordered not to leave the county. Is that clear?"

Alex swallowed and found his throat dry. He could barely afford his lawyer. Where was he going to get a half-million dollars in bail? He looked back, and his eyes met Fran's again. He knew what she was thinking, and he didn't like it. "Charlie," he whispered to his lawyer. "There's something else I need to tell you."

"In a minute," Smith told him. Smith turned back to the judge. "Your honor, we are filing a motion to suppress and a motion to dismiss. The evidence, in this case, has been seriously compromised. There is no way my client can get a fair trial."

"Not exactly a novel argument, Mr. Smith. Do I get a synopsis, or should I wait for the book?" the judge asked.

"The synopsis will suffice." Smith pulled a handful of glossy 8x11 photos out of a manila envelope, handed a copy to the prosecutor and a copy to the bailiff to give the judge.

"And these are?" The judge asked, slipping on his glasses and studying the photos.

The prosecutor didn't ask. He just sank into his chair and tossed the photos to the side.

"Those are pictures of the chief investigator on this case, taken the night of the murder, in an amorous embrace with the victim," Smith said. The courtroom was deadly silent. "The same chief investigator who coincidentally found her body hours later, just after she allegedly had sex with my client. The same chief investigator who led the forensics team that combed her house and the defendant's condo for evidence. The same chief investigator who, as of Friday, is the new director of the crime lab."

Alex had never before seen a judge go from cynical, to calm, to furious, to icy so fast. The judge looked to the prosecutor. "Well?" he asked.

The man stood up slowly. "This is all news to us, your honor." The look on his face said he was telling the truth.

"I just bet it is." The judge frowned. "What happened to the last director - what's her name - Knight?"

"Dr. Knight," the prosecutor stated. "She was discharged."

The judge grunted. "They're going through directors pretty fast over there these days," he noted.

"One more thing," Smith interrupted.

"Please, Mr. Smith. Enlighten me," the judge said with a note of sarcasm.

"The prosecutor stated that the only other prints in the apartment belonged to the landlord, at least according to Director Elliott's report. However, the report fails to note that the landlord," Smith paused for effect, "is Sheriff George Randall."

The judge's fingertips met in a tent shape, and he pressed them to his lips as he eyed everyone in the courtroom. Reporters were writing furiously. The prosecutor looked like he was about to be sick. Smith had an irritating smirk on his face.

The judge's icy gaze finally fell on the prosecutor, but he spoke to the clerk close to him. "Didn't Paulutto just settle?" he asked in a restrained voice.

"Yes, your honor," the clerk said, her fingers flying over the keyboard of her computer. "I was going to move the Fidele case into that spot...." she never got to finish.

"I want Mr. Warner's motions heard ASAP." The judge nodded quietly, then shifted his voice towards the prosecutor. "You may have just lost your murder case. Better come prepared." He glanced back at the clerk. "Date and time?"

"Week from tomorrow, 9 a.m."

"Did you hear that gentlemen?" the judge asked.

Both men nodded.

***

"Don't you dare go to Max!" Alex yelled at Fran in one of the visiting rooms in the detention facility. "Shit, Fran! You know what he wants from you! I won't stand for it. I'd rather sit here and rot than have you go crawling to him! You know what he'll do to you? To us? To the firm? For all we know, he's behind all this shit."

"Look, I don't want to go to Max, but do you have any better ideas? Do you know what will happen to you if I leave you in here?" She paced the floor on the other side of the table.

Alex turned to keep his good ear towards her. He studied her with a sidelong look. "Focus on the firm, Bella. Take care of business. Take care of the Callas case, for god's sake! That's what matters. Maybe your hunch is right. Maybe that's what's behind this."

195

"Alex, wake up and smell the press releases! The firm was in trouble the minute you...." She hesitated.

"Screwed Carol?" His voice was barely a whisper.

Fran's heart froze in her throat. He was confessing to her and she didn't want to hear it. Swallowing her wounded pride, she began again.

"The minute you were arrested. You're page one news. CNN picked it up. Hell, even the goddamn Enquirer has your mug shot plastered all over it: Vegas Playboy Slays Sexy Cop."

Alex's boiling point rose a notch higher. "Damn!" His jaw tightened.

"Come on, Alex. We're a team, you and I, all of us. The avalanche has happened, and we're all buried up to our goddamn necks. Digging you out means digging us out. We're in this together."

She quickly glanced at the guard. She wanted to touch Alex, just one little touch to let him know that she understood. She didn't.

"I'm sorry, Bella." He spoke slowly and sounded almost normal for the first time in two days. "I never meant to hurt anyone. Not Toni, not you, not anyone."

"A lot of people got hurt, Alex, but it isn't your fault. You didn't do anything wrong," Fran said, although she believed he had.

A moment of tense silence passed between them as they both assessed the lie in that statement.

"Alex?"

"I'll resign. I'll leave the firm. You can take it over. You're good. You can handle it," he told her.

"God damn you! Don't you dare do that to me!" Too many emotions tried to break down the wall between them. "Talk to me, Alex."

"I can't."

"If you're worried about hurting my feelings, it's too late for that." Fran leaned against the wall, her arms crossed defensively.

196

"They'll put you on the stand. They'll ask you what I said," he explained.

"I'm your lawyer," she argued.

He glared at her, his face turning red. "Fuck, Bella! Did it ever occur to you that I just don't want to tell you?"

She caught her breath a second and weighed his words. "If you didn't kill her…."

He stiffened up, startled. "You think there's even a chance that I did?"

"That's not what I'm saying." She leaned forward and slammed her knuckles on the table. "I KNOW you didn't kill her so how can anything you tell me be used against you?"

She didn't seem to get the point he was trying to make. He detoured: "Stop being naive. You know better. You know how this works."

Fran sank into a chair and clasped her hands together as she hung onto her own fragile sanity. "I didn't come here to argue with you. We're going to clear your name, and that's all there is to it."

As she stood up to leave, Alex suddenly said, "I'm not perfect, Bella."

"No kidding, Sherlock!" she yelled. She straightened up and took a deep breath.

"I know what you think of me. You made that quite clear more than once. All I care about is my career. Since Sarah…. But you don't understand. I need you," Alex said.

"Now you need me? Now? After someone is dead?" She remembered years of arguments. She planted her fists on the table and leaned into his face. "What about when I needed you? What about when Sarah died? She was my best friend! You think you were the only one hurting?"

He flinched.

"What about when Paul left, and I was alone with Lauren? I needed you then and you shut me out. Now you need me? After what you did to that slut? After…. Damn you!"

His dark eyes pleaded with her to understand. "I'm a man, Bella. I have certain needs. I just don't bring them to work."

"Or to me." She was surprised at how much anger went into that response.

"You didn't want that from me," he said. "You didn't want anyone to touch you that way and you know why."

"It's the bondage I can't take, Alex. The bondage, not the sex." The image of Tom pinning her down flashed through her mind.

"That's not how I operate, and you know it," he told her.

"It wouldn't have killed you to try." Her red hair flew about her face as she spun around to march out the door.

"Bella?"

She froze and turned around. "What, Alex?"

"I didn't kill her. I swear I didn't. And I didn't gag her or torture her, either. She wanted to be tied up. She begged me."

Fran was chilled by the images that flooded her mind. "Anything else?" she interrupted, her voice bitter. She didn't want to hear any more.

"I'm sorry."

Fran slowly inhaled and tried to block the image of him and Carol from her conscious mind.

"Will you be alright?" he asked when she didn't say anything.

"I don't know yet." She walked away.

Tom waited for her in the parking lot, arms crossed, leaning against the sun-heated car. His shirtsleeves were rolled up to his elbows. Mirrored sunglasses covered his eyes. "How's he doing?" he asked as he opened the door for her.

"About what you'd expect." A whoosh of hot air hit her in the face as she got in. She hesitated a second and then looked up at him as she waited for the next question.

"And?" He looked at her with worried eyes.

She shook her head. "Did he kill her? No. As for the rest, who the hell knows." It wasn't a question. Tom's earlier words echoed in her mind: Any man can rape, and every man knows it.

But can any man murder?

Tom reached inside and gently squeezed her shoulder before he shut the door. "You deserve better," he mumbled.

CHAPTER 14

MONDAY AFTERNOON

A burly man in a black suit loomed in the doorway of Fran's office. His bald head shone in the overhead light. He arrived unannounced until his shadow fell across the pile of papers on her desk.

Fran removed her reading glasses and looked up. She recognized him. "Jerry," she said coolly, suppressing a shudder.

"Looking good, Fran." He offered a curt smile.

"I had court this morning, but I suppose you know all about that." She closed the folder in front of her and rested her hand protectively on it.

"Max wants to see you," Jerry said as if announcing the time of day.

"Max always wants to see me." Fran pushed her chair back and let out a deep sigh as if she could exhale a lifetime of resentment. "Tell Max I don't want to see him, I don't want any more of his damn flowers and I don't want him calling me. I'm busy."

"Sorry, kid. Just doing my job." Jerry looked apologetic but was unmovable.

Fran reached for the phone and hesitated. Who would she call? The police? Paul? Alex? Where the hell was Rick? She tried to remember.

"He said it's about your partner. He's got..." Thinking hard, Jerry searched for the right word, "…exculpatory evidence. I think that's what he called it."

"Damn." Angry, Fran abandoned the phone, picked up her purse and followed him out the door.

Margo, startled that a stranger had gotten past her and into the office, nearly jumped out of her seat as they walked by her. "Where did you....?"

"It's okay," Fran assured her. "I'll be back in an hour or two." Before Margo could respond, Fran added, "Call Rick and tell him I've been summoned to the mayor's office."

***

Fran had never been intimidated by the mayor's office until her father occupied it. Occupied, that was the word: as in occupation, as in an invading army camped out in occupied territory. An oversized desk and massive high-backed leather chair sat on a raised platform, framed by the skyline of Las Vegas and humbling even tall men who stood before it. They always stood because Max Simone provided no chairs for those brought before him. If Simone wanted to entertain, he went elsewhere. If he wanted to relax, he stretched out on the sofa in the corner, far from his desk and far from the use of any guest. His office was a seat of power, a throne whose purpose was to intimidate. Fran feared the man himself, not the room with its oppressive dark red paint, heavy furnishings, and thick rug. She should have worn different shoes, she realized, as she stepped across that carpet and tried not to fall. Or maybe it wasn't the shoes, maybe her knees just weren't working.

Simone, at 62, had aged a lot since she'd last seen him. He seemed tired and much older than his age. His wavy salt and pepper hair was thin. His lanky frame was gaunt. Normally he was surrounded by a small army of bodyguards, but none were present when Fran was deposited at the office. He didn't need bodyguards to stand between him and his daughter. A lifetime of shared history was enough.

"Okay, Max. You finally got me here. What the hell do you want?" Fran planted herself in front of him with her arms crossed defiantly. She felt as if the room could swallow her up like a drop of rain and no one would know.

"Hi, honey," Simone said, grinning at her from behind his desk. "Happy belated birthday. Have a nice ride?"

Fran glared at him. "I think everyone should be kidnapped by a limo," she snapped.

"Well, at least you got my birthday gift." His grin broadened.

"The flowers? I got them. I burned them."

For a few seconds, his face froze as he stared at her. "And the disc? What about the disc that came with the flowers?"

"What disc...." she started to say, then stopped. "Oh. I burned that, too."

Disappointment and rage settled into a stony glare on Max's face. "You never even LOOKED at it?"

She shrugged, suddenly wishing she had but not wanting to give him the satisfaction of knowing how she felt.

He shook his head. "You could have made this easy on yourself, you know. You could have just watched the disc, called me back, anything, instead of ignoring me like I'm dead and buried already. Besides, I'm trying to do you a great favor." His voice turned patronizing. "All I want is a little something in return, something I have a right to have."

"What the hell are you talking about?" Fran's hands went clammy. She allowed her eyes to slip out of focus, so she could look straight at him and not really see him. Without thinking, she noted that he was badly in need of some sun.

"I'm your father, honey, and like any good father, I have always loved you. I only want what's best for you and for Lauren, that's all. I want to take care of you and my granddaughter. I want to protect you from that homicidal boyfriend of yours and all the dangers out there on the street."

The mention of her daughter's name made Fran shudder. "You're worried about him? You've got to be kidding! You dragged me all the way down here to tell me that? What the hell do you want, Max?"

Her father's brow narrowed into an angry V, but he kept his voice calm. "I'm not getting any younger, Frannie. I miss you. I want you to move in with me. I want us to be a family, again."

Fran's skin crawled. She hugged herself tighter. "We had this discussion years ago. You didn't listen to me then and you're not listening to me now. For years you left me alone; now you want a relationship. Well, I don't. I want you out of my life, the further the better, and you will not come

203

anywhere near my daughter. Not now, not ever. If you do, I swear to god, Max, I'll kill you with my bare hands."

He leaned back in his chair, studied her and said, "Your boyfriend is in a bit of a jam. The disc could have fixed that. Well, somewhat, anyway. Nothing can fix stupid."

Fran leaned back on her heels a bit and forced herself to focus. "How?" she asked.

He slowly pushed himself up from the chair and stepped down from the platform. He towered over her. "I was doing you a favor. It was a gift. I should have realized you wouldn't appreciate it."

She shrank from him. It didn't matter that he looked thin and weak, he moved like a cat, and she very much felt like the mouse being stalked, like she was five years old, powerless. Being in his presence clouded her judgment and her instincts.

He stopped a moment to read her body language but didn't comment on it. "The state's case is circumstantial." Max carefully circled her and walked to the mahogany bar. He poured himself a scotch but didn't bother to offer her anything. "I can make it a lot worse. I could deliver his head on a platter." He looked at her with piercing eyes, and she suddenly felt nauseous. He indicated she take a seat on the leather sofa in front of the television. "Or I could make it a lot better. It's all in the editing."

She didn't move. "You set him up." Fran's voice was low and threatening. She was sweating.

"No, honey. I didn't do that. I liked Carol a lot. She was special. She reminded me a bit of you." He took another drink. "Just shows you what kind of a man that sick bastard really is."

Fran held onto her growing rage. Her blue eyes flashed fire. "What are you saying?" A fear gnawed at her. What if Alex was guilty? Tom's words rattled in her mind. She shook her head to drive out the doubts. Exculpatory evidence, that's what Jerry had said. That was a good thing.

Simone put down the drink and picked up the DVD from the bar. He held it tauntingly in the air between them. "This," he said, his eyes gazing fondly on it, "could seal De la Rosa's fate forever – or not. It's all up to you."

She stared at the disc and choked down her initial reaction. "What is that?"

He chuckled softly, glanced back at her and smiled. "I sent it to you. You watched it. I know you did, so let's not play these games." His voice felt like slime on her skin.

"I told you, I didn't watch it. I trashed it." Her stomach twisted into a sickening knot. "I trash everything you send me."

He frowned a little and then shrugged. "Perhaps you did. Perhaps you have no idea what's on this. Perhaps Alex didn't tell you about him and Carol. So much for honesty and trust in a relationship. Oh, well, in that case, let me enlighten you."

He slipped the DVD into a player and, using the remote, turned on the television above the bar. It took Fran less than five seconds to realize she was watching Alex – naked and having sex with a bound Carol. The cord was snugly wrapped around the victim's neck and wrists. She was screaming. The screen went dead and Fran realized with a chill that Max had hit the remote.

"Give me that!" Fran yelled. She took a step forward and froze as he turned to face her. She stepped back. Her high heel caught on the rug and she tripped, falling into the leather sofa behind her. It smelled of cigar smoke. It smelled like Max Simone. Repulsed, Fran quickly pushed herself back to her feet. "How the hell did you get that?" she demanded to know.

"You didn't know Carol, did you? I did. I knew her very well. For years. She was a beautiful girl once." A flash of grief crossed his face. "I never believed those stories about Alex killing his wife. Now I know he didn't. But Carol, she was a lot of fun. She had a thing for handcuffs...." He seemed to

205

drift into a fleeting memory. He leaned against the bar to steady himself, his voice shaky. "She liked to keep mementos of her – What shall I call them? Liaisons? I'm sure your boyfriend was fully aware of that little fact. Although...." His voice grew quiet.

"Although what?" Fran asked.

He didn't answer.

"How did you get that? The police were...." Her voice choked in her throat. "You fucking bastard! You did do this to him! You did!"

"You know better than that, honey. I'm just an opportunist. I'm taking advantage of the situation, that's all." He still seemed distracted as if unraveling a puzzle.

"How the hell did you get that?" she asked again.

"How doesn't matter." He removed the disc and looked it over as if it was a rare diamond. "I have it and, trust me, you don't want the police to get it. Not now and not ever."

"He didn't kill her! You know he didn't and that thing proves it!" She stood up again as if to tackle him, but her fear kept her frozen to the spot.

"Is that what you saw? I saw an angry man having forced sex with a woman who winds up dead. Are you sure he didn't kill her?" His warning sliced like ice through her. "Like I said, it's all in the editing."

Fran gasped and clenched her fists.

"You know he could have killed her," Max said, assessing the look in her eyes, "or at least you've entertained the idea."

"You're crazy! How would I know? I didn't even know that thing existed!" Her mouth felt dry. She licked her lips.

His eyes went back to the disc. "I could just give this to the police. Then at least they'd have the rape, complete with the cord around her neck."

"He didn't rape her," Fran insisted. "She was into it. You know that, too. That's how she did it with him and with everyone else she screwed, including

206

you." It was a calculated guess, but she could tell by his pained expression that she was right.

"Alex is into it with everyone he screws," he reminded her.

I'm going to kill him, Fran thought, not sure if she meant Max or Alex.

Max smirked. "You think the police will see it your way?"

"I hate you!" The familiar chant reminded her of her daughter. A ghost possessed Fran. Memories. Trapped. Watery sunlight. Tears. A child's screams. She couldn't believe how fast he had reduced her to childish behavior. "You can't have Lauren. I won't let you do to her what you did to me."

Simone looked sad. "I never hurt you. I never gave you anything you didn't want."

Fran shuddered. She was close to throwing up. "You raped me."

"No." His face turned red. "I loved you. No one ever loved you as much as I did, as much as I still do. And you loved it. You wanted it. You'd sit on my lap for hours."

"I was a child! I didn't have a choice!" she screamed.

"I was gentle with you. Kind. And you're throwing your life away on this philandering bastard?" He angrily waved the disc in her face. "You know who he's screwing now, don't you?"

"I don't care. You're blackmailing me, Max. Is that how you treat everyone you love?"

"Call it what you like, honey. We're a family. We belong together. I can take care of you. I can give you and Lauren anything you want. I can protect you, both of you. The mansion is big and empty, especially with Carol gone." He swallowed hard.

Fran gasped.

"Is it wrong for a man to want to be surrounded by his family? By those who love him?" Max asked.

207

"Love you?" Fran stepped backward towards the door. "I wish you were dead."

"You may have that wish filled sooner than you think, honey, but in the meantime…." He held up the disc again. "It's your call. I can make this mess a whole lot worse real fast." He followed her across the room, one step at a time.

Fran thought her heart was going to explode. "I need time, Max. I need to think this through."

He handed the disc to her. "Take it. Take it home and watch it. Make sure my grandchild isn't there, of course. It might be a bit embarrassing."

Fran reached out a shaking hand and plucked the disc from his grasp. "It's a copy," she said, more to herself than to him. "How many copies did you make?"

"Think about my offer, Frannie."

"I need to know he's going to be alright." She slipped the disc into her purse. "You have connections, even on the inside. You have to protect him, and you can't have Lauren ever or, I swear Max…."

"I know, I know. You'll kill me with your bare hands. I'm impressed." He didn't sound like it.

He moved closer to her and she continued to back away until he had her backed up against the door, his acrid breath hot on her cheeks, the stench of tobacco seeping into her nostrils, his hands planted on the door behind her, one on each side of her head. She closed her eyes and turned her face away from him.

"You never know, honey, I just might grow on you again." His lips fell on her cheek and she struggled to control her breathing.

"I'm too old for you, Max."

He pulled away slightly.

"Anyone lays a hand on him in prison and the deal is off," she added, mentally crossing her fingers behind her back and offering up a silent prayer.

"Then it's a deal," Simone whispered in her ear. His hand cupped her chin and turned her face to his. "I'll be waiting."

He kissed her softly on the forehead before reaching around her waist, turning the door handle and letting her fall through the open door and into the empty corridor.

Fran scrambled to her feet and ran out of the building in tears.

Max, looking exhausted, leaned against the door frame and watched her go.

***

Fran dashed past Margo, locked the door to her office, took the phone off the hook and fell into the chair behind her desk. She was shaking so hard she could barely pull the DVD out of her purse. Nothing was written on it – no clue to the darkness hiding inside. A part of her wanted to heave it out the window and never see it again. A part of her wanted to watch it from beginning to end, even though she knew how it began and how it ended. She closed her eyes, held her breath and offered up a silent prayer. She knew what was on that disc was enough to destroy everything and everyone. Alex didn't kill Carol. That was the one litany that ran through her mind and grounded her. He didn't. He couldn't have. He'd sworn.

A frightening thought kept gnawing at Fran's mind and she didn't know what scared her most, that she was right or that she was wrong. Either way, Max had her back against the wall in more ways than one. She winced at the memory of his touch and reached into her desk for some cologne to drive the scent of him off her. A soft knock sounded at her door. She jumped.

"I don't want to be disturbed!" Fran shouted.

The knock went away.

Fran glanced at the clock and wondered how long she could put this off. She turned the DVD over in her hand and sighed. It wasn't any good. She simply had to face the fact that what was on it would change her life forever. She slipped it into the computer, put on her earphones and turned on her player, then watched the bar fill from left to right as the download counted: 5%... 12%... 22%... She almost clicked cancel but stopped herself. 35%... 47%... Almost halfway there. 53%.... Fran toyed with the mouse. She wanted to distract herself with a game or some music, anything so she wouldn't have to think about what was coming. 68%... 73%... 91%.... Fran was always amazed how much faster a download went near the end. 98%... 99%....

The screen opened on darkness. The darkness peeled away. Alex in all his nakedness crawled on top of Carol and pinned her down. The DVD kept playing. Fran muted the sound. Seeing what was happening was torture enough. Hearing it was too much. Fran felt dirty watching them, like a kid surfing porn on the Internet while his parents watched the news in the next room. Worse, because she knew Carol would end up dead and because she was watching Alex with a voyeurism that surprised her. She saw Carol's screams, she saw their argument, she saw Alex slap Carol several times. Fran saw him leave. Without warning, she saw Carol brutalized and murdered.

Fran cried.

***

"We need to raise Alex's bail and we need to do it now," Fran said to Rick, Tom, Margo, and Toni in the conference room of the law office. It was late Monday night. Outside, the city's lights sparkled seductively.

Fran was still shaken from viewing the DVD and had just gotten off the phone with Alex's lawyer. Tom hovered near her as if expecting her to collapse.

"Why not use a bail bondsman? They only need ten percent." Rick twirled the dregs of his coffee around in a paper cup. He'd been on the streets all day and looked discouraged. He settled into the sofa next to Toni, who looked much the same as she had that morning – perhaps paler.

"Can't get one to touch it. Too much political heat," Fran said.

"From whom?" Margo asked, her fingers toying with a dangling, gold necklace. She leaned against the doorway where she could still hear the phone ring in the front office. Gone was the pink running outfit, and, in its place, she wore black, from her nearly hip -high boots to the short-cropped leather jacket over her straight skirt and camisole.

"Who do you think?" Rick countered. He decided to chuck the cup; he hit the trash can dead center.

"How much do we need?" Margo asked.

"Half a mil," Toni replied.

"Wish I could help," Margo said, "but I'm mortgaged up to my neck."

"I got some money saved up," said Toni.

"How much?" Fran asked without looking at the woman.

"About thirty thou," Toni told them.

Fran looked up. Even Tom did a double take.

Rick whistled. "On your salary? How the hell did ya do that?" He stared admiringly at her.

"Easy." Toni shrugged and untangled a lock of hair with her fingers. "I don't eat, I don't sleep, I don't date, and I put in a lot of overtime."

"I thought you were dating Tom?" Margo asked.

Everyone stared at her until she blushed.

"Sorrrrrrryyyyy," she drawled.

"Well, I can put in two hundred thousand," Fran said. Everyone stared at her. "It's what I have left. I spent the rest."

"Your ex-husband's money?" Brandt asked. "He'll appreciate that!"

"Yes. From the property settlement," Fran said.

"Why bother to work?" he asked.

"Because nothing lasts forever, Rick, not even money," Fran said, "and in the big scheme of things, two hundred thousand isn't that much. Besides, I get bored."

A woman's voice intruded. It floated on the air with the deep scent of musk. "I can make up the difference."

Fran turned to find Alex's favorite actress, Autumn Bartlett, standing in the doorway just behind Margo. Fran bristled and then reined in her instincts. For good or ill, the actress was Alex's ticket out of jail.

Son of a bitch!

Autumn casually slid by Margo and tossed her long auburn hair over her tanned shoulders. She was dressed in a clinging sweater that showed off her voluptuous figure. She had the height of a runway model. Full lips and emerald eyes completed the vision. One look and everyone believed the elevator story.

"You can barge in anytime," Margo said with a smile, only partially under her breath as she admired the woman's striking beauty. "I don't know if you remember me. Margo? I worked on your case." She offered her hand.

Fran shook her head in amazement as Autumn accepted it. Fran then glanced at Tom. He was very quiet, she noticed. Too quiet. Their eyes met a moment before she turned back to Autumn.

"You've got that kind of cash?" Toni asked impatiently.

"I've already called my accountant," said the actress. "The money will be waiting first thing in the morning."

"Just how much will Alex owe you then?" Fran asked, her voice dripping with contempt. She couldn't help it. She just had to say it. She cursed herself the minute the thought escaped her lips.

Autumn frowned. "He won't owe me a thing if he doesn't skip bail. Besides, the publicity alone is money in the bank."

"You're exploiting this?" Fran asked incredulously, her eyebrows going up.

Autumn just stared at Fran a minute. "You know, we need to have a

212

serious discussion someday."

"Fine," Toni interrupted as she stood up and stepped between the feuding women, "but not now. Let's get Alex out first. Then we can argue about who owes who what."

Fran drew in her claws and took a deep breath. "That's fine by me."

Autumn shed a warm smile on the others and said her goodbyes. "I'll be here as soon as the bank opens." She turned on her high heels and glided out of the office.

Margo stared at the actress as she left, the tip of her tongue protruding unconsciously through her teeth.

"Close your mouth, woman!" Rick snapped.

"Spoilsport!" Margo shot back.

Rick turned to Fran. "You're better than her," he said.

Fran shook her head and relaxed.

One by one they filed out of the room, leaving Fran alone with Tom.

"Nothing to add?" she asked as she leaned against the table.

"What's wrong?" He stepped closer and rested a hand on her arm.

"What's wrong? What do you think is wrong?" she snapped. "I've got Callas in jail and evidence he's an innocent man. I've got Elliott set for a deposition and I've barely had time to prep for that. I've got Alex being framed for murder. Anything else you had in mind?"

Tom nodded as if he was ready to accept her explanation, for now. He gently stroked her arm with his thumb. "You need sleep, Fran," he said softly.

"What I need is a stiff drink," she said, but the tone in his voice had seeped through her defenses. She leaned forward into the safety of his arms and wept.

CHAPTER 15

LATE MONDAY NIGHT

"Are we the only ones who care about the Callas case?" Tom leaned against the bar at Circus Circus and finished his beer. His elbow rested on a large brown envelope with no markings. He'd managed a few hours of sleep, found someone to cover for him for the day, and tracked down Rick.

Rick thumbed the poker chips in his pocket and tried the bourbon. "Maybe we should pass on that. Let another firm take it," Rick suggested. "We kinda got our hands full here."

Tom shook his head. He scratched absentmindedly on the bottle's label with his thumbnail. "Nope. Not good. No one's going to do for Callas what Alex is doing. It's a big one. It's hot, and it's ours."

"Ours?" Rick grinned at the slip.

"Yours. Whatever." Tom wasn't up to arguing.

"Alex ain't doing it. Least not anymore," Rick studied his drinking partner's face for a bit. "Okay, whatcha got?"

Tom looked up, his eyes floating for a moment over the chaotic atmosphere around him. Then he focused on Rick. "I got lab reports, DNA tests from the latest victim, an anonymous memo from that friend of Margo's, inside info from Candy, and copies of the crime photos." He slid the envelope in Rick's direction while looking him steadily in the eyes. "All confidential and you didn't get it from me."

Rick nodded and looked surprised. "And?" he encouraged without opening it.

"This isn't a copycat. This is the real thing," said Tom. "Fran should file a motion to dismiss as soon as possible and get that man out of jail."

"Randall will fight it." Rick lifted the envelope in his palm, mentally weighing it.

"I'm not so sure." Tom took another swig of his beer. It slid down his

215

throat like salve. "I've been watching him. He sides with political correctness, not with incompetence. He's given Elliott a lot of room to screw up. If he does, Randall is sufficiently distant to watch the man drown without counting the bubbles."

"He promoted him to set him up?" Rick asked.

It was a leap Tom hadn't taken, but he nodded, following Rick's logic. "The man's been a liability for some time. Makes sense."

"What about the DNA?" Rick asked. "If it's a match to the first victim, then...."

"Then the lab report generated in Callas' case is a phony. Exactly. Probably taken from Elliott's own samples."

"How would he know to use the real rapist's DNA?" Rick asked.

Tom looked up a minute. The impact of that statement rattled him. "Interesting question. Who's to say the DNA on either victim is the real one?"

"No idea who it belongs to, huh?"

"No known hits so far other than a match to whoever did Amelda Pena," said Tom. "I'm still waiting on results from the Emily Walkins case. If the DNA is the same, that alone should clear Callas. We need to get Fran focused on that, if only for 10 minutes."

"Why not have an independent lab do the DNA work?" Rick asked.

"That's your job. I work for the good guys, remember? I have to catch a serial predator who targets 12-year-old girls. You need to get Fran on this." Tom pointed to the envelope.

"Easier said than done," Rick noted. He continued to play with the chips. "Well, at least we'll have Alex bailed out tomorrow."

Tom grunted.

"You don't sound very happy," Rick noted.

"I'm beginning to seriously dislike that man," said Tom.

"Yeah, I know the feeling. Anything else?" Rick asked.

"Oh, yes." Tom pulled a second, smaller envelope from his jacket. Inside was a pin drive. "Do you remember what you and Toni were doing the night Alex was arrested?"

"Sure? She was being an ass, I was being nice, and…."

Tom gave him a warning look.

"We were following Roger Rabbit, why?" Rick asked.

"With Alex's camera," Tom reminded him. "The same camera Toni had with her when the police searched Alex's place. The same camera Toni brought back to the apartment. The same camera that produced these – the photos Smith sprung on the prosecution in court." He handed the envelope to Rick.

Rick's face brightened. He grinned.

Tom stood up and stretched.

"I thought you were off for the day," Rick said, still grinning.

"I live for these moments," Tom said sarcastically.

***

TUESDAY MORNING

Fran was relieved when Rick met their car in the garage of Turnberry Place early Tuesday morning. He was leaning against his Jeep. A splash of pink sunlight invaded the garage through the entrance. As Tom drove up, Rick dropped his cigarette butt to the concrete floor and flatten it with the heel of his black, alligator boot. He approached the driver's side of Tom's car as it rolled to a stop.

Tom opened his window and a blast of heat filled the vehicle. Fran, Autumn, and Toni stepped out of Tom's car. Fran was gripping Alex's camera.

"Is he here?" Toni was the first to ask.

"Upstairs with Margo, safe and sound. Went without a hitch," Rick told

217

her. He then turned to Tom when he realized the man wasn't getting out. "You're not staying?" Rick asked. "I think the ladies got an orgy planned." He gave Tom a wink.

"I've got a lead. I'm going to strike while the iron is hot, as they say," Tom responded.

"What lead?" Fran asked, approaching the men. She was still in her jeans and a light sweater, her hair pulled back tightly.

"If it works, I'll tell you," said Tom.

Fran was unhappy with the brush-off but too tired to argue. She glanced at the others. "Go on up. We'll be right there," she said.

Toni was already gone, and Autumn followed her to the elevator and out of sight.

Rick nodded to Tom. "Don't do anything I wouldn't do."

Tom grinned. "Or anything you would do." He waved at Fran and Rick as he drove off.

Rick took hold of Fran's elbow and steered her to the elevator. "How ya holding out, boss?" he asked.

"You seem to be asking that a lot these days," Fran commented.

Once inside the elevator, she slipped her arm through his. "As long as I got you to lean on, I'm fine."

He chuckled. "One of these days, boss," he said with a wink.

When Fran entered Alex's condo, she found the curtains closed and the phone off the hook. What had once been a familiar and welcoming landscape was suddenly foreign to her. She didn't know where to sit. She didn't know where to stand. She wanted to busy herself doing something, but she didn't know what. Images of the murder scene flipped through her thoughts as if displayed on an old stereoscope. She watched Alex ease himself into the sofa and look around. Toni sat curled up next to him, her arm through his. Rick hovered protectively nearby. Autumn disappeared into the kitchen. The atmosphere balanced somewhere between that of a welcome home party, a summit and a siege. Fran put the camera down on the kitchen counter.

"I don't know what to say," Alex began.

"Try thank you," Rick told him.

Alex smiled. "Thank you."

"Don't worry," Toni chimed in, leaning against Alex. "We'll fix this. We won't let that little whore or the cops set you up. I'm going to fix this. You'll see. I promise."

Fran shuddered, slipped behind the kitchen counter and pulled drinks out of the fridge. As the others talked, Autumn pulled out a platter and started making sandwiches, laying slices of roast beef on the bread and reaching around Fran for mustard and mayonnaise. At one point, Autumn leaned toward Fran and whispered, "Someone's got to straighten that girl out before she screws up this case, and I don't think Alex is going to do it."

"What do you mean?" Fran pulled a towel out of a drawer and wiped the condensation off the bottles.

"You heard her. She can't go around calling the victim a whore or saying the stuff she's saying without it getting back to the cops and the press and making Alex look worse. She's either got to shut up or get out of town. Something has to be done. You're the lawyer. You know how this works."

"She knows. I'm sure she knows," Fran argued. "She wouldn't say anything in public." Fran, her hands full of beer bottles, elbowed the refrigerator door closed.

"She's a loose cannon. We have to talk to her," Autumn insisted.

Fran stiffened, resenting the woman's intrusion. "I'll do it," she said as she set the drinks down.

"We can do it together. It'll make it easier," the actress said.

"Easier?" Fran kept her voice low. She was going to put up an argument but decided against it. "Okay. We'll talk to her together."

"Today."

Damn bitch, Fran thought. What she said was, "This is not a good time. She barely got him back. You see how she's taking this. She's...." Fran glanced at Toni. The detective looked strangely fragile as she clung to her brother. Fran forced her eyes away.

"This is the right time – and it may be the only time." Autumn poured a bag of chips into a bowl, grabbed a plate of sandwiches and headed back to the living room.

As Fran passed around drinks, Rick sat down on an ottoman, stretched his legs and took the lead. "I gave everything the once over. Fran and Tom checked out Carol's apartment." He nodded a thank-you to Fran as he grabbed a beer.

Margo jumped in. "I got copies of the coroner's report," she said, barely containing herself within the confines of her chair. "Still waiting on the DNA results."

"Carol's?" Rick asked, making sure they were on the same page.

"Uh-huh," Margo said as she nodded yes.

Autumn smiled at her. Margo beamed.

"This whole thing is fucked up," Rick continued. "There are so many inconsistencies in the evidence, I don't even know where to begin."

"Not that many," Alex said. He frowned at Rick.

Rick continued. "For starters, Carol never really moved into the house. She had so few possessions there that Fran asked Tom to check on her history in L.A."

"Nearly everything there was brand new – shampoo, toothpaste, that sort of thing," Fran said.

"Were her prints on them?" Rick asked.

Fran looked startled. "They were in the apartment. No one dusted them for prints. Why?"

"Maybe someone replaced them after she was dead; someone who didn't want his or her prints found for some reason," Rick explained.

"What did Tom find out?" Alex asked.

"She apparently left L.A. in a hurry, a big hurry," said Fran. "In fact, she was reported missing at first until she contacted the LAPD and told them she was alright. She just got in her car about four weeks ago and drove away without a suitcase and without a word to anyone."

"Sounds like an abusive boyfriend," Margo interjected.

"Sounds like her," Alex said at the same time. "She just drives to Las Vegas, walks into another job and moves into an apartment, just like that?" he asked.

"That's the good part," Rick interrupted. "Apparently, Max had the job waiting for her, and Randall set her up in the apartment."

"I heard," Alex noted with a grimace.

"And Max and her were...." Fran looked up at Alex to gauge his reaction, "...sleeping together."

Alex grunted softly and shook his head. He didn't seem to be surprised or to care.

"And she suddenly came into some money. Ten grand, to be exact, deposited over three different accounts in three different banks," Margo added.

"Of course, she was paid. I told you. She was a whore," Toni spat. "She was sick. Twisted. She had it coming."

Fran caught Autumn's eye.

The actress nodded and looked at Toni. "Hon, we need to talk."

"What's going on?" Alex asked, looking confused.

Toni drew her knees up to her chest. "What?" she asked, suddenly nervous. Her eyes darted back and forth between the two women.

"This case has taken on a life of its own," Autumn told her. "You know

221

that. The press is all over this and they're saying things about Alex that you probably don't want to hear, but you're going to hear them, whether you like it or not."

"This isn't any of your business," Toni said coldly.

"I know how much he means to you. I know how hard this must be with everything…. With your past and…. Well, knowing him like I do and…. What I'm trying to say is…."

"What are you doing here, anyway? Why did you come?" Toni turned to Alex. "She's not one of us. I don't want her here."

Autumn's words froze in her throat and she glanced at Alex for reassurance.

"Toni, she's only trying to help," Alex said. "Listen to her."

"Do you really want to save Alex's ass, or don't you?" Fran interjected impatiently. Her voice was hard as she spoke to Toni. "You can know what we know, when we know it, and work with us, or you can get out now. You might even consider leaving the state for a while. It would be easier on both of you. Either way, we'll respect your decision, but either way, you've got to keep your mouth shut."

Rick scowled.

Autumn and Alex both stared at Fran.

"Well, don't you think it would be best?" Fran asked them defensively. "She can't go around calling the murdered woman a whore, or a bitch, or whatever else comes to mind. She can't be running around getting into fights and causing trouble with the police department. She can't be spying on people. She can't be part of the investigation. We got our hands full. We can't afford to be worrying about what she's going to say next or do next." Fran faced Toni again. "Carol was the victim. She didn't ask to get murdered," Fran said bitterly. "She got used, by everyone, apparently. If anyone – police, press, anyone – hears you talking like that, it makes Alex look worse.

Understand? You may not have liked the woman, but she didn't ask to get killed."

"I know Alex didn't kill anyone." Toni came bounding out of the sofa in rage and stopped just short of plowing Fran over.

Rick stood up. He stepped partly between the two women.

"I know you know." Fran's head spun as her carefully directed conversation suddenly veered off course. "This isn't about that."

"We're not saying he did," added Autumn, "but the case looks bad, very bad."

"Shut up," Toni barked at Autumn.

"Talking like that only makes it worse," Fran said.

"Calm down, sweetie," Rick told Toni.

"You're not saying he didn't, either." Toni ignored Fran's comment.

"Alex was there that night," Fran said as if restating the obvious would somehow bring everything back in focus. She heard Alex shift uneasily on the sofa and she ignored him. "You already know that. They had dinner, they drove to her place, they showered together…," She shivered. "…then he tied her up with the extension cord and they had sex. After that…." Fran closed her eyes a moment, trying to drive the images from the DVD out of her mind. "It was consensual. They had history, but his DNA and fingerprints are all over her place, and that's all the D.A. needs to convict him." Her arms tightened around her chest.

"Bella." The tone of Alex's voice was a warning.

Rick, tense, moved closer to Toni.

Autumn hesitated a second before adding in a soft and sympathetic voice, "I'm sorry, Toni. I don't know how to fix this, how to make this easier for you." She looked to Alex. "Or you."

Toni's eyes flared. "What the hell is the matter with you two? You think I don't KNOW what went on? The bitch seduced him and set him up. Plain and

223

simple. I know it. You know it. The world needs to know it. What's your problem?"

"The problem is you can't say that! The problem is you have got to get yourself under control or you're going to make this worse, for everyone!" Fran barked.

"That's enough, Fran," Alex ordered. "Leave her alone."

Fran didn't look at him.

"Honey, I know you idolize Alex, but you need to understand his part in all this," Autumn said, resting her hand maternally on Toni's shoulder.

"Don't touch me!" Toni jerked away. "I know." She turned and glared at her brother. "I know what you do. I know who you do it with. I've always known. I KNOW!"

"Toni, please, stop," Alex pleaded.

"Bondage," Toni said, spitting out the word. "The bitch was a damn whore and she was into bondage. You think I didn't know that? Think I'm that naive? She seduced you. She set you up. She...." Toni choked on the words and her eyes spit fire. "Somebody has to tell them!" She waved her arm as if encompassing the entire world.

Fran looked helplessly at Rick. He wasn't happy.

Toni glared at Fran. "You think he killed her, don't you?" she asked, eyes darting from Fran to Autumn. "That's what you're saying. You think he's guilty and you want me to shut up."

"You don't have to be guilty to be convicted," Rick said quietly. He'd been holding back, waiting, watching.

"No, Toni. They're not saying that," Alex stated. He turned back to the women. "I told you two. Enough. Stop it."

"I know you'd never hurt anyone, at least not on purpose," Autumn said to Alex.

"Not by accident either!" Toni objected.

224

"With the charges against you and all the press, everyone is going to be speculating about it," Fran said, turning her attention to Alex. "They'll dig into your past. They'll drag up Sarah's murder. Randall still wants to pin that on you, too. You know that. He can't bury that bone. They're going to point out the similarities. They're even going to talk about what happened to your parents." She focused back on Toni. "You need to be aware. You need to be ready. You need to be strong, Toni. If you can't keep it together, then you need to get out."

Rick moved to Toni's side.

Toni looked like she was about to explode. "Leave me alone," she said emphatically. "It's not his fault. I know it's not his fault. I know he didn't kill her. You're idiots. Both of you. You don't know him like I do. You don't understand!" She stood up, ran into the bathroom, and slammed the door behind her.

"That went well," Autumn muttered sarcastically.

"She totally missed the point," Fran said.

"What did you expect?" Alex stated. "I warned you, Fran, right from the beginning. She can't handle this. I told you to stop. Both of you. What are you trying to do?"

"You could have gone easier on her," Autumn told Fran.

"I did go easy," Fran stated. "Or do you think I should have just told her that he did it?" The question was rhetorical. Autumn didn't answer. Alex stared at Fran.

"Will she be alright?" Autumn asked, glancing over her shoulder at the bathroom door.

"She hasn't been all right since this thing started," Rick said.

Margo was on her cell phone in a corner of the kitchen. She came out with a sullen look on her face. "They got the DNA results," she said, oblivious to the drama going on a few feet away. She didn't have to say

225

anything else.

"No surprises there," Alex said.

Fran nodded.

Toni found her way out of the bathroom and back into the group. "I don't feel good," she said, studiously avoiding Alex's eyes. "I'm going to go home and get some rest."

"I'll take you," Rick offered, slipping his arm around her shoulders. "You're going to need help getting through the vultures out there."

Toni nodded. They were half-way to the door when she stopped and looked back at Alex. "It's going to be okay, right? You can get out of this, can't you?"

"Yes, sis. It's going to be all right." Alex watched them slip out the door. His shoulders slumped.

"You probably need some rest, too," Fran said to Alex. She wanted out of there before he started yelling at her about Toni, again. "We can finish this later, now that you're home." She gave him a kiss on the cheek and left with Margo in tow. Only Autumn remained, her presence filling the now silent apartment.

She pulled away from him, creating a vacuum that seemed to suck him towards her. She moved to the window, drew back the curtain and looked out. Protected by the tinted glass, she was invisible to those below.

"If I were you, I wouldn't want to face the press either," Alex commented as he struggled to get up.

"They didn't see me come in," she said.

"But they'll see you go out." He moved closer to her and felt her tingling heat on his skin as he pressed his chest into her back. His chin rested on her head. His arms encircled her waist.

"They know who I am. In some strange way, this has actually been good for my career." She was trying to make light of the situation. "You know the

226

old adage: It doesn't matter what they say about you as long as they spell your name right."

"Did I thank you, yet?" Alex bent his head and tasted her neck.

She curled her arms over his, leaned back into him and smiled at their reflection in the glass. "You don't have to thank me. Just knowing you has been thanks enough." She looked down at the press. "How do you want me to handle this? Should I tell them I'm the cleaning lady?"

"It doesn't matter what you say, they'll spin it the way they want." Alex looked over her at the group below.

She smiled, turned and kissed him on the lips, then slipped out of his arms and out the door. He was alone for the first time in days. He licked his lips, still tasting her kiss, and slid the door to the terrace open a notch to spy on her and to hear what was being said.

When Autumn appeared on the front steps of the building, her sunglasses shielding her eyes and a security guard at her side, the press surrounded her.

"Miss Bartlett! Miss Bartlett!" They snapped photos of the dark beauty and threw questions at her as she stepped into the sunlight. "Did he do it? What's he like? What's your relationship with Alex de la Rosa? Is it true he was sleeping with four women at the same time? Is he your lover? Is the elevator story true? Did he murder the policewoman? Did he murder his wife? How well do you know him?"

Alex felt the rage coming back as he watched her smoothly work the press. He couldn't understand how people could be so cavalier about destroying a man's life. A part of him wanted to confront them, but he held back. He knew Autumn would do a better job at defending him than he could. Unseen, he scowled at them.

Posed at the top of the stairs, Autumn faced the news-hungry mob and offered up a seductive smile. "I have just one thing to say about Alessandro de la Rosa," she said, tossing her hair over her shoulder and slipping off her sunglasses. His name rolled gently off her tongue. She shielded her eyes against the sun with her hand. "He's the kindest, most decent man I know. He would never hurt another human being. These allegations have been completely trumped up by someone obviously obsessed with destroying Alessandro's political career, someone with an agenda and a thorough knowledge of the law. You want a story? That's your story. Go find out who is framing this man!"

Alex smiled. He'd said from the beginning that Elliott had set him up but, deep down, he didn't think the man was smart enough to pull this off. Still, Autumn had managed to toss a bouncing, red rubber ball in that direction, and the press would follow that ball like a happy puppy.

Making sure the doors were locked, Alex entered the darkened bedroom, put Diana Krall on the CD player, took some sleeping pills with a scotch chaser, removed his glasses and fell asleep in his own bed. He never wondered where the clean sheets had come from. He didn't even miss his cat.

CHAPTER 16

WEDNESDAY

Randall stood in the air-conditioned conference room, his hands buried deep in his pockets, a litter of newspaper clippings and magazine articles spread across the tabletop. He was waiting, glancing from time to time at the clock on the wall, swiping a tissue at his now raw nose and taking deep breaths to stay calm. His eyes moved to the door as the handle turned and Tom and Toni slouched in.

"About time you got here," Randall snapped. A heavy knot settled in his chest as he watched them. The cough medicine he'd taken earlier left him slightly dizzy and his mouth dry.

"Sorry, boss," Tom said, his coat slung over one shoulder in feigned nonchalance. "What's up?"

Toni sulked behind her partner. Her black hair was wet and pulled back tightly. Her mouth was clamped shut.

Both ignored the papers on the table.

"What the hell are these?" Randall asked, pressing the fingers of his large hand like paperweights on the articles. He didn't want to be here. He didn't want to have this discussion. The knot tightened. "Are you trying to destroy this department? Well? Are you?" He didn't wait for an answer. "Aiding a rapist and murderer. Conspiring with his accomplices. Obstructing justice." He looked at Toni. "Bailing him out of jail?"

"I didn't…." Tom began, flustered.

"Shut up." Randall interrupted. He almost felt sorry for the guy. Almost. "You're not stupid, Sadler. You have a good career here, a good track record. You're an honest, hardworking cop, but these days, if there's a pile of shit on the floor, you're going out of your way to step in it." Randall turned to Toni. "You work for the City of Las Vegas. You're a police detective, for god's sake, although how you ever passed the psychological is beyond me. You

229

want to tank your career? Fine. That's your business, but I won't let you take this department down with you."

Tom shuffled back and forth as if caged. Toni glared defiantly at the sheriff.

"You're an embarrassment to this department. Both of you. What do you have to say for yourselves?" Randall demanded to know.

Toni turned, stormed out of the room, and slammed the door behind her. Randall could feel the knot loosen a bit. He was hoping she would quit. He was hoping she'd move to Timbuktu. He was hoping he'd never have to see her again.

Tom stared after her, his mouth hanging open, before turning back to his boss. "You can't blame her, sheriff. It's her brother. She's caught in the middle."

"Exactly my point. We're all caught in the middle. What's your excuse?" Randall asked.

"I thought the prosecutor pulled the case from the department," Tom said. "Didn't he hire someone to investigate it out of his office? We're not on this, anyway."

Randall could hear the panic in the man's voice. "How'd you know?" Randall asked, then shook his head before Tom could answer. "Never mind. You gotta pull the damn shades to think around here. By now, the press has it too." His shoulders slumped. "Candy. He hired Candy Knight as a special investigator to prove to the world how fucked up this department is. How's that for a kick in the ass?"

"Sorry, boss," Tom said.

Randall couldn't tell if the detective meant it or not. "You're on suspension as of right now," Randall said. "I hate doing it, Sadler, but I got no choice. If I had replacements in the wings, you'd be fired, but I hate losing a good cop. As it is, you go anywhere near that perp or this case again and you can kiss

230

your job goodbye." Randall marched out the door. The news articles flew off the table behind him.

Tom flopped into a chair, buried his head in his hands and swore to himself.

When Randall emerged from the conference room, he found Toni pacing the hall floor. "My office. Now," he ordered.

"I'm waiting for Tom," she objected.

"Now."

He stepped back, making sure she was in front of him and herding her toward the office door. As they broke a path down the hall, staff members scattered out of their way. Once the door to Randall's office was shut, he plopped down in his squeaking seat and stared at her a full minute before interrogating her. For the life of him, he couldn't figure her out.

"Where the hell did you get a half-million dollars to bail that loser out of jail?" he demanded to know. "That's Max Simone's money, ain't it?"

"No." Toni stood in front of him, eyes glaring, arms crossed in front of her. "The mayor didn't have a damn thing to do with it. Alex would never allow that. Some of that money was mine."

"Some of it was yours?" Randall asked.

"Yes, mine. The rest was raised from friends. He does have friends, you know. People who know he's innocent."

"Who put up that money?" Randall asked again, leaning forward and trying to stare her down.

"That's none of your damn business," she said.

"If you got that money illegally…," he snapped.

"You think I would do that?" Toni yelled. "You fucking prick."

Randall rose menacingly to his feet. "You have a serious conflict of interest here." He wagged a finger at her. His jaw hurt, and he realized he was clenching his teeth.

231

"I have a conflict of interest? What about YOUR conflict of interest?"
Toni asked.

Randall froze. "You're out of line, detective."

"You dragged McEnroe here from L.A. The mayor snapped his
fingers…," Toni snapped hers. "…and you jumped. You gave her a job. Hell,
you put her up in a house. You don't think this whole damn department has a
conflict of interest?"

Randall's jaw locked. For a moment, the laughing face of Carol McEnroe
flooded his memory. He pushed it out, along with the wave of grief and guilt
that came with it. "It wasn't like that. I was helping the kid out. That's all. She
needed to get out of L.A. She needed a job."

Toni, studying the man's body language, suddenly laughed. "Shit. You
were screwing her, too. Is there anyone who wasn't sleeping with that
whore?"

"She is not – was not – It wasn't like that." The knot exploded.

Randall charged around his desk, grabbed Toni by the arms and shoved
her against the wall. His flushed face was an inch from hers. He could easily
have killed her. Easily. And if she had been Alex…. He realized what he was
doing and suddenly backed off, letting her go.

Furious, she slapped him hard across the face.

He covered the cheek with his hand and resisted the urge to hit her back.
"You're fired."

Randall watched as Toni stormed out of the office and straight into Tom.
She nearly knocked Tom over. He and a handful of others had been standing
in the corridor, listening to the fight. At the sight of Randall in the doorway,
they galloped away like startled sheep.

"You're going home," Tom said, grabbing Toni by the arm and pulling her
down the hallway and out of the building.

She didn't resist.

Randall shut the door and leaned back on his desk. "That murdering son of a bitch," he muttered under his breath. "You're gonna pay, you bastard. I'm gonna make you pay."

***

"Have you seen my cat?" Alex asked Toni as she entered his condo. She'd had some time to cool down, but not much. She bristled with tension.

"He's at my place." She crossed the room, looked out the window and watched Tom drive away. He'd refused to come up with her. "I see the vultures have thinned out," she said, referring to the media still camped out in the parking lot.

Alex nodded but he was watching her. In the glow of the setting sun, she seemed frail and tired. He reached over and rested his hand on her tense shoulder, turning her to look at him. When she didn't meet his eyes, he knew she was in trouble.

"What happened?" he asked.

"I got fired." She stuck her chin out defiantly. She didn't need to tell him more. She didn't want to tell him more.

"Because of me?" he asked.

She blinked back tears. "Yes - and no. Because I screamed at Randall and slapped him."

Alex chuckled. "Wish I could have seen that," he said, letting go of her. "How'd it happen? And I want all the gritty details." He headed to the kitchen to pour them some soda as she collapsed into his sofa with a heavy sigh.

"Well, first, that bastard said we couldn't be seen with you or we'd be fired. Then he tried interrogating me about the bail money. Wanted to know where it came from," she said.

"Why didn't you just tell him? He's going to find out anyway," Alex said.

She shrugged. "I didn't want to do him any favors. Anyway, then I called him a prick." She smiled a little, enjoying the memory.

233

"Go on," he said. He picked up the drinks and joined her.

"He said you got the bail money from illegal sources. I said he was screwing Carol." She looked up at Alex as she took the glass. He didn't react. He was standing there like a man who'd been sleepwalking for days.

"Was that it?" He asked.

She shook her head. "Then he fired me." Her voice was weak, and her hand went to her arm, rubbing it.

"Are you alright?" he asked.

"Yeah. I'm alright," she lied. She sipped on her drink and screwed up her nose. "Got anything to put in this?" she asked.

"You know better. I can't afford to have you go off the wagon on me." Alex paused, quiet a minute, thinking, until Toni shifted restlessly in her seat. "I wish there was something I could do," he said.

Toni put her drink down, stood up and went to him. "You're not going to do jack shit," she said sharply. "You so much as breathe wrong and you're back in jail and we all forfeit our money. I don't know about you, but I worked long and hard for that cash and...."

"You think it's true?" he asked her, unexpectedly.

"What?"

"Him and Carol? You think he slept with her?" Alex asked.

Toni frowned and shook her head. "How the hell would I know? He slept with me, didn't he? He didn't deny it. Besides, what do you care? She's gone." Just thinking about Carol McEnroe got Toni worked up again.

"You sure you're alright?" he asked.

She took a deep breath and nodded, forcing the tension out of her. "Yeah. I'm fine, really. Don't worry about me. Tom's picking me up in a few minutes. He had to run an errand. I just wanted to see you."

Alex reached over and squeezed his sister's hand. "Don't worry, sis. Everything will be fine. I'll take care of this. I promise."

"I thought it was my job to take care of you." She gave him a halfhearted grin.

Alex shook his head. "Not anymore."

***

"That's what you told her? Everything will be fine?" Fran asked. She was curled up on her sofa, wearing a terry robe and watching the late-night news. She cradled the phone between her shoulder and her ear as she painted her fingernails and listened to Alex rant.

"What was I supposed to tell her?" Alex asked. Back at his place, in sweatpants and a tank top, he stretched out on the sofa, a stiff drink in one hand and the phone in the other. "She's not as strong as you are, you know. I'm just glad she doesn't have to go back there. I called Rick. He's watching her back for me."

Fran shook her head. "You know, Alex, I'm not as strong as you think I am, either," she said quietly, half hoping he'd hear her, half hoping he wouldn't. She heard him groan and shift his weight in the sofa. "How are you holding up?" she asked.

"I feel like shit, but at least I'm not in jail," Alex said.

"For now," she reminded him. "You know, Rick could probably get you out of the country, send you somewhere with no extradition agreement. We'd all be out our life's savings, but…."

"Fran, stop it. I won't do that to you, to any of you," Alex said.

She sighed. "I just don't want you back in prison. Every time I think about it, I get sick to my stomach."

"Damn, girl. Don't remind me." He sat up and considered getting another drink. "Want to keep me company?" he asked. He had that hesitancy in his voice that always managed to surprise her.

Fran put down the nail polish and took hold of the phone. "Keep you company? What, like a sick aunt?"

"No." He almost laughed. "Like old times. Remember? Getting drunk. Watching old movies. Telling war stories. Fooling around." He made his way to the bar and poured another scotch.

She leaned back and sighed. "Oh, like THOSE old times," she said. "Those were not good times, Alex. You were a mess back then. Hell, I was a mess back then. Not good times."

"I'm a mess now, Bella," he said, "and I need you. Please? Promise I'll be good."

It was her turn to laugh. "Well, that would be a first," she joked.

"You could even bring Lauren." He was trying to soften her up.

"She's at Paul's. Tom filched her from me. He got her out of here before one more reporter called." She screwed the cap onto her polish. "Besides, there are some things she should never see, and us reliving old times is one of them."

"They're calling you, too?" he sounded worried.

"It's okay," she said. "I'm screening my calls." She blew softly on the wet polish.

"Then come over. Keep me company. I'll even make popcorn."

Fran smiled and gave in. "Okay. I'll be there in forty minutes, but I swear, Alex, if I get there and find that damn actress…."

He hung up before she could change her mind.

***

Rick knocked on Toni's door for nearly fifteen minutes before she answered it. She was wearing pajama pants and a tank top with no bra. Her eyes were bleary and bloodshot, her hair was mussed, and she smelled like the longneck beer that dangled precariously from her fingers. "What are you doing here?" she asked, her voice slurred.

Rick frowned, looking worried. "Can I come in?" he asked.

She shrugged her shoulders and threw back the door.

She had somehow managed to fill the sink with dirty dishes and more beer bottles since his last visit. The dirty laundry was piled where he'd left it. Books and papers had multiplied in his absence. Curled up in the middle of the round kitchen table, as if he was afraid to step on the littered floor, was Black Velvet.

"Are you alright?" Rick asked, glancing around at the mess. "Tom told me what happened."

A bitter laugh escaped her lips. "Alright? You goddamn self-righteous bastard."

Startled, he stared at her. She took another swig and leaned precariously against the kitchen counter.

"I just came to check on you," he said, standing in the middle of the room, hands in his pockets. She hadn't offered him a seat and he wasn't sure she wanted him to stay.

"Do I look alright to you? Huh?" She staggered towards him.

Rick grabbed her arm to steady her, but she yanked it away.

"You're not the one whose whole goddamn life just got flushed down the toilet," she said. "You smug son of a bitch."

She lunged for him and nearly fell, but Rick caught her easily, put her beer on the table, picked her up and dropped her into the bed.

"Toni, let me help you," he said, pinning her shoulders to the bed when she struggled to get up.

"The fuckin' blind leading the fuckin' blind," she yelled, sobbing and trying to shove him off her, but his powerful arms wouldn't let her go.

His head hung down sadly and he spoke softly to her. "I'm an addict. I know," he said. "I gamble. You drink. Different party, same dance. That's why I'm here. I'm your friend. You've been my friend, now I'm here for you."

She seemed so fragile, not the feisty, wild woman who tried to beat up Tom Sadler in the office parking lot. She was crushed. Every instinct Rick had wanted to rescue her; every ounce of logic told him he couldn't.

"Did Alex send you to babysit me? Did he? Bastard. Get out. Get out. I want to be alone."

She tried to swing at him, but he caught her wrists and held them to her side. His face was inches from hers.

"I'm not leaving you, Toni, not like this," he said.

"Why? I've lost him. I've lost everything. I've lost Alex, my family, my job, my career, even Tom, all over some shit-faced whore. And what have I got to show for it? What? They'll send him to jail for life or worse. It's all my fault. Damn it, Rick, it's all my fault!" She sobbed.

"You haven't lost me," he said. "You idolize Alex and you shouldn't do that."

"Don't tell me what I should do," she snapped. "He's my baby brother. I'm supposed to take care of him. That's the one thing I'm supposed to do. The one thing, and I failed him."

"Stop it!" Rick yelled back.

"I fucked it up. Don't you see? It's all my fault."

"Alex is just a man. He's a smart son of a bitch, but he's no different than me, or Tom, or anyone else, but you see him differently. All you see is the kid brother you have to protect, not the man he really is. Open your eyes, Toni. You can't go on like this."

She stared at Rick as if he was a stranger.

"I'm your friend. I care about you," Rick said. "I can't just sit by and let you do this to yourself. It's got to stop. It's all got to stop."

She collapsed under his hands. When he let go, she curled up into a ball.

Rick gathered her in his arms and held her until she cried herself to sleep.

***

The night air chilled Fran's cheeks as she stepped out of the security of her apartment building. She pulled up the hood on her sweatshirt to hide her

238

flowing red hair. Her eyes darted down the street, watching for the watchers. Hoping to avoid detection from stray reporters, she left the distinctive Mercedes coupe sitting in the garage as she jogged to the bus stop. Two strangers joined her on the corner, huddled against the cool night air, drawn into themselves, and avoiding eye contact. Fran breathed a little easier but kept her eyes on the ground.

She was still looking down when she boarded the bus and dropped her change into the box. It clattered to the bottom. The driver passed her a transfer without looking at her. Fran moved towards the back of the bus, sidestepping a wad of chewing gum and some unrecognizable sticky substance. The air was bitter with the smell of diesel and the plastic seats were stained from years of hard use.

On the floor, beneath the seat in front of her, the remnants of the daily news flickered in the passing streetlights like an old silent movie. The Cubs had beaten the Nationals. Mayor Max Simone had announced the formation of a task force to deal with the increase in violent crimes in the city in response to the McEnroe murder. Murder suspect Alessandro de la Rosa had been released on bail.

Fran stared at the photo, which captured Alex leaving the detention center. She sunk lower into the seat and pulled the hood closer around her face. She was relieved to finally get off unnoticed near Turnberry Place.

A few straggling reporters were still camped in the parking lot. They sipped hot coffee and shared the recent celebrity gossip, as they glanced from time to time at the fourth-floor window, where heavy drapes and tinted glass blocked out the light from Alex's condo. Fran jogged casually past them, her heart pounding in her throat, her eyes straight ahead. She turned the corner and disappeared around the back of the building without drawing their attention, then she slipped behind some vehicles and into an employee entrance. As the heavy metal door slammed shut behind her, the security

239

guard, a cup of steaming black coffee in hand, looked up from the sports pages of his newspaper. Fran threw back her hood.

"Miss Simone," he said, recognizing her with a smile. "Headed up?"

"Yes, Matt. Can I use the service elevator? The vultures are out front," she told him.

"Sure thing." He set his mug down, got up and led the way. He opened the elevator with one of the many keys clanking on his belt and pressed the button for the fourth floor.

"There you go, ma'am," he said, holding the door open for her. "Good luck." He gave her a small wink.

"Thanks," Fran said, leaning against the back wall as the mirrored doors slid closed in front of her. In the graying, fluorescent light, her ghostly reflection peered back - pale, exhausted, with dark circles under the eyes. Fran dropped her gaze to the floor, wishing she'd brought her make-up.

When the doors opened, she glanced nervously up and down the quiet, carpeted hall, making sure she was alone before finding Alex's door and softly knocking.

He was waiting for her. He was still in his sweatpants and tee-shirt, his hair a mess and a drink in his hand. He staggered to the door, opened it, and startled Fran by immediately pulling her into his arms. Assailed by the thick odor of scotch and cigars, she caught the glass before he dropped it. The door slammed shut.

"Bella, Bella," he slurred, draping himself over her for support. "I'm so sorry. So sorry."

For the first time since Carol's murder, they were alone. Fran wrapped an arm around him and held on, feeling the bandages where his ribs had been cracked and noting he needed a shower. "It's alright, Alex. It's alright," Fran said, resting her hand on his chest. "I'm going to fix this. I promise. I'm going to fix this." She realized she sounded like him and Rick and Tom. They

240

were all repeating the same mantra.

He pulled away slightly, swaying on his feet, his swollen and bloodshot dark eyes peering into hers. "Oh, Bella, honey, sweetheart," he said, the alcohol on his hot breath burning her cheeks. "I love you, you know? You know I love you."

"Yes, Alex, I know," she sighed, hearing the alcohol talking. "I promise...."

He planted two shaky fingers on her lips to hush her. "Bella, don't, honey. Don't make promises you – can – you – can't – keep."

He staggered backward, and she grabbed his arm, steering him towards the sofa, where he collapsed. She set the glass down on the end table and knelt in front of him as he buried his face in his hands. She ran her fingers through his thick hair, carefully avoiding the fresh bruise and remembering the damaging disc and Max's hold on her. 'I can make this mess go away,' he had said. 'Or I can make it a whole lot worse.' All she had to do was surrender to Max and Alex would be free.... maybe, if she could trust Max, which she didn't. And if it wouldn't cost too much. And it would. Alex would never forgive her. She would never forgive herself.

Fran grasped Alex's hand in hers. "I'm not going to lose you," she said.

"I love you, Bella," he mumbled again, leaning back into the sofa and fighting to keep his eyes opened.

"I know. I know. Every time you're drunk, you love me," she said.

His face twisted in agony as deep sobs wracked his body. "Why?" he cried. "Why did she want to leave me? Oh, god, Bella, I still love her. I still need her. I can't do this without her."

Tears threatened to burn through Fran's eyes as memories of Sarah boiled to the surface. "I'm going to make you some coffee, okay?" Fran patted his hand and pulled away from him. "We'll eat popcorn and watch movies, just like the old days, and everything will be alright."

241

"Popcorn. I made popcorn," Alex said, struggling to focus his thoughts.

"Where?" Fran stood up and headed for the spotless kitchen; she glanced around.

"In that thingamabob," he said, his hand shaking as he tried to point at some obscure place in the distance. "You know, that popcorn cooking thing." He grasped the edge of his shirt and pulled it up to wipe his face.

Fran opened the microwave and found a flat, hard bag of popcorn in it, uncooked. She set the machine on high for four minutes and tried to wipe the fatigue from her eyes. A thud drew her attention back to the living room.

"Bella," Alex called weakly.

She found him flat on the floor in front of the sofa.

"I fell down," he said. He dropped his head to the carpet and passed out.

Fran shook her head and sighed. As she watched him, looking so incongruously sweet and innocent, the images from the DVD played over and over in her mind until the beeping microwave dragged her back to the present. The popcorn had burned.

CHAPTER 17

THURSDAY

Rick awoke to a hangover and the smell of bacon and eggs. He couldn't remember where he was. He stretched, stiff from sleeping curled up around Toni. She was gone. Sitting up and looking around, he saw her standing at the stove, scrambling eggs in an iron skillet. Memories broke through his headache.

Her long dark hair was wet, and she was dressed in a short, faded, yellow terry cloth robe. For a second he admired her silky legs, then cleared his throat. She glanced back and smiled at him, tucking her hair behind one ear.

"Bacon?" he asked, rubbing the sleep from his eyes and trying to find a clock. "You didn't have to do that. What time is it?" He slid his legs off the bed and put on his shoes. He was still wearing his pants, but he'd lost his shirt sometime during the night.

"Almost eight. You need to get to work." She scraped the food onto a plate, turned off the stove, shooed the cat off the dining room table and wiped it down before setting it for breakfast.

"Where's the clock?" he asked, standing up and looking around.

Reading his look, she pointed towards the bathroom door. "I don't use a clock. Go wash up."

"Then how do you know what time it is?" he asked, heading for the bathroom.

She shrugged. "I just know."

Toni had hot coffee, juice and a bottle of Ibuprofen waiting for him when he came out.

"You really didn't have to do all this." Rick took a seat and admired her handiwork. His stomach was growling with hunger and he needed the caffeine for his headache, but a handful of pills went down first. She handed him his shirt and he slipped it over his head.

She stood tall and stared at him indignantly. "How many times have you been to my apartment?"

He frowned, somewhat embarrassed. "I don't know. Three, four times?"

"That makes you company. I cook for company. Now eat."

"Bossy little bitch, aren't you?" he asked with a smirk.

She gave him a gentle cuff on the back of the head and went back to the kitchen area to pour herself a cup of coffee.

Rick gave her a wary look. "You're not having any?" he asked, noting only one plate of food on the table.

"I ate already." She set her cup down and began cleaning up the pile of dishes, rinsing and stacking before filling the sink with hot soapy water.

Rick ate hungrily while keeping an eye on her. He couldn't stop wondering what she was wearing under that robe. It occurred to him that this wasn't what Alex meant when he'd told Rick to watch her back.

"Need some help?" he asked, bringing her his dishes when he'd finished. He felt uncomfortable in her place, like he was too big for it and would knock something over if he turned around. Or step on something, maybe. He noticed the cat kept his distance.

"When I need help, I'll ask for it," she snapped. Her eyes met his and her tone instantly changed. "Besides, it's not like I got anything else to do today. I got fired, remember?"

She slumped against the sink, a dishtowel wrapped around one hand, the wet strands of her hair falling into her face.

He rested a warm hand on the back of her neck and nodded. "We still have the Callas case. With Alex out of the picture, you could help me with that," he offered.

She closed her eyes and let out a soft sigh.

He brushed the strand of wet hair back from her cheek and pulled her into an embrace. She melted into his arms and buried her face in his strong chest.

244

"Why didn't you hold me like this before? Before all this shit happened? Before...." Toni asked, her eyes closed, her arms wrapped tightly around him for support.

He frowned, thinking. "Because you're Alex's sister," he said. "Besides, you and Tom...."

She looked up at him and rolled her eyes. "I never went out with Tom. How many times do I have to tell people that? I never took you for a coward, either," she snapped. A moment of silence followed between them before she continued. "You'd better get to work." Her fingers drifted over the tattoo on his neck.

"I know." He didn't let go. His eyes were drawn to hers with the force of gravity. It seemed the harder he tried to pull away, the more he was sucked in until his lips landed hard on hers.

Toni pushed away and stared up at him a moment before slipping her arms around his neck and pulling him into a long, deep kiss. He was more than willing, yet, as he absorbed her body heat through the robe, he knew the clock was ticking. This wasn't the time. He finally pulled back, drunk on the smell of her and nervously licking his lips.

"Call me if you need me," he said as he headed for the door.

"Rick?" She softly called his name just as he opened the door; he turned part way around to look at her. "I need you," she said with a smirk.

Rick grew warm under her gaze. Resisting the urge to smile, he grunted, "I'll be back." He barely escaped.

***

Fran awoke on the sofa in Alex's apartment, still wearing her jogging suit and covered in a soft, warm blanket. Fingers of sunlight poked through gaps in the curtains. She reached down to the floor. The spot where he'd passed out was empty. She looked around the room but didn't see him. Getting up, she tiptoed to his bedroom and found him stretched out on his bed and softly

245

snoring, an open bottle of painkillers still in his hand. Quietly closing the door, she went to the bathroom to clean up, then she started breakfast.

Alex woke up a few minutes later. His nose followed the aroma of her cooking. "What are you doing?" he asked, coming up behind her and eying her curiously. He was rumpled, groggy and still in a tee-shirt and boxers.

"Hold still," she said. Fran took a tissue and carefully wiped away the sleepy seeds from the edges of his eyes. "There, that's better." She turned back to the stove. "I'm hungry. Want some?"

Sober and stunned from the unexpected display of intimacy, he didn't have time to respond before she spoon-fed him a taste of her omelet.

"Mmmm. That's good. How did you do that?" he asked, licking his lips and smiling.

"Magic," she said. "I used the leftovers from your welcome home party."

"Potato chips?" he asked.

"No. Beer and French onion dip." She rolled her eyes.

"Smartass," he said, smacking her lightly on the butt. Digging a clean fork out of the drawer, he scooped out a bite of omelet and put it to her lips. "Turnabout is fair play," he said.

She closed her eyes, opened her mouth and took a bite. For that moment, her life seemed normal and sweet. Then she opened her eyes again and knew better. She tried to ignore the knot in her stomach.

"Mmmm. Not bad," she said, licking her lips. "I should really do this more often." She turned back to the stove.

"Do what?" he asked.

"Cook. Have a normal life."

Alex leaned against the counter and watched her as she continued her work. He was smiling to himself.

"Something funny?" she finally asked, giving him a cursory glance.

"I just never thought I'd see you in this context," he said, his eyes roving her body. She was still in her sweats, her hair was tumbled and unruly about her face, and she wasn't wearing any make-up. "You look sexy."

"You think just because I'm a brain and I work all hours of the day and night that I don't know how to cook?" She pretended to be insulted, but she felt a slight flush at the base of her neck.

"I'm sure you can do anything you put your mind to," he answered softly.

She heard the tenderness in his voice and looked at him, wondering how much she should read into that comment. He hurriedly turned to avoid eye contact and started collecting silverware and glasses. Fran dished breakfast onto a couple of plates and carried them to the table.

"Where do you usually sit?" she asked, holding the plates and trying to break the unexpected tension between them.

"What?" he asked in confusion.

"Everyone has a place at the table where he or she usually sits. Where do you usually sit?" she asked again.

"I don't know." He looked down at the table. "Well," he said. "Let's see." He tried one chair, moved it around a bit, shook his head and got up and tried a second chair, deliberately antagonizing her. Fran patiently held the plates as he shook his head and tried a third chair. By now, she was ready to heave the plate at him. He didn't seem sure, so he tried the fourth chair, just to check it out. Shaking his head, he went back to the third chair and smiled. "This one," he said.

"Are you sure, Goldilocks?" she asked.

"I'm sure," he said with a broad grin.

She set the plate down in front of him.

"You know it's all your fault, don't you?" he asked, taking his first bite. A small moan escaped as he savored the food.

Fran sat down in the chair next to him, picked up her fork and glared. "What's all my fault?"

"The chair thing. I never really thought about it before. If you had just set the food down, I probably would have sat down wherever it was." He continued to eat, pretending not to notice her irritation.

He probably would have, she thought. *Now, who's the smartass?*

"You can do the dishes," she told him, finally giving in to her own hunger. They both began to laugh.

"Fran, you are one of a kind," he said, reaching across the table and squeezing her hand. Their eyes locked and the laughter stopped. Alex looked down at their hands joined together. "You were right," he said, nervously swallowing the surfacing emotions.

"About what?" she asked, playing innocent.

He gently rubbed her hand and his eyes met hers. "It should have been you." He paused. "When I lost Sarah, when all hell broke loose, when I needed someone, I should have come to you."

She was silent a few seconds, absorbing his admission, trying to ignore the flutter in her heart. "Why didn't you tell me what you were going through?" she asked, dodging the obvious bait. "I could have helped. You didn't have to go to anyone else." She didn't have to say Autumn's name. Or Carol's.

His fingers slipped out of hers. His eyes fell back to his plate. He pulled away and began playing with his food. "I couldn't. You had problems of your own. You didn't need mine."

"Your problems were my problems," she said. "Sarah was your wife and my best friend. We could have faced it together."

"Autumn is different. I can talk to her differently." He shrugged. "Do things with her that I wouldn't dare do with you. She understands how I am, what makes me tick, and I couldn't explain that to you, even if I'd wanted to." He was embarrassed and avoiding her eyes as he picked at his breakfast.

"Yes, you could have," she countered. "Besides, I found out anyway and

I'm still here, right?"

"I wanted to tell you."

"About the bondage? Or about the women you were sleeping with?"

He nodded. "Both."

"But?"

"I didn't want to lose your respect." He smirked as if trying to lighten the moment with a bad joke.

"Bullshit."

He shrugged.

"And you had to tell someone."

He swallowed hard, trying to find the right words and failing. "I also told Carol," he said. He looked up sheepishly.

Tension and heat rose up Fran's neck. "About Autumn?"

"No, about the other stuff – the bondage, the BDSM, the lifestyle. I told her back then, five years ago. I didn't even know Autumn, yet. I had these feelings and I didn't know what to do with them, so I thought—"

"Excuse me? You found it easier to talk to Carol than to talk to me?" Fran was furious and nearly yelling.

Alex shrunk under her glare. "There's a difference," he tried to explain.

"I certainly hope so," said Fran, dropping her fork on the table. "I'm your best friend and she was, what? A quick affair? A one-night stand?"

"That's just the point," Alex said. "With her, it was just sex, and she was into it. With you…."

Fran frowned, trying to make sense out of what he was saying. "If we'd had sex, would you have been able to talk to me then?" she demanded to know.

Alex, flustered, got up from the table. "I can't talk about this. Not with you," he said, picking up his dishes and dropping them in the sink. "I'm sorry. I just can't." He gripped the edge of the counter and silently counted to ten.

249

"You don't want to know me, not the real me. You could never accept what I am, what I do."

"What you DO got you accused of murder! If you hadn't tied her up, if you hadn't left her there, if you hadn't...." She stopped and caught her breath.

"You're a self-righteous bitch," he said softly.

"I gotta get home. I'll call later," Fran snapped. She pushed her chair back and stood up quickly, grabbed her purse and headed for the door. She had barely seized the doorknob when he stopped her.

"Fran," he called out.

She turned around angrily, but her heart nearly broke when she saw the look of devastation on his face.

"Don't go." His words formed a plea.

Reluctantly dropping her things, she slowly approached him and gently placed her palm on his chest. He took a deep breath, sensitive to the warmth of her touch.

"Then talk to me," she said.

"Will you still respect me in the morning?" he asked, resorting to cockiness.

"Alex—" There was a warning in her voice.

Covering her hand with his own, he asked, "Where do you want me to begin?"

"Anywhere."

He closed his eyes a second, uncovering a memory. "Do you remember when Sarah said she needed to get away and you convinced me to start spending more time with her?" he asked.

"Is that who you want to talk about now? Sarah?" she asked, drawing closer, her eyes searching his, noting the slight nervous twitch of his lips.

"I was madly in love with her. You know that. She was everything to me," he said.

250

"So far, so good," she encouraged. She wondered if they should be sitting down for this.

"Then I found out— I found out about him—" He winced.

Fran closed her eyes and took a deep breath as the memory hit her square in the heart. "How?" she finally asked.

"It doesn't matter, now. She was going to leave me. I knew that. And I knew you knew, but you never said anything."

"No, she wasn't."

"She was having an affair. She wanted to TALK. I could see what was coming. That's why I was avoiding her."

"She was *not* having an affair," Fran said. "She had a friend. A married friend. Someone she could confide in. You know, someone she could talk to. What made you think she was having an affair, anyway?"

"Well, Toni. She saw them together and...."

"They were friends. That's all. She was at the end of her rope, Alex." She pulled away, feeling the need to defend Sarah. "She really did love you, you know," Fran said. "She just couldn't bear being alone so much. It ate at her, like cancer in her heart. She needed attention. I told you. She needed you."

"And I thought we were going to make it. I really did. I was trying. And then—" He let go of her hand and walked swiftly towards the window of the living room, throwing the curtains back to let in the sun. The tinted glass made him invisible to anyone in the parking lot below. "I never found out who he was," Alex said, "but I had suspicions. And I thought maybe he was the one who killed her." He looked back at her, waiting for her to tell him, but she didn't.

Fran came up behind him and rested her hand on his arm, feeling the warmth and strength there. "Why didn't you tell me?"

"Because you should have told me. Because that's what friends do."

Trust. Nasty business, Fran thought. Fragile trust. Shattered as easily as

251

Humpty Dumpty and just as impossible to glue back together.

"After that, things got weird. I didn't want anyone to know, not even you."
He winced. "Now, everyone knows."

"No. They're only speculating. The only ones who know are Autumn and
me, and now Toni."

"She's angry with me," he said, meeting her eyes.

Fran nodded.

"She's not as strong as you are, you know," he added.

"She's a hell of a lot stronger than you think she is." Fran turned to look
out the window.

"I mean it. She's not. You don't know her. All that talk-tough stuff and
carrying a gun, it's her way of compensating. It's how she copes. But here,"
he pointed to his heart, "inside, she's very fragile."

Fran's eyes narrowed. "You want me to talk to her again?" she asked,
glancing back at him over her shoulder.

Alex nodded towards the reporters camped out below his window. "Don't
they have anything better to do?" he asked.

Realizing she wasn't going to get an answer from him, Fran picked up her
purse. "It's late and I need to be in court today."

"Just a few more minutes," he pleaded. "It's so quiet up here in the
morning."

She frowned. She had been reassessing her opinions of both Alex and
Toni the last few days. She wondered how she could have known them both
so long and still not known either of them at all.

***

"I tried to stop him!" Margo yelled, jumping up from her seat and coming
around the desk as Fran charged into the law office.

"Who?" Fran demanded to know, dumping her briefcase on the chair. She
was dressed for court and gripping a manila envelope tight enough to tear it

with her fingernails.

"In Alex's——" Margo never got to finish.

Fran crashed into the office and threw the envelope down on the desk. "What the hell is this?" she asked.

Tom was in Alex's chair, leaning back, his booted feet on the desk and his hands tucked comfortably behind his head. "I tried to warn you," he started to explain.

Fran grabbed his feet and unceremoniously shoved them to the floor, nearly toppling him out of the chair.

"You said this was a hot case. You said everyone would be watching it. You NEVER said they'd be watching ME." She glared at him as she dumped the 8 x 11 photos out of the envelope. They showed her coming and going from Turnberry Place, dressed in her sweat suit, jogging through the parking lot and getting on the bus.

"You weren't listening, Fran," Tom argued, sitting up and growing irritated. "You never listen. Alex is a murder suspect. He's accused of raping and killing a cop. Everything he does and everyone he sees is under surveillance. What did you expect? Kid gloves? You should feel damn lucky I bothered to let you know."

"You've got to stop this," Fran countered.

Tom was on his feet, his face flushed. "Then stop sleeping with him!" he yelled.

Fran's eyes went wide, and the words froze in her throat. Tom grabbed his jacket and headed for the door, but she intercepted him, roughly shoving him back into the desk.

"That's what this is about? You're jealous?" she asked, shocked.

"No...." He started to object.

"Now, you listen here, Tom," she said, "I have never – NEVER – had sex with Alex."

"Bullshit." Tom retorted. "I saw how you were all weepy over him, hanging onto his every word. I'm not blind and I'm not stupid, Fran. I know you're in love with him."

"I don't give a shit what you think you know. I NEVER slept with him," Fran yelled.

They both stared at each other for a few minutes, letting their tempers cool. Fran picked up the photos and slapped them into Tom's chest. He took them without looking at them.

"Maybe you're used to people lying to you. Maybe you lie to me. Maybe you arc having an affair with Toni and you're just denying it like the scumbag you are. I don't know, and I don't care. It doesn't matter. Max is playing you," Fran said. "He set Alex up and he's using you to tear us apart."

"For the last time, there's nothing between Toni and I and— Damn it, Fran. Don't you think I know what I'm talking about? I got my hands full just with the Callas case, something you seem to be neglecting, by the way. Plus, I'm running interference for you. I'm trying to do you a favor. And whether you like it or not, Max is the mayor of this city and I'm already on the department's shit list."

"Max Simone is a fucking son of a bitch who is capable of anything," she growled.

"Can you prove it?" Tom asked.

"No—Yes— Maybe," Fran stammered, her gaze faltering.

Tom's eyebrows went up. "You're that sure?" he asked. He saw the sudden fear in her eyes.

Fran took a deep breath and closed the office door before turning to face him. "Sit down," she said, indicating the sofa. "There." She wanted him away from Alex's chair.

Looking skeptical, Tom obliged. Fran leaned against the desk, her arms crossed in front of her. For a moment, she collected her thoughts, trying to decide where to begin, how much to tell and what to leave out.

"I was summoned to Max's office," she said, taking a second to brush her bangs back with her fingers.

"I heard." Tom leaned forward, elbows on his knees. He clasped the photos and waited patiently. His hazel eyes targeted hers.

She was surprised that she was surprised.

"I know he set Alex up." She looked defeated, growing uncomfortably hot under his stare.

"He admitted it?" Tom asked.

"Well, he didn't come right out and say it, no."

"Then...."

"He showed me a disc, a DVD, of that night...." A surge of panic gripped her.

Tom paled. His mouth twitched. "He has Alex and Carol on....? Where did he....? How did he....?" He stopped.

"Yes. Having sex. That's all," Fran finished for him. "He played a part of it for me." She blushed. "I asked how he got it. He said Carol recorded all her encounters, but he wouldn't tell me who gave it to him. Elliott is my guess. First on the scene, right? Max said—" Fran stopped a moment. A lump had formed in her throat and she pressed her fingers to her temples, warding off a tension headache.

"It's evidence, Fran. You knew about it and you didn't tell me. You expect me to trust you, to work with you, to help you, and then you screw me over by withholding evidence."

"I don't have it. Max does," she lied.

"But you should have told me," he argued. "You had a duty to tell me."

Fran leaned forward. "I have a duty to disclose evidence I'm going to use in court to the prosecutor. That's all the duty I have. Period."

"Is it? You're an officer of the court, Fran. You're sitting on a smoking

255

gun. Worse, you know this loaded gun MIGHT clear your client, and you are STILL sitting on it. What in the world are you thinking?" Tom stared at her with a look of astonishment.

"How many times do I have to tell you, I don't have it! Max does. You want to give me a lecture on ethics, fine. But not now. Max said-"

The office phone rang. She jumped but didn't answer it. It stopped after two rings, and she knew Margo had gotten it.

"Max said?" Tom pressed, rocking nervously on the edge of the sofa and trying not to stand up and shake her. "What did he say?"

"He said he could make this all go away or make it a whole lot worse."

Tom's mouth was dry. He swallowed hard. "What else was on the disc?" he asked.

She shook her head. "I didn't get to see it all," she lied, "but from what Max said, there's enough to prove Alex didn't kill her." At least that part was true. Almost.

Tom's eyes narrowed as he looked up at Fran. "Does it prove who did?" he asked quietly.

Startled, Fran's eyes widened at the dreaded question and she stared back at him. "I didn't ask."

"Why?"

"I don't know." She scrambled for an excuse. "I guess I was so shocked. So scared—"

"No," he interrupted, "I mean, why did he do it? The mayor? Why would he set up Alex?"

Fran bit her lip. Turning away from him, she walked to the oversized, arched window and looked down on the sunlit parking lot below. This all began with a rainstorm, she recalled— puddles of water, a power outage, lightning, and thunder — a freak of nature in the middle of the desert, like Max.

"Fran?" Tom asked, getting up to join her. He stood behind her and gently rested his hands on her shoulders.

Fran shivered and pulled away. She closed her eyes and forced her voice to stay calm, feeling the warm sun on her face. "Politics," she said. It was only a half-lie. "He wants Alex out of the mayor's race." She couldn't bring herself to tell him the only other reason she knew.

"That doesn't add up, Fran," Tom said. "Level with me."

Fran turned to face him. "What are you talking about? What doesn't?"

Tom leaned back against the edge of Alex's desk. "Okay, let's say you're right. The mayor wants Alex out of the race, something he could have easily done without resorting to murder."

"Max didn't resort to murder. He just.... He just got lucky, that's all."

"Wait. You just said he set Alex up."

"Set up the encounter, yes. To get dirt on Alex. To blackmail him. Something like that. But he didn't plan on the murder. I'm sure of that." She sighed. "At least I think I'm sure of that." She lowered her head a moment and shut her eyes. "At least as sure as I am about anything these days."

"Well, what about Sheriff Randall? And Elliott? You think they'd set up Alex for murder just so Max could stay mayor? That doesn't make sense, either."

Fran shook her head, following his argument. "Max probably has them on his payroll," she said.

"Of course, he does, Fran. He's the goddamn mayor, but...."

"What then?" she asked. She stared at him defiantly, daring him to come up with a better reason and afraid he just might.

Tom studied her a minute. "How much do you know about Sarah's murder?" he asked.

"I was there, remember? I called the police."

"And you saw the body?"

257

"Yes." She got a cold chill and turned to look back out the window again, seeking the warmth to drive the memory away. A sickening tension knotted her stomach.

"You know Randall is convinced Alex murdered Sarah, right?"

Tears burned the back of Fran's eyes. "I don't give a shit what Randall thinks. I know Alex didn't do it. He loved her. He still loves her. There isn't a day that goes by that he doesn't feel—"

"Guilty?" Tom supplied.

Now she was angry. "He didn't kill her. You know that, Tom. You know that." She buried her head in her hand.

Tom's eyes looked steadily at the smooth arch of her back. He started to reach for her, to comfort her, then thought better of it. He drew back. "No, I don't know that. I know there was no evidence against him. I know he was never charged with it, but, face it, Carol's murder was almost exactly like Sarah's—"

"Why do you always have to be such a cop? It only proves the killer is familiar with the facts of Sarah's case," Fran argued, facing him again, her eyes flaring.

Tom shrugged. "Or the same person killed both. Either way, if you want a motive for going after Alex, that's it. He got away with it once, they won't let him get away with it again."

"Tom, I used to like you," Fran said bitterly, "but I've decided you're a prick."

She started to march out of the office, but he caught her arm and stopped her. He drew her close, his eyes borrowing into hers. "I'm not a seven-year-old kid anymore, Fran. I care about you. I really do. Probably a hell of a lot more than you realize. I don't want to see you get hurt. I don't want you to throw your life away over this guy whether he's guilty or not. You deserve better."

For a second his touch burned like electricity through her skin, but all she heard was echoes of Max.

"This guy is my partner and my best friend," Fran snapped, jerking her arm away and fighting off the unexpected reaction. "If you're not going to help me clear him, then I don't want to see you around here again."

Tom backed off. "Okay. You say Max set him up. Maybe he did. Maybe he was even in on the murder."

"I didn't say that. I'm sure he didn't kill her," she argued.

"You seem to be sure about a lot of things," Tom shot back.

"I know him. He wouldn't go that far."

Tom looked at her quizzically. "Just how far would he go?"

Fran shuddered at the thought of Max pushed up against her, his breath on her face. She looked away. She remembered Tom's words: *Any man can rape, and every man knows it.*

Tom watched her reaction and frowned. "How far did he go, Fran?" he asked, rephrasing the question.

She closed her lips tight.

Tom tilted his head and examined her body language. He didn't like what he was reading. "Okay. Let's try it this way. If you're right and Max didn't kill her, I can rule him out, right?" He was playing a hunch.

"How?" Even as she asked the question, the answer came to her. "DNA?"

"Exactly."

"You'll never get a DNA sample from Max," Fran scoffed.

"No, but I can get one from his daughter. That will at least establish if a relative was in the room, right?"

"My DNA?" Fran nodded slowly. "Right."

CHAPTER 18

Tom drove up to the address Candy Knight had given him. He stepped out of his vehicle and stared at the warehouse structure. The Adult Super Store stared back. Tom pulled the slip of paper with the address out of his pocket to check it. "Yup, that's the one," he murmured. Swallowing his nervousness, he walked bravely forward.

After a few minutes of searching, he found her standing in a far corner and admiring some men's latex chaps on a slender mannequin. She was dressed in black stiletto boots, tight leather pants, and a laced corset. Her hair was slicked back, and her makeup was extreme for Tom's taste.

"Strange place for a date," Tom quipped, trying to sound nonchalant.

"You'd be surprised," Candy responded, giving him a little smirk and a wink. "You like these?" she indicated the chaps with a flick of her wrist.

"Well, actually, I don't think they'd fit me." He glanced skeptically at the item.

She laughed. "They just might. Nice tight ass like yours."

"I wasn't thinking in terms of size." The back of Tom's neck burned as he turned towards her self-consciously, keeping his ass out of her line of sight. He studied her for a moment while she dug through her purse, then he cleared his throat.

"You have a cold, detective?" she asked, pulling out a credit card.

"I heard the prosecutor hired you to handle Alex's case," he said.

She turned to face him, nodding. "Go on."

"Does he know about your taste in – chaps?"

Candy chuckled softly. "What he doesn't know can't hurt me."

He glanced about. "Is it safe to talk here?"

"That's why I picked this place, hon," she told him. "The four rules of BDSM: Safe, sane, consensual, and confidential." She smiled. "You don't think the sheriff or his cronies would be caught dead in here, do you?"

"I'm surprised you're here," he admitted.

Candy tapped her lower lip with the credit card, eying him. "There are a lot more people in the lifestyle than you think."

Revelation. "Alex. That's why you're trying to help him. He's one of you." Tom blushed as he realized how stupid that comment sounded.

Her smile broadened. "Confidentiality, remember? But I can assure you, I wouldn't be 'helping' him at all if I thought he was guilty. Now, what can we do for each other?"

Tom pulled a small plastic bag out of his shirt pocket and handed it to her. "I found these hairs at the crime scene," he told her. "They didn't seem important at the time, but when I thought about it, I figured, no stone unturned and all that." He had practiced the lie over and over in the car on his way to meet her. He wasn't comfortable lying to Candy. They were Fran's hairs, of course; something for comparison.

Candy fingered the bag gingerly. "At the crime scene, huh? Which crime scene?"

Tom hesitated a second too long before saying, "I need you to tell me. I need a blind match. It's the only way I can trust the results. It might be something or it might be nothing," he said. "Can you check it out?"

She nodded and dropped the bag into her purse. "Done and done."

"Don't you want to know why I'm not going through channels?" he asked.

"I am channels," she said.

"On Alex's case, but not...." He stopped.

She chuckled. "I worked there, remember? I know why." Her attention was drawn back to the chaps. "Are you sure you wouldn't want to try these on for me?"

"Not in this lifetime."

***

Fran got back to Alex's condo around 10 p.m. and found him standing in the kitchen and taking some more pain medication. He was sober and shaved but wearing the same clothes he'd had on that morning.

"You okay?" she asked, worried. She had expected him to be his usual fashionable self. His choice of outfit unsettled her.

"I've been pacing the damn floor all day," he said. "You?"

She covered her mouth and yawned. "Long day. Sorry you missed it."

"I just bet you are." He smiled. "Come on." He put his glass down, took her hand and pulled her back to the bedroom where Bocelli floated softly in the air. "Lay down, Bella," he ordered.

"Alex, I can't. No way. I shouldn't even be here." She started for the door.

"No shenanigans. Promise," he said, grabbing her arms and gently pulling her back. "You're beat and you're here. Just lay down. Keep me company."

"This is a bad idea," she argued.

"I can't sleep, Fran," he stated, a look of panic on his face. "I keep seeing Sarah. I keep seeing Carol. I just... I can't Fran. Just BE there for me, okay? That's all I need. I need to sleep."

For a second she considered telling him about the photos from Tom, then thought better of it. She started to object but he put his fingers to her lips and hushed her.

"Just rest. No funny stuff. Don't you trust me?" The question sealed the deal.

"I don't have...."

"Here." He pulled a clean shirt out of his closet and tossed it to her. "I'll even turn around." He obligingly did so.

Slipping off her suit and shoes, Fran put on the fresh-smelling shirt and crawled under the toasty comforter. She drew it up to her chin. "You can look now," she said calmly.

To her surprise, Alex crawled in behind her and pulled the comforter over them both. He wrapped his arm protectively around her and nestled his head

263

on the back of her neck. As his heavy arm went limp and his breath became steady, she allowed herself to be lulled to sleep. When she awoke the next morning, he was already up.

FRIDAY

Fran waited impatiently outside his bathroom door for the better part of a half hour. When he didn't come out, she rapped on the door for the third time. "Are you alright?" she asked.

"Yes. Just a minute," he yelled from behind the door before letting out a definitive "Damn!"

"Alex, what's the matter?" she asked.

"Bella, just give me a minute, will you? I'm going as fast as I can."

Inside the bathroom, Alex stood in front of the wide, chrome-trimmed mirror that hung over his pedestal sink. He had undressed down to his boxers and had removed his bandages. His ribs, side, back, neck and shoulders were covered in deep, yellowing bruises. A pile of bandages cluttered the floor at his feet. He was trying to wrap fresh bandages over his cracked ribs but was having trouble reaching around his torso. Whenever he tried to turn, the pain stopped him. "I can do this," he told himself, gritting his teeth and staring in his mirror.

"Alex? Are you alright?" Fran pounded on the door.

She was right there, a little more than an arm's length away. All he had to do was open the door and let her in, but he didn't want to do it.

"Alex? What's wrong? Talk to me."

His pulse started to race, and the pain increased. It had been hours since he'd taken his medication. The effects were quickly wearing off.

"Damn it, Alex! You're scaring me! Let me in!"

He tried one more time to twist around and reach his back but ended up doubled over in pain. "Bella!" he called out through labored breathing. "Help me!"

She had already found a paperclip and was two seconds from picking the lock when he reached over and turned the knob. When the door opened, she gasped and quickly covered her mouth. She was still wearing his shirt and held her clothes and purse in her arms. She dumped everything on the floor.

"Oh my god, Alex! What are you trying to do?"

Slowly he pushed himself into a semi-upright position. "My ribs," he said. "I need to wrap the bandage around them."

Fran backed up and looked him all over. "I need to take pictures of this," she said quietly.

He stared at her in the mirror. "I don't want anyone to see me like this, and I don't want any reminders."

She shook her head. "You can sue those bastards over this. What those people did to you was criminal. I need to take photos."

He knew she was right, but he didn't want to go through another photo session of his body. He shook his head. "I need my pills."

"Hey," she said, gently resting her hand on his arm, "if it was me, you'd insist."

Their eyes met. He relented.

"You have your camera?" she asked.

"Toni borrowed it," he told her.

"No, I mean yes, she did, but she brought it back," Fran explained. "That's where the photos came from that we used in court. I took the card and left the camera here."

Alex thought a minute, then nodded. "Right. Top right side of my bedroom closet. Don't drop it."

She quickly got the camera and began photographing his injuries. She moved slowly, gently, noting the placement of each bruise with her fingertips but never pressing on them. She had him turn slightly so she could get the best light. Then she stood on the edge of the bathtub to photograph his

265

shoulders and neck.

"Bandages?" she asked.

"In my gym bag," he told her.

"Stand still," she murmured when he tensed up. "I won't hurt you."

Her touch was gentle. She carefully encircled his chest with her arms as she passed the end of the gauze from one hand to the next and wrapped it around him, and yet Alex felt as if every pass was restricting his breathing. She straightened out each band and made sure it was secured but not tight. Then she cut off the end and affixed it with more tape.

He stood perfectly still, swallowing his panic and gazing down at her, letting her envelop him in her tender care and wondering why he had been so afraid to let her in.

"Lean on me," she ordered.

"Bella?"

"Lean on me. I'll help you to your room and get you some meds. Then you can rest."

"I just got up," he objected.

"Just 'til the painkillers kick in," she said.

"And then what?" he asked, feeling foolish.

"Then I can finally take my shower." Fran grinned at him.

She helped him to his bed. Then she brought him painkillers and a glass of water, found him a magazine, and left him lying on his back, reading.

Within minutes, he had fallen asleep, the magazine on his lap and his reading glasses slipping off his nose.

***

"Where is he?" Rick asked the moment he stepped into Alex's apartment. He carried a laptop and a large file.

Fran's hair was wet, she wore fresh clothes and had a rosy look on her cheeks. "Sleeping," she said.

A pained look crossed Rick's face.

"What have you got?" Fran asked, clearing off the kitchen table and making room for them to work.

"Film and photos at eleven." Rick held up a large brown envelope. "The pix came with the discovery material this morning, hand-delivered by the way. I got a vid of the wedding from the dead girl's father. I talked to him Sunday, but he couldn't get his hands on it 'til today."

"Which girl? Which wedding?" Fran asked.

"Tom didn't tell you?" Rick asked. "There was a third murder: same MO, two years ago, Walkins' girl. When I was goin' through the files I came 'cross a note about a video of a wedding, the last place the girl was seen alive. Turns out the groom was cousins with the little girl in the Callas case."

Fran opened the envelope and spilled its contents on the table. She shuddered when she saw the crime scene photos. Twelve-year-old Emily Walkins, the flower girl at the wedding, had turned up raped and choked to death in a dumpster behind a dance hall on Freemont Street. She was dressed in a torn, pink silk gown and missing her shoes; her mass of blonde hair tangled with garbage.

"What a waste," Fran muttered. She looked up at Rick, unnerved by the way he was studying her.

"Problem?" she asked.

He shook his head no and looked away.

Fran frowned. "So, what's her story? Give me the bottom line. What does this have to do with our case?"

"It's a mirror of the other two cases. She attended the same school. She was the same age. She was dumped in the same place. That Saturday, she went to her cousin's wedding. The reception was at the Crowne Plaza off Flamingo. One second she's there and the next she's gone. No one saw her again."

267

"Until trash day," Fran finished, nodding. "Do we have preliminary discovery on the latest victim?"

"Not yet. I'm hoping today. Margo is working on it," said Rick.

"Let's see the wedding clip," Fran directed.

Rick picked up the DVD and headed for Alex's computer. He sat down in the leather chair, slipped in the disc and waited for it to download. Fran watched the bar fill from left to right, 2%... 5%... She turned and walked away, the memory of another DVD too fresh in her mind. She poured them both some coffee and returned in time to see the 99% mark. The screen went blank and then cleared, showing a gathering of friends and family enjoying a wedding reception. A band played an old-fashioned polka in the background. The film was shaky. The camera had been handheld. Fran gave Rick his cup of coffee.

"Hold on a minute," Rick told her, setting the coffee to the side. "The good part is coming up."

A few seconds later, the camera panned over the girl. She was deep in conversation with the accused, Ivan Callas.

"How did he end up at the wedding?" Fran asked, leaning on Rick's shoulder.

"Cousins, remember? Pay attention, Fran." He took a sip of the coffee and looked up, startled. "That's actually good." He smiled.

Fran nodded, watching the screen. "All he's doing is talking to her," she noted.

"Or trying to pick her up."

"Same difference." Fran set down her coffee and glanced back at the photos. "Nothing. Can't say he did it; can't say he didn't."

"Except for the strands of hair with his DNA on it," Rick said, looking back at her.

"From the Walkins' case?" she asked.

268

He nodded. "At least that's what Elliott's report says. He claims, under oath, mind you, that he didn't know whose hair it was until the other two cases. Once they got Callas' DNA, they matched it and, well, you can figure out the rest."

"Convenient," she muttered. "Just because he got close to her doesn't mean he raped or murdered her. It's all circumstantial." She was holding onto threads of hope.

Rick arched an eyebrow. "You sound like a lawyer."

"Besides, does he look like a man about to rape a young girl?" she asked. She knew how foolish that sounded the second she said it.

"I don't know, Fran," Rick said sarcastically, leaning back in the chair and crossing his arms. "What does a rapist look like?"

"You're beginning to sound more like Tom every day," she snapped, heading back to the kitchen. "That still doesn't explain the murder of the third child while he was in jail," she yelled as she ran some water over the dishes in the sink.

Rick turned his attention to the screen and Fran heard a sudden, "Whoa there!"

"What?" she asked, turning off the water and hurrying back to his side. "What have you got?"

Rick turned the monitor slightly, so she could see it better. "I guess our janitor wasn't the only person of interest at the wedding," he said.

As Ivan drifted away from the victim, another figure emerged, homing in on the girl like a bee to honey. His statuesque figure filled out the expensive tuxedo to a tee, and his silver hair and goatee were immaculately groomed.

"Max," Fran hissed. "What the hell is he doing there?" Her stomach knotted up and her legs weakened. She leaned against Rick for support. "Alex has to see this. This is it. This is...."

She looked in Rick's curious eyes and realized he didn't have a clue what

269

she was talking about. "Alex has to see this," she repeated.

"What's going on, Fran?" Rick's voice was quiet and even, like a tightrope walker testing his line.

"What's going on, Bella?" Alex interrupted them. He had stepped out of the bedroom, dressed in jeans and a sweatshirt. "What's on the computer?"

Startled, Fran swung part way around to see him, looking for and not finding the telltale sign of pain in his eyes.

"A video of a wedding from the Walkins' case two years ago, featuring Ivan Callas, a third twelve-year-old who turned up dead later, and...." She glanced back at the screen. The name forced its way out of her tight throat. "...Max."

Alex moved swiftly to the computer. "Move," he ordered Rick, who quickly gave up his seat. "Son of a bitch!" Alex said, turning to Fran. "This is it, isn't it? This is why he set me up! He knew we'd figure it out. Sooner or later, we'd figure it out."

"What are you talking about?" Rick looked from one to the other and read old history in both their eyes.

Fran took a deep breath. "Max murdered her." She choked on her words. "Max raped and murdered that child."

"Or had her murdered," Alex corrected.

"Don't give me that bullshit," Fran countered, tears welling in her eyes. She felt sick and ran to the bathroom. Blinded by tears, she ran into the door jamb, before falling hard to her knees on the cold tiled floor. Fran leaned over the porcelain bowl and threw up. She shivered as her stomach knotted again, forcing more up. She was sweating, exhausted and weak when she finally stood and flushed the toilet. She turned to the sink to wash her face, catching Rick staring at her from the doorway.

"What's your problem?" Fran snapped.

He crossed his arms, scowled, turned and walked away.

270

"Are you going to bring me into the loop or am I just here for my good looks?" Rick asked Alex.

"I need you to find out everything you can about Max Simone's whereabouts the day of the murders," Alex responded.

"Carol's?" Rick asked.

Alex thought a minute. "Yeah, hers too, but I was thinking of the girls."

This time, both of Rick's eyebrows went up. "You really think *he* did that?" he asked, surprised.

"Let's just say he's capable of it." Alex faced his investigator. "If he did, if we can prove he did, it'll go a long way to clearing me."

Rick nodded. "I'll get on it," he said. He glanced back at the kitchen where Fran was getting a glass of water. "She going to be okay?" Rick asked Alex. "She isn't pregnant by any chance, is she?"

Alex snorted. "Pregnant? You're kidding, right? That's not possible. I mean, I don't think she's...." He was about to say, "even seeing someone," but he realized he didn't know. "No. Couldn't be."

"You do know where babies come from, right?" Rick asked with a smirk. He picked up the photos and disc and headed for the door. "Have fun, you two," he said, as he left.

"What the hell was that all about?" Alex asked Fran after Rick was gone.

Fran choked on her water, wiped her face and stared at him. "They think we're sleeping together," she said.

"What?" Alex looked stunned. "They who?"

"Tom and Rick and," she shrugged, "everybody, I guess."

"What the hell?"

"Well, we did sleep together, and this was the second night I've spent here. What did you expect them to think?"

Alex turned red, partly from embarrassment and partly from anger. "It's none of their damn business who I sleep with, or who you sleep with, for that

271

matter. And you're not pregnant." He paused a second. "Are you?" he asked.

"Alex, do I look like an idiot?" Fran asked. She gathered up her things and headed for the door. This time, when he tried to call her back, she ignored him.

CHAPTER 19

Fran was wilted and exhausted from surviving a difficult morning and dodging the paparazzi. She was worried about her blowout with Tom and preoccupied with the new evidence in the Callas case and her unusual night with Alex. She felt like she was going around and around on a carnival ride.

Fran slipped into her apartment as the hot noon sun perforated the curtains. She dropped her briefcase on the bar and pulled out a cell phone, laying it on top of the case. She shed her shoes and light gray suit jacket, untucked her pink silk blouse, skipped her usual scotch and poured herself a cognac. Rubbing her eyes against a looming headache, she picked up the remote control and headed for her favorite chair, only to find Max Simone already in it. Fran froze.

"What the shit? Get the fuck outta my home!" She threw the remote at him.

Simone easily batted it away. His feet were propped up on her ottoman, an unsettling reminder of Tom in Alex's office. "Nice chair. My place is completely furnished, you understand, but I won't complain if you bring your stuff with you. In fact, I insist. I'll have my men pack everything up in the morning." A smile crept across his lean face.

"Get out of my home, Max! Now!" Fran backed up until she was pressed against the bar, still holding her drink in one sweaty hand. Her heart raced. Her eyes darted to the door.

"We had a deal, honey. Remember?" Max stood up slowly, watching her tremble. "Look at you; Francesca Simone, famous attorney and political strategist, a woman of independent means, and you can't even handle a surprise visit from your dear old dad." His voice was laden with sarcasm.

"This is a hell of a time to play daddy," she snapped. The sickening sensation had returned. She couldn't contain her rage.

He took a step toward her. Fran dropped the drink on the bar and seized her cell phone. In a few quick steps, Max was in front of her. He snatched the phone from her hand and threw it on the floor, then he grabbed both her wrists, squeezing until tears came to her eyes. She wanted to fight him, to hit him, to push him off his feet, but her lifelong fear paralyzed her.

"I can't take much more of this from you, Frannie," he snapped. His eyes clouded over in pain. "I need you in my life! You've got to listen to me! You've got to come home!"

"Go! Please! Leave!" she begged. She hated that feeling of helplessness that he always gave her. It was almost ingrained, a conditioned response. As thin and pale as he was, he left her trembling and weak in her fear.

"Is this how you respect your father? Is it? Who were you going to call, anyway? You want Alex to spend the rest of his life behind bars? Or maybe he'll be executed. Tell me, honey, who do you trust that much? Who would you trust with his life?"

"Stop it! You're hurting me!" she screamed.

"We had a deal," he hissed. "I'm keeping my part of the bargain. You'd better keep yours."

"I can't do this! Not now!" She turned her face away from him. "I've got an office to run. I've got to help Alex! I've got to…." She needed more time. She needed to focus. She needed to drive the screams out of her head.

Max tightened his grip on her wrists and the pain stopped her words. He scowled and glanced nervously around the apartment. "Where's my granddaughter?"

Fran's skin went cold. She shuddered and gasped for air. "The deal was for me, not her!"

"She's my granddaughter! I have a right to see her! Where is she?" His gray eyes bore into her green ones.

"At her father's. He has her this week. Visitation. He's bringing her. He'll be here soon. That's why I came home early," She lied. She struggled to breathe between the words.

Angry at the potential interruption, Simone let go of her wrists and backhanded Fran across the face. She crumpled to the floor, covered her cheek with her hand, and shed hot tears. She was afraid he would rape her, even though she knew that wouldn't happen. He didn't want her. He wanted someone much younger. He wanted what she used to be.

She looked up at him with a vague, haunting sense of seeing a man she had once known well and now didn't know at all. *When did he get so old? So thin?* In her mind, he was always so much bigger and stronger than she was.

He leaned against the desk a moment for support. "Well, I'll have to do something about that," he said quietly as he pushed himself up and moved toward the door.

"No!" Fran screamed as she clawed at his jacket. "No! You can't have her! You can't! I'll call the police! I swear, Max. I will!"

Simone stopped a few moments and studied the woman groveling at his feet. "You realize what's at stake here, don't you? You know what's on that disc, or should I say who?"

"I'll die before I let you get your hands on Lauren!"

"Don't be a fool." Max's voice was even and deadly quiet. "Now, get up and stop begging. You're embarrassing me. You're my daughter, for god's sake. I thought you were tougher than that." He watched as she pulled herself back to her feet. "My people will be here first thing in the morning for your things. Be ready."

Simone strolled out the door and shut it firmly behind him.

Fran, dizzy and hyperventilating, clutched her chest as a cutting band squeezed her heart. Collapsing back to the floor, she snatched her cell phone and hit speed dial. "My place. Now. Hurry." She passed out.

Across town, Rick slammed on the brakes and made a U-turn in the road, crossed four lanes of traffic and defied a tractor-trailer truck. The driver

275

pounded on his horn and gave Rick the finger.

***

It took Fran a few minutes to realize she was in a hospital bed. Soft voices drifted past her as nurses, doctors and orderlies pattered about in soft-soled shoes and tended to other emergency room patients. A cold air chilled the skin on her exposed arms. She shivered.

Fran heard a woman say, "She's in here, detective," and the shower-stall-styled curtain that encased Fran's bed swished back on its metal rings.

Tom Sadler, his shoulder holster under his arm, looked every bit the professional cop working on a case. "Ms. Simone? How are you feeling?" His tone was guarded and formal, but his eyes looked worried. He instinctively reached for her arm and then stopped short. Instead, his hand rested on the bedrail.

He seemed much bigger than Fran had remembered. Much taller, stronger. Or was that Max? Fran shook her head slightly and immediately became nauseous. In a moment of drug-induced paranoia, she wondered who was watching them.

"How are you feeling?" he repeated.

"Like shit." She raised her hand in the air and counted her own fingers. "Yeah, they're all here. Where's Rick?"

"In the waiting room," Tom told her, stifling a small grin, "but I need to get a statement from you, first."

"How did you know?" she asked.

"Rick called me." Tom pulled out a pad of paper and a pen from his coat pocket.

"A statement? What for? I collapsed in my own home. You don't need a goddamn statement. Besides, aren't you...." Suspended, she thought, biting her sentence off in the middle. For some reason, he was pretending to be on the job. Or was he pretending?

Tom gently touched the side of her cheek. She cringed.

"Since when does collapsing in your own home leave a swollen jaw?" he asked. "Did Alex do this to you?" There was an angry bite to his voice that set her off.

It only took a second for her anger to boil to the surface. "No! Bastard! You're watching him! You know where he is! You, you, dickhead!"

Fran's breathing suddenly became labored and Tom, worried, signaled for the nurse, who checked Fran's vitals.

"Please, Ms. Simone," the nurse said. "You need to relax. Your blood pressure is still too high."

"You want me to relax?" Fran snapped. "Get that jackass the hell out of here!"

The nursed scowled at Tom. He had withdrawn his hand but refused to move.

Fran had to swallow hard, forcing herself to remain angry when she saw the hurt in his eyes. He didn't deserve that, she knew, but she had to get rid of him. "I want Rick in here, now!"

Tom closed the notebook and slipped it back into his pocket.

"I'm sorry, sir. You have to go." The nurse ushered him to the door.

Tom glanced once over his shoulder as he let himself be dragged down the hall and out of sight.

Fran closed her eyes and let out a deep sigh. A few minutes later, she felt a presence at her side and inhaled the familiar scent of tobacco. She opened her eyes to see Rick leaning on the safety rail of her bed and smirking at her.

"I swear, girly, some days you're more damn trouble than you're worth." His eyes crinkled with humor in his worn face, and Fran suddenly felt safe.

Despite her pain, she smiled. "What happened to me?" She gripped his hand.

"Well, whoever hit ya must have given ya a damn good scare. The doc

277

ruled out heart attack so, best guess, panic attack – or just plain stupidity. I ain't decided yet."

Fran glanced around the room and whispered. "We need to talk privately. Get me out of here."

"I'll see what I can do. Hold tight." Rick didn't bother to challenge her.

She felt the safety of his hand dissipate as he wandered off in search of assistance.

Fran, her eyes closed, allowed whatever medication they were pumping into her arm to lull her back to sleep.

"Ms. Simone?" A man's voice roused her.

"Huh?" She opened her eyes and saw one of the young doctors leaning over her. She noted that his glasses seemed too big for his face. When he smiled, her body went tense.

"How are we feeling?" he asked.

Fran frowned as she focused on his name tag. It read Dr. Dick. She almost laughed, reminded of an old television show. Whatever they were giving her was working. Feeling dizzy, she closed her eyes.

"Ms. Simone? Are you still with us?" he asked.

"Oh." She forced her eyes open and tried to keep the room from swimming. When it settled down, she continued. "Better. Thanks. What happened?" Her mouth tasted dry. She licked her lips.

"Best we can tell, you had a serious panic or anxiety attack. We believe you hyperventilated until you passed out. Can you tell me what happened?" the doctor asked.

Someone beat the crap out of me, you ass, she thought. Fran choked back obscenities and shook her head no. The room swayed. She closed her eyes. "Just stress. Everything came to a head."

He shook his head disapprovingly at her. "I know it's hard to talk about these things, but we have counselors here who can help. I promise that

278

anything you say to them will be strictly confidential."

Fran went from confused to frightened to furious in a heartbeat. "Don't patronize me. I'm not talking to anyone. Got it? Back off." Plucking at the thin white blanket, she tried to cover her cold arms.

The doctor frowned and looked at her chart. He wasn't rattled by her reaction. "Well, your BP is still high, so I'm going to give you some meds for that and something for your anxiety. We'll see if we can't reduce some of that stress and make sure this kind of attack doesn't happen again, right?" He looked at her over the top of his glasses. "Right?" he repeated when she didn't respond.

Right, dickhead. "Right."

"Make sure you don't take them with alcohol." The doctor crossed his arms and frowned. "As for the beating, there are no broken bones or serious injuries, just some bruising and swelling for a few days, maybe a week."

Fran kept her eyes clamped shut. She wanted to scream.

"Very well. I'll have the nurse give you some materials on domestic violence. There are people you can call, places you can go, and there's always someone here when you're ready to talk." The doctor patted her leg gently.

She jerked away from his touch and nodded silently. He was the kind of condescending son-of-a-bitch who patted a woman's leg, she thought. She could picture him patting his wife's leg, picture her turning away, picture him raising his hand to strike. Fran shuddered. She had no reason to think that any of that was true, of course. It was just a reaction triggered by a touch.

"I'll call your primary care provider and fill him in." He glanced again at her chart. "Fill her in," he corrected. "In the meantime, there's somebody here to see you."

Fran, expecting Rick, opened her eyes. Instead, she saw a tall figure with a gray goatee. She paled and grit her teeth. "Get him out of here!" she

279

shrieked. She seized the doctor's jacket. "Get him out, now!"

"But…." The young man looked trapped between his hysterical patient and the mayor of Las Vegas. Before he could speak, Rick ran into the room.

The investigator inserted himself between Simone and Fran. "You heard the lady." Rick gave Max an icy stare. "Time to go."

The two men were nose-to-chin, Max being the taller of the two. They were close enough to breathe each other's air.

Simone pursed his lips together and glanced at the curious hospital staff. At a different time, in a different place, Max might have taken Rick on, but not here and not today.

"I understand." Simone, speaking loud enough for anyone passing to hear, addressed the doctor. "I'm sure, with the proper medication and counseling, my daughter will be back to her old self in no time. I appreciate all you're doing to help her."

Simone walked away. Rick turned, dashed to the bed and seized Fran's wrist, stopping her from nailing her father in the back of the head with a flying bedpan. Rick pulled the bedpan from her grasp. Fran yelled at the pain of his touch on her already injured wrist. He let go.

"You want to end up in the goddamn psych ward?" Rick tossed the bedpan out of her reach.

"Take me home," Fran pleaded. Her rage gave way to sobbing. "Please, Rick. Take me home. Now." She clung to his arm.

"Right away, boss," he told her.

"I'll get the paperwork," the startled doctor said to Rick. "You can get her prescriptions filled at our pharmacy if you like." He paused and looked back at Fran. "Remember, we're here when you want to talk."

When the doctor was gone, Rick pulled the curtain closed again, cutting off the looks of the curious. He leaned on the bed's safety rail and eyed Fran. "Spill," he ordered.

She scowled. "Not here."

***

Fran didn't speak about the incident again until they were well on the road. The dizziness had receded, but the pain in her cheek and wrists was coming back. Rick had given her a spare pair of sunglasses that were too big and somewhat scratched. She slipped them on without a word. He'd also given her one of his fleece jackets. Despite going from the hospital's cold air to the sunny heat outside, Fran was still shivering. She draped the jacket over her shoulders and pulled it tight around her.

Rick puffed on a cigarette as he drove, flicking the ashes out the partially open window as the air conditioner blew cold in their faces.

Fran resisted the urge to write WASH ME on the dust-laden dashboard. Instead, she stared at her window and focused on bringing her heartbeat and breathing to a much calmer state.

A small bug was pinned to the outside glass by the force of the air going by. It wouldn't be swept away, but instead crawled along the edge of the pane, looking for a way into the safety of the vehicle. Fran finally lowered the window a half-inch and the bug disappeared somewhere behind her.

About two blocks from her apartment building, Fran rested a hand on Rick's muscular arm and told him to stop the car.

Without a word, Rick drove into a gas station parking lot, pulled up to the shady side of the building and turned off the engine. As the hum of the air conditioner went silent, they unrolled their windows. A hot breeze sifted through the Jeep. When he looked at her, she was trembling.

"What happened?" he asked.

"Oh god." Fran tipped her head back and closed her eyes behinds the shades. "I don't even know where to begin."

"Just about anywhere will do," he said softly. He squeezed her hand, careful to avoid her wrist.

281

She sighed. "Max is blackmailing me." She didn't look at Rick.

Rick's eyes narrowed. "Explain."

"Carol…." Fran swallowed hard. "She recorded…. There's a DVD of them, of her and Alex." Fran shook her head. Tears welled up in her eyes and splashed down her cheeks. She swept them away with the sleeve of her silk blouse.

It wasn't much information, but it was enough for Rick. "He's got it," Rick finished.

She nodded. She looked at him and indicated the cigarette. "Can I have one of those?" she asked.

Rick handed her one. He didn't ask what was on the disc. If she was this upset about it, he could guess. "What does Simone want from you?" he asked.

"Trust me, Rick, you don't want to know."

"Don't fuck with me, Fran. What does he want?"

Fran leaned forward as Rick lit her cigarette. She inhaled deeply. She hadn't had one in years and now the smoke made her cough slightly.

What does he want? Max's words came back to her. *Tell me, honey, who do you trust that much? Who would you trust with his life?* The answer was simple. She trusted Rick.

"He wants Lauren. The filthy prick wants my daughter. He's got this crazy idea that we're all going to just move into the mayor's mansion and be a happy family. You know, Walton style – only not." She shuddered and closed her eyes again. The smoke rose around her.

Despite the heat penetrating the vehicle, a cold chill streamed up Rick's spine. "Fuck, girl!" Rick tossed the remnant of his cigarette out the window and shook his head. He fought to contain his rising fury as his mind worked the puzzle. "He did you, too, didn't he?" he asked, eying her. "That's why you think he did them other girls. That's why you think he killed 'em."

She didn't answer.

"Who else knows?" he asked.

"Alex. Tom. Paul, of course," Fran said.

"Why didn't you go to the cops?"

It was the question Fran had asked and answered in her own head a million times. "I was twelve. I told my mother. She tried to leave him." She tipped her head back again as the tears kept coming.

"Your mother? Your mother's dead. Didn't she die in an accident of some kind?"

Fran nodded. "Yes. An accident, of some kind."

"Fuck!" Rick slammed the steering wheel and she jumped. "Max did this to you. He beat you up. That's why you screamed at him at the ER."

Fran bowed her head and sighed. "He was waiting for me at my apartment. I don't know how he got in."

"You gave him hell and he beat the crap out of you," said Rick.

"Yeah, well, I went off on him. I should have known better."

"No excuse." He reached into the back seat, felt around, and dug up a roll of toilet paper.

She took it, tore off some to wipe her face, and nodded.

"Probably got his own set of goddamn keys." He paused. "Where's Lauren?" he asked.

"At her dad's, thank god." She took another drag on the cigarette before pinching it dead between her fingers. She ignored the pain and dropped it to the ground.

Rick stared at the ceiling of the Jeep as if it magically held the answers to his questions. "How'd he get it? The disc?"

With the engine and air conditioner off, the vehicle was quickly heating up despite the open windows.

Fran shrugged the jacket off her shoulders. "Elliott, I guess. He was the first one on the scene."

"You know Randall was fucking her, too, right?" Rick asked.

"Who?"

"The cop, Carol," Rick said.

Fran shook her head. "Damn, she was screwing everyone."

"I bet Elliot thought Randall was on that disc," Rick mused. "Politics, man. Serious leverage. Either that or covering Randall's ass."

She shook her head. "No. I don't think so. I'm not sure why Elliott took it, but he gave it to Max, not the sheriff. He wouldn't have done that unless he was sure Max needed it."

"The whole fucking thing was a setup," Rick growled.

"Yes, and Alex was stupid enough to walk right into it, but I don't think they planned on Carol getting murdered. That was extra."

Rick lit another cigarette and deeply inhaled.

She turned and stared at him a second.

"What?" he asked.

"You didn't ask the sixty-million-dollar question," she said.

He took a moment to calm himself. His hand gripped the steering wheel tightly. "Tell me."

"I only saw a part of the disc," she lied. "Max showed it to me. I saw Alex and Carol, what he did to her, but not the very end. The last thing I saw, he was walking out, and she was still alive."

Rick blinked. "If Alex had killed her, why not just…." His voice went silent in thought for a few seconds. "We need to get that disc and any copies Max or Elliott have."

"You think Elliott's got copies?" Fran squeaked, staring at him. The thought hadn't occurred to her.

"He'd be an idiot not to. I hate the little shithead, but he's not stupid." Rick thought a minute and then frowned. "Elliott didn't put the disc in the

284

discovery packet, did he? You know what that means."

Fran nodded. "Of course. Alex didn't kill Carol."

"And the disc shows who did."

"Maybe," Fran admitted. She looked away.

"Kinda takes the teeth out of the blackmail, don't it, boss?" Rick asked.

Fran bit her lip. "It still puts Alex in that bitch's bed, screwing her with a cord around her neck. Pretty damming from what I saw. At the very least, it supports a charge of rape and it implies the murder. If the rest of the disc is erased, the implication...."

"Is enough to convict," Rick finished. He was still watching Fran. "You think you know who killed her, don't you?" He was quiet a second. "You saw the disc. You must have an idea."

"The disc ended with Alex walking out." She looked at him. "All I know is he didn't do it, 'cause if he had, either he would have taken it with him and it wouldn't be kicking around at all, or it would be in the hands of the prosecutor and we'd all know about it."

It was Rick's turn to look away. When he looked at her, he said, "What aren't you tellin' me, boss?

She chewed on her lip. "We'll get the disc. Then you can see what I saw." Fran's head and face hurt. "Take me home, Rick. I'm tired. I don't want to think about it anymore." The medication was wearing off. The bruises hurt. She wanted to crawl into the quiet safety of her bed and pretend today hadn't happened, except her bed – her entire apartment – wasn't safe anymore.

Rick started the Jeep, put it in gear and pulled back into the traffic. "What are you going to do?" he finally asked as he pulled in front of her modest apartment building and parked.

"Max is sending his guys in the morning to get my stuff. He insists we live with him. If I do that, he'll help Alex." She shuddered.

Rick's fists tightened on the steering wheel. "What are you going to do?"

he asked her again.

"I'm going to get into that house. I'm going to try and find the disc and every last copy, and I'm going to get the hell out." She glanced at him, reading the anger and disgust on his face. "I don't know what I'm doing anymore. I know Max is lying to me. I know he's full of shit, but I've got to do something. I've got to play out this hand. I need to find evidence that Max set up Alex. I need to clear Alex. I'm begging you, Rick, as my friend, don't try and stop me."

"You're pushing me pretty hard against the wall, boss. I don't like it."

"I know."

He grunted, clearly unhappy. "And Lauren?"

"She's at Paul's and she's going to stay there," Fran said.

Rick turned off the engine and got out, pausing before he came around the back of the Jeep and opened her door. He felt the sun pour over him like a hot cleansing shower. Fran stepped gingerly out of the vehicle. Together, they leaned against the Jeep and stared ahead in thought, their arms crossed, their shoulders touching.

"Don't. It's not worth it. Alex isn't worth it. We'll find another way." Rick dug out another cigarette and lit it.

"I wish the hell people would stop telling me that."

"Telling you what?" Rick asked.

"That Alex isn't worth it. That I shouldn't be – that I shouldn't care so damn much about him." She shook her head.

Rick didn't react. "Who else told you?"

"Tom. Paul."

"They know you're going in?" He tensed, surprised.

"Hell, no." She looked up at him. "You're the only one I trust. You know that."

"Don't go. Max is slime. It won't work. It's another setup." Rick looked

286

down at her and studied the determination in her jaw. "Is that why Paul split? 'Cause of Alex?"

She groaned and pushed the oversized sunglasses up her nose. "If only it was that simple."

He nodded and returned his gaze to the distance. "Don't do it," he reiterated.

"I don't have a choice," she argued.

"You always have a choice." He put an arm around her shoulders.

"Okay, wise guy, what's your brilliant solution?" she asked, staring up at him.

"Run. Pack a bag and run like hell."

"You wouldn't, perhaps, have a personal agenda behind that suggestion?" she asked bitterly.

"Very personal," he admitted. "I don't want to see you hurt."

She felt chastised. "Where do I go? How do I pull it off? Who's to say he won't find me?"

Rick faced her. "No one knows more about running than I do, Fran. I was a bounty hunter, remember? When I get done with you, Max will never find you, or Lauren, or anyone else for that matter."

Fran shook her head and gently rested a hand on Rick's unshaven cheek. "You're a good man, Rick. I trust you with my life, but I got to try this. I owe it to Alex to try."

"Bullshit," he said.

"Rick...."

"Trust me, Fran. Trust me." He pulled her into his arms and hugged her. "Just trust me."

***

She trusted him. Or at least she thought she did. What did she have to lose? Her life, her job, her relationship with Alex, custody of Lauren, any hope of getting back at Max. The list went on and on, clicking in Fran's head as she rode in Rick's Jeep through the desert. She had rolled down the window for some fresh air, closed her eyes, and let the wind whip her hair about her face. She didn't know where they were going, and she didn't want to know. It was enough that, at least for these precious minutes, she didn't have to think about a damn thing.

"You'll like this place," Rick said between teeth clenched down on his unlit cigarette. "It's clean and quiet. No neighbors in sight. No one will bother you."

He turned the vehicle onto a narrow dirt road that wound into the hills.

Fran peeked open her eyes for a bit, assessed her location, then closed them again. She didn't speak. She must have dozed off because, when they arrived, it seemed like the trip had been very short, yet she couldn't orientate herself to her surroundings. "Isolated," Rick had said. *Barren* was what came to her mind. Fran dropped her legs out of the Jeep and stood up slowly, stretching.

He had pulled up next to a minivan with California plates, but no one was around. The air was cooler here. A slight breeze ruffled the brush around her.

"You get the suitcase and I'll get the boxes," he instructed.

She nodded. Rick might have been her chauffeur to this place, but he certainly wasn't her lackey.

Fran picked up her bags and turned to look at the house itself. The building was designed like a log camp, only with modern amenities. It wasn't as large as her condo, but it was comfortable. A weathered porch looked down the mountain to what Fran suspected was the west. Here, she could sit and watch the sunset, she thought.

"I'm waiting," Rick interrupted, carrying two large boxes and standing behind her.

"Oh." Fran dismissed the remaining quasi-romantic notions and headed up the porch and into the rustic kitchen. The floorboards creaked slightly beneath her. She held the doors open with her elbow to let Rick in. After he passed, she moved away, and the door swung shut with a slam.

What hit her immediately was the faint scent of sage. "Indian?" she asked.

"Bedrooms are through the living room and on the left," Rick instructed. He plopped the two heavy boxes on the kitchen table.

Fran nodded and wandered slowly through the main room as she headed for the bedroom: fieldstone fireplace, terra cotta tile floor covered in worn Persian rugs, heavy leather furniture, and a large, box-style television in a painted armoire. At the back of the room were two large windows that looked over a small garden of rocks and cacti.

Fran carried her luggage into the bedroom and smiled slightly, careful not to trigger the pain in her cheek. The heavy, wooden furniture looked like maple but smelled like cedar. *It must be whatever they clean it with*, she thought. The bed was covered with a handmade quilt. On the dresser, photos of native flowers were lined up in a decorative way. She looked for something more personal but didn't see it.

Fran plopped the suitcases on the bed and opened the small one. She removed a five-by-seven, framed photo of Lauren and set it on the dresser.

"Who lives here?" she shouted out to Rick as she walked up to the window to look out. Lauren would like this place, Fran thought, if the television worked.

"Seasonal," he said quietly from right behind her.

She jumped slightly and caught her breath as she looked up at him.

"The people who own it rent it out to tourists, especially the artistic types who want some privacy." He handed her a set of keys. "For the house and the van, but only leave if it's an emergency, and I mean a real emergency. Being out of scotch doesn't qualify."

She smiled. "It'll do," she said, taking the keys and slipping them into her pocket. "Expensive?"

He shrugged. "I don't know. They just let me use it now and then."

She nodded. He wasn't going to tell her more, she knew.

Rick handed her a cell phone. "No one has this number. No one. It's not listed to you or me or anyone at the office. Use it ONLY to call me. No calling Alex. No calling Paul. No calling out for pizza. Got it?"

Fran took the phone and nodded. "Does this place come with something to drink?" she asked.

Rick smiled and lead the way back into the living room. He opened a small, distressed wood hutch with a few bottles and some glasses inside. "It ain't much, but you got the basics: gin, vodka, whiskey, and…." He picked up a bottle, looked at it oddly and put it back. "…crème de menthe? Why?" Rick shook his head.

"Goes good on ice cream," Fran suggested.

"Speaking of which," Rick said as he put the bottle down, "I brought in some groceries for you, but it may not be what you want. You can figure that out and call me later with an order. I'll bring up more tomorrow."

She nodded. Her gut tightened slightly. "You're leaving then?" she asked.

"Yup." But not before he pulled a .32 out of his pocket and placed it gently on the table.

"I won't need that," she said, itching to get her hands on it.

"I hope you're right, but you never know. Stick it in your purse. It's loaded, so be careful. Last thing I want is you shooting yourself."

She nodded.

"I gotta lot to do, boss, but I'm sure that will keep you busy." He indicated the boxes on the kitchen table. He'd brought the Callas case.

Fran avoided looking at it. All the crap in her life seemed to be condensed in those boxes. What if, unlike Pandora, she didn't open the lid? "We were supposed to do a deposition." To her "supposed to" sounded almost hopeful;

290

maybe they wouldn't have to, now that the police had another killing.

"I know. It's still scheduled." Rick headed towards the door, turned at the last minute and gave her a wink. "Trust me," he said.

"Rick!" she called out.

"Yeah?"

"Thanks," Fran said.

Then she was alone. The tears returned.

***

"I got it! I got it! I got it!" Margo, wearing a big grin on her face and waving a piece of paper in the air, dashed into the law office.

"You got what?" Rick asked, straddling a chair in the conference room and glaring at her over his coffee. The sandwich he'd bought for supper was half eaten on a small paper plate. A recently minted copy of the Callas file was spread out on the table in front of him. Now that he knew its secrets, he needed to look at it with fresh eyes.

"I'm not telling you!" Margo sing-songed, skipping down the hall to Fran's office. When she found it empty, she rushed back to Rick. "Where is she?"

"What's going on?" Tom asked as he stepped into the office. He carried a large manila envelope of his own.

"Oh, no! I'm definitely NOT telling you!" Margo stated. She turned back to Rick. "Where's Fran?"

Rick glanced nervously at Tom and then Margo. "She's gone for the rest of the day," he said.

"Why?" she demanded to know.

"Personal reasons."

Margo looked deflated and Tom looked wounded.

"She checked herself out of the hospital, didn't she?" Tom asked.

"Hospital? What hospital? What happened?" Margo's eyes widened with

291

worry. She looked like she was about to crawl out of her jeans.

"She collapsed this afternoon," Tom explained. "Stress. Or so she said."

Margo headed out the door and was suddenly stopped by Tom grabbing her arm.

"Just where do you think you're going?" Tom asked.

"Well, if she's not here, then she's got to be home, and I have got to talk to her now." Margo yanked her arm out of the detective's grip and sailed down the hallway.

"We really should check on Fran." Tom looked to Rick.

Rick nodded silently. He knew Fran wouldn't be there. He could have just told Tom and Margo that she was gone, that she was someplace else, sitting this out. He could have avoided the trip to her place, but he didn't. Somehow, being drawn into her conspiracy of silence made it hard for him to do the obvious.

Together, the men headed for the parking lot and took separate cars, weaving in and out of early evening traffic and following Margo to Fran's apartment building. Once there, they ignored the elevator and hurried up the stairs. Margo stood in the hallway, staring fearfully at a half-open door.

Tom leaned against the wall, signaled Margo to stay back, pulled his gun and gently pushed the door further open. Rick was close behind. Despite what he knew, Rick was still surprised when he stood next to his companions and stared into the empty apartment. Nothing was left: not a book, not a curtain rod, not a piece of furniture. All that remained was the carpeting and slivers of dust drifting in the rays of sunlight.

Tom stared into the empty room. "What the hell?"

"Son-of-a-bitch," Rick muttered. He crossed the floor and stared out the window, his hands planted on his hips, his back to the door. "She's gone," he said.

"Gone? Where?" Margo raced frantically from room to room as if that would uncover Fran.

Rick didn't answer.

"What's going on?" Margo asked.

"Go back to the office, Margo," Rick ordered. "Tom and I need to talk."

"You and I need to talk, first, mister!" Margo insisted. "Alone!"

"Margo!" both men yelled.

"Now!" Margo yelled back.

Rick's attention turned to Margo. "Okay," he said, slowly. "You got me. Spill."

"Not 'til he's gone." Margo nodded her head towards Tom.

Tom let out a deep sigh, stepped into the hall and slammed the door. He was still grumbling when he crawled into his unmarked cruiser and spun out of the parking lot as a few straggling reporters gawked at him.

"This better be good," Rick snapped, angrily crossing his arms over his chest and glaring like an irritated drill sergeant at the young woman.

Margo pulled the piece of paper from her pocket where she'd unceremoniously jammed it. She made a brief attempt to flatten out the wrinkles and then handed it to Rick.

"It's a copy of the latest crime lab update on Alex's case," Margo said excitedly. "One of the cigars had a third set of DNA on it, saliva, unidentified so far. Probably from lighting or relighting it. And trace found several dark blue fibers on the masking tape that don't match anything yet. Oh, and they found a camcorder in the vic's closet. Seemed she liked to record her foreplay, for starters. No DVD though. Too bad. That would have helped."

Rick's lips were suddenly dry. He licked them as he took the report and studied it carefully. Margo, shifting impatiently back and forth, tried not to interrupt him.

"Margo, did you read this whole thing?" he asked quietly without looking up.

"The whole thing? Well, no, of course not. I just read the summary at the bottom, you know, where it says it isn't Alex's DNA." She grinned, but when Rick didn't look at her, Margo's grin faded. "Why? What did I miss?"

"You were right to bring this to me. I'll make sure Fran gets it. but I need you to do me a big favor," Rick said.

"You know where she is?" Margo asked excitedly.

Rick put his finger to his lips to hush her.

"Sure. Anything. What?"

"Don't mention this to anyone, including Alex. Not until we know what it means." He raised his eyes and they met hers.

Margo shivered. "It means someone else killed her!" she said almost frantically. "Doesn't it?"

"Yes, but who?" Rick asked. "If we let this out, we could spook the real killer. We gotta find out what we're dealing with here, first. We got to find out who set him up. Got it?" He watched and waited, wondering if she'd go along with his plan.

Margo nodded. "You'll talk to Fran?" she asked.

"Yep."

"When?"

Rick rolled his eyes. "Soon," he said, challenging Margo to ask anything else.

Margo headed for the door and glanced back once before stepping into the hallway.

Rick stood staring out the window into the oncoming night, his hands balled into fists and the paper crumpled in his grasp. He closed his eyes against an agonizing darkness. Somewhere, in the cluttered backdrop of his imagination, he thought he heard the mournful cry of a cat.

CHAPTER 20

The day had stretched into evening and then night as Fran cried herself to sleep on the leather sofa. She hadn't bothered with a blanket and, when she awoke, she shivered in the cool night air. Goosebumps ran the length of her bare arms. She pushed herself up to sitting and wiped the crusty remnants of her tears from her eyes. Every muscle in her body ached. When she coughed, a sharp pain pierced her face where Max had struck her.

"Damn!" she muttered with a groan as she cradled her jaw in the palm of her hand.

She had lost so much, and it was all her own fault – well, almost all. Some of it was his fault. *Bastard.*

Her obsessive attempt to revenge herself against Max had backfired. Alex, for whom she had harbored a romantic fantasy for years, had betrayed her in more ways than she could count. Her loss of that fantasy stung not just because it was gone but because she was glad it was gone. She was over Alex. Years wasted, she told herself. The pain in her chest lessened.

The law firm was in shambles and likely would never be resurrected no matter who took the helm. Her condo, the one she'd bought right after the divorce, her sanctuary, decorated with care, her security blanket and her home – gone. Max had stolen the safety of it when he found his way inside. She wondered how long he could have done that and didn't. Now, she couldn't go back. That part of her life had been wiped out of existence.

Finally, Loren. Paul had her. He'd keep her. He had more ammunition than ever against Fran. She'd lost so much and now she was losing her child. The tears began again.

"Idiot!" Fran yelled at herself in the dark. "Goddamn idiot!"

Someone had told her once that depression was anger turned inward, and right now she was very, very angry with herself.

She stood up, wiped away the fresh tears and tried to rub some heat into her arms. From where she stood, the furnishings were little more than black on black shadows, but a bright moon cascaded through the window and threw light on the rug and fireplace. She fumbled in the dark and found a lamp. The light was soft but sufficient.

Fran made her way around the house, closing doors and windows and locking them, pulling drapes together and shades down, and turning on lights. She checked the purse to see if the gun was there or if she had imagined it. She shuddered when her fingers brushed the barrel. She snapped the purse closed and went back to the bedroom and rummaged through her things until she found her hooded sweatshirt. She pulled it on and zipped it up, found the thermostat in the kitchen, and turned up the heat. The quiet hum of the furnace filled the house.

"Now, what?" she asked herself. She returned to the kitchen to face the boxes on the wooden table.

"First, food."

She wondered if Rick had gotten any ice cream.

SATURDAY

"You know where she is, don't you?" Tom asked Rick.

The sun was low on the horizon and splashes of pink and orange floated above the city outside the large law office window. A few stars pierced the ascending darkness. Margo had popped in once or twice to get updates. Fran, of course, never showed up, but Rick had spoken to her a few times. The two men were alone in the library, Rick looking like he didn't know what sleep was and Tom finally looking like he did.

"What do you mean?" Rick avoided looking at Tom, concentrating instead on a computer printout of the crime scene that he'd generated from the court files. He was stiff and sore from pouring over the evidence all day and he was starting to get hungry for a real meal.

Tom pulled a chair up to the table and sat down. "Look at me," he

296

ordered.

Rick turned his head just enough to eye the detective. "Don't give me orders, kid. Not if you want two good eyes to see the sunrise with."

Tom ignored the threat. "Where is she? Why is she hiding? WHAT is she hiding? What happened?"

Rick's eyes went back to the computer screen. He blinked as he focused. "What makes you think she's hiding anything?" He typed in some information.

"How long have we known each other?" Tom asked.

"Too long."

"Then don't play stupid with me," Tom said. "She must have told you about the disc. I'm sure Max is somehow using it against her. Blackmail? Does it prove Alex is guilty? Is that why she's running scared?"

Rick shrugged. A ping of pain rippled through the muscles with that move. He straightened up and rubbed his shoulder a few seconds before continuing to type. "If she told you about it, then she also told you that she doesn't know." Rick frowned. He held his fingers suspended over the keyboard a few seconds before balling his hands into fists. "What are the chances she's lying to us?" he asked without looking up from the keys. The words came slowly. "What if she has the disc?"

Tom sat on the edge of the table. For some inexplicable reason, the thought took the wind out of him. "Why? If what she knows could free Alex, why would she do that?"

"It's the rape, or the rough sex, depending on how you look at it," Rick answered, still not looking at the man. He typed a bit more as he spoke. "That's what's on the disc. Alex and the dead girl. Enough to put him away for life." He was trying to justify an action he couldn't accept with reasons he couldn't believe.

"Any good lawyer can create reasonable doubt around that," Tom

297

answered, "and Charles Warner Smith is one damn good lawyer. So, all that's left is who killed Carol. If it's Alex...."

"It's not Alex," Rick said.

"You know that because?" Tom leaned forward, placing his hand over the keyboard to stop Rick from typing.

"Because there IS a disc." Rick sighed as he pushed back from the table and looked up. "If Alex had killed her and known about the disc, he would have taken it. In fact, any killer would have taken it. The fact that it didn't turn up in evidence means...."

"Elliott took it. First one at the scene, and he knew her – well. Naturally, the first place he'd go would be the recorder," Tom surmised.

"If it proved Alex killed Carol...." Rick continued.

"It would be in evidence," Tom finished.

"It's not Alex," Rick repeated, his hand tightening in fists.

"Everything I have says it is." Tom stretched his back.

"I said it's not Alex." Rick barked. He stood up to challenge Tom.

Tom got to his feet and the two men faced off, both ready for a fight.

"You gonna bust me up now? Or later?" Tom asked. "One way or the other, I'm going to get that disc and, when I do, we'll all know who killed Carol McEnroe. Which brings me back to my first question. Where is Fran?"

"She's safe." Rick's voice softened as he backed off and looked away.

"Safe from whom?" Tom asked.

"Safe from the goddamn world, for now." Rick picked up his jacket and slipped it on.

"You know who killed Carol," Tom said, a sickening sensation crawling through his body. "You know and you're hiding it."

"No, I don't know, but I can guess. So, could you, if you thought about it," Rick snapped. The muscles on his neck tightened into rods.

Tom wiped the sweat from his upper lip as a short list of names sprung

298

into mind. His gut clenched. "Tell me it isn't you."

"Me what?" asked Rick.

"Who killed Carol?"

Rick stared angrily at him. "It's not me."

Tom made a fist. "Or Fran."

"For Pete's sake, stop being stupid," Rick said.

"What did Margo have to say?"

"Nothing you and I didn't already know." Rick stomped toward the door. "There was another set of DNA, and it wasn't Alex's, this time."

"Hey, we're not through here. Where are you going?" Tom demanded to know.

"For a steak and a cigarette – and as far away from you as I can get." Rick slammed the door and left Tom standing alone in the empty office.

The computer clicked into sleep mode and the sunset poured through the window and bathed the office in a soft golden glow. Tom's eyes followed the streams of light to the library table. He sat in Rick's seat, looked around, and struggled to keep calm as he searched for the inevitable. With a little digging, he turned up the crumpled lab report. A third DNA strand on the cigar, he read; no match yet, nothing in the database, but the readout suggested.... Tom suddenly felt ill.

He called Candy.

"Nice to hear from you, sweet cheeks," she piped over the phone. "Finally taking up my offer on the chaps?"

"Any luck on the DNA?" he asked, getting right to the point.

"Well, yes and no. Depends what you're looking for."

Tom nodded on his end. "Tell me what you have."

"Nothing to match it with the McEnroe case," she said.

"But?"

"The hair belongs to someone related to Alex's client, Ivan Callas," she

299

continued.

Tom leaned back in his chair. He hadn't expected that answer. "What do you mean by related to him?" he asked. "How did you get to that conclusion?"

He could imagine her sitting on a velvet throne in her dungeon with a crop on her lap. He quickly erased the thought from his mind. His eyes went to Rick's abandoned cup of cold coffee. Tom's stomach growled.

"The sample has enough characteristics in common with the Callas sample to indicate a relative," Candy explained.

"The Callas sample...." Tom's voice trailed off in thought. *The Callas sample was a ruse. It wasn't Callas' DNA at all.*

"I smell smoke, sweetie," Candy said, breaking into his thoughts. "You're thinking too hard."

"I've been assuming that Elliott took a sample of Callas' DNA and swapped it for the real killer's, to make Callas look guilty. Now I'm wondering if it's the other way around. Maybe he swapped the real killer's DNA for Callas' instead."

"I'm not following," Candy admitted. "What's the difference?"

"Let's say the killer's DNA is sample 1, Callas' is sample 2, and the strands I gave you are sample 3, okay?"

"Go on," she urged.

"Two things could have happened. Either Elliott collected the hair from the scene, sample 1 – the unknown killer, and swapped it for hair taken from Callas at another time, maybe at the arrest, sample 2, to make it look like Callas was at the scene."

"I can't imagine why he would do such an idiotic thing, but go on," Candy said.

"Or Elliott collected hair from the scene, sample 1, and switched it for an unknown sample, one not in the equation, someone completely outside the

300

scope of the investigation, someone he was trying to frame."

"Then how would Callas' DNA end up on the girl's sweater?" Candy asked.

"He knew the girl, remember? If his story is true, he had her sweater. He cut himself. Hence, his blood was on her sweater but no other DNA of his was on her." Tom's head was beginning to spin with the possibilities. "Or, Elliott matched the sample taken from the scene, sample 1 – subject unknown, with another sample that didn't belong to Callas but may have belonged to the real killer."

"Why do you say that?" Candy asked. "That would presume Elliott knows who the real killer is or..." she thought a minute. "No, that's not right. If he knows who the killer is, he has no reason to switch the hairs. That means he's setting someone up and Callas just got in the way."

"Damn, this is confusing. There's no way in hell that sample 3 is related to Callas. None," Tom admitted.

Candy was quiet a moment. "Who is it related to?" she asked. "Or do I want to know?"

Tom sighed. In for a penny, he thought. "Sample 3 came from Fran Simone, Alex's law partner. Unless I miss my guess, that proves the DNA at the murder scene belongs to her father, Max Simone."

He could hear Candy gasp. "Oh, shit. Elliott is trying to frame Simone for child rape and murder?"

"Or Simone is guilty."

"Can you email me that information in affidavit form?" Candy asked.

"On its way. And, Candy?" Tom continued, feeling suddenly weak and exhausted. "I have something I need to send to you too, from Alex's case. The DNA...."

"I already have it," she said, her voice soothing.

"Why didn't you tell me?" His throat tightened. His chest hurt. He had to focus to breathe. Something about sharing that information openly made it real - made it painful.

Candy hesitated a minute. "It's my investigation, Tom, not yours. I couldn't. Not yet. Not until I know what it means."

"It's exculpatory evidence," he pointed out, his voice weak.

"Is it?" she asked. After a few moments of silence, she continued. "What are you going to do, sweet cheeks?"

The last sliver of sunset disappeared from the window. The darkness was broken by brittle shards of light from the city. The conference room bore the weight of the silence in the once active law office.

"Tom?"

"My job, Candy. I'm going to do my job." Tom hung up. Remembering it was Saturday, he called Randall at home.

Randall's wife answered. "He's not here. He's at the goddamn office – again!" she yelled before slamming down the phone.

Tom hung up, locked the office door and trudged to Randall's office. Tom hoped Randall really was there and not gallivanting around town with another woman. This wasn't about Alex anymore or Fran. It was about justice and the perversion that had spread its tentacles throughout the city. It was about Max Simone and the murder of three innocent children. Tom realized who had beaten Fran up and why. He wondered what else he didn't know. He thought about Lauren and all the other little girls at her school. He broke into a run.

***

Charles Warner Smith banged on the door to Alex's apartment. He looked surprised when Toni answered. She looked like she hadn't been sleeping well. Her eyes were puffy, her clothes wrinkled and her hair unkempt.

"I need to see my client." Smith charged into the room and dropped his briefcase with a thud on the kitchen table. He looked like he'd just stepped off the golf course.

Alex stepped out of the bedroom, pulling on a shirt. "It's late. What's going on?" he asked.

Smith glared at Toni. "Alone."

"She's my sister. She's not going anywhere. What's going on?"

Smith turned his anger back on Alex. "What part of don't-talk-to-anyone don't you get?" He began pacing the floor.

"I haven't been talking. I've been listening." Alex buttoned up the shirt and stared Smith down.

"To a cop?"

"You mean Tom?" Toni quickly came to her partner's defense.

Smith didn't acknowledge her. "What about Rick? What about your secretary? Your law partner? What about that actress you're sleeping with? You know the cops have photos of who comes and goes from here, don't you? You know they are required by law to provide me with that stuff, right? You're charged with murder and rape of a cop. You're under surveillance every minute of every day. You're sleeping with two women...."

"I'm what? Who the hell said that?" Alex demanded to know.

"The photos say that." Smith pulled them out of his briefcase and threw them on the table. Toni just stared at them, her lips taut. Fran, Margo, Autumn, her, Rick, Tom. They were all there.

"In the first place, I have never had sex with Fran, and I'm getting damn sick and tired of constantly telling everyone that." Alex tore angrily through the photos. "She's my friend and my partner and that's it."

"I don't think a jury would believe that," Smith responded.

"In the second place," Alex resumed, "my private life is none of their goddamn business." He threw the photos back at his lawyer.

"Don't think for one minute that this case isn't about your moral character." Smith shoved the photos into the briefcase. "You're playing with fire. You want to get burned, that's your business, but I'll be damned if I let you take me down with you."

Toni backed away from the two men and slunk into the living room. She curled up on the sofa and pulled a throw over her, trembling.

"My job is to make sure the state can't win its case," Smith continued.

"Mine is to clear my name," Alex yelled back. "Do you know that Roger Elliott has a history of tampering with evidence? Did you know the sheriff fired my sister when she accused him of sleeping with Carol?" He angrily pointed to Toni and suddenly grabbed his side as the pain returned. "I've been beaten and labeled a murderer and a rapist. I can't just be acquitted. I have to be vindicated, and the only way to do that is to find the killer."

"You have someone in mind?" Smith asked.

"Yes. I just can't prove it, yet," said Alex.

"Max Simone." Toni's voice rose softly from the next room.

Smith turned to stare at her. "The mayor?"

"He's Fran's father," Alex explained. "He's a suspect in the Ivan Callas case. We're pretty sure he raped and murdered a young girl two years ago, and he knows I'll get to the bottom of it. He wants me out of the picture. That's why he set me up."

"You think he murdered McEnroe?" Smith looked incredulous.

"Why not? He rapes kids," Alex said.

Smith bit his upper lip and considered the statement. "You're sure about that?"

Alex nodded. "Dead sure." He thought only a few seconds before betraying his partner. "He raped Fran when she was twelve."

Toni sat up, surprised. This was new information to her.

"They all knew about me and Carol. Carol probably told them. They paid her cash and they got her back here just to set me up. Randall even got her a job. He was her landlord," he continued. "Why am I telling you this? You know all this stuff. You knew it before I did. You don't think that's a bit suspicious?"

"I know all that. Randall thinks you killed Sarah and got away with it. That's his beef with you," Smith explained.

"Of course, he does," Toni stated without elaborating.

"He was probably hoping Carol would drag it out of you," Smith continued without acknowledging Toni.

"She couldn't have. I never killed my wife."

"As for Elliott, that's another matter. Simone?" Smith thought a minute. "Okay, I'll have my people look into it."

"Before or after he kills again?" Alex asked.

"We need evidence," Smith reminded Alex.

"That makes me feel real safe." Alex didn't hide his raw sarcasm.

"You want to feel safe?" Smith countered. "Ditch the damn actress!"

As the slamming door echoed in the apartment, Toni looked up at Alex. "Listen to him," she said quietly. "He knows what he's talking about. All she's going to do is hurt you, just like the others. Just like that cop. Stop seeing her. Please, Alex. Just stop."

"For once, Toni, stay the hell out of my business!" he yelled.

***

Tom walked into Sheriff George Randall's stuffy office unannounced and with an air of confidence driven by desperation. He plopped down in the plastic chair in front of his boss' desk.

"Did I send for you?" Randall asked, glancing up from his paperwork. His blinds, closed behind him, shut out the nightfall. He was twisted half-way in his chair to stretch his legs to the side. A baseball in a Plexiglass box held down a stack of papers on his desk.

"No, but you should have," Tom said.

"What do you want?" Randall tossed down his pen, took off his glasses

305

and leaned back in his chair. It squeaked.

"To negotiate."

"Why should I do that?" Randall asked. "Negotiation is what happens when both sides have more to lose than they have to gain. I have nothing to lose."

"Don't you?" Tom asked.

Randall eyed Tom suspiciously before pushing the intercom for his secretary. "I don't want to be disturbed." She didn't answer. He remembered it was Saturday. He stood up, shut the door and locked it before returning to his seat. The chair squeaked again.

"I see we're on the same page," Tom said. He kept his hands buried in his pockets to hide his nervousness.

"You want to negotiate? Tell me what you've got," Randall snapped.

Tom straightened himself and looked the sheriff in the eye. "I know Roger Elliott and Max Simone have a DVD of Carol's murder." From the startled look on Randall's face, Tom knew Randall was in the dark. "I know Alex didn't kill her or the disc would have been in your hands by now, which means your lab is withholding exculpatory evidence from the defense."

"It's the prosecutor's investigation, now, remember? Go on." Randall squirmed a little.

"I also know you were sleeping with Carol, as was Elliott, Simone, Alex and god knows who else, which means there probably is a disc of you and her somewhere, too."

"If you think I'm going to be blackmailed, forget it. I'm fifty-five years old and on the verge of a divorce. This is Vegas. If I want to get laid by some hot young thing, that ain't going to hurt my career none." The tension in Randall's voice betrayed the anxiety under his apparent bravado.

"True, but she's a dead hot young thing, and the fact you were involved with her at all compromises your case against de la Rosa, and I know how

306

badly you want him for murdering Sarah, even if he didn't do it."

"He did it," Randall asserted.

"Maybe." Tom nearly choked on the word. The earlier nausea was still with him.

"Sarah and Carol. He did them both. I know it in my gut." Randall's eyes flashed. "Make your point." He shifted his weight and the chair squeaked again. He grimaced.

"Whether you like it or not, whether you're aware of it or not, Elliott and Simone have you over a barrel," said Tom. "I know the disc will clear Alex of the murder. We both want the same thing, justice. Give me my job back and I'll solve both cases and cover your ass."

"Both cases?"

"The serial child murders and Carol's case. I've got all the pieces in my hands now. I just need to put the puzzle together."

"I told you, this is the prosecutor's case now. That damn dominatrix, Candy Knight, is handling it," Randall said.

"We're – cooperating," Tom stated, "but I can't do what I need to do if I'm not officially back."

"Tell me what you got," said Randall.

Tom thought a minute. "I have enough evidence to establish probable cause that Max Simone is our serial child killer, that Elliott planted evidence on the dead girls, that Elliott took the DVD of Carol's murder from the crime scene and that he gave a copy to Simone. Once I have the DVD, I can prove who really killed Carol."

Randall pursed his lips together. He didn't seem surprised. "How will you do that?"

"You get warrants for their properties - work and home - and I'll find the DVDs and sort through them. I'll pass on what Candy needs for the prosecutor and give the rest to you, to do with what you want."

307

Randall squinted at Tom and reassessed him. "That's tampering with evidence."

"No, that's handing evidence over to a supervising officer. As long as the prosecution gets their legitimate pound of flesh, what do you care?"

Tom was sweating, but he was not about to let Randall see it.

"You're asking for a warrant for the mayor's office," Randall said. "That's political suicide."

"And his home, and the crime lab, and Elliott's property," Tom clarified.

Randall groaned as if in pain. "Do you have any idea what this is going to do to any case Elliott has ever handled?"

Tom lowered his head a bit and sighed. He was banking on Randall being one of the good guys, but maybe he was wrong. He waited.

Randall leaned forward, rubbed his chin, and tried to ignore the irritating squeak of the chair. "How do I know I can trust you?"

"As compared to whom, Simone or Elliott?"

Randall thought quietly for a minute.

Tom nervously continued his argument. "Look, if anyone is committing political suicide, it's me, not you. You reinstate me, and I'll get the warrants if you want. There's got to be at least one judge in this town who isn't afraid of Simone. If I'm wrong, fire me. If I'm right, you could be the next mayor of Las Vegas. That is what you want, isn't it? Carol's killer in jail, the child murders solved and Simone out of power? Three birds with one stone. What have you got to lose?"

Randall growled. "Consider yourself reinstated, but you'll have to get the warrants, and I don't want to know about it." He reached in a drawer and threw Tom's badge at him. "Don't expect much help from your buddies in the department, either. You sided with a cop killer in an ongoing investigation. That makes you persona non gratis around here."

Tom caught the badge with one hand, smiled, stood up and unlocked the door. "Good move," he said over his shoulder. "Better get that chair fixed." He entered the corridor, his heart pounding in his ears. He took a deep breath of relief.

Randall leaned back, the chair squeaked again, and he erupted. Clearing his desk with one sweep of his arm, he picked up the chair and flipped it upside down on the desk. "Margie!" he yelled. "Get me some oil!" No one answered.

Brandt, leaning against the unmarked cruiser, was waiting for Tom in the parking lot. His black leather vest glistened in the streetlights. He hung up his phone and obliterated the remains of a cigarette under his heel.

"I thought you couldn't get far enough away from me." Tom unlocked the door and opened it.

"If we're going to do this, we gotta work together," said Rick.

"How the hell do you know what I'm going to do?" Tom asked.

"You're after the disc, aren't you?"

"What are you after?" Tom studied Rick.

Brandt straightened up. "Justice," he said with a smirk. "What else?"

"For whom?"

Brandt didn't answer.

"Careful there, Rick. Justice has a way of biting you in the ass," Tom stated.

"I've been bitten before, and I got the scars to prove it," said Rick.

Tom didn't doubt it. He realized they both knew who killed Carol. The shared pain was tangible between them. He smiled weakly. "How about I buy you that steak?"

CHAPTER 21

Alex pressed Autumn against the door of his apartment, his hands wrapped tightly around the tender skin of her waist, under her shirt. His lips were hungry on hers. He inhaled her scent, letting it seep through his pores. "Are you sure you have to go?" he asked in a plaintive voice, as his mouth moved to her neck and she groaned.

"Alex! Enough already." She reveled in the power she had over him. "Toni could be back anytime, and she doesn't need to catch us."

"She knows I'm sleeping with you," he murmured, pulling her tighter and finding her lips again.

Autumn gave in to him a few more minutes before gently pushing him away. "No. She knows I slept with you. Past tense. There's a difference."

"Stay." His voice was muffled as his lips found her breasts.

"She doesn't like me, you know." Autumn squealed and playfully hit him on the head. "Stop that!"

He reluctantly straightened up to look in her deep jade eyes. "She doesn't like anyone I date. She thinks she's my mother, protecting me from the world." He sighed. "I want you. Stay. I'll make it worth your while."

Autumn smiled and nuzzled him. "You always do," she said, "but I think we've done enough of that for one day."

He groaned in resignation and finally pulled away from her. "You don't know what you do to me." He gently brushed his fingers through her thick long hair.

"I have a pretty good idea."

"You saved my life."

"Not yet." She gave him one last kiss. "Time to go."

He pulled the door open behind her as she slipped out of his arms. Halfway down the hall, she turned and threw a kiss over her shoulder. Alex smiled, closed the door, and rested his head on it for a moment. He checked the clock. It was getting late and he hadn't heard from Fran or Toni all day. He was worried.

Outside, the night sky was bright from a million city lights. Autumn pulled a sweater over her shoulders and quietly slipped through the parking lot to her car. She glanced about nervously, noting the media van, then clicked the lock open and slid behind the wheel.

From the moment she closed the door, she knew something was wrong. The car smelled funny, oily and yet like cinnamon. Something cold pressed against the back of her neck and she went to slap it away, glancing in the rear-view mirror as she did so. A shadowy figure in a black stocking mask stared back. Without thinking, Autumn pulled open the car door, fell to the ground, and rolled away from the vehicle. She heard her assailant hiss and exit the car. Autumn got to her feet and ran for the television van. The reporters, stunned to see the actress running towards them in high heels and screaming, dropped their coffees and grabbed their cameras. A bullet, whizzing past Autumn, shattered a window in the van. The reporters ducked for cover. Another bullet skimmed her shoulder. She cried out in pain and fell forward.

"Call the cops, you idiots!" Autumn screamed, crawling for shelter behind another vehicle.

One of the reporters pulled out his cell phone and made the call while the other continued taking photos. The svelte figure in black stopped, suddenly aware of an audience, then turned and ran into the darkness. Autumn trembled on the pavement and hid her face as flashbulbs went off around her.

Alex heard the shots from his condo. Startled, he stared through the curtains at the commotion below and saw the flash of camera bulbs and a figure on the ground. His gut wrenched. Barefoot, he grabbed his keys and ran out of the condo and down the stairs. The hot night air hit him in the face as he charged out of the lobby and into the parking lot.

312

Two reporters hovered around the actress. She sat on the ground and leaned against the car. One grabbed a jacket and was placed it under her head, while the other held a handful of paper towels to her shoulder.

"Autumn!" Alex yelled. He ran to her and dropped to his knees. In that second, everything else was forgotten. He saw the blood oozing over the reporter's fingers. "Hold on, honey," he told her. "It's okay. Just hold on."

Her face was pale, and her eyes looked dazed.

"I called 911," the reporter with the paper towels said.

The other reporter stood up and tried to decide if he should take a picture or not. He backed up a little.

Autumn smiled through clenched teeth. "It hurts like fucking hell."

"Who was it? Did you see him?" Alex asked.

"I was too scared." Autumn began to cry.

"All I saw was someone in black. Looked skinny. Could have been a teenager," one of the reporters said.

Alex sat down next to Autumn and held her hand. "Don't worry, honey. It'll be okay."

A siren grew louder as an ambulance approached. The reporter with the camera took the picture.

***

Alex paced the floor of the hospital waiting room. He didn't have a shirt or shoes, but he'd managed to borrow a phone. His feet were dirty, and his hands were covered in blood. He tried calling Fran with no luck. Then Toni, also no luck. Then Rick. He stopped pacing when he heard the investigator's calm voice on the phone.

"Autumn's been shot," he said in lieu of hello.

Rick's voice was taut. "How is she?"

"Okay. She got lucky. We're at the hospital."

"What happened?" Rick asked.

"Some idiot was stalking her. Stalking her! Do you believe it? Fucking piece of shit. He was hiding in her car and she ran. Got her in the shoulder. If I find that asshole…."

"Calm down," Rick ordered.

"Mr. Bartlett?" an orderly asked, tapping Alex's arm.

"I gotta go," Alex told Rick. "Keep me informed." He hung up the phone and handed it back to a man sitting in a nearby chair. Turning towards the orderly, Alex said, "I'm her boyfriend, not her husband."

The orderly nodded. "Well, your girlfriend wants to see you, but you can't go in there like that."

"Got any better ideas?" Alex asked.

The young man thought a moment, then motioned for Alex to follow him. A few minutes later, Alex sidled up to Autumn's bed, cleaned up and dressed in greens.

Autumn, drowsy from pain medication, smiled up at him. "Well, well. Look at you. One day you're a lawyer, and then a political candidate, and then an accused killer, and now you're a doctor. You're practically your own soap opera."

Alex smiled, took her hand, and squeezed it gently. "I thought I'd lost you there for a moment," he told her. "Scared the hell out of me."

She saw the sincerity in his eyes. "I love you too, Alex," she whispered.

He kissed her. "I guess it was my turn to save your life."

The emergency room doctor came in to check on Autumn. Stepping around Alex, the doctor smiled briefly and went through her vitals. "You're a very lucky lady. I'd normally send you home tonight, but you banged your head when you fell, and I want to make sure you don't have a concussion." He took a moment to check her eyes. "I'm going to keep you overnight for observation and, if all goes well, as I suspect it will, you'll be on your way first thing in the morning."

"Thanks, doc." Autumn offered up one of her famous smiles.

The doctor glowed and turned to Alex. "I hope your friend is feeling better."

"Friend?" Alex asked, confused.

"Yes. Ms. Simone. She is your…." He glanced at Autumn. "Oh. I'm sorry. I must have made a mistake." He quickly slipped out of the room.

Autumn giggled. "Well, he wouldn't be the first one to think she's your girlfriend."

Alex wasn't smiling. "I just spoke to Rick. He didn't say anything about Fran being in the hospital."

Autumn shrugged. "Then it must not have been serious." When she saw how intent he was, she squeezed his hand. "Why don't you go find out, hon. I'm not going anywhere tonight, and you won't be happy until you know. Go on."

Alex gave her another kiss before he headed back to his apartment to get dressed. When he arrived, he found Toni's jacket flung over his sofa and heard the shower running. A few minutes later, she emerged, wearing his robe and dripping water on the carpet.

"Hey," she said casually. "Where have you been?"

"Never mind where I've been," he snapped. "Where have you been?"

"At my apartment." She scowled at him. "I had to do some grocery shopping and feed the cat. What the hell's the matter with you?"

"Autumn was shot. Why didn't you answer your phone?"

"Shot?" Toni looked startled. "Where? When?"

"Why didn't you answer your phone?" he screamed at her.

Pouting, Toni went to her jacket, pulled out her cell phone and glanced at it. "Battery's dead," she said. "I'll have to recharge it." She slipped it back into the pocket.

"Why don't you shower in your own goddamn place?" he asked.

315

"Because you're my brother. Because I love you. Because I wanted to be here with you. I wanted to make sure you were okay." She crossed her arms defensively as tears brimmed in her eyes. "Besides, I got no place to go, no one to talk to, except the cat. It's not like I'm getting up and going to work every day."

"How many times have I told you to stop mothering me!" His voice was slightly quieter, but only slightly. "I can take care of myself, Toni. Stop it."

"No, you can't, and sleeping with Carol and that slutty actress proves it," she snapped. "Didn't you hear your attorney? Weren't you paying attention?"

Frustrated, Alex stomped to his bedroom and slammed the door behind him. Once alone, he picked up his slacks from the bed and pulled his cell phone out of the pocket. He dialed Rick's number.

"What's up?" Rick asked.

"Why didn't you tell me Fran was in the hospital? What happened? I've been calling her all day and she doesn't answer."

"She's fine. She left her phone at the office and no one's there," Rick lied. "I saw her earlier. She's up to her elbows in the Callas case."

"Why was she in the hospital?" Alex asked as he relaxed a little.

"Nothing serious. Exhaustion. She passed out, but she's fine. I took care of it," Rick assured Alex.

"Probably too much scotch," Alex muttered.

"How many times do I have to say she's fine? Now get some sleep. It's late and we got a pile of shit to do tomorrow." Rick also sounded tired.

"Like what?" Alex asked.

"I'll fill you in over breakfast."

"Okay." Alex closed the phone and collapsed on his bed. He reached over and turned on the CD player.

***

SUNDAY

316

Fran, in her double bed, held Lauren tightly and drew the blankets around them both. A nightlight shone in the corner.

Why are you afraid of the dark?"Lauren asked, yawning wide.

It's silly. I know.'Fran stroked her daughter's hair and sighed softly. I'just have bad dreams, that's all. Besides, I don't like sleeping in someone else's home. I need your company. You'll keep me company, right? You won't go anywhere?"

Lauren nodded as she drifted off to sleep. Fran felt under her pillow for the gun and breathed a little easier. She slipped it into the drawer of the nightstand, rolled over and curled protectively around her daughter.

Fran awoke from the dream. She'd fallen asleep at the kitchen table in the safe-house. The sun was just beginning to rise, and a pale gray light slipped through the drawn shades. A large file was opened under her arms, half read. Next to it was a pad of lined, yellow paper scrawled with notes. She stared at it, frustrated. It stared back at her.

"I can do this," she said. "I can stop this monster from killing again."

She glanced at her notes and yawned. Coffee, that's what she needed – a lot of it – and breakfast.

She stood up and ran her fingers through her unkempt hair. The house seemed too quiet for her, so she turned on the radio. Operatic strains tried to escape into the air, but she quickly turned the knob. She had enough drama in her life right now. She didn't need more.

She caught the news. "Actress Autumn Bartlett was injured last night when a gunman shot her in the parking lot of Turnberry Place. The actress was rushed to the hospital where she is reportedly in fair condition and is expected to be released sometime today. With her at the hospital was her reputed boyfriend, accused killer Alexander Rose."

They got his name wrong, Fran thought. *How could they get his name wrong?*

317

She flipped off the radio, looked at the phone Rick had left her and wondered if this was a good time to call him. As if on cue, the phone rang.

"Too late," she said, skipping the hellos. "It was on the radio. What happened?"

"Alex was worried about you. I finally told him you collapsed from exhaustion, but you're okay and working on the Callas case. He was okay with that," said Rick. "You are okay, right?"

"I am. What happened?" she asked impatiently. At this point, she didn't give a damn what Alex thought.

"Well, we're not sure," Rick replied. "Autumn got into her car and somebody was already in it. The assailant pulled a gun on her, and Autumn ran. He managed to get a shot off and hit her in the shoulder but didn't do any real damage. The who and why parts were still a mystery. The guy probably would have killed her but for the press being there. They all started yelling and taking photos and the guy turned and ran."

"Alex?" she asked.

"Alex is fine. Alex is always fine." Rick oozed sarcasm.

"Don't go there," Fran told him, her shoulders drooping. "It's not worth it. It's over, and I know it. Don't say I told you so, either. I have enough to deal with."

Rick was quiet a moment. "You alright, boss?" he asked again.

Fran cleared her head. Her eyes went to the file. "We have a problem with the Callas case," she said. "Elliott tried so hard to do – whatever the hell he was doing – that we're missing evidence."

"What kind of evidence?"

"Well, a full DNA panel for one. He's got Callas, of course, but those girls must have been in contact with a dozen people: teachers, family members, kids on the school bus, and so on," said Fran as she looked at her notes. "No one tested all the samples to see if there are any other matches. Also, all three

318

girls went to the same school, but no one interviewed people at the school or, if they did, they didn't include any statements in discovery. And I don't know what these girls had in common, other than going to the same school and being about the same age. Did they have the same teachers? Live in the same neighborhood? All belong to the choir? We need their school records to figure this out. No one – and I mean NO one – has done a real investigation on this case."

"What about the stuff from Tom?" he asked.

"Stuff? What stuff?" She tugged the box towards her and started fingering through the file folders.

"The envelope. I stuck it in there, sealed and unmarked. There's some lab reports from the latest victim, some memos, emails I think, crime photos. I didn't look at it all."

Fran's fingers lighted on the envelope and she pulled it out of the box. It was heavy in her hand. The edge was sealed twice, once with its own glue and then again with scotch tape. She turned it over and back and found no writing on it.

"I think I found it," she said. She set the phone down while she found a kitchen knife and sliced the envelope open. Then she dumped the contents on the table and quickly rifled through them. She picked up the phone. "Yes, I got it. I'll go through these. Thanks."

"Hopefully, there's something there," Rick said.

"Looks like Tom's been hard at work."

"He's reinstated." Rick hesitated for emphasis. "Randall is letting him pursue Elliott and Max on these cases. Tom's going to spend the day finding a judge, any judge, who will sign a search warrant for these guys."

"What's he after?" she asked as she smiled.

"The discs, of course, and anything else incriminating."

Fran froze for a minute.

319

"You still there?" Rick asked.

"Yes," she said, barely above a whisper.

"Fran...," This time his voice came softly, comfortingly. "...I know who killed Carol – so does Tom and so do you."

"You saw the disc?" she asked, grabbing her purse and searching through it to reassure herself it was still there. She held it up.

"No. I saw the latest DNA report, and I suspect so did Tom. At least he should have if he's half the cop I think he is."

Fran, startled, sat back down at the table. "Then why would he pursue this?" she asked. "He's got to be going out of his mind."

"I'd better go, kid," Rick said, not answering her question. "It's going to be a long, hard day. I'll pass on your discovery request to Tom and see what he can dig up. Stay put. I'll be in touch."

"Be careful, Rick."

"Always, boss," he said.

Rick hung up. He started his vehicle and drove off, his meeting with Alex forgotten.

Fran closed the box and sat down to go through the contents of the envelope. She forgot about coffee. It occurred to her that Callas was probably unaware of what was going on. She had to see him, but not today. She wanted to be in the heat of things. She needed to know what was happening. The house that was supposed to be her refuge now seemed more like her cage. She went back to work.

***

This is poker, Tom reminded himself, as he trudged through the crime lab looking for Elliott in the late Sunday morning hours. Tom used to be good at poker, a very, very long time ago. He had spent all morning going door to door and had so far found only one judge who would issue a warrant of any kind, and that was a search warrant limited to Roger Elliott. Tom found

320

Elliott in the locker room, changing his clothes. The smell of sweaty socks and Right Guard hung in the air.

"Imagine my surprise when they told me you worked weekends," Tom said.

"I thought you were suspended." Elliott pulled on his khaki pants and buckled his belt.

"I was. Things change."

"Good," said Elliott. "Maybe you can find something more constructive to do with your time than hanging out with perverts." He pulled a polo shirt over his head and reached for his lab coat.

"Like you? Or like the mayor?" Tom asked.

Elliott glared at him. "Bad career move, Sadler," he snapped.

"Just tell me two things and I'll leave you alone," said Tom.

"What?" Elliott slipped on his jacket and buttoned it up, then stuck his feet in his loafers.

"Who's on the disc and where are the copies?" Tom asked.

Elliott tried not to react, but the slight pause was enough to give him away. "What disc?" He stared at the mirror inside his locker as he ran a comb through his hair.

"The disc Max Simone is using to blackmail Fran."

Elliott turned and stared at him. "I don't know what you're talking about."

"Don't bullshit me, Roger. I know all about it, from more sources than you can count on one hand," said Tom. "You should have realized that Max would pull a stunt like that, and Fran would come to me about it."

Elliott didn't respond.

"Well, let's try this on for size," Tom began, approaching Elliott and straddling one of the benches. He sat down and pulled out a blank disc. "A copy. Corrupted, of course, with only the rape remaining. It's the one Max gave Fran." As he spoke, Tom realized that Fran must have a copy. It would

321

explain so much. His mouth went dry. "I really need the whole thing if I'm going to solve this case," he continued, "and I am going to solve this case, with or without you. Now, you were the first one on the scene, you were the one having an affair with her, you knew about the DVD recorder, and you took the disc. That means…."

"That means shit." Elliott stared at the disc. "Nice bluff."

"Suit yourself." Tom put the disc back in his pocket and turned to leave. He stopped at the door. "By the way, you know I don't need a search warrant for the crime lab, right? I mean, there's no expectation of privacy here. Everything already belongs to the police department." He grinned and walked away, leaving Elliott sweating in his gym socks.

***

"He's on the move," Rick told Tom over the cell phone. Rick slipped on his sunglasses, put his rented sedan in gear and pulled out behind Elliott's red Mustang.

Rick dogged Elliott to Barry's Boxing on Highland Drive. The investigator kept a safe distance and relied on the tracker Tom had taped to Elliott's bumper. Rick called his location into Tom, who hung back and followed the same route. When Elliott finally parked, Rick drove by.

Elliott checked the street before entering the building. He carried a gym bag with him. When he emerged a few minutes later, the bag was gone, and Rick and Tom were waiting. They each grabbed an arm, lifted the short man a foot from the ground and carried him back into the locker room of the gym as he squirmed and hollered to be let loose. When onlookers stared, Tom flashed his badge.

"How are you doing, Roger?" Tom asked, opening Elliott's locker and seizing the gym bag. "Did I give you a bit of a scare?"

"You can't do that," Elliott squealed. "This isn't the lab. You need a warrant."

Tom fished in his jacket, pulled out the paper, and handed it to Elliott without looking at him.

"Checkmate," Rick said, gripping Elliott by the collar.

"Roger, you are under arrest for tampering with evidence in a homicide investigation," Tom said, "being an accessory after the fact – maybe even before the fact – to blackmail, obstruction of justice, maybe even jaywalking. I don't think Randall is going to be happy about all this." Tom shook his head sadly.

"Randall? He's behind this?" Elliott demanded to know.

Tom plucked three discs in jewel boxes out of the bag. He had hoped they wouldn't be there. "You want to search him?" Tom asked Rick.

"Can I?" Rick leered.

"Well, it's against protocol but what the hell. Committing a felony while being director of the crime lab is, too, right?" Tom nodded.

Elliott dug his hands into his pockets and produced two more discs. "There, that's all of them."

Rick pushed Elliott against the lockers and patted him down anyway for good measure. "Any chance you want to tell us what the hell is really going on?" Rick asked.

"Can't do that, Rick. Gotta do Miranda first," Tom reminded him.

"This isn't over," Elliott yelled. "I'm not the only one mixed up in this. You'll see. You can't fight…." he stopped.

"City hall?" Tom finished. "It figures you and Max Simone would find each other."

Rick nearly choked on a laugh. "City hall? Damn, man, I thought you could do better than that!"

Elliott glowered at him, spun around and darted out of the gym.

Rick turned to Tom. "Crap. Are we gonna let him get away?"

"Hell, no." Tom, gym bag in one hand and discs in the other, took off running with Rick close behind.

The two men caught up with Elliott just as he was getting into his car. Rick grabbed the still open door and dragged Elliott out.

"Hey!" Elliott yelled. "This is harassment. Police brutality. I'll sue."

"Shut up," Rick barked.

Tom handed the evidence to Rick, turned Elliott towards the car and kicked his legs into position, then patted him down.

"I didn't find anything on him last time," Rick said.

"I know." Tom smiled. "I just wanted to do that."

"Arrest me or let me go," Elliott demanded.

"He'll make a cute little prison bitch," Rick teased.

"Yeah, too bad," Tom agreed.

"Let me go!" Elliott yelled.

"Sorry. Can't do that," Tom said. "In addition to all the crimes you've committed, you're a material witness in a homicide investigation. Actually, you're a material witness in four homicide investigations." Tom stopped to count in his head. "Make that five. And now you attempted to elude police and resist arrest. You're looking at serious time there, Roger."

"Five?" Rick asked.

"Four? I'm losing track," said Tom.

Elliott swore.

"Now what?" Rick asked as Tom cuffed Elliott.

"That's up to the sheriff. It's his call."

"This could screw up every case the crime lab has ever processed," Rick noted.

Tom nodded.

"The D.A. probably won't charge him, not if it fucks with the cases." Rick talked as if Elliott wasn't there.

"Probably not."

"The disc?" Rick asked.

"Got someplace quiet to watch it?" asked Tom.

"You don't want to do that," Elliott said with a sneer.

"I thought I told you to shut up," Rick told Elliott. He looked at Tom. "You sure you want to watch that thing? It's not like you don't know what's on it."

"I don't want to. I have to, as soon as I figure out where to put this guy." Tom sighed.

"Bad idea." Rick shook his head.

"I thought you wanted justice," Tom said.

"I thought you said it would bite me in the ass," Rick countered.

Tom frowned and held up the discs. "I can watch these," he said, "or you both can tell me what I already know. Which is it going to be?"

Elliott swallowed.

"We're on the same side," Rick said.

"Are we?" Tom shook his head and glanced at the disc. "Thing is, this changes everything." He recited Miranda Rights to Elliott.

CHAPTER 22

"Where the hell were you this morning?" Alex wanted to know as he marched into the law office.

It was nearly 10 a.m. Autumn was safe at his apartment and Alex had changed clothes and come looking for someone, anyone. He found the place empty except for Rick, who was sitting in the conference room, the sun at his back, his eyes buried in a computer screen. "I've been calling you for the last two hours! Nobody picks up the goddamn phone around here anymore? I thought you were going to come by my place and brief me."

"We don't work on Sunday," Rick snapped sarcastically, a cup of cold coffee at his side and a pile of discs on the table. He looked like someone had dropped an atomic bomb on him. His face was pale, his eyes red, his expression pained. "Guess you don't want the good news," he said without looking up.

Alex didn't hear him. "Where's Bella?"

"You've got bigger things to worry about than Fran," Rick said sharply. "Sit down." Rick motioned to a chair with his hand.

Alex slipped into one of the conference room's leather chairs and stared at Rick. "Where's Bella and what happened?"

"Elliott was arrested this morning. He's in jail."

Alex was stunned. "For what?"

"Obstruction of justice. Tampering with evidence. Hell, I don't know. Tom came up with a nice long list. Oh, and we got the disc," said Rick.

"What disc?" Alex asked.

Rick leaned back in his chair and looked at Alex for the first time. After all this time, all this work, all this chasing around, it had never occurred to Rick that Alex, of all people, had been left out of the loop.

"The video disc Carol had running when you were in bed with her. The disc that proves you didn't kill her," he spat. "The disc Max Simone has been using to blackmail Fran. The disc that shows what a total ass you are."

Alex's jaw dropped. His eyes widened. He seemed to melt into the seat.

"What the hell! Where? Who?"

"Elliott had it. First one on the scene, remember?" Rick reminded Alex. "That fuckin' weasel knew exactly where to look, and he took it."

"Does that mean I'm free?" Alex asked weakly.

Rick looked away, disgusted. "Not yet," he said. "We got to get this to the prosecutor, first."

"Well, what are we waiting for?" Alex asked as he started to get out of his chair.

Rick shook his head. "Well, for openers, it's Sunday, or didn't I just mention that?" He took the discs and slipped them into a paper bag to take with him. "I've downloaded it onto the computer," he told Alex. "When you have the stomach for it, you can watch, you should watch. In the meantime, we need to find out who really killed those three girls." Rick pushed himself up slowly. "Take your time," he said. "Call me when you're done. We'll talk."

"What are you doing? Where are you going?" Alex asked, panicked.

"Tom and I got some business to finish up. We think we can solve the Callas case, but we still got a lot to do. I'm meeting him at the crime lab." Rick grabbed his jacket as he started walking out the door. He was heavy on his feet like a soldier headed for his last battle.

"Rick," Alex said, stopping him in his tracks.

Rick didn't turn around.

"You've seen the disc."

"Yes," Rick acknowledged.

"Who killed Carol?"

Rick walked away without looking back.

Alex took Rick's abandoned seat and turned on the computer. He saw the file on the desktop, waiting, taunting him. He nervously clicked on it, trying to still the apprehension that threatened to drown him. The life seemed to drain out of Alex as he watched the hooded figure approach the bed. Carol, still bound with the electrical cord, struggled to get free and screamed as the figure sat on her, pulled off the mask and lit a cigar.

"Whore."

Alex's fingernails dug into the chair. He wanted to scream. He wanted to cry. Every cell in his body was collapsing in on itself. He'd shut the video off if he could just remember how to move and how to breathe.

***

Tom called Candy from the quiet of his car. He had pulled up to the forensic lab, still holding onto the gym bag and arguing with himself over what to do next. "Any luck?" he asked when she answered.

"On the DNA from the girls? I think so," Candy said. "I went through the files. The full panels were already done, but they were ignored."

"Well, that brings us one step closer," Tom said. "When can I pick up your report?"

"That depends. What's in it for me, sweet cheeks?" she joked.

He wasn't in the mood. "Does there have to be something in it for you? Doesn't catching a child rapist and serial murderer count as its own reward?" Despite himself, Tom's voice came out bitter and attacking.

Candy was silent for too long.

"Still there?" he asked.

"I know you arrested Elliott," she said calmly. "There's a rumor going around that you have evidence that could clear Alex. If that's true, I want it."

Tom swallowed. "Max Simone has a disc that shows Carol screwing Alex. It also shows who killed her, but I don't have it yet," Tom lied, happy he wasn't looking her in the eye. "I'm trying to get a warrant to search his house and office. I know he has it."

"How do you know?" she asked.

"Because Elliott found it and gave it to him, and because Max is using it to blackmail Fran," he said.

"Blackmail? But if Alex is innocent…." Candy started to say.

"It's complicated," Tom interrupted.

"Okay." She hesitated a moment, thinking. "Come on in from the cold and let's see what you need."

"Where are you?" Tom asked.

"At the lab."

Tom looked at the building in front of him, surprised. "The crime lab?" he asked.

"Yes. Randall called me. With Elliott in jail, he needed an interim director on short notice. So here I am. Are you coming in or not?"

"And you said yes?"

"I have a hidden agenda," she answered. "Okay, not so hidden. Get over here."

"What about your work at the D.A.'s office?" Tom asked.

"I'm moonlighting," Candy told him.

"I'll be right there." Tom hung up the phone. He was sweating, shaking, sick to his stomach. He had kept several copies of the now infamous disc, tucked into Elliott's gym bag. Rick had the rest of them. Tom wondered how many times a man could copy a scene like that and if Elliott got off on it.

Tom stepped out of his vehicle and went to the back. He unlocked the trunk and settled the gym back on a spare tire. Then he shut the trunk and walked slowly toward the building. He could not remember when he ever needed to be somewhere so bad and yet hated to get there so much.

Rick was waiting for him in the lobby.

"You found me," Tom commented as he pocketed his keys.

"Two plus two. Got the discs?"

"In the car," Tom said.

330

"What do you expect to learn here that we don't already know?" Rick asked.

Tom stopped a moment and turned towards Rick. The bustle of the station seemed to fade into the distance. He remembered a busy diner, the streak of sun dancing off cars in the parking lot, a pot of decaf coffee carried by a pretty waitress. "I take it you have somewhere else you need to be," he said.

Rick just nodded as he chewed on one of his unlit cigarettes.

"What are you going to do?" Tom finally asked.

"I'm taking the fifth," Rick responded. He glanced around to make sure no one was listening. "I'm not really sure, yet."

It was Tom's turn to quietly nod. "Candy is waiting for us. Just let me do the talking. No reason to screw up one lie with another."

They picked up their visitor's badges and were passed through security to the lab. This time, no one tried to stop them.

"That was fast," Candy said, glancing up as the men entered her workspace. "I've been digging through the files and, believe it or not, I think I've found something helpful." She looked as sharp and professional as ever, her short hair tucked behind her ears, her lab coat crisp and neatly ironed.

"What?" Tom asked. He angrily shoved away a sliver of hope. He couldn't afford to go there, not yet.

Candy leaned against the table, her arms crossed. Her eyes seemed to be sizing him up. She barely looked at Rick.

"There were between seven and ten samples of DNA on each child. Three came back identical. At least three others were family members or, in one case, a police officer," Candy told them. "Of the three identical ones, we have, of course, Max Simone and Ivan Callas. The third sample, however, can't be identified, at least not yet."

"You mean it's not on file," Tom stated.

Candy nodded. "Oh, it's on file, but with no name to go with it." She reached for a report on the desk and smiled. "It matches a strain of DNA taken from a half-dozen other murder scenes, in Seattle, Washington." She handed the paper to Tom. "You find out who was in Seattle at the time of those murders, compare it to this one, and you got your killer."

Rick shook his head. "Needle in a haystack," he muttered, discouraged and obviously distracted.

Candy shrugged. "It's a start. Maybe the Seattle police had a lead or suspect. What do you lose by trying?"

"You're right," Tom nodded, staring at the report. Rick was right, too. It was a longshot.

"While you're at it," Candy said, "I called Judge Wilburn. He'll give you that search warrant for Max Simone."

Tom looked up, startled. He smiled. He didn't have to ask how she'd done that. His phone rang. Glancing at it, Tom said, "Sorry, I have to take this." Tom stepped out of the lab and found a quiet corner. He pressed the cell phone to his ear. "Hi, mom. I'm sorry. I completely forgot."

"You forgot lunch with me on Sunday?" she asked at the other end. "It must be a big case – or a new girl."

He could almost hear her smile, but he knew her feelings were hurt.

"I'll make it up to you, I promise," he said.

"I'll hold you to it."

Tom hung up the phone and took a deep breath. It was Sunday. How could he forget it was Sunday? He looked up as Rick came out of the lab and joined him.

"All set here?" Rick asked.

Tom nodded.

"Good, I got some stuff I gotta do. Let me know how the search goes, what turns up," said Rick.

Tom frowned. "You don't want to be there?" he asked.

"Like I said, I got some stuff I gotta do."

The two men walked to the door.

"Care to tell me what that something is?" Tom asked, his voice taut, his eyes straight ahead.

"Nope. Bad idea," Rick said.

Tom nodded. The two men stopped, turned, and looked at each other.

"Be careful, Rick. I wouldn't want to lose you in the crossfire," Tom said. "Don't forget to call Fran. She will probably want to know if you're going to work tomorrow."

Rick nodded, gave Tom a friendly slap on the back, and walked out of the building.

***

The apartment building's elevator was too slow for Alex. Too slow and too fast. His fists were gripped tight. His heart pounded. He felt like he was going to faint. He could hear the music blaring from his radio before he entered the apartment. His hands shook as he fumbled with the keys, swung open the door, and yelled for Toni.

No one answered. The door closed behind him as he went from room to room looking for her, but she wasn't there. The music continued to blare. Finally, in a fit of anger, Alex yanked the plug out of the wall, grabbed the radio, threw it across the room, and slammed it into the kitchen counter.

The phone rang but he avoided it. The answering machine softly intoned its message and then Autumn's voice could be heard asking if he was alright. He walked over to the phone, picked it up and threw it hard against the wall. He was shaking all over now. His knees gave out under him and he sunk to the floor. He was curled up and crying, the images from the disc burned deep into his mind.

***

Rick pulled his Jeep in front of Toni's apartment building, like he'd done so many times the last few days. He sat there wondering, again, if he should go in. Once, he'd seen her leave but hadn't followed her. The two times he'd knocked, she hadn't been home, but this time…. He saw the reflection of the early afternoon sunlight dance against her window. The cat was sitting on the windowsill and licking his paws. Rick had to see Toni. He didn't want to see her, but he had to.

Rick rubbed his tired eyes and called Fran. She answered on the first ring.

"What's going on?" she asked. "I need to get out of here, soon. I'm going stir crazy."

The connection was weak and choppy.

"You may get your wish," Rick said. "Elliott is in jail and Tom has a search warrant for Max's home and office. At least, he's on his way to pick it up. They should execute it in an hour or so."

Fran stopped breathing. "Thank God. It's almost over," she finally said. "What are you going to do?" she asked softly.

Rick shook his head and chuckled. "Boss, I'm still trying to figure that one out."

"Does Alex know?" Fran asked.

"Yes," said Rick.

"Shit."

"It couldn't be helped, boss," Rick told her. "You know that."

"Yes, yes, damn it, yes. I know."

"I'll check in with you later," he said.

"Right." The phone went dead.

Rick pocketed his phone, got out of his vehicle, took a long, deep breath, and trudged slowly up to Toni's apartment one last time.

When she answered the door, he smelled the familiar odor of beer on her, but she looked better than she had in a while. She was wearing her usual tight jeans, a tee-shirt bearing the logo of a local bar, and her sneakers. Her dark

334

hair was wet and slicked back.

"Come in, sexy," she said with a playful grin as she swung the door open for him.

Rick almost smiled. He stepped through the doorway and into the main room. His eyes swept the place and noted that she had done some cleaning. Only a few beer bottles were on the counter. The cat, still in the windowsill, was curled up and purring. A scented candle burned in a jar next to the bed and the covers were, to some extent, straightened and neat.

"You've been busy," he said, nodding approvingly.

"Well, when you don't have a job, you have time on your hands. Want a beer?" Her hand rested on the door to the fridge.

"No. Next time," he said, realizing there would be no next time.

She didn't argue with him. She plopped onto the bed and sat, cross-legged, watching and waiting. "So?" she finally asked. "Why are you here? Other than to see my pretty face, that is."

Rick grabbed a kitchen chair and placed it in front of her, the back of the chair facing her. He straddled it and sat down, his arms resting on the back. "I have a problem," he finally said after some thought. "A dilemma. That's what they call it, right? Dilemma?" His eyes focused on her face. He watched for any twitch of a muscle, assessed the tilt of her chin, and looked for a telltale sign in her eyes. He gripped the back of the chair tightly and tried to quell his fear.

"Depends what you're talking about," she said, leaning forward slightly with a flirtatious smile.

"I'm conflicted," he continued. "On the one hand, I'm crazy about you. You know that. I'd do just about anything for you."

"The feeling's mutual," she said.

"On the other hand, I know you killed Carol McEnroe."

Toni paled and began to tremble. "What do you mean you know?" she

335

asked, her eyes quickly avoiding his. "What are you talking about?"

There it was, he thought: the twitch of a muscle, the tilt of a chin, the way the eyes avoided him. It couldn't be helped.

"Carol recorded her little parties. I've seen the DVD, all of it, and you're on it, baby, cigar and all." His voice was heavy with sadness.

"That's crazy!" Toni objected. She jumped out of bed and began to pace the room.

Rick stood up, watching her, posting himself between her and the door as the knot in his gut tightened. "I wish it was. I wish I understood it. I do understand it, some. Carol was a piece of work. She was a threat to Alex. I get that. But Sarah? Why the hell did you kill Sarah?"

Toni stopped pacing and stared at him. "Did she have a DVD recorder too?" she asked sarcastically.

"No, she didn't, but she had your MO burned into her." He swallowed. His head hurt. He watched her every move, anticipating what she'd do next. Would she bolt? Scream? Try to kill him? Try to kill herself? He waited.

"Who else did you tell this wild story to?" she demanded to know.

Rick sighed. "Everyone knows about Carol, Toni. Everyone, including Alex."

"He won't believe you! He'll believe me! I'm his sister. I take care of him. I look out for him. That's my job. Understand? I'm the one who cleans up after his messes! I'm the one who keeps him out of trouble! HE NEEDS ME!" She paced faster as she became hysterical. Her voice was loud and high.

Rick winced. "It's not about him believing you. By now he's seen the DVD. He knows."

Toni stopped pacing, crossed her arms in front of her chest and glared at Rick. "What are you going to do now?" she taunted him. "Arrest me? Take me to jail? You'd like that, wouldn't you! You're supposed to be my friend,

336

my lover, but you're a bounty hunter, through and through, and I'm the catch of the day. What else could I expect from someone like you?" She spat out the words.

"Why did you kill Sarah?" he asked again. She was wearing on his nerves. He wanted to grab her, scream at her, shake her, pound some damn common sense into her. The pain in his gut was almost more than he could handle. He fought with himself to act calm. "Alex loved her, adored her, wanted to have children with her. She was a good woman. I don't get it."

"She was a bitch! She was going to destroy him! Don't you understand? She was a worthless whore! He told me. He knew. He said she was sleeping around. A slut, just like that cop! Just like Miss Autumn prissy pants actress! They should have left him the hell alone. He's MY brother, MINE. I'm responsible for him!" Toni collapsed in the chair Rick had just abandoned. She sobbed. "Get out of here!" she screamed. "Get out of my sight! If you're not going to arrest me, then go. Now."

Rick approached the chair and placed a comforting hand on her shoulder. He couldn't leave her like this; he had no idea what she would do next. He didn't trust her. "I'm not going anywhere, baby," he said finally. "I'm not leaving you."

Rick could feel the creeping weight of darkness seep into his body as he closed his eyes. He could barely stand. The air was being sucked out of the room and all light faded away. He stroked her hair as she sobbed. "Get your things. Pack a bag. Make it light. We're getting out of here."

What else could he do? He thought of Fran alone in the safe-house. He'd have to get word to her somehow. She'd understand – he hoped. Leaving was a decision he knew he'd regret, but it was the only choice he could bring himself to make. He wondered how long it would be before Toni killed again and what he'd have to do then.

***

337

After Rick was gone, Tom found a quiet office in the lab and pulled out his phone. Reading from the report Candy had given him, he called Seattle. When a dispatcher answered, Tom cleared his throat and charged ahead.

"Hi. This is Detective Tom Sadler from the Las Vegas Municipal Police Department. We are in the middle of investigating a serial child rapist and killer, and it looks like our perp may be related to some cases you had about four years ago." He checked the date on the report to be sure. "Yes, four years. Who do I talk to?"

"Probably Assistant Chief Joe Stafford," the dispatcher said. "He heads up our criminal investigation bureau. He's out of the office today, but I can patch you through to his voice mail if you want."

"Is there anyone I can talk to today?" Tom asked. "I wouldn't push, but we've already got three dead girls and I really don't want to see another one."

"I understand. Hold on, let me see who's around," said the dispatcher.

The phone went quiet for a while, and Tom wondered just how far professional courtesy would get him in this case.

When the dispatcher returned, her tone had changed. She was clipped, intense. "Can you give me a few details?" she asked.

Tom thought that was an odd question coming from a dispatcher, but he launched ahead anyway. "The victims were all females around 12 years old. They attended the same private school." He could hear her repeating the words to someone behind her. "All found with some kind of rock in their hands, although that may have been planted evidence."

"Just a moment," the dispatcher said. "I'm patching you through to the chief of police."

"He's in the office?" Tom asked, surprised.

"No, he's going to take this at home."

Tom leaned against the desk and waited. A few minutes later, he heard the man's voice on the phone.

338

"Chief Barber here. How many girls? What age?"

"Three. Twelve," Tom answered. "The earliest one was killed about two years ago. The second was about six months ago and the other just happened." He could hear what sounded like someone cooking in the background.

"He's decreased the time between hits. That's not good," Barber said. "Where's your investigation at? How can we help you?"

"Our investigation is in the toilet," Tom said. "The chief investigator screwed up the case. He planted evidence to frame someone, although I haven't figured out why, yet. He's currently locked up. In the meantime, we found a DNA sample report that matches one from your area. We were hoping to find something, anything, that could get us a hot lead."

"Who does the sample belong to?" Barber asked.

"That's just it," said Tom. "We don't know."

"Idiot," Chief Barber mumbled.

"Pardon?"

"We had a series of those murders. Seven of them. The perp must have moved to Vegas 'cause the murders stopped just about three years ago. The investigations were so badly botched we couldn't get anywhere. We had to fire one idiot over it, from the crime scene unit. A bloody mess! The only good news is the perp apparently moved on. Good for us, that is. Not for you, I take it," Barber explained.

Tom frowned, thinking. He played a hunch. "Who was the investigator? Do you remember?"

"Oh, yeah. I remember. I wanted to beat the crap out of him," Barber said. "His name was Elliott. Roger Elliott. Ever heard of him?"

Tom almost laughed. "I don't know whether to be relieved or furious," he finally said. "Roger Elliott is the man I arrested for tampering with evidence. He's in jail as we speak."

"Good! That's where he belongs! That bastard shouldn't be within a hundred miles of a crime lab!"

Tom rubbed his forehead. "Anything else you can remember about the case?" he asked.

"Not off the top of my head, but I can have a copy of my report faxed to you, or emailed, or whatever the hell they do with it these days."

"Great." Tom gave his contact information to Barber and hung up. *Elliott. That little piece of...* Tom's thought was cut off by his cell phone ringing. "Yes?"

"Where are you?" Candy asked.

"Still in the lab. I found myself a quiet place to call Seattle. What have you got?"

"You first," she said as she strolled through the door with her phone to her ear. She shut it off and slipped it into the pocket of her lab coat.

Tom turned off his phone as well. The first thing that struck him was the scent of her cologne. The second was the unshakeable image of her with a crop. He shook his head to clear it and focused on the work.

"Seattle doesn't have a name to go with the DNA sample because the investigation was botched up by some idiot lab tech by the name of – get this – Roger Elliott." Tom shook his head. "Do you believe it? He screwed up the same cases there as he screwed up here. What the hell is the matter with that guy?"

Candy froze in her steps and stared at Tom.

"What?" Tom finally asked.

"Oh – my – god," she exhaled. For a moment, she looked like she was about to be ill. She rested her hand on the back of a chair to steady herself.

"What?" he asked again, alarmed.

"Tom, we are looking for a man who was in Seattle during the earlier murders and in Vegas during these murders. Roger Elliott IS that man."

340

"Naw! It couldn't be! I mean…. That's impossible!" Tom tried to imagine Elliott in the role of a child molester and the image wouldn't gel in his head. "That's just bizarre."

"It makes sense," Candy argued. "The real child molester, if he had the chance, would tamper with the evidence and frame someone else. It explains everything. It's motive."

"I just don't believe it," said Tom.

"Believe it."

"Okay." Tom took a deep breath. There wasn't enough oxygen in the room. "We need a DNA sample from Elliott, right? With what we have, I should be able to get a court order. Elliott's in jail, so…."

"He made bail," said Candy.

"What the hell?" Tom straightened up. "You've got to be kidding!"

"The mayor bailed him out. Got any other ideas?" she asked.

Tom thought a few minutes. Then he remembered the gym bag. "Yes," he said finally. "I have an idea. I'll be back in two minutes."

Tom returned with the bag. The discs, however, were still safely tucked in his trunk.

"What's that?" Candy asked, eying the bag.

"It's Elliott's. He had it with him when we arrested him this morning. I haven't inventoried it yet." Tom opened the bag and pulled out a pair of gym shorts, some sneakers, and a couple of towels.

"You'd better do the inventory paperwork now, so we don't get screwed on illegal procedure," she told him. "I'll run the DNA sample. It will take a while, though."

"How long is a while?"

"Two, three, four days." Candy looked apologetic. "I'll push it, but that' the best I can do."

Tom felt the frustration knotting in his chest. "What do I do until then?"

he asked.

"You didn't find any evidence of kiddie porn when you searched his house this morning?" she asked.

"I never searched his house." Tom quickly dug the search warrant out of his pocket. "I arrested him at his gym. I never executed the warrant."

Candy shook her head. "Well, you'd better get going."

"I need to find someone to take with me," he said as he headed towards the door. "I don't have any friends in the department, right now, not after this mess with Alex."

"Wait," Candy called after him, "I'll go with you."

He turned, surprised, and saw her drop her lab coat and hurry towards him.

"Just let me get my piece. I'll meet you in the parking lot," she said.

"The DNA?" he asked.

"Hon," she said, resting a hand on his shoulder. "This is why I'm director. I can have someone log and babysit it while I'm gone."

It was nearly two in the afternoon by then. Tom stepped out of the cool, air-conditioned building and into the parking lot. The hot sun was well into baking the cars. The door was hot when Tom opened it, and a draft of warm air escaped from inside. As he sat with one leg outside, the windows down and the AC running, he thought about what they would find at Elliott's house. More discs? Was Elliott telling the truth when he said that what he had at the gym was all he had? What if they didn't find anything else? Would Elliott be dumb enough to keep evidence of his violent activities in his home? Tom had told Elliott about the warrant. Elliott would have cleaned up by now. If he was still in the state.

Tom rubbed his tired eyes.

Candy strolled across the lot, sunglasses perched on her nose, a lab kit in her hand, her gun holstered on her hip. She opened the back door to the cruiser and dropped the kit on the seat, then got in next to him.

"You shoot?" Tom asked as he eyed the gun.

"Not really," Candy admitted. "Some, but I'm not very good at it. I just wear it to scare people." She buckled up. "We should pick up the search warrant for Simone's place while we're running around," she said. "Maybe even go there first."

"I'm not sure we can afford the time." Tom shut the car door, rolled up the windows, and let the AC take over. "If Elliott is the monster you think he is, we have to catch up with him before he leaves the state."

"If he is, he's long gone," she said. "It's your call. We can still hit them both today."

Tom shrugged, pretending not to care. Even if they went to Simone's, he argued, they wouldn't have time to look at the disc before going to Elliott's place. Did it matter, really? In the end, would it matter?

CHAPTER 23

Fran's frustration was growing by the minute. Rick wasn't answering his phone or returning her calls anymore. She wondered if his battery had died, although it wasn't like him to let that happen. She wondered if he was out of a service area. That could be, she reasoned, but for hours at a time? She wondered if he was in trouble. The last time she'd spoken to him, he was headed to Toni's place. That was trouble, she thought. She was worried.

"Don't call anyone else," he'd told her, but now anyone else seemed to be the only person she could call. She had made a discovery, or what looked like a discovery, if she was right. She felt as if small worms were crawling under her skin and she had to tell someone.

She had poured over the papers for the last hour, matching the reports in Tom's envelope with the official discovery package. She had read and reread the emails between Candy and Elliott. Her mind didn't have to stretch very far to realize that everything Alex had been telling her about Elliott was true – the man was manufacturing evidence. Not just screwing it up and not just being lazy, but manipulating it, changing the reports, lying to his superiors, and covering up his lies with more lies. Why?

If Elliott was trying to cover up for Max, he was doing a bad job of it. In fact, it appeared he was trying to frame Max, which made even less sense. The tiny rocks appeared to be meaningless. Not only were they common, they apparently had never been used. According to the lab report in Fran's hand, no water, and hence no residue, had ever touched the rocks. That was contrary to what Rick had told Tom, and it assumed the lab report was true, the lab report in her hand, of course. Maybe there was a second report. Was that before or after Candy was fired? Fran couldn't remember, and she didn't know what or whom she could trust.

She looked again at the e-mails: Candy was constantly reprimanding Elliott, telling him to "get your shit together," to finish lab results, to follow up with reports, to check the evidence. Elliott was constantly responding with promises he apparently never kept or, in at least two cases, lies that he had done something that he hadn't. He spent more time and energy dodging Candy's bullets than he would have if he'd done his job, Fran realized.

Fran had reached frustration level when she found something unexpected, a reference to a website. Elliott had forwarded a link to Candy that, when opened, included a compromising photo of the criminologist. Blackmail? Fran asked herself. Candy never acted like Elliott had anything on her. Maybe he'd tried; maybe he'd failed.

Fran tried to access the rest of the link but kept banging against a password. After four or five blind tries, she was about to give up when she saw the link that read, "Have you forgotten your password?" She clicked on it. In exchange for a name, email address, and date of birth, she could have the password sent to Elliott's account. Stymied, she was about to throw her laptop across the room when it occurred to her that she didn't need to access Elliott's account, she just needed to open her own.

A minute later, Fran stared at something that made her ill, something that, whether she wanted to see it or not, could send her directly to jail. She was looking at child porn.

As fast as the photos appeared, Fran logged off. Her hands shook as she closed the laptop. This was it, she told herself. This was why Elliott had taken so many risks. This was why he had manipulated the evidence. This was....

Fran felt sick to her stomach as she dialed Tom's number. She expected to hear his reassuring voice on the other end of the line. Instead, she got a curt response.

"Where are you? Never mind. Look, I can't talk now. Things are breaking fast," he said before she could say anything. "I'll call you later." He hung up.

Stunned, Fran frowned and stared at the phone a minute. "What do you mean, things are breaking fast?" she yelled into the dead phone. "Damn it, Tom!"

She tried the number again, and this time she got a voice mail message.

She tried Margo and, again, got nothing. Margo *would* let her battery die, Fran reasoned.

Alex? She started to dial his number and stopped. Not Alex. Anyone but Alex.

Paul. No way in hell.

Rick? Damn him. Why couldn't she reach him!

Slamming the phone down, Fran paced the kitchen floor, her heart racing, her arms wrapped tightly around her. She was trying to swallow the nausea that threatened her. She turned on the radio but got only music, or what passed for music. She went into the bedroom and stuffed her clothes back into her bag. She checked the purse and reassured herself that the gun was still there.

Should I go back? Where will I go? I've got nowhere to go!

She paced some more before loading the case files into the vehicle and grabbing her purse, feeling the weight of Rick's gun settled in the bottom of it. She couldn't remember where Rick had put the keys. By then the anxiety had built to the point of explosion. Fran stood outside the house, her suitcase on the porch as a falling sun cast long shadows behind her. She doubled over and screamed. She dropped to her knees in the dusty driveway and screamed some more. She screamed until she was hoarse. She screamed until all she could hear were her sobs.

"Damn it! Damn it! Damn it!" she screamed, angrier at herself than at anyone else, including Max. "How could I let this happen? How. Damn it! Stupid! I'm a goddamn idiot! If I'd just read the Callas file! If I'd just believed Alex! If I'd just...."

She stopped and buried her head in her hands as a throbbing headache

347

took hold.

Enough, she told herself. *Enough.*

She wiped the tears from her face with the back of her sleeve, pulled herself to her feet and leaned against the vehicle until her legs steadied under her. *Enough of this self-pitying shit. It's done. All done. All over.*

She entered the house and searched until she found the keys on top of the refrigerator.

Her hands were shaking as she started the vehicle and pulled out of the driveway. Half-way to the city, she decided to call Paul. At least she could check in with Lauren and see how the child was doing. After seeing those photos, Fran needed to do that. She needed to hear her daughter's voice. She didn't have to tell Paul she was hiding from Max. She didn't have to tell him anything.

She didn't get the chance.

Paul was hysterical and screaming out of control the minute he answered the phone and knew it was her. "What did you do, change your number on me? Where have you been? Do you have any idea how irresponsible you are?"

She tried to interrupt. He wouldn't let her.

"Lauren disappeared this morning after church. We had an argument. She didn't want to go but she didn't have a choice. You have got to start taking that child to church, Fran!"

"What?" she tried to interrupt again.

"She's gone! You understand me? Gone! I've looked everywhere. I went to your place thinking she'd go there but you don't live there anymore. Since when don't you live there anymore? Why didn't you tell me? What the hell is going on? Where's Lauren?"

"Why ask me?" she screamed back, swerving the van. Swearing, she veered into the breakdown lane, dust flying up around her. She brought the vehicle to a sliding halt and yelled back at him. "You're the one who had her! You're the one who lost her! Oh my god! Lauren!" Her stomach twisted, and she bent over. "Did you talk to Tom?" she asked.

"Another one of your adoring fans?" he spat. "I called the police. There's an Amber out on her. Get back here!" He slammed the phone down.

Fran fought back a wave of panic as she stared at the phone. She tried Tom's number again, but still no luck. She had to find him. She had to find out.... She sat there in the heat, in a state of shock, as the only logical answer occurred to her: Max. He had Lauren. He had to have her. Her hand went to the purse and she patted it to make sure the gun was still there. Then Fran threw the vehicle back into gear and stepped on the gas.

***

"Nothing," Tom muttered as he flipped Elliott's mattress over and searched under the bed.

Candy walked into the room and wiped a fine sheen of sweat from her forehead with her sleeve, careful not to get any on her purple gloves. "Nothing here," she agreed. "Blank. You think we're wrong about him?"

Tom shook his head. "It makes sense. He should be the one, but this place is cleaner than...." He stopped a moment in mid-sentence.

"Than what?" Candy asked, noting his change in body language.

Tom straightened up and looked at her a second, the thoughts still racing through his head. "Cleaner than Carol's place. Not a cereal box opened. No perishables in the fridge. Everything is so clean you wonder if anyone uses it."

Candy smiled. She turned and went back through the house, room by room. "You're right," she called out. "That bastard doesn't live here."

Tom joined her in the main room. "Now what?" he asked.

"Well, we could start with Simone. Maybe he knows where to look."

"He would," Tom agreed.

Together they headed out the door as empty-handed as when they came in.

***

Tom took the lead as they marched into the Simone mansion. If you're going to get a tooth pulled, he reasoned, you might as well get it over with fast. Only this wasn't about a tooth. It was about a murder, about a friendship, and about his career.

He was surprised when Max's man let him in without hesitation. "He's waiting for you," Jerry said, his lumbering body pulling them along like a huge magnet to the study.

Simone was in a large leather chair by the fireplace, wearing his smoking jacket, his feet propped up on an ottoman, a blanket over his legs and his pipe in his hand. The darkened room was thick with the smell of tobacco. The curtains had been drawn against the sun.

Tom wondered what all the drama was about, but as he approached Max, the mayor held up two discs in jewel cases.

"Looking for these, I take it," he said, offering them without hesitation.

Candy beat Tom to the chair and seized the discs, then slipped them into an evidence bag and marked them.

"That's all of them?" Tom asked, mentally kicking himself.

"All that I have, but you can search if you want. Just clean up after yourselves." Simone turned to face the cold fireplace and puffed on his pipe.

"What do you mean, all that you have?" Candy asked.

Tom swallowed involuntarily. This was it. This was where he got his ass kicked.

"Roger had his, of course," Simone said. He glanced at Tom and frowned, but didn't add to the statement. "Then there's the one I gave Fran."

Even though Tom had already figured that out, hearing it still stunned him. His shoulders sank.

350

Candy was quick to pick up on both men's body language. Her jaw tightened, and her hand gripped the evidence bag tightly. "Where's Elliott?" she asked.

Max shrugged. "How should I know? I posted bail. He left. As long as he shows up for court, I don't care."

Somewhere in the next room, the phone rang. Jerry left to answer it.

"We have to find him, now," Tom stated. He kept his focus on Max.

"Try his home. He's probably licking his wounds."

"Don't be a fool, Simone," Candy snapped. "He doesn't live there. It's a front. We have to find him now, immediately. Understand? Where is he?"

Jerry appeared in the doorway, a phone in his hand. He cleared his throat.

"Not now," Max said, waving the man away.

"It's important, sir," Jerry said. He glanced nervously at the others.

Candy ignored the exchange. She marched towards Max and the words spit out of her mouth like nails. "Roger Elliott has been raping and murdering those girls and planting evidence to frame you for it, and we need to find him NOW before another child dies. If you don't think I won't wring his whereabouts out of that scrawny neck of yours, you're wrong."

"Sir, please, it's important!" Jerry interrupted.

"Not now!" Max yelled at him, his eyes on Candy, assessing her.

"It's Roger Elliott," Jerry stated.

Everyone turned and stared at him.

"Give me that damn phone," Max ordered.

Jerry quickly approached, and Max snatched the phone out of the man's hand.

"Roger! Where the hell are you and what the fuck have you been doing?" he screamed. "I got cops here saying you're the serial child rapist. You hear me? What the hell is going on?"

Max was silent a few moments as he listened to the man on the other end

351

of the phone. The mayor's face darkened. His eyes narrowed, and his hands shook. Still listening, he threw back the blanket and pulled himself to his feet. He gripped the edge of the chair for balance.

Despite Max's height and menacing stance, Tom immediately knew something was wrong with the mayor. Tom glanced at Jerry, who hovered around his employer.

"You don't want to do that, Roger," Max snapped. The room crackled with anger. "I swear to all that lives, I will hunt you down and skin you alive!"

More silence.

"When? Where? How?" Max demanded to know.

A minute later, he grunted and threw down the phone. He looked around the room as if surprised to find people in it, then his eyes focused on Candy. "He has my granddaughter," he said. "He wants two million and safe escort out of the country." He turned to Jerry. "I need two million in unmarked bills, in a satchel. Now. You know where it is," Max barked.

Tom felt his heart stop and his knees weaken. He inhaled deeply to clear his head. Lauren, of all people, Lauren.

"Yes, sir." Jerry turned and started out of the room.

"Where is he?" Candy asked again.

"You show up and she's dead," Max told her.

They were interrupted by someone yelling in the hallway. Tom jumped at the sound and he turned towards the door. He knew that voice. If there was one person he dreaded seeing at this moment, it was Fran Simone, and yet there she stood, screaming at a maid and hitting Jerry with both fists as he gripped her arm.

Max walked slowly out of the room and stood in the hall, frozen, quiet, watching her, until she noticed him and turned towards him, her face red with rage. "Where's Lauren?" she demanded to know. "You son of a bitch, where is she!"

352

Tom hurried forward and grabbed Fran by both arms as Jerry, with a sharp look from Max, went for the money. "He doesn't have her," Tom said quietly. "She's not here. How did you know?"

"I called Paul," she yelled. "He's frantic. He's never frantic! Where is she? Where's my daughter?"

"Roger Elliott has her," Candy said softly. "He's holding her hostage until he can escape."

"Elliott?" Fran glanced from Candy back to Tom. "But he's... He's...."

Tom held her tight in his arms, his hand pressed to the back of her head, cradling her against him. The soft scent of her perfume cut through the odor of tobacco that clung to Max. She was trembling, barely standing. She didn't cry but held onto him as if he were a life jacket in a turbulent sea.

"I know," he said softly into her ear. "I know. I'll get her back. I promise. He doesn't want to hurt her. He wants money from Max to make a clean getaway. She's going to be okay. I promise, Fran. I promise."

"But he's...." she tried again, her voice a whimper. "I can't lose her. I can't."

"I know."

"No, you don't know. Elliot is the one. He's...." Fran shuddered, and the words garbled in her mouth.

"The child killer. I know Fran." Tom looked calmly into her blue eyes. "I'll get her. I'll bring her back. I promise."

Jerry reappeared, a small, blue gym bag in hand.

"You keep two million dollars lying around the house?" Candy asked.

"We're going to talk about this now?" Max rebutted.

"I'm going with you," Tom stated, lowering Fran into a chair. She clung to his arm.

"No, you're not." Max barked.

Jerry took Max's smoking jacket and helped him put on a windbreaker.

"You're in no condition to do this alone," Tom stated.

Max looked up at Tom and frowned.

Tom continued. "He doesn't want to hurt her. He knows better. He might be able to escape the police, but he'd never escape you. No, he won't hurt her, but if you go alone, there's a good chance he'll kill you and take her and the money and disappear. I can't – I won't let that happen. This is a police matter. We're doing it by the book." He nodded to Candy. "Put in the call."

While on the phone with Sheriff Randall, Candy turned to Max and asked, "Where is Roger Elliott?"

Max took a deep breath. "Fremont Villa," he said.

She conveyed that information to the dispatcher and shut the phone. "Let's go." Candy headed out the door with Max and Jerry in tow.

As Tom turned to leave, Fran squeezed his arm and pulled herself up. She didn't have to speak. He took her hand and they headed out the door together.

CHAPTER 24

SUNDAY EVENING

Fran sat in the back seat of the unmarked cruiser, her body pushed hard against the door, her cheek pressing against the warm window and her oversized purse tucked securely under her arm. Every bone in her body ached and every cell was on fire. The air conditioning wrapped its tendrils around her, crawled inside her pant legs, and left her shivering. She didn't react. She didn't move.

Maybe it was shock. Maybe the crying had run its course. Maybe.... She abruptly stopped thinking about the "maybes," she only knew she was being shredded apart, caught up in something overpowering her. She was walking on the bottom of a cold mountain lake, her soul battered by invisible currents and unable to keep her balance. The hysterics were over. All she could do now was put one foot in front of the other and breathe. The breathing was the hardest part, especially while underwater.

Max sat on the other side of the leather seat, the small tote bag on his lap, his long legs stretched out as he leaned back against the door and kept his eyes on Fran. He hadn't spoken to her since they'd left, but that didn't matter to Fran. In fact, it was a relief. She didn't want to feel his unique presence. This way, he was just another current in a roiling sea.

Candy was driving. Tom, sitting in front of Fran, turned part way around to check on her.

"We have undercover units on their way," he said. "They'll meet us there. We'll keep things low key. I don't want to spook this guy." He reached back to touch her hand.

She nodded but didn't look at him.

"It's going to be alright, Fran," he told her. "He wouldn't dare hurt Lauren. Not now. He can't afford to."

For a brief second, Fran felt comfort and hope in Tom's words, then the darkness flooded her again and she leaned back, her arms wrapped around herself, her eyes closed.

Just outside the complex, Candy slowed the car to a stop, rolled down the window and spoke to a man in work clothes.

"How we doing?" she asked.

Tom returned his attention to the front of the car and listened while the two talked.

"We got the area secured," the man said, nodding to Tom and glancing at the passengers in the back seat. "If he makes a run for it, he's not going anywhere."

"He may try to take the hostage with him," Candy said.

"We're ready."

She nodded and drove forward.

The apartment village was innocuous and inviting. The sun was setting, and a soft orange glow wove its fingers through the buildings and trees and kissed the top of the pool. The setting was seductively and deceptively serene. A few minutes later, they parked near Elliott's building.

"Okay, kids," Candy said, her voice lacking the confidence she was trying to achieve. "Let's get this show on the road."

Tom stepped out of the car and opened the door for Fran. "We'll wait here," he told her. "Let Max make the drop. Then we'll see what happens."

Fran looked up at him with an icy stillness. "I'm going in," she said, tightening her hold on the purse.

"Fran, you can't," Tom's voice had an edge of panic to it. "You don't know what he'll do. We can't risk it. I won't allow it."

"I'm going in," she repeated, her voice softer as she recognized the deep worry in his eyes.

"He could kill you, Fran," Tom argued, grabbing her upper arm to stop her.

356

"If he kills Lauren, it won't matter what he does to me," she said.

"It matters to me!" His voice was tense and louder.

She stood on her tiptoes, kissed Tom on the cheek and slid out of his grasp. Her eyes looked past him to Max. "Ready?" she asked.

Her father nodded and tapped the tote bag of money.

Fran Simone had never thought of herself as a killer, except when she thought about Max. Lately, she'd been thinking about Max a lot. Now, as they stood together in common cause, side by side, killing her father was the last thing on her mind. Anger, revenge, repulsion – all those feelings she'd been simmering and stewing for several decades – had lost their flavor. In their place was the bitterness of regret and the acidic taste of fear – the kind of deep down, bone scraping fear that set her on autopilot, that made her put one foot in front of the other without hesitation. Tom would have said that she was in shock, but shock couldn't begin to explain it.

She pushed the strap of her purse further up her shoulder and brushed her bangs back from her eyes.

"Let me hold that for you," Tom said, reaching for the purse, but she pulled away and clasped it tightly to her side.

"Don't go," he said again. His hand grasped the air in desperation.

She wasn't listening.

"You don't have to do this," her father told her, and she wondered if he was reading her mind.

"Yes, I do," was all she said. She turned away from Tom and headed up the stairs to the apartment, her sneakers padding softly on the wood and her emotions balancing precariously on the strained line between her and Max.

Behind her, Candy grabbed Tom's arm to stop him from following.

Max, gripping the tote-bag that held the money, followed close behind Fran. When they got to the painted door with its "Welcome" brass knocker, she stepped aside and inhaled deeply. Max rapped twice in staccato on the door, and they heard Elliot's voice yelling for them to come in.

They left the cool of the evening behind them and stepped into the stifling apartment, its dim lamp casting shadows on the walls, its pulled blinds and closed curtains, and the heavy, acrid odor of old tobacco in the warm air. For some reason, Elliott hadn't turned on the AC. Fran couldn't imagine it was because he was saving pennies.

"Where is she?" Max asked before Fran could get the words out.

Elliott was seated in the center of a small, rose print sofa; a maple coffee table was between them and he held a pistol, aimed at Max, in one trembling hand. He had shaved off his signature handlebar mustache and dyed his hair black. He was dressed in dirty old jeans, roughed up sneakers and a sweatshirt.

Max smirked.

Elliott motioned towards a coat closet.

It was clear he had carefully positioned himself in the room, had probably rehearsed this moment, and now, face to face with Max, found himself too weak-kneed to stand up.

All of that didn't matter much to Fran as she hurried to the closet and opened it.

Lauren was crouched in the dark on a small floor littered with boots and shoes. She was shaking, tucked into a collection of coats that surrounded her head. Her wrists and ankles were bound with duct tape, her mouth was gagged, and tears flowed down her face. The stiff, Sunday best, pale blue dress her father had forced her to wear was now rumpled and torn. She had been crying so hard that her nose was stuffed up and she could hardly breathe.

Fran gasped as if the wind had been knocked out of her. She dropped to her knees on the soft carpet and pulled the child into her arms as she carefully peeled away the gag. Lauren, sobbing, leaned into her mother; Fran rocked her. "You're safe. You're safe," Fran said quietly, shaking the sticky tape from her fingers, kissing her daughter's head and face and stroking her hair. "It's all over. Shhh. It's all over."

"Get her out of here," Max ordered Fran, never taking his eyes off Elliot. He set the bag on the coffee table and waited.

"I'm working on it," Fran snapped. Frustrated, she reached into her purse, pulled out a metal nail clipper and used that to stab at the threads of the tough tape. Once she broke through, she unwrapped the wrists and ankles.

"No one is going anywhere until I get my money," Elliott barked.

"I wouldn't be here if I hadn't brought your damn money," Max shot back, his eyes narrowing angrily. "I always knew you were stupid, Roger; I just didn't realize how stupid." Max reached into the bag and pulled out a bundle of bills, then tossed it at Elliott. The bundle fell into the man's lap.

Elliott picked it up and gave it a cursory look. "All of it, on the table, now!" he ordered.

Max grunted, upended the bag and dumped the bundles onto the coffee table. A few fell to the floor and the others were heaped in a pile.

"Fran, are you done yet?" Max demanded to know without looking at her.

"Yes, yes, almost," she yelled back, standing and pulling her child up with her. She half-carried, half-dragged Lauren to the door and opened it. "Tom is waiting downstairs," she whispered in the girl's ear as they stepped over the threshold and onto the landing. "Go to him."

"But mommy!" Lauren squealed, clinging to her.

"I'll be right behind you," Fran told her. "I'll be right there. Please." She squeezed her daughter tightly.

Fran waved to Tom, who was pacing at the bottom of the stairs. He froze.

"See, there he is; now, go to him, quickly." Fran gave Lauren a gentle shove forward. Tom, realizing what was happening, met the girl half-way up the stairs.

359

Lauren screamed, "No! No! Mommy. No! Please!" Tom picked up the child and glanced back.

"Fran!" he yelled. "Get out of there! Now!"

"Soon," she said. Her heart skipped as she watched him leave with her screaming daughter safe in his arms. For a second, she paused, her hand gripping the doorknob. All she had to do was take that one step and close the door. That was it. Just that one step, and whatever happened next wouldn't matter. She wouldn't be part of it. None of it would be her fault. Her mouth was dry. Her thoughts were racing. Her hand, gripping the purse, was suddenly stiff and cold.

The memory of her own abuse flooded over her like hot lava as she turned and stared at Roger Elliott – the child rapist, the child murderer, the man who had dared to put his hands on her daughter.

Max glanced at her, startled. "I thought you were gone," he said. His eyes darted back to Elliott.

Fran stepped into the room, closed the door behind her, let go of the knob and looked at her father – really looked at him. For the first time, she saw him for what he was, not the man of her nightmares. She could see how strained his features were as he fought to stand straight and tall. She noted how thin and pale he was. She wondered what had happened to the dragon of a man she'd feared for so many years.

"Not yet," she said. She was still looking at Max when she reached into her purse, pulled out Rick's gun, turned and aimed it at Elliott.

"Shit!" Elliott screamed, his gun going from Max to her and back again. "You shoot me, and I'll kill him!"

Fran smiled. The tension left her shoulders. "I got nothing to lose, then," she said softly as she pulled the trigger.

The jolt from the bullet threw Elliott's aim off and, when his gun fired, the discharge missed Max and lodged in the wall. Fran lowered her gun. Max, angry, seized the weapon from her hand, used his shirt to wipe down the handle, and gripped it.

"What the hell do you think you're doing?" he asked. "I told you, you didn't have to do this!"

Fran looked in his eyes and realized she was no longer afraid of him.

"I did to him what I should have done to you, years ago," she told him as she reached for the gun. "You don't have to cover for me."

"Yes, I do. I owe you that much." He lowered the gun to his side, out of her reach, as footsteps rushed up the stairs. Someone banged loudly on the door. "I'm sorry, Frannie. For everything," Max said. His shoulders fell as he held her gaze.

The words were like dandelion seeds in the air. She saw them, she appreciated them, but they floated by as if they had no life of their own. Fran, watching, didn't try to catch them. She didn't need to forgive him, and she probably never would. It just didn't matter, anymore.

Max yelled to the police outside, "It's safe. Come in!"

As several officers charged around them, Fran looked over at Elliott, sprawled on the sofa, blood splattered on his chest and seeping out, the gun still in his hand. She suddenly felt lightheaded and stepped back, nearly falling over, but Tom caught her in his arms. She turned and leaned on him. It was as if firing the gun had discharged all the anger in her. She was no longer angry or afraid or anxious. She was tired – very, very tired. Max was an old man who happened to be a relative. The bullet was a period at the end of a chapter of her life. And Tom – Why hadn't she noticed before how much he cared for her?

"Thank you," she whispered.

He held her close and steered her out the door and down the stairs where Lauren was waiting in the back of Candy's car. Candy, at the open car door, was bent down and holding the girl's hand.

361

Fran crawled in next to Lauren, slid her still shaking body across the cool seat and pulled the girl into a tight hug. "It's all over," Fran said.

"What about grandpa?" the girl asked.

"Grandpa is fine. He'll be down shortly."

The fatigue and relief were overwhelming.

A week later, Max was dead.

Fran, the legal documents from her pending custody battle gripped in her hand, was at her desk when Jerry called. Max had succumbed to cancer that he had refused to treat. No more phone calls. No more text messages. No more flowers. She put her head down on her arms and cried.

***

Fran sat cross-legged on the library table at the law office in the late morning hours, cradling a large potted rose plant. She was dressed in stretch pants and a tank top, her red hair pulled into a ponytail. She looked more like a college student on break than the new head of one of Las Vegas' leading law firms. She was watching a morning news feature on the sensational life and death of her father, Mayor Max Simone, and his connection to the murders of Carol McEnroe and Roger Elliott. The television, tucked into the bookcase, flashed a clip of Alex's interview with Holly Butterfield on LV:AM, and Fran felt goosebumps make their way up her arms. A few clips from a press release of Sheriff George Randall followed, announcing his candidacy for mayor. The young reporter craned his neck slightly to get a kink out of it before continuing.

"De la Rosa, who was cleared of all charges involving the horrific rape and murder of policewoman Carol McEnroe, is reported to have wed actress Autumn Bartlett in a private ceremony in Los Angeles. Friends close to the couple report they will honeymoon in Italy."

Whoopee. Fran tightened her grip on the pot.

"This announcement comes on the heels of a manhunt for Antonia de la

362

Rosa, who is now the chief suspect in the McEnroe murder, and her purported lover, Richard Brandt, a former Marine who is described as armed and dangerous. The Las Vegas Crime Lab confirmed that a third sample of DNA taken from a cigar at the scene matches Miss De la Rosa, and fibers found on the duct tape used to gag the victim are consistent with clothing found in the suspect's apartment. The motive for the killing and her whereabouts are still unknown."

Good luck, Rick.

"Finally, police still have no leads in the attempted shooting of Autumn Bartlett, but they suspect it was a botched carjacking. Interestingly, the assailant was frightened off by the paparazzi."

Right.

"Francesca Simone, the mayor's daughter, who took control of the De la Rosa law firm, refuses to comment on recent events. Stay tuned tonight for a special hour documentary on the strange life and death of Max Simone."

Fran's phone rang. She stared at the number a moment before answering it. "Where are you?" she asked.

"If I told ya that, I'd have to kill ya," Rick joked half-heartedly.

Fran lowered her head and bit her lip. There was so much she wanted to say to him, but nothing would come out.

"I won't be in work anytime soon," he said.

She nodded. "I know. What in hell am I going to do without you?"

It was his turn to be quiet.

She sniffled.

"I'm sorry," he finally said. "I heard about Lauren. I should have been there. I never thought…. Well, I just never thought. I was focused on you instead of the big picture."

"Will you ever come home?" Fran asked.

"If I can," he told her. He paused. "Take care of yourself, Fran. I'll be

363

thinking of you."

"Same here." She hung up.

Fran hadn't asked about Toni.

"Why are you torturing yourself?" Tom had slipped silently into the room and was watching her, wondering if he should intrude.

Fran jumped at the sound of his voice but didn't look at him at first. She picked up the remote and clicked off the television. "Closure, I guess." She tossed the remote to the side.

Tom dropped his jacket in a chair and came around the table to face her. "How are you feeling?"

She picked up a slip of paper from the table and handed it to him. It was a note from Alex, asking her to attend the wedding. "You're my best friend, Bella. I want you to be here," he'd written.

"I take it you didn't go."

She shook her head. "He sent a plant." She indicated the pot. "Weeping roses. They used to grow around his home in Italy. I guess he thought…." She couldn't imagine what he thought.

"It's just a gift." Tom gently lifted the pot and set it to the side. "Weeping roses. How ironic."

"He never got it," Fran admitted. "After all these years, he never knew how I felt."

"He knew, he just didn't want to know. He couldn't give you what you needed, Fran, and he was smart enough to realize it." Tom stroked her cheek with his thumb. "I heard about Paul suing for custody of Lauren. I'm sorry."

Fran's shoulders drooped. "We're negotiating." She looked up at him. "There's still so many unanswered questions."

"Like why Max would decide to make your life a living hell, now, after all these years?"

"I know that one," Fran said. "In the end, he wanted exactly what he said he wanted, his family around him when he died, and he would have done anything to get that."

Tom nodded. "Well, there's still a few loose ends to wrap up." He gently squeezed her hand.

She didn't resist.

"Toni," she said, watching his expression.

Tom turned away from her a second. The pain of that revelation still cut through his gut. He remembered milkshakes and hamburgers at the diner, Toni kicking him under the seat, the times he'd wanted to shake some sense into her, the times he'd enjoyed pretending they had a romantic relationship. He shook his head.

"In her twisted thinking, she thought she was protecting him, I guess." He shrugged. A part of him struggled with the impulse to come to Toni's defense.

"Protecting who? From what?" asked Fran.

"Alex – from Sarah breaking his heart, from Carol setting him up, from Autumn endangering his criminal case; she had her reasons." He paused a moment. "She was damaged, Fran. None of us realized just how much, except maybe Alex. He knew, or he seemed to know. But this...." He couldn't go on.

"I guess it's a damn good thing I didn't marry him, then," Fran said with a smirk. "Toni would have come after me. That would have been a bitch."

Tom smiled.

"After all this time, how could I have known them both so little?" Fran asked. It was a rhetorical question.

"You were blinded by love," he said softly. "You think you'll ever get over him?"

"I've been told I can do anything if I set my mind to it," Fran answered, her eyes narrowing as they focused on his.

"Can I help?" Tom leaned over, cupped Fran's chin in his hand, tilted her face up, and softly kissed her. He sighed when his cell phone rang. He checked the caller ID and smiled. "What are you doing for dinner on Sunday?"

Printed in Great Britain
by Amazon

46993523R00210